THE SEPARATED

ARE THE MAGIC SPELLS OF THE KEEPER strong enough to keep the world in balance against the sorcery of evil Lord Maldici, who wants to conquer the land?

Can young Giovanni, the son of a pirate, fight the temptation of gold to vanquish a monstrous sea dragon?

Can Marina escape her powerful sea-witch mother and her own destiny as a witch to live on land, no longer a feared outcast?

Will the three, separately and together, save their world from certain disaster and slavery?

NOVELS BY TROON HARRISON

The Separated
(First Book of the Tales of Terre series), 2006

Storm Lion of Penzance, 2005

Millie Book II, 2005

Millie: Ride the River, 2004

Eye of the Wolf, 2003

Goodbye to Atlantis, 2001

A Bushel of Light, 2000

THE SEPARATED

by Troon Harrison

First book of the TALES OF TERRE

Brown Barn Books
Weston, Connecticut

Brown Barn Books
A division of Pictures of Record, Inc.
119 Kettle Creek Road, Weston, CT 06883, U.S.A.

www.brownbarnbooks.com

The Separated
Copyright © 2006, by Troon Harrison
Original paperback edition

Library of Congress Control Number 2005935280

ISBN: 0-9768126-1-4
       978-0-9768126-1-6

Harrison, Troon

Printed in the United States of America

For Edith Brown

who wanted more than three chapters

While the writing of a book may appear a solitary undertaking, the nurturing of creative endeavor is a community effort. The final stages of this particular book were completed in fall 2005 during a period of great personal stress. Throughout, I was sustained and nurtured by a community of wonderful friends. Each one extended to me wisdom, kindness, and loving support. Each one of you has been a light in my darkness. Heartfelt gratitude:

- to Patricia Stone, for being truly a friend in deed, and always a superb listener with a loyal and empathetic heart;
- to Jane and Henry Fernandes, for the depth of your caring;
- to Mary Breene and to Barb Mitchell, for open doors, tea and hugs;
- to Florence Treadwell for a plate of food, and to others who gave me warm support at the same gathering: Jane Collins, Cathy Rowland, Lea Harper, Julie Johnstone, Julia Bell and Betsy Struthers;
- to all of you who cheered me with sympathetic emails and phone calls, and offered me help: Esperanca Melo, Maggie Crawford, Dave and Ann Heuft, Carol Francisco, John Forde, Jed Vallings, Shelley Bates, Stephen Brown, Elizabeth Orsten, Judy Langdon, Eleanor Hayden, and Nancy Dunford.
- to Jill Suggitt, for being so understanding;
- to Michelle McLean, a caring and expert massage therapist;

- to Nancy Hammerslough, a publisher with a sense of humor—you are a pleasure to work with;
- my parents, Glyn and Judy, for all their incredible effort on my behalf, and my lovely sister, Gwedhen;
- to my very dear son Ripley, for giving my world a centre, for being a comfort and joy, and for sharing your wise words at age nine: "Unicorns are a gift from God. When you look into their eyes you feel gentle because they are so beautiful."

CHAPTER ONE

THE SORCERER'S RED HAIRED DAUGHTER stood at an open window in the castle's highest tower of pale stone. Far below her, the tiled rooftops of Genovera tumbled down the slopes of the hills, interspersed with the spires and towers of noblemen's city palazzi. The awnings of a market formed rectangles of brilliant color in a cobbled square. Farther down yet, in the valley, the river Arnona gleamed like a silver thread in the sunlight. Barges labored upstream to the docks, laden with traders' goods: spices from islands far to the south, salt and gold from the desert of Terre. Other barges sailed downstream more easily on the Arnona's current. They were loaded with goods from Genovera's docks: porcelain and terracotta, wine and wheat, and dried figs to the delta where the huge ships docked.

The sorcerer's daughter stared farther, out across the fertile plains of central Verde, the green land. Her golden hawk eyes seemed to pierce the heat haze, roving across the fields of wheat and grapes, the scattered farms and villages and country towns. Far to the south, in Verde's misty distance, her uncle—that incompetent fool—ruled a portion of the land. He was her father's older brother and should have ruled all of Verde, but her father had beaten him long ago in combat and banished him to the dry south with its rocky fields. Soon, now, she and her father would vanquish Lord Verona completely and rule all of Verde themselves. Rumors of war eddied on the warm air, escaped from the mouths of wandering singers, sighed in the leaves of the olive trees.

To the west, and south of the delta, jagged blue mountains guarded secrets and separated Verde's inland plain from the coastal villages strung like beads along the Golfo d'Levanto's salty waters.

The girl licked her pouting red lips and stared hungrily toward the mountains. Who knew if the old stories were true, if the mountains hid a great secret, a great power? Since her father had unlocked the library of his ancestor, Lord Morte, he had learned many things about the black arts, and the history of Verde, written by the sorcerer himself. Perhaps, now that he possessed the knowledge of Lord Morte, her father also possessed the future of the land. If indeed the books spoke the truth about what existed in the mountains.

"We must make haste, and act in secret," she said sharply, turning away from the window. The folds of her gown of green Barbari silk shot through with golden threads, sighed as she paced across the room to where her father, the sorcerer Lord Maldici, scowled thoughtfully.

"I will join the spies," she said. "My uncle must not know what we search for, lest he find it first."

Lord Maldici stared at her, his eyes as sharp as knives in the thin, hard planes of his face. "You will go?" He laughed, a hawk's cry. "You, born and bred to luxuries, will wander in the countryside?"

His daughter glared at him, her lips tight. "I will go in disguise," she said obstinately. "If war is declared before we find the beast and its Keeper, we may lose all. The country people

2

favor my uncle. But with the missing beast found and united with its mate, you will possess greater power than my uncle could imagine. You said so yourself."

"This missing beast and its Keeper may all be a myth," the sorcerer reminded her. "We do not know whether they exist." Nevertheless, his eyes gleamed hotly with greed as he spoke, and his daughter smiled.

She pointed at the huge book lying on the floor beneath her father's chair. Its covers were black, mildewed from all the years it had lain, forgotten behind locked doors and rusted hinges in the library of Lord Morte, the first great sorcerer of Verde. Its creased pages of heavy paper were inscribed with faded ink, in the old tongue. For many hours the girl and her father had pored over the lines, translating their words, feeling the dark power rise from the page to coil about their hearts with a fierce, consuming grip.

"If the book is true, the greatest power lies in the Keeper's protection," the girl reminded her father now. "We must find out whether this is myth or truth. I will leave Genovera today. If there is a Keeper and a beast, I will find them and bring them here. The two beasts will be united, twice as strong. You will claim their power for your own uses. We'll crush the forces in the south and the whole land of Verde will be ours. You will become Emperor, for already Verde is the most powerful of nations. The riches of the world will come to our door; foreign princes will kiss my feet."

The sorcerer nodded, his dark hands clenched on the carved arms of his chair.

"It will be a great victory, with great power," he snarled. "Go, you witch. Find them, the Keeper and the beast, if they exist in the mountains. Bring them back alive."

The girl's red lips curled in a smile both cruel and victorious. She pulled a pair of tiny silver scissors from one pocket and began delicately to cut her long, sharp nails.

"There is the other book too, which we read of in Lord Morte's book," she reminded her father. "The other book was written by the moon goddess, and belonged to the Keeper, but it disappeared. It may contain spells and power that we need."

"Yes," he agreed. "Search for it, too."

The girl nodded and began to pull golden hairpins from the intricate mass of coiled braids that crowned her head and, when she reached the tower door, they were tumbling down her back. The hem of the green silk dress swept the pins across the tiles. As the door thudded shut behind her, closing off her sharp cries to servants, the sorcerer bent to the black book and opened it. His face grew intent as his hard fingers traveled along the lines of ink, and his mind claimed the dark powers of Lord Morte for his own.

CHAPTER TWO

IT WAS THE FIRST MORNING of the spring equinox when Vita came alone out of the mountains. She paused on a grassy slope above the waters of the Golfo d'Levanto. Shading her eyes, she stared toward the valley, hidden by a fold of the land, where her home waited. Already, she could see the smoke from village chimneys lifting straight into the still air like brush strokes of translucent gray. At this reminder of cooking fires and bread ovens, Vita's stomach rumbled hungrily. She had traveled light in the mountains for two days, eating only the figs and the goat's cheese that her aunt, Aunt Carmela, had packed into the sack that she carried slung over her thin shoulders.

I'm almost home, Vita thought. I should be happy.

She sighed and continued along the path as it wound down-hill, her sandals beating softly in the dust. Her legs felt as heavy as though sand filled them, and a weight seemed to press on her shoulders along with the hot sunlight. She remembered how, when she was small, she had skipped down this path beside her mother, how she had picked wildflowers and sung simple tunes.

It had been easy then, to be joyful. Today she felt old, much older than fifteen, and too miserable to sing. What was wrong with her?

She should have been satisfied, for yesterday she had completed the magic circle around the mountain realm of the Corno d'Oro. As she did at each equinox and each solstice, she had sung the ancient spells, drawn the sacred symbols with her fingertips on trunks of towering catalpa and fragrant acacia and gnarled olive and onto the backs of warm rocks. She had chanted the incantations over pools of water and rushing rivulets. Now the secret ways and places of the mythical Corno d'Oro were protected for the year's quarter—its paths invisible to the eye, its places of rest hidden behind the veil of magic she had created, its grazing meadows peaceful and secure.

When the next solstice or equinox drew near, she, the Keeper, would travel once more alone into the mountains, the villagers averting their eyes as she passed through their terraced gardens, their groves of nut trees. They had vowed to protect the Corno d'Oro from the evil that swept across the land, but only the Keeper could work the ancient magic and they didn't wish to spy on where she went or what she did when she climbed the slopes alone behind their houses, her eyes shining with old wisdom.

Now, leaving the path, Vita plunged abruptly downhill on a shortcut of her own. Around her, twisted olive trees cast a thin shade, their pale leaves fluttering above swathes of crimson poppies and of cyclamen in shades of white, pale rose, and deep crimson. Tiny butterflies of palest blue danced over the flowers. The trees quivered with bird song: the long warble of the olive thrush that was like water falling, the chitter of moon wrens, the sleepy hoot of a distant gufo. Thick spring grass swished against Vita's bare legs, and the smell of the land filled her nose: the warmth of tilled earth, the aromatic whiff of rosemary and thyme, the tang of salt from the beaches below. She knew that she should have felt content in the midst of such beauty, not miserable. Moodily, she kicked a pebble down the path before glancing up to notice a plump girl of her own age seated nearby on a rock.

"Beatrice!" Vita shouted.

The potter's daughter turned and waved. Vita quickened her stride and climbed onto the flat rock beside her friend, who was rubbing dried clay from her fingers.

"You're back," Beatrice said, her cheeks dimpling as she smiled. "All is well?"

"All is well," Vita said shortly, but she didn't feel as though all was well. She felt as though a nest of snakes was uncoiling in her heart, restless and dangerous.

Beatrice stared at her for a moment. "I thought you might be hungry," she said, and held out a stack of almond cakes wrapped in a grape leaf.

"You're right," Vita agreed. She bit into a cake's crisp, golden edge. She munched through its soft centre, sticky with honey, and then silently ate a second one.

"Is something wrong?" Beatrice asked at last.

Vita shrugged. "No," she said. "Not really. Maybe. At least— it's me, Beatrice. There's something wrong with me."

"What do you mean?"

"I wish I wasn't the Keeper. At least, not yet. Other Keepers, in other generations, haven't had to be responsible at my age. I just wish I could do something else first. Travel. Have fun. See the inland plains and visit the cities. Buy from the merchant ships unloading treasure in the delta."

"But the Corno d'Oro's safety is in your hands," Beatrice pointed out. After a pause she asked shyly, "Have you ever seen him?"

Vita shook her head. "No. My mother said that if I ever see him, it will be at a time decided by him and not by me. And that, in the meantime, I see his spirit when the village children laugh, or the fish jump in the sea, or the wind and sun pass through the olive trees. But Beatrice, we know what he looks like from the Keeper's Tale: wondrously beautiful, with purple-brown eyes, rippling mane and tail, a noble face and tapering, spiral horn of pure gold growing from his forehead."

Beatrice sighed in awe, with lips parted and eyes gazing away down the slope. "You're lucky, to follow in your mother's steps," she said. "Since she was the Keeper, you must be the next one."

Vita swallowed, feeling tears close to the surface. She rested her elbows on her knees and bent her face into her hands, staring into the red darkness behind her eyelids.

"I wanted to grow up and be just like my mother—only not so soon," she said, forcing the words out. Beatrice's warm hand squeezed her arm. If only her mother had been more careful, eleven months ago, picking herbs on a mountain ledge. If only she hadn't fallen so far, landing on rocks below...Vita pushed away her grief, letting resentment take its place. Straightening, she rubbed a hand across her lavender eyes and brushed away the strands of silver-blonde hair that had fallen across her face.

"Don't you ever wish you could wear a silk dress and eat food from faraway places?" she asked passionately, staring at Beatrice. "Don't you ever wonder what it would be like to live in a palazzo in Genovera? Don't you wonder about the parties they hold in the cities, with fireworks and exotic animals, games and street shows and dancing?"

Beatrice frowned, clasping her plump fingers together. "Not really," she said. "It's very beautiful here, Vita. I'm happy painting pots and living in the village. And I thought that being a Keeper was something special, a sacred trust—"

"Of course it's a sacred trust," Vita interrupted impatiently. "But I don't want it, at least, not yet. I want to—oh, I don't know. I want to be free first. This time, I almost didn't come home."

"What?" Beatrice sounded shocked.

"I could have walked down into the plain, on the other side of the mountains. There was no one to stop me."

Vita remembered how she had lingered on the eastern ridge of the mountains and gazed across miles of blue distance to where the plains shimmered. Restlessness had gnawed at her with a kind of hunger. She had longed for the freedom to walk down into the plains and explore the cities that spread by broad, shining rivers. In her imagination, she viewed the city's tall towers and huge squares, their cafes with bright awnings, their slender spires where bells tolled. She had heard about such sights from the wandering tale-spinners who occasionally passed through her coastal village. They talked about the nobili too, those rich merchants and princes who lived in the cities, riding on spirited red horses with hooves that struck sparks from the cobblestones. According to the tale-spinners, the nobili wore fabulous clothes of silk and velvet, ate from plates of gold, and could have whatever their hearts desired.

Balanced on her rocky outlook, Vita had fingered her own dress of coarse blue fabric with discontent. What would happen if she simply took the path winding down into the plains and journeyed to the nearest city instead of returning to her village? What an adventure that would be! And there was no one there to prevent her from going, or to see her leave. For what had felt like a long time, she'd lingered on the ridge and fought temptation while the breeze on her shoulders seemed to nudge her forward. As shadows lengthened, she had turned her back on the plains and her longings, and begun her journey westward toward the coast. For she was the Keeper, bound to the Corno d'Oro—and dreams of silk and dancing were not for her.

Although she knew that to be the Keeper was a great honor, lately she'd felt that it was a load that she carried, or a rope that bound her tight. She hadn't asked to be fulfilling the expectations of others: her dead mother and all the previous generations of Keepers, Aunt Carmela, the villagers.

"If you hadn't come home, there wouldn't have been anyone to tell the Keeper's Tale at the Feast of Dragomar this afternoon," Beatrice reminded her.

Vita followed Beatrice's gaze across the Golfo d'Levanto's wrinkled surface of water that stretched to the pale horizon. Two miles offshore, the rocky archipelago of twenty-two pirati islands floated on the surface of the sea.

"Another of my responsibilities," Vita sighed.

She would be expected on the largest of the islands, in the village of the pirati, to tell the Keeper's Tale before the feast. For most of the year, the pirati did not encourage mainland visitors to their islands, and the mainland villagers for their part preferred to keep to their mountain terraces and their small fields. But at the Feast of Dragomar, the Keeper always visited the islands to tell the Keeper's Tale because it was a story important to the pirati as well as to the villagers.

"Never mind," Beatrice said, poking Vita playfully in the ribs. "Giovanni will take you across the water."

Heat rose up Vita's neck when she thought of Giovanni's changeable sea eyes dancing over her face, of Giovanni's brown hand steady on the tiller, of his boat with its pale yellow sail and blue hull.

"Maybe there was something to come home for?" Beatrice teased, but Vita leapt to her feet and jumped down off the rock.

"Don't you have pots to paint?" she teased in return. "Let's go."

She scrambled over a stone wall, taking a shortcut through old Tomie's meadow where a sturdy jennet raised her head to watch. The jennet and her foal had golden coats striped with cinnamon lines, and their short horns made whorls like snail shells below their huge creamy ears. Old Tomie bred the finest jennets in the village—they were always in demand for riding and for carrying loads of firewood and panniers of grapes. Vita scratched the mother jennet in the warm spot behind her ears while she waited for plump Beatrice to scramble over the wall and catch up to her.

Suddenly, from the far side of the meadow, drifted the sound of a reed pipe and of a drum being beaten slowly, and children's laughter. Vita shaded her eyes and saw, visible above the stone wall, the top half of a curious procession moving along. Huge lurching puppets waved stick arms while their flimsy costumes fluttered in the sea breeze. Their faces, scowling or sad or laughing joyously, peered into old Tomie's meadow, and leading them all along was a shining bald head.

"It's the beetleman!" panted Beatrice, catching up to Vita. "Come on!"

They ran across the field while old Tomie's jennets watched. Vita sprang easily to the top of the far wall, then turned and hauled Beatrice up by the hand before they both dropped down into the lane.

The procession halted. At its front, the beetleman stared gravely at Vita, his bulging stomach stretching the shiny fabric of his striped yellow vest. Around his bald head the beetles, their wings flashing brilliant green and yellow, fluttered in circles at the ends of their thread harnesses, which were fastened at the bottom to a huge silver button on the beetleman's striped vest. In contrast to his restless flying menagerie, the beetleman's face was curiously still: a placid moon with three chins that nothing seemed to disturb.

The drum on the back of the piper, a scrawny man with wizened cheeks and hair like feathers, fell silent, for its sticks were attached to the man's legs and it only beat when he walked. The puppets swayed in the breeze, over the legs of their human puppeteers whose bodies were hidden inside the puppets' gauzy gowns. Only the puppeteers' eyes, bright and mischievous, peered out at the girls.

"Dear ladies," the Beetleman said calmly. "The Keeper and Beatrice, the potter's daughter. A delight." And he swept them a low bow that the wizened piper and all the puppets copied.

Vita grinned with delight; she couldn't help it even though she knew she was too old to care about beetles and puppets any longer.

The beetleman stared at her gravely, as though he knew secrets about her. Vita felt her grin waver.

"There are rumors of war, dear ladies," the beetleman informed them sonorously. "Dark and ancient powers stirring in the north. Swords being beaten on anvils in the south. Be vigilant. Be courageous. Be true." He stared at Vita as he spoke, his deep eyes pools she might fall into. It was strange that in all the many times the beetleman had visited the village when she was a child, she'd never noticed his eyes before.

Then he bowed low again, and all the puppets bowed, and the piper winked at Beatrice and Vita and placed his reed pipe to his lips. He capered to his sprightly tune on his bow legs, and his drum boomed and the puppets swayed forward, jostling up the lane toward the path that led on to the next village. Ahead of them all, the beetleman's bald head shone in the sun amidst the flashing beetles.

"What did that mean?" asked Beatrice anxiously, but Vita shrugged.

"Who knows?" she said dismissively, but still she felt herself falling into the beetleman's soft, wide eyes that were like pools where no wind ever blew.

CHAPTER THREE

As Vita and Beatrice continued down the rocky lane, the roofs of the village came into sight below: a jumbled mass of terracotta tile glowing in the sun. The tall narrow houses—painted rose and ochre with wooden slatted shutters of green and blue framing every window—struggled for standing room on the slopes of the valley. Lines of washing hung limply above cobbled alleyways. At the mouth of the valley the houses formed a half-circle, around the tiny harbor with its wall of golden stone where even now, Vita could see figures of pirati and villagers bargaining over goods for the Feast of Dragomar. The pirati would have brought their fish packed in silvery layers in wooden crates, and the villagers would have brought casks of olive oil and red wine and also the first tender endives and chicory from their gardens.

At an angle to the village and its river valley lay another, smaller valley down which a tributary of the main river, a mere stream of burbling water, flowed. A lavender colored gate stood at the top of the garden that filled this valley. To one side of the gate, a shrine to Luna, the moon goddess, held a bunch of almond blossom and a pot of honey.

Vita stopped at the gate. "Are you coming with me?" she asked Beatrice, but Beatrice shook her head.

"I said I'd be home by the noon meal. My mother wants help in the kitchen. And anyway, you have to meet Giovanni this afternoon." Her eyes, dark as olives in her plump face, sparkled mischievously, and she hurried down the hill, waving goodbye before Vita could reply.

Vita pushed the gate open and followed the path in the bottom of the valley. Nut trees—mandolo, sweet hazel, and fragranti—held aloft a froth of pink and white blossoms. The air was perfumed by the flowers on the apricot and tangerine and lemon trees, and filled with the sound of running water. Vita smiled, feeling her restlessness soften and become still. Even on this beautiful coast, nowhere was more beautiful than her own valley, for generations of Keepers had lived in it and thus a little of the power of the Corno d'Oro touched it. Flowers brushed her ankles as she followed the path downhill toward the red roof of her home.

She crossed the courtyard with its well of golden stone, and paused by the open back door to slip off her sandals.

Greetings, Keeper, said the soft, sleepy voice of the wombo in Vita's mind. She glanced up into the spreading limbs of the chyme tree that grew beside the house and shaded the courtyard. The wombo was halfway up the tree, clinging to a branch with its paws, its soft gray fur blending into the bark. Its huge, round eyes peered down at Vita.

You're awake late, she told it in her thoughts.

I was waiting to see the Keeper safely home from the mountains. All is well?

All is well, small one, she replied. *The world will not slip further out of balance. The magic is completed.*

The wombo blinked sleepily and nodded, then opened its small mouth wide in a yawn that revealed a tongue of pale, cyclamen pink.

Sleep, all is well, Vita said gently but the wombo's eyes were already shut. It had spent the night catching moths by the light of the moon.

Vita slipped through the back door, into the kitchen's welcoming smell of wood smoke and the aroma of the dried herbs that hung from wooden beams in bunches. She crossed the red tiles toward the fire where Aunt Carmela—her aunt and the village witch—bent over a griddle. She straightened at Vita's approach, wiping her hands down the front of her apron, her face breaking into a smile that sent lines chasing each other like rivulets of water. Her smile seemed to spill over her face and into her green eyes.

"Vita." She pulled the girl into her bony grip and held her. "All is well in the mountains?"

"All is well. I didn't omit anything. Every path is invisible, every pasture safe, and every valley secure. The Corno d'Oro is in peace."

"You are very young for such a task. Only fifteen. The balance of the world trembling on such young shoulders," Aunt Carmela muttered, sighing, her hand stroking Vita's pale hair. "But with your mother dead..." She trailed off, sighed again, then straightened up with a determined jut of her chin.

"You are wise beyond your years," she said. "You have learned everything your mother could teach you. Now, for some griddle bread."

Returning to the fire, she lifted the golden flat-bread from the hot griddle and passed it to Vita on a plate. Vita carried it to the wooden table beneath the window and lifted the bread to her mouth, its flavors of basil and pepper and olive oil rising into her nose. There was no reason for Aunt Carmela to worry, she thought. It was true that she had learned everything her mother told her before she died...no, don't think of this. Her thoughts shied away from the grief that lay in her like a hard kernel in the center of an apricot. She tried to forget that moment of temptation too, when she had almost chosen the path that led down to the plains and cities. What would Aunt Carmela think of her, if she knew about that moment of indecision? She would not say then that Vita was wise beyond her years.

I will never break my trust, Vita thought with sudden resolve. I will not think of the cities anymore. I will be content, like Beatrice.

She swallowed hard on her bread, turning her glance from the empty silence of the big room—where only Aunt Carmela was left—toward the bright square of light in the window. Craning her neck, she could just see the furry outline of the wombo asleep in the chyme tree. The tree's hard, metallic leaves rang softly as the breeze passed through them.

Suddenly, the light flickered. Vita jumped back, her chair legs squealing on the tiles. The window filled with a great beating of gray, barred wings and the glare of golden eyes. The bird's talons scratched across the shutters, and air thrummed between its huge feathers. Vita leapt to her feet.

"It's a gufo!" she exclaimed, flinging the back door open. She lifted her arm and the bird landed on her wrist, its talons biting into her skin and its weight almost more than she could hold. Its golden eyes, ringed with orange, gleamed fiercely at her and its feathers settled slowly down along the sweep of its folded wings.

A chill of fear ran up Vita's arm into her body.

What is wrong, night brother? she asked it in her thoughts, for it was unusual to find a gufo awake by day. It was a bird that preferred to hunt in the dark, the moon mirrored in its eyes, its hooting cries drifting through the acacia trees as it swept down onto unsuspecting mice.

It is the assassini and the brutti of Lord Maldici—they are coming. They are in the next valley, the gufo replied, its voice urgent in her mind.

The assassini! Are they coming this way?

They are coming. You must hide, Keeper.

"What is the matter?" Aunt Carmela asked, coming to stand beside Vita.

"The assassini are coming, and the brutti." Fear made Vita's voice thin, and panic poured through her body like a wave. Her arm shook under the gufo's weight and the bird flew up into the tree where the wombo slept deeply, its breathing barely lifting its soft gray chest.

"You must go to the islands at once!" Aunt Carmela said. "The assassini will not go there today; they are afraid of the dragon on his feast day. You must flee to the beach!"

In a whirl of black skirt, Vita's aunt turned to the kitchen and emerged after only a minute with a shawl that she flung over Vita's bright hair. "Go! Go now!" Her thin hands shoved at Vita's back.

"You too! You come too!" Vita cried.

Aunt Carmela's arms, fiercely strong, spun Vita around and shook her. "Run!" she ordered. "They do not want old women! I will warn the village."

"Tell Beatrice!" Vita shouted. She sprang forward, her sandals pounding up the valley path, making the birds cry out and flutter in alarm. Behind her, as the gate at the top of the garden swung shut, Vita glimpsed Aunt Carmela strewing the path with herbs, muttering her spells. The gufo was sweeping the ground with its wing, erasing her footprints. Oh, that their efforts might protect her from the tracking noses of the brutti packs! And that Aunt Carmela would be safe! Vita's heart clenched into a fist.

Gasping, she raced across the grass and past the grazing jennets. At the crest of the ridge above the valley she paused, threw herself flat on the ground, and glanced back at the village. The first assassini were running down the far slope of the valley, into the village streets. The sun glinted on their short bodies covered in sparse, wiry red hair, and Vita could see the blue smudge of the brands tattooed on their foreheads. Below this, their bulbous noses were always damp, and their soft long ears flapped against their swarthy necks. Their black boots rang on the cobbles black whips cracked and snaked, looking for victims. At their side the brutti ran baying, their coats red as blood, their keen noses skimming the ground.

Vita lay like a statue. They would run right through the village, run up the slope and find her here like a hare in the grass;

they would kick her ribs in with their boots and beat her with their whips and let their brutti tear at her. A sudden scream from the village roused Vita from her frozen state. Pottery broke with a bright shattering, a man yelled, the crackle of fire clawed upward. Vita slid on her belly down the far side of the ridge until the village was out of sight. Then she ran between the man-dolo trees, ran and ran until she reached the oldest tree, the one with the hole in its trunk. She slipped in like a shadow and crawled on hands and knees into the tunnel below.

Darkness took her, but she was not afraid of it. She felt her way carefully, smelling earth and roots, touching stones. Gradually, the tunnel grew larger and she stood up and went forward, touching rough rock. The surge of waves filled her ears, the rock became smooth. Weed squelched underfoot and a gull screeched close by as she burst out into the dazzling sunlight of the secret beach, protected by rocky arms of cliff.

A Mara woman, sitting on a rock and combing her green hair with a silver comb, glanced at Vita, her eyes changing color from blue to green as waves change color as they swirl around rocks.

"I greet you," Vita said courteously, her heart thudding and her stomach sick with fear.

The Mara slid from the rock and paced across the sand, her body covered in tiny, soft scales that changed from pale pink to aqua green and lavender as she moved. Against her scaled legs, her tiny skirt of cowry shells chimed softly, and green scallop shells swung against her breasts. She stopped before Vita and regarded her regally.

"You are the Keeper. Something is amiss in the world of man. Not that it is any of my affair." And she arched her green brows delicately to show her disinterest.

"Please," Vita gasped. "Please, help me. The assassini are raiding the village, they are from the north, from the army of Lord Maldici. I must reach the pirati. Please could you swim out for me and find Giovanni, the pirati boy?"

"Giovanni? It is a long swim," the Mara replied with a lazy

smile and a toss of her long hair. She was very beautiful, sleek and slender on the sand, with bangles of gold around her wrists and ankles. Vita tried not to stare at the gold—some said that the Mara aided the pirati, pulling shipwrecked sailors to their death, stripping them of their wealth. But others said that the Mara simply took what drifted to the bottom of the sea in the hulks of wrecked ships, that they only rescued what would otherwise have been buried in the sea bottom by swirling tides.

"I could find this Giovanni," the Mara decided. "He is a friend of yours?"

"Yes. Please, ask him to meet me here with a boat. To come now, sooner than we planned."

"If I find him."

The Mara undulated across the sand and slipped without a ripple into the surf; she waved goodbye to Vita with one slender green arm and a flash of gold. Then she sank beneath the surface, not to reappear, for the Mara could breathe underwater as well as on land.

Vita hunched against a rock and stared out to sea. She wondered what was happening in the village, heard again the sickening scream of a woman and the sound of glass breaking. The nobili of Genovera to the north were commanded by Lord Maldici. They warred with the nobili of Piso to the south, who were commanded by Lord Maldici's brother: Lord Verona. It was said that the whole land should have been Lord Verona's, for he was the elder son. When they were youths, his usurping younger brother had driven him from Genovera, and now Lord Maldici plundered the land of Verde with his packs of brutti and cruel assassini. The nobili were always hungry for more, for wealth and fame, for pleasure, for food they had not labored to nurse from the earth.

Vita listened to the hard rhythm of her heart, a sound louder in her ears than the crashing surf that sluiced the golden sand. There is no reason to fear so much, she told herself. They are not looking for me but for crops to strip and young men to take into bondage and gold to steal. They do not even know that I exist. She imagined the quivering, drooling noses of the brutti skimming her garden path, picking up her scent, tracing her to the tunnel. No! No, the gufo and Aunt Carmela had covered her footprints, and in the high mountains the Corno d'Oro was safe. She had performed the magic to keep it so. She had nothing to fear. Still, her heart pounded.

Vita waited for a long time. The Mara were fickle; perhaps the woman had not delivered her message to Giovanni after all. At last, a speck became visible bobbing on the bright horizon. The pale wing of a yellow sail licked the sky above it. Vita ran down the coarse sand as the blue hull crunched onto shore, carried by the surf. Giovanni leapt from the boat and grasped Vita by the arm.

"Come!" he said. "Hurry!" And he swung Vita over the gunwale as the surf lifted it, and then he thrust the boat back into the sea. At the tiller, the Mara woman shot Vita a glance of cool amusement as the sail caught the wind and the boat scudded northward, tacking toward the pirati archipelago.

They were a quarter of a mile out to sea when they passed the village. Black smoke rose in choking columns from burning houses, and the brutti ran baying along the harbor wall amongst the spilled casks of oil and wine. A jennet cried on the hillside and there was a confused tumult of swords clashing and men roaring. There was a yell as Giovanni's boat was spotted, and three assassini archers ran to the end of the wall and drew their bows. Giovanni pushed Vita down into the bottom of the boat and drew Aunt Carmela's dark shawl over her head. The archers released their arrows; there was a whistle of air, but the arrows fell short and hissed into the sea. Giovanni trimmed the sail, pointing the bows close to the north wind, and the boat shot forward.

Vita struggled up onto her elbows, noticing that the Mara woman had gone overboard into the sea without a sound. For a long time she stared over the gunwale, watching the village burn and wondering if Aunt Carmela, the only family she had left, would be alive by evening.

Finally she turned to face the islands that were so close now that she could see the tide pools shining along the rocky shorelines, and the crooked salt-pines. Giovanni tacked, pointing the bows into a narrow inlet in the cliffs and expertly steering the boat between submerged rocks where the surf boiled white. At the head of the inlet, a harbor wall reached out to meet incoming boats, and beyond it the village crouched low, sheltered from the west wind by the island's hills. Vita sat on the gunwale of the boat, keeping out of Giovanni's way as he let their sail down with a rush of cloth. She leaned out to fend them off from the harbor wall. When Giovanni had tied the bow rope to a ring in the wall, she stepped out carefully and climbed the slippery steps to where a huddle of pirati children watched curiously. "The Keeper. It's the Keeper," they whispered, shuffling away from her as she stared at them uncertainly, feeling small and alone on the wall under the watching windows of the pirati houses. She had never been to this place before, for villagers were not welcome here.

Then Giovanni sprang to the top of the steps and flashed her a crooked grin. "Ignore them," he advised. "Let's go home and my mother can give us something to eat."

Gratefully, Vita went with him into the alleys of the village, where fierce eyes seemed to glint at her from every window and every corner.

CHAPTER FOUR

WHEN IT WAS TIME for telling the Keeper's Tale, the pirati children gathered around Vita. The youngest urchins crowded at her feet as she perched on the rough stone wall encircling the village well. Behind these youngest children, cross-legged on the cobbles, clustered older brothers and sisters, all with the same cheeks burned dark by wind and sun, the wild dark hair, the bright splashes of festival clothing. Here and there, the sun glinted off a gold hoop in pierced ear or nose, and a restless sea of blue eyes stared at Vita—eyes that changed from blue to gray, indigo to aqua as the sea will change under varied skies. It was said that, generations ago, the pirati had loved the Mara and that, as a result, they had come to possess Mara eyes.

Behind the rank of older children the adults lounged against the salt-pines that surrounded the square. They had heard the Keeper's Tale every year, at the Feast of Dragomar, since they were youngsters themselves, barefoot and scratched on the cobbles, with sand between their toes. In those days the Keeper had been a woman, not a girl too young for the task of protecting the

Corno d'Oro. Yet now, with the death of the Keeper, this girl Vita was the only one who knew the spells and the ancient singing magic that protected the mountains. She alone could make the paths of the Corno d'Oro invisible to all eyes, keeping hidden its resting places in the valleys and its grazing places in the high meadows. And so, the adult pirati held themselves still and prepared to listen to Vita retelling the old story, with as much attention as the youngest children on the cobblestones.

Vita glanced once around the crowd, gathering them in with her lavender eyes. This was her first time to tell the Keeper's Tale at the Feast of Dragomar but she was not nervous. Every word of the tale was familiar to her; she had begun to learn it as soon as she could talk, her mother leaning over her bed at dusk and asking her to repeat sentences in her drowsy, child's voice while the gufos hooted outside in the valley. She would tell the story as it had been taught to her by her mother, who had learned it at the knee of her grandmother, who had learned it in turn from her great-grandmother. These words had been passed down as a sacred trust through many generations.

"In the high and far-off days," Vita began, and a satisfied sigh, like a breeze in the salt-pines, rose from the children.

"In the high and far off-off days, a queen reigned in the Moon Mountains on the roof of the world. In that place, the stars were closer and larger, and the magic was young and strong. This queen was a moon goddess with starry eyes and silver hair that fell to the ground and her name was Luna. She could speak to all the animals of the night: the moon wrens and the silver bats, the moths and spotted panthers and gentle wombos.

"But the most important animals that Luna befriended were the Corno d'Oro, the Golden Horns. These beasts were silver in the moonlight and golden in the sunlight, and they had the power to maintain the balance between the forces of darkness and light. Where they lay down, star lilies of pale gold sprang up. Where they grazed, the grass and meadow flowers grew thick and lush. As long as they were free and alive in the mountains, the world was at peace and untroubled. No frost harmed the flowering mandolo trees, or the tender grapes on the young vines. The great power of the Corno d'Oro maintained the balance in the world.

"They were wondrously beautiful, with purple-brown eyes like the finest ripe olives; with manes and tails of rippling silken hair and nostrils of velvet; with legs as delicate as the limbs of the fleetest deer. Where the Corno d'Oro trod on the mountains, the mare left hoof prints shaped like sickle moons, and the stallion left hoof prints round as the midday sun. Their faces were long and noble, and from their foreheads grew a tapering, spiral horn of pure gold.

"The fame of these magical beasts trickled down into the valleys and plains of the world, and seeped like rainwater into the ears of men. In the city of Genovera, in the north of Verde, their fame came to the ears of Lord Morte. He was born a prince of the house of Maldici, but he had fallen into evil ways and had studied the black arts. He had become a great and powerful sorcerer and he wanted to possess the Corno d'Oro, thinking to wrest their power to his own uses. His greed became so great that it was beyond his control. It escaped into the world, like a spell, slipping into the hearts of many other men. In the taverns of the cities, wandering singers lay their tongues against the beauty that was the Corno d'Oro. Adventurers began to seek them, longing for fame and to have their names recorded in the chronicles of the world. Rich men ached to possess the beasts and control their powerful magic; greedy men, both rich and poor, lusted after their golden horns.

"But Luna, the moon goddess, wove strong magic around the mountains and made the Corno d'Oro invisible in their meadows beside the crystal mountain rivers. Thus she protected them from the greed of Lord Morte that had slipped into the world.

"The power of Lord Morte increased as he aged. His will reached out like claws and sank like talons into people's hearts. He was greedy for power, for wealth and gold, for fame and fortune. He seized land by force, stripped the crops, and levied harsh taxes. Where his armies trod, the earth lay scorched. He reigned with cruelty and terror, and his greatest desire remained to find the Corno d'Oro and steal them from their mountains, bringing them to his city of Genovera where he would bend their power to his will. To this end, he sent cunning spies to the city of the moon goddess high on the roof of the world, for he had heard that she was dying in her bed beneath the carved stars. And this rumor on the wind was true.

"To take her place, Luna had trained a young girl, the first Keeper of the Corno d'Oro, and to this young girl she taught her strong magic and the secret songs and signs to protect the beasts and keep them invisible. Some said the Keeper was Luna's daughter, and some said she had been found as a baby abandoned on the mountain peaks. She had lavender eyes and silver-gold hair, and to this day all Keepers look like her.

"When Luna died and returned to the skies, Lord Morte's men tricked the young Keeper into betraying her spells and they captured the two Corno d'Oro. They tied the beasts' slender legs with ropes and muffled their wild cries and covered their olive eyes with strips of cloth. They transported them to the sea, and loaded them into a ship and set sail for Genovera where Lord Morte waited. And with them traveled their Keeper, the young girl who had betrayed her trust and lay in the ship's hold near death with a broken heart.

"But there was power still in the Corno d'Oro even though they were captive. They cried to the sea and to the moon, and the tides rose higher and higher, surging over the land. In the heavens, the stars fell and the moon turned dark as a bruised aubergine and hid behind the gathering clouds. A cold, relentless rain began to lash the earth, filling the valleys and flooding the plains with its angry power. The rain waters mingled with the rising tides and slowly the world began to disappear into the waves.

"Then the great sea dragon, Dragomar, which lives in the Golfo d'Levanto, grew disturbed in his deep-sea lair by the tumult in the world, and rose up through the murky depths to thrash at the waves with his scaly tail. As the ship with the Corno d'Oro sailed toward him, he opened his gaping jaws and broke the ship into pieces with his blue teeth, and Lord Morte's men, and the young Keeper girl, and the Corno d'Oro fell into the waves. The men drowned, and the sea dragon sank to the seabed and began to collect all the gold that had been in the ship, the gold that Lord Morte's men had stolen from the towns and cities they had sacked. So the greed of Lord Morte entered into the heart of the old sea dragon and all year he lies in his deep caverns, covering his golden hoard with his slimy belly. But once every year, at the Feast of Dragomar, he rises to the surface of the Golfo d'Levanto, and the fishermen throw him gold to appease him. And so the fishermen too fell under the shadow of Lord Morte, for they became pirati, sinking ships to steal gold that was not theirs. And some of it they throw to the sea dragon, but some of it they hoard for themselves."

"But what happened to the Keeper girl and the Corno d'Oro?" piped the voice of a small girl in the front row, while the other children shuffled to look at her.

Vita gave the children a grave look and continued with her tale.

"The Keeper girl had a small sharp knife hidden in her clothes. When the ship was wrecked, she used the knife to cut loose the ropes and cloth that bound the two Corno d'Oro, so that they might swim free and save themselves if they could. They both turned toward shore, but the sea dragon was beating the sea into a mighty froth as he whipped and stirred it with his tail, searching for every piece of gold. In the spray and waves, the two Corno d'Oro became separated. The stallion swam in circles, crying for his mare, but at last he was too weary to swim much farther and began to sink low in the wild water. Then he turned for shore once more with the Keeper girl clinging to his mane, and when his hooves touched land, the rain ceased and the waves calmed. But the sea never gave back the land it had stolen, and that is why now the world is almost all water.

"The villagers found the stallion and his Keeper on the shore and took pity on them and hid them. They nursed the Keeper back to health, and they let the stallion go free into the mountains. They vowed to protect him, to keep him wild and free, to save him from the greed of Lord Morte. The Keeper wove her spells and sang her magic again, to keep the stallion invisible. And gradually the story of the Corno d'Oro passed into myth and people in the cities forgot about the beasts. And the Keeper married a man of the village who grew mandolo nuts on the terraced slopes. They had two daughters, one with black hair and one with hair of silver-gold. The fair daughter had eyes colored lavender, like an evening sky. She could speak to the animals of the night. She grew up to be the next Keeper. The dark daughter had green eyes, and the power to understand green growing things, to foretell when to plant and when to harvest the crops. She grew up to be Carmela, the wise witch of the village. This is the way it has been ever since: in every generation of my family there are two daughters: a Keeper and a girl called Carmela.

"But the Corno d'Oro mare perished in the stormy waves, and the stallion runs alone in the mountains. As long as he is free, the villagers' tender grapes are not touched by frost, and the olives cling thick as bees in the ancient trees on the mountain terraces, and the jennets deliver foals with strong legs and soft ears. And where the stallion rests alone in the mountain valleys, the star lilies spring up. But because he is alone, the balance of the world cannot be healed, and the nobili of Genovera and Piso war and fight, and tax the villagers and bind their sons to carry swords. The assassini stalk the land, carrying the greed of Lord Morte in their hearts, keeping it alive long years after that old sorcerer has died. And the brutti hunt in packs, sniffing out secrets, leaving messages in blood. And wherever the assassini and the brutti packs tread, everything shrivels and dies as though the earth has been scorched."

There was silence in the square at the end of Vita's tale, a silence that the cry of gulls and the sigh of wind and the slap of waves against the harbor wall could not penetrate. The children stared at Vita, motionless, their eyes clouded dark with grief. Even the youngest felt the profound grief of that moment: of the thought of the Corno d'Oro stallion alone in the mountains, of the balance of the world swinging precariously. And Vita, watching their smooth upturned faces, wondered which amongst them would let the greed of Lord Morte trickle into their hearts, so that they plundered the trading ships and hoarded gold and spices in sacks and chests deep in the island caves. It was said by the mainland villagers that you could never trust a pirati child, that in each of them was the seed of Lord Morte's greed. But the pirati scoffed at the villagers, who knew nothing of tides and storms, and said that they lived life at the speed that a jennet toiled up the steepest mountain path.

Suddenly a voice broke the silence and, as though released from a spell, all the children sighed and stirred, shuffling their skinny legs on the cobbles, rearranging their brilliant dresses over their knees, picking at scabs.

"But if you're the Keeper, how come you don't have a dark sister?" asked a boy of about nine, his eyes bright with curiosity.

"I had a dark sister, but when we were both infants, my mother took us to visit relatives far down the coast. And a wave swept my sister into the sea. And she was lost," Vita said. "And my father was a wandering tale-spinner; I have never known him. And my mother...my mother died eleven months ago. She was gathering thyme in the mountains when the rock gave away and she fell and died."

Vita swallowed on the hard, familiar lump of her grief her mother's name swollen in her throat. For one moment the pirati shimmered before her eyes, but she willed her tears not to fall while the children gazed at her with a philosophical sympathy. They were familiar with sudden death: boys washed from rocks by a sudden wave while fishing, women lured to sea by Mara, men who sank in small boats in fierce autumnal storms.

"There's a rhyme about you," said a teenage girl from the edge of the crowd.

Vita stared into her green eyes and felt a sudden touch of

cold, like a dribble of water, slide down her spine. There was something intent and knowing about the girl's look.

"What rhyme?" she asked.

"They sing it to babies in the cradle, " the girl replied with a touch of scorn at Vita's ignorance. "It goes like this:

When the dark and fair part
And greed sings in the heart,
The shadows gather; the balance trembles.
Amongst poppies lies the Corno d'Oro
While the New Moon Keeper
Betrays the world's tomorrow."

"What does it mean?" asked a younger child, but Vita shook her head. She felt cold all over now, numb with cold, as though she had been swimming in the waves for too long.

"That rhyme is not about me," she retorted, aware of the adult pirati shifting uneasily against the sea-pines in the periphery of her vision. She rose to her feet, moving more sharply than she'd intended, the children scooting backward to get out of her way as though afraid that she might tread on them. But she waited, willing herself to be still, until the children had stood up too, shaking out their clothes, grabbing each other by the arms, stretching and calling to one another. Quickly, they dispersed in a bright stream, like a shoal of fish navigating the familiar reef of the village, its squat houses hunkered low to withstand the blast of storms.

The girl who had chanted the rhyme lingered until last, watching Vita intently. Where the sun shone on her long hair, tints of blue and green shimmered iridescent like the plumage on the neck of a black bird. She tossed her head as the last children streamed past, then turned on her slender bare feet and flounced away, her deep green dress, with its border of starfish, swinging over her slim hips. Vita stared after her uncertainly. What did this stranger know that she didn't?

"Vita? What's wrong?" asked Giovanni's voice and his hand was a warm pressure on her arm, bringing her back from the cold place she'd gone to. She had forgotten that he had been nearby the entire time, leaning in the shade of a sea-pine over to her right and listening to her tale, waiting for her. She glanced at him now: his familiar sea eyes, his hooked nose and strong teeth, and the bright red cloth knotted at his brown throat. Something stilled within her.

"Who was that girl?" she asked.

"That's Marina, the daughter of the sea witch who lives at the northern tip of the island."

"I'm afraid," Vita whispered. "What does the rhyme mean?"

"I don't know. They say it's very old; the grandmothers sing it."

"I am the first Keeper to be parted from my dark sister," Vita said. "And Keepers are born at the full of the moon, Giovanni. All of them—except me. I was born in the early morning, when the moon wrens were nesting. My mother said the sickle moon was framed in the bedroom window at my birth, hooked in the mandolo trees on the terraces. Perhaps I am the New Moon Keeper. But I would never betray the Corno d'Oro—never!"

"Hush," Giovanni soothed, for her voice had risen loud and sharp, and heads were turning in the cobbled street that led down to the harbor. He caught Vita by the elbows and swung her around to face him. "I know you would never betray your sacred trust. I believe you," he said firmly.

Staring into his eyes, now brilliant blue as the Golfo on summer mornings, she felt a wave of gratitude for his friendship. He had been steadfast since she'd first met him, when they were both four years old and he had come to the village with his father in a boat shaped like a cockleshell, to play on the beach while his father bartered fish for casks of smooth olive oil and of rough red wine with a taste of oak fires and dry earth. When she and Giovanni were five, they had poked sticks through their belts and swaggered around the village. Giovanni had dived off the harbor wall to pull her from the water when she fell in, for he could swim like a fish. At age six, they had used a fish gutting knife to their fingers and mix their blood; they had vowed to be true to each other until death. At seven they had stolen a boat for an afternoon's sail and been rescued far out to sea. At age eight, they had toiled into the mountains, gathering herbs for Aunt Carmela. Already then, Vita knew some of the smaller magics and simpler songs of all the vast store of knowledge that she would learn and use to protect the Corno d'Oro when it became her turn to be Keeper. But she never spoke of these things to Giovanni. She had taken a vow of silence at her mother's knee. When they were both nine, Giovanni took her swimming with the dolphins—for he could speak to them.

When Vita had told Aunt Carmela this, she had nodded her thin face and gripped Vita's wrist with surprising power in her bony fingers. "Listen to me," she had said, her breath smelling of garlic and bitter herbs and wood smoke from the cooking fire. "In every generation of pirati, there is one and only one who can speak to the dolphins. This one is pure in heart, untainted with the gold greed of Lord Morte. With the pure of heart, keep your trust. Remember what I tell you." And she had given Vita's wrist a shake before turning away to her black pot suspended over the hearth by stout chains, and taking up her long handled spoon had begun to stir her sweet, stewing tomatoes.

"Vita," Giovanni said now, shaking her from her thoughts. She saw that they had reached the harbor, where pirati women and children lined the wall with their bright clothes flapping in the wind. Behind them, the waters of the Golfo sparkled and swung.

"Don't look so worried," Giovanni said. "What do the old grandmothers know anyway, chewing their fish paste by small fires in dark kitchens? Forget them. Forget the rhyme about the New Moon Keeper."

And he slipped a candied sea-snail from one pocket and gave it to her with a flourish. Vita laughed and let the sweet dissolve slowly on her tongue as she and Giovanni stood watching the crowd of pirati gathered on the harbor wall. Soon, the water of the Golfo d'Levanto would heave and dance, parting to let the writhing bulk of Dragomar, the sea dragon, rise into view. Already, the little ships were putting out from the harbor, flying bright pennants, their crews stern with courage, and their decking strewn with sacks of plundered gold with which to appease the dragon. The pirati did not take out their gun ships today, for fear of accidentally antagonizing the dragon. These two ships lay instead against the harbor wall, their sleek golden hulls formed of the finest-grained fragranti wood polished like silk, their crimson sails furled against the booms, the slender masts raking the sky, the cannons hidden from sight in the gun ports. To take out such boats, it was felt, might incite Dragomar to rage and so today only the small fishing boats left the harbor's shelter.

Vita watched every detail of the spectacle, but fear nagged at her. The old grandmothers knew plenty; they guarded the village wisdom, the knowledge of generations. What did they know about her and betrayal?

Now the little boats were bobbing out over the Golfo, their sails belling taut in the wind as they tacked to and fro, waiting for the dragon. Alongside the boats, the sword whales leaped into the air, slicing through the bow waves, their tapering horns flashing in the sun. It was said that the black of heart amongst the pirati could commune with the sword whales, and that man and beast worked together when there was a ship to attack—the whales piercing the hulls with their horns and letting water into the holds while, above water, the pirati boarded with hooks and ladders, their cutlasses drawn. It was said that the sword whales would eat man-flesh when they could get it.

On the harbor wall, silence fell. Even the gulls, hanging overhead in the clear air, became silent. This was the moment that the pirati thought of all year with a shiver of dread and awe; there was always the fear that Dragomar would open his huge jaws and crush the little boats into kindling wood, that the women would see their men falling defenseless into the water with that mighty, scaly body lashing its coils around them. Would there be enough gold to propitiate the dragon?

Eyes strained, focused on the swinging dazzle of the waves and the fragile, brightly painted hulls.

"Ohhh!" A collective gasp, almost a moan, rose from the crowd and beside her, Vita felt Giovanni tense like a coiled whip.

For the sea was parting and from the waters, in a boiling mass of foam, rose the shining hulk of the dragon's back ridged with spikes and covered in tightly overlapping, metallic, lead-blue scales. Water streamed off its back as it rose higher. The boats, circling in closer, pitched on the waves as the sails, deprived of wind, luffed and hung empty and booms swung across with startling *cracks* that carried clearly to the watchers on the wall. Higher and higher the spiked back rose, the thrashing tail lifting clear with its deadly pointed barb of silver-blue. Women pressed their hands over their mouths and a baby whimpered. Vita found that she was squeezing Giovanni's arm and she loosened her grip.

Now the dragon's head broke the water, streaming foam, and its thunderous roar buffeted the watchers on the wall and made the boats rock. The air smelled putrid, like slime and dead things stranded in stagnant pools above the reach of all but the equinoctial tides. The crew heaved the gold over the tilting gunwales, watching with mingled regret and satisfaction as it plummeted into the sea's darkness for Dragomar to hoard in his caverns. The dragon roared again, its wide maw dark crimson, its curved teeth blue and smooth as glass. Vita shivered, remembering how Lord Morte's men and the first Keeper had fallen through those teeth into the water. But the first Keeper had deserved this ordeal, for she had betrayed her sacred trust—whereas she, Vita, would never betray the Corno d'Oro living free but alone in the mountains. She would guard it with her life, she thought fiercely, her fists clenching against her sides. Hadn't she turned away from the temptation of that path leading down into the plains and their cities?

The last bag of gold fell over the gunwale and the dragon swiveled its head in a great circle, its eyes—glassy and green as fishing floats—mirroring the tossing boats. Then with a coil of its shining scales and a slap of its tail that sent a wall of water rushing toward the boats, it began to sink back into the depths. Slowly the great spiked back disappeared from view, until the boats circled only a heave in the water, a circle of drifting foam. A great cheer rose from the wall and the women clasped one another and danced in circles as the men angled their sails to catch the wind and tacked back toward the harbor. The most dread moment of the Festival of Dragomar was completed for another year. This evening, lights would burn late under the sea-pines as the pirati danced and drank in the streets, between the stout houses of beach stone, while children tried to retell to each other Vita's tale of the Corno d'Oro...and around the fires, grandmothers fed fish paste to babies, and crooned songs of betrayal.

Vita shook her head anxiously, and grabbed Giovanni's hand.

"I'm starving! " she complained. "Let's find something to eat! And then I must go home."

"It might not be safe to go home yet. Stay here tonight; in the morning, we'll go for a sail and see if the assassini have passed through and left the village."

"But—Aunt Carmela!" Vita protested, tears stinging her eyes for the second time that afternoon. Giovanni slung his arm around her shoulder.

"It's a worry," he said gravely. "But you won't make things better for her by returning too soon. And who knows—if the assassini commandeer boats, they may even come here tomorrow."

Vita knew that this was true, but she pulled away from Giovanni's arm and strode scowling over the cobbles, surrounded by noisy pirati. They jostled toward the village square to lay tokens of thanks at the shrines of Luna, the moon goddess, and of their own special goddess, Sirena, whose graceful form, carved on the shrine, ended in a tail instead of legs and on whose forehead sat a crown of starfish. Passing by, Vita noticed that frolicking dolphins, their graceful leaps frozen in stone, curved around the edge of Sirena's shrine. Then she was pushed by the crowd toward the slow, communal fires over which flat bread and fish broth—thick with plump mollusks and juicy sea grapes—steamed in the late afternoon sun.

Vita leaned into the steam, her stomach cramping with hunger and anxiety.

CHAPTER FIVE

IN THE PEARLY DAWN, while the sea lay flat and the little waves barely licked the beaches, Vita and Giovanni slipped from his parents' house and walked down the cobbled alley to the harbor. Against the wall, the gunships lay motionless, and the fishing boats flared in bright chips of color in the dawn light. Vita saw that the two scouts, adult pirati who had sailed over to the mainland under cover of darkness, were laying sails out on the harbor wall to be mended. The men had volunteered the previous evening, after the feast, for this dangerous task of spying on the assassini, and they had promised to return before dawn. Now they laid out the sheets of tough sail fabric with strong tosses of their bronze arms, and flashed Vita a smile as she rushed toward them, as though their work had been no more than an amusing diversion in a day's routine—but it was said, Vita reminded herself, that the pirati thrived on danger. The sails were indigo colored, dyed with pigment from the mullosks that clung to the island rocks, and around the fabric's periphery stood other pirati, watching the scouts and talking about the assassini raid.

"Hurry. I must know," Vita said breathlessly to Giovanni, her long legs striding forward. She reached the scattering of men and came to an abrupt halt with her toes grazing the edge of a sail.

"I need to know about the assassini," she blurted out. "Have they gone again?"

The assembled pirati shifted, turning to look at her.

"The Keeper. It's the Keeper," they muttered and stared admiringly at her unusual hair streaked with silver and gold that hung unbrushed and tangled down her back this morning.

"The assassini are sleeping off the excesses of their night," one of the scouts said. "They roasted a suckling pig in the market square, and opened the wine casks. Wine and blood ran down the streets into the sea."

The pirati watched intently, their gazes shifting between the scout's face and Vita's wide, frightened eyes.

"My Aunt Carmela—" she began, but the other scout shook his head.

"We did not venture far ashore," he said. "We spoke only to old Tomie, who was wandering along the shoreline. He said that the assassini talked last night of moving on today. By noon perhaps, when they have all woken up and freshened their brains with a dunk in the sea."

There was a snicker of laughter from the pirati, but Vita turned away and paced to the end of the harbor wall with Giovanni beside her. She gnawed on her lip anxiously, every muscle in her body tight with dread as she stared across the stretch of water to the blue mountain slopes and the golden jumble of pebbles at their base that was the houses of her village. Despite the clear morning, an acrid smell of burning mingled with the tang of salt, and a smudge of dark air hung over the village as though a dirty finger had been rubbed across the sky's pure, rosy pigments.

"Please, Giovanni. Please, take me back now. I must see if Aunt Carmela is all right."

"It's too early. The assassini might not have left. Come on, we'll sail around the island instead. This morning has the lowest tide of the year, did you know that? It's the Tide of Dragomar, the tide of the spring equinox. The water sinks so low in the Golfo d'Levanto, it reveals caves and caverns and tiny beaches that we never see for the rest of the year. And it's a wonderful morning. Come on." He tugged on her arm, and with a worried sigh she turned to follow him down the steps to the water, where his blue boat floated only a few feet above the sandy bottom.

As Vita stepped lightly down into the boat, it dipped beneath her, coming alive. Giovanni ran the sail up as Vita rowed out into the Golfo, where the slightest of breezes played with the sail fabric and the boat skimmed gently forward, barely rocking on the quiet, shining sea. The pirati harbor slipped slowly astern and the coastline of the island drifted past, rimmed with craggy gray rocks where twisted salt-pines leaned over the ripples and the scent of flowering salt-grass drifted to Vita's nose. A group of Mara dove from a rock, waving to Vita and Giovanni as they passed, and presently three dolphins began to swim alongside the boat, smiling joyfully and leaping into the air where the sun sparkled on their sleek sides and through their blue flippers.

Vita let go of her worry for a moment and laughed aloud with sheer pleasure; the dolphins were her favorite sea creatures. Giovanni leaned intently forward and Vita, glancing at his face, knew that he was talking to the dolphins. His eyes shifted in color as he talked: pale blue, silver, dolphin green.

"What do they say?" she asked curiously.

"That the sea witch's daughter is paddling around the point in a small boat, and going in and out of caves. They ask why she is always alone."

"Because she's horrible," Vita snorted.

"No," said Giovanni thoughtfully. "She's lonely. The sea witch isn't interested in people. She works magic only for the well being of the sea creatures, and knows the ways of tides and winds. I'm not afraid of her but the pirati are, because she's mysterious. The pirati don't mix with her. And so the village children have always been scared of Marina, because of whose daughter she is. She is used to being scorned, and outcast, and alone—so she acts scornful in return. But she's not mean; she's kind to the creatures of the sea."

"Lucky them," Vita muttered sarcastically. She had lain awake long into the night in the spare bed that Giovanni's mother had made up for her with sheets that smelled of seagrass. For hours her mind had worried around the edges of the verse that the sea witch's daughter had chanted at the Feast of Dragomar, as well as fretting over Aunt Carmela's safety.

Giovanni ignored her sarcasm. "Let's find Marina," he said. "She knows the caves better than anyone. We'll all go exploring."

Vita shrugged; the sun and the gentle rocking of the boat were making her feel relaxed and sleepy after her restless night. "If you want to," she agreed.

They neared the northern point of the island shortly after, but the cliffs and rocks seemed bare. Giovanni tacked around the point itself, staying well offshore for a jagged reef of black rock ran out from the point and menaced passing boats. Vita watched the sea swirl around the rocks with lazy rolls. Then she saw Marina. The girl had her back to them and was rowing northward between three small islands.

Giovanni followed her; as they rounded the end of the third island they had almost caught up to her. She was heading into a tiny cove on the eastern side of the island's point.

"Look at that!" Giovanni exclaimed with excitement. "It's a beach I've never seen before, Vita. This tide is lower than ever I remember it being."

"You're only sixteen, not an old pappa," Vita teased.

Giovanni grinned as he dropped the sail and began to row after Marina, his oars dipping into the clear water without a sound. Nonetheless, the sea witch's daughter must have sensed them coming, for she paused suddenly in her own rowing and glanced over her shoulder. Iridescence shimmered in her black hair. She didn't smile, only sat waiting as Giovanni rowed closer.

"Can we come with you?" he asked. "I've never seen this beach before!"

Marina smiled scornfully, a mere twitch of her thin lips. "You pirati," she said. "You think you know the sea, but if it were a body you'd know only one little finger. If you knew anything, you'd know that this is the seventh low tide since the full moon, falling on the seventh day of the seventh year. Such a tide happens only once in a hundred years. On this one day, you can walk barefoot between some of the islands in the archipelago and you can pick golden whelks from the reefs with your bare hands instead of diving down for them."

"Well," Giovanni replied cheerfully, "it's a good thing we met you today so that now we know." And he dipped the oars into the shallow water so that the boat shot forward and crunched onto the wet sand of the tiny, crescent-moon shaped beach that lined the cove. The beach was a mere sifting of sand that might have fallen from the pocket of a careless giant.

Marina's boat crunched ashore a moment later, and Vita gripped the gunwale and hauled it higher onto the beach. Marina gave her a surprised look and jumped lightly out, watching her with wary curiosity. Suddenly, Vita realized that she and Marina were almost the same height, and their tangled hair was the same length, and they had the same thin, strong legs and slender wrists. Something like a tingle ran over Vita's skin although she didn't know why. She remembered what Giovanni had said about Marina being lonely, and so she smiled at her—but Marina only stared, and didn't smile in return.

Giovanni was already clambering over rocks that were slippery with wet green weed, and rough with mullosks, their pink translucent shells glowing in the light.

Vita climbed up to join him, wishing that Marina wasn't following her, that she'd just climb back into her boat and row away into her own lonely space.

"There's a crack here!" Giovanni cried. "Maybe a cave!" and Vita saw the black jagged line in the rock, that would normally have been below water level. On an impulse, she turned sideways and edged slowly into it, clutching at the rough walls. Weed tickled her neck like cold fingers but the floor of the crack, or tiny passageway, was soft sand under her bare toes. She edged away from the bright line of blue sky where she had entered, and where Giovanni and Marina's curious faces hung in silhouette. The light grew dimmer as she went farther into the rock, but she had the night vision of all Keepers and the gloom did not deter her.

"What can you see?" Giovanni's voice echoed around her but he was too broad shouldered to slip into the crack as she had done.

"Nothing much!" she shouted in reply, but at that very moment she did see something in the dimness: a small box, wedged overhead in a crack. The box was dry, for the slender passage had been angling upward through the cliff and even the highest tides would not reach it. With a sudden excited snatch, Vita dislodged the box; its leather casing was smooth and cool and she could feel strange symbols embossed on it. She scanned the cave, but it ended only a few feet farther on and there was nothing else hidden in it. Awkwardly, with the box in her hands, she edged back toward the daylight, being careful not to step on the sea stars that lined the passageway where the sand became damp again.

"What is it?" Giovanni asked, as she stepped out beside him, and his eyes shone at the sight of the box.

"It's a treasure chest," she teased, for this is what they had spent long hours hunting for on the beaches when they were children with sticks jammed in their belts.

"It's been there at least a hundred years," Marina said with awe.

Vita nodded, realizing that this was true, and suddenly the box seem heavier in her hands and she felt almost afraid to be holding it. There was power in it; she couldn't recognize its source but she felt its tingle in her fingertips.

Their three heads bent over the box, fair and dark hair mingling, their bare feet forming a circle in the sand. The leather covering of the box was chestnut brown and still held a soft gleam, despite its age. The embossing was of sheet gold, hammered into symbols that resembled a foreign tongue and that ran in a single line all the way around the box's four sides. In the center of the lid was embossed a full sun and sickle moon, and when Vita saw this, something leapt inside her. She traced the designs with one fingertip, and saw the sudden awareness kindle in Marina and Giovanni's eyes.

"The Corno d'Oro," Giovanni said softly, and Vita nodded.

"Open the box," commanded Marina in her clear voice, and Vita tugged at the lid. For a moment nothing happened, and she thought with sharp disappointment that it was locked, but then with a slight sigh the salt corrosion on the metal lip released and the lid rose. Vita lifted out the book that was the box's only contents. It too was bound in chestnut leather and embossed with the sun and moon design and when she opened the covers she saw that the pages were of a strange, thick parchment with the ghostly shapes of star lilies contained in their weaving. There were very few pages, and they were written on with golden ink in the same strange symbols that were on the outside of the box. But the final page was blank and smooth. Vita lay her hand on it and felt its power thrumming in her fingertips.

"I cannot read any of these pages," she said and for some reason she felt a great sadness, so that her throat closed and her eyes burned.

"Look, there's something else," said Giovanni, and he held up a single piece of parchment that had been pressed flat in the bottom of the box, below the book. He handed it to Vita and she unfolded it, the thin ordinary parchment rustling in the breeze. The lettering on it was also different from that inside the book, written not with gold ink but with black charcoal, and using plain language in an uneven scrawl.

This book I stole for it belonged to the Keeper of the Corno d'Oro, and washed onto the beach after the storm, Vita read aloud. *And now, before my death, I hide it in a secure place under a spell from the sea witch on the point, that it may remain hidden until she who needs it most shall come. And this I do to make amends for my great crime regarding the Corno d'Oro. Of which I have told no-one. Marco, Captain of the pirati.*

They stared at each other in puzzled silence. "Your mother, the sea witch, put the spell on this book?" Vita asked Marina at last.

"This is too old to concern my mother," Marina said haughtily. "There have always been sea witches on the point. It must be about another witch."

"*Until she who needs it most shall come,*" Vita read again. "Does this mean me, since it was me who found the box? And what great crime has been done?"

But Marina and Giovanni could only return her troubled look in silence.

"My mother can read many tongues," Marina said. "We should take it to her."

"Yes," Giovanni agreed.

Vita dug one toe into the sand. She didn't like Marina, and she didn't know if she should take her treasure to Marina's mother who was a witch.

"Come on," said Giovanni, and gave her a smile of reassurance. She shrugged and followed him down the beach, clasping the box and the book to her chest.

The sea witch lived beneath a huge salt-pine at the very tip of the pirati island, in a small house of golden pebbles bound with a pale mortar of crushed shells. The courtyard was paved with slabs of cliff stones and the flowerbeds were filled with yellow salt-grass and the blue blooms of sand poppies, and bordered with the shells of scallop and golden whelk and triton, scoured clean by tide and sun. Vita and Giovanni followed Marina in through the green front door, to a round room where in every direction a window looked out over the sea and where the wind played amongst strange furniture of twisted driftwood.

"Mamma!" Marina called and the sea witch came into the room swiftly on bare feet, her black hair woven with silver shells and reaching almost to her ankles, and her silver eyes regarding Vita and Giovanni with stern assessment above her unsmiling mouth. Vita felt another spasm of doubt; she could feel the witch's power and she wondered if she had done the right thing in bringing the box here.

"We've been exploring," Marina said, "and we found this but we can't read the pages."

The witch took the box from Vita in her long fingers weighted with silver rings in the shapes of fish and sea serpents and dolphins, and examined it before a window, her face suddenly still and narrow in thought. Then she opened the box and removed the book.

"Can you read it?" Vita asked.

"Carry in some wood," was all that she replied, and Marina slipped out the door and re-entered with an armful of driftwood that she flung down into the fireplace with a clatter. The witch moved to the hearth, and Vita saw that her thin dark ankles were twined around with anklets shaped like seaweed and ropes, and hung with tiny scallop shells and silver crabs that chimed as she walked. She leaned over the wood and signed with her fingers and spoke words that Vita had never heard, and the wood broke into tiny, flickering blue flames that filled the room with the smell of a sea wind. Then the witch scooped powder from two glass jars on the mantle, and tossed handfuls of it onto the fire so that the flames leaped up, crackling white and green and sending a column of whirling sparks up the chimney. The witch held the pages of the book open to the light of the flames and ran her hands over them, signing with her fingers and muttering.

Vita knew suddenly, in her bones, that this book was important to her and that she needed its words.

"A word here and there is all that I can read," the witch spoke at last. "They are riddles, perhaps. Here is a phrase: *when the Keeper tries to...something....and her shame.* And here: *When amongst the ...something...the Golden Horn...falls, seek the high ...peak, something, something, lay in yellow earth to heal...wounds and dry tears.*"

The fire was dying. The witch bent closer to the flames, turning the pages to the last one. "There is something here that I feel, yet cannot see," she muttered. "I can read no more. It is written in a very ancient tongue, one that might be as old as the kingdom of the moon goddess on the roof of the world. Maybe that old…I have seen this tongue before, inscribed in a great rock pillar that stands in the center of the Middle Sea. Though no one now can read the inscription, it is said to be an ancient prophecy."

"What prophecy?" Vita asked.

"Until the powers of the earth god and the moon goddess unite, peace will not dwell in the world," the witch repeated.

"But who is the earth god?"

The witch shrugged. "I do not care for the riddles of men's affairs," she said.

Straightening from the flames, she handed the book back to Vita. Vita hugged it against her chest again where it seemed to tingle with a power that felt strange and ancient. Why did it warn of tears and wounds, the fall of the Corno d'Oro and the Keeper's shame? Did it tell of things past or things to come?

"It is about me?" Vita asked, her voice quivering,

The sea witch bent a considering look upon her, the silver shells dangling motionless from her ears. "It is about a Keeper," she said. "Whether it is about you, Vita, I cannot say. But these are dark times, and strange things have happened in your lifetime."

Vita nodded. She could feel the witch and Giovanni and Marina watching her, while the fire sank into embers that glowed silvery blue, and the sea wind teased round the window frames and tugged at wisps of the witch's black hair. Vita knew that she needed all the words to the verses, or the riddles—but she didn't want to leave the book with the sea witch.

"Aunt Carmela will not be able to read it," Marina said haughtily, as if reading Vita's thoughts.

"You don't know anything about my aunt," Vita retorted. Yet she felt sure somehow that Marina was right and that Aunt

Carmela would not be able to read the book. Her magic was concerned with spells for crops and the birth of jennets and children, for falling in love with the right village man, and for healing fevers, wounds and broken bones. Her magic was not fierce and complicated, the way that Vita felt the sea witch's magic to be.

"If I left the book with you, could you find out the meaning of the words?" Vita asked.

The witch's bony shoulders twitched. "I am not interested in the world of people," she replied coolly. "You may leave the book if you wish, but I don't promise you anything."

Her eyes, silver and strange, stared away over Vita's shoulder to the sea beyond. Vita shifted her weight indecisively from one foot to the other. What use was the book if she didn't know the meanings of the words? To whom else could she take it for help? Perhaps the sea witch would work on it some evening when a storm beat against the rocks below her house.

"I will leave it here," Vita decided, and she placed the book into its box and laid it on the driftwood table. The witch nodded once, a jerk of her sharp chin, without speaking. She took the box and stored it in a narrow cupboard to the left of the fireplace, locking the cupboard door afterward with a silver key in the shape of a fish that hung around her neck. Then, still without speaking, she took a bent staff of silver wood from where it had leaned behind the door, and strode outside with her anklets chiming. Vita watched her cross the garden and stride to the end of the point, where she stood stiffly erect, gazing far out across the water.

Giovanni nudged Vita's arm with one elbow. "Ready?" he asked.

"Yes."

"Goodbye," Giovanni said, turning at the door, but Marina did not reply. She too simply stared out the window, as the witch had done, and ignored them.

"Arrogant cuttle fish," Vita muttered as she followed Giovanni across the garden. His lips twitched with amusement. "Sounds like a pirati insult."

"You should know."

"But she's not actually arrogant." Giovanni began as they climbed down the path to the beach.

"I know, she's just lonely," Vita interrupted impatiently. "No wonder. Who would want to be her friend?"

She helped Giovanni to push the boat back into the water, its hull grating on the sand, then jumped in beside him as he raised the sail. She felt a sudden rush of anxiety, for she had almost forgotten about the assassini in the wonder of the box's discovery.

"Can we go home now?" she asked and Giovanni nodded.

"The tide has turned," he said, "and the assassini have probably moved on. We'll be at Aunt Carmela's for the noon meal."

The Golfo was alive with wind now, the waves tossing and the light swinging. Giovanni's sail pulled taut, and the boat bounded forward with the gurgle of water sluicing fast under the planking. Vita strained her eyes toward shore as they rounded the pirati harbor and began to cross to the mainland under the scudding shadows of white clouds.

They moored against the village's harbor wall. Vita looked up at the empty casks rolling in the wind and felt dread, hard and dark, thicken in her chest. "Come with me?" she whispered and Giovanni climbed onto the steps and reached for her hand, enclosing it in a firm grip. Together, they threaded their way along the wall, between stains of wine and slick pools of oil—the fragrant oil that the people of the village had labored to harvest, shaking the olives from the trees, packing them to the presses, straining the pale gold liquid through muslin. And the casks, rolling empty in the wind or lying still with sides smashed in, had been made by hand too, lovingly—the trees selected and felled by bright saw blades, the thin planks smoothed to a sheen, the boards bent over steaming water as the fires roared.

At the end of the wall, the village lay ominously silent. Vita and Giovanni entered the first street, threading their way past shutters that swung loose from broken hinges, and blackened rooms that reeked of smoke—not the sweet smoke of cooking fires, but the bitter smoke of ruin and despair. Outside the baker's, small mandolo cakes and a loaf of bread were squashed into crumbs, and outside the pottery a thousand broken shards littered the cobbles in a crazy mosaic. At the sound of their feet crunching on the shards, Beatrice came out into the street, her soft eyes swollen with tears. Vita wrapped her arms around her.

"They took all the best pots, the biggest," Beatrice whispered. "They filled them with wine and oil, with honey and dried figs, and loaded them onto the jennets. Then they smashed everything that was left and threw my father's clay into the harbor. They took my brother Sandro to be a soldier. My mother won't get out of bed today."

"I'm sorry," Vita whispered and she hugged Beatrice tighter. "I'll come back and see you again later. But Beatrice, I have to go to Aunt Carmela."

Beatrice nodded and stepped back, and Vita and Giovanni continued up the hill.

In the doorways of houses, women huddled together, weeping for their sons taken away to carry swords in the armies of the north, and for their daughters taken to slave in the kitchens of the nobili houses in the cities. They flung their aprons over their faces, freeing their grief onto the wind in hoarse wails. And old Tomie staggered down the street like a drunk, his legs weak with grief.

"They have taken them all, all my jennets," he mumbled as he reached Vita, and she understood his sorrow for the jennets were like children to him. "And they took Paolo's suckling pig, that was to produce piglets for his whole family, his nine children. And they whipped all the men in the square until they bled and begged for mercy, and promised taxes of oil and wine and cheese and gold. We shall all starve! We shall perish!"

And Tomie staggered on downhill toward the water, crying the names of his jennets.

In shocked silence, Vita and Giovanni toiled up the steep slope to where a side alley branched off, leading to the fifty steps worn with the passing of many feet over hundreds of years, that led to the lavender colored gate at the top of the Keeper's valley. Vita saw that the gate hung from one hinge, and the gravel path beyond was scratched and marred by the trampling of black leather boots. "Please!" she breathed toward the shrine of the Luna, the moon goddess, with its wilted flowers and its carving of stars and sickle moon. The dread swelled larger in Vita's chest and she gripped Giovanni's hand more tightly as they stepped into the valley. The grass and flowers—that had been so green and sweet—drooped, charred and blackened: scorched where the assassini had touched them. The blossoms hung shriveled on the trees and the birds were silent. On the sill of the kitchen door, the wombo's furry form lay motionless and when Vita stooped with a cry and turned it over, she found it was drenched in blood, its throat cut. She snatched it up—cradling its velvet fur, its tiny paws, and its closed eyes against her chest—and remembering the many nights she had sat with it under the chyme tree, talking by the light of the moon while the leaves rang around them.

"Bastardi! Sons of sea slugs!" Giovanni cursed, clenching his fists, his eyes turning almost black. Then more gently he said, "We will bury it later," and he took the wombo from her and laid it beneath the tree. Then he pushed the kitchen door open and Vita followed him inside.

"Aunt Carmela!" she cried, her voice ragged as torn cloth.

The village witch was hunched by the dead hearth, her shoulders sagging as though under a great weight. Vita flew to her across the floor and clasped her dry, cool hands and cried her name again.

The woman's eyes opened in her bruised face.

"Vita," she croaked.

"But what's happened here?" Vita cried, for she suddenly saw the chaos in the room: the smashed pottery on the floor, the spilled goats' milk, the slash through the center of Aunt Carmela's weaving on the broken loom.

"They were looking for you," Aunt Carmela croaked. "The Lord Maldici has learned something. They say he has become a sorcerer as evil as his ancestor, Lord Morte. He has learned something and decided to hunt the myth of the Corno d'Oro. He will start by finding its Keeper in the coastal villages. But we did not betray you. We kept silent. "

And she covered the purple welts on her face with her apron while Vita squeezed her shoulder in sympathy.

Giovanni took the broom from behind the door and began to sweep the tiles clean.

"Why did they kill the wombo?" he asked.

"Because everything they do is for greed," Aunt Carmela replied. "And when there is nothing else to take, they take life."

Vita crouched against her aunt's knees, pressed her face into their bony warmth and tried to still the trembling that shook her limbs.

CHAPTER SIX

IN THE WEEKS FOLLOWING the assasssini raid on the village, spring swept along the coast in a wave of greenness and light, blossom and bird song, that washed away the blackened footprints of the raiders. In the Keeper's valley garden, the shriveled stems grew fresh again. Vita replaced the wilted flowers in Luna's shrine. Old Tomie wandered in the mountains, searching until he found one of his jennets that had escaped from the assassini with a broken rope trailing from its halter. When the old man rode the jennet into the village, his wrinkled face was wet with tears of delight.

Beatrice swept the broken shards from her father's pottery floor, and at night his kilns glowed with incandescent heat as new pots were fired to hardness for Beatrice to paint with soft, bright colors. Aunt Carmela spent long hours in the red tiled kitchen, bent over her iron cauldron suspended above the glowing coals of olive wood. Young women came to her for love potions, and older women came with requests about the fruitfulness of their olive and mandolo trees. Day and night, her upright figure, its sharp angles wrapped in a shawl, could be seen hurrying from pigpens to bee hives, from garden plots on terraced slopes to the village well where the young women met to fetch water for washing clothes and on to dim bedrooms where babies slid, bawling lustily, into the world.

In the midst of all this activity, Vita too was kept busy. Under Aunt Carmela's direction, she planted their garden of tomatoes and hot peppers, sweet onions and gourds that would swell, shaped like turbans, from their pale blue flowers. Early in the mornings, when the red earth was damp and friable beneath her hoe, Vita worked on the terrace, pausing sometimes to gaze out over the where the water lay smooth and pale. She wondered what Giovanni was doing, whether he was on the water somewhere, catching slippery silver fish. She wished he'd sail into the harbor, far below her, and climb the hill to her garden with his grin flashing bright and crooked in his wind-burned face. She imagined how he'd wipe his forehead with his red bandana and sprawl in the shade of the nut trees, pulling her down beside him and telling her about pirati raids and rip tides and that he'd missed her.

She thought too about the sea witch and wondered if she'd been motivated by curiosity to open the locked cupboard with her silver key and lift out the book, to bend over it and try to translate its words from the ancient tongue. A shiver of fear prickled over Vita when she thought about the book, about the witch's thin mouth reading the words "shame, wounds, tears".

In the hot afternoons, when the cicadas chirred in the mandolo trees, Vita scrambled across the hills, gathering herbs for Aunt Carmela: the aromatic eyebright, feverfew, verlaini, sweet marjori. At home, she tied them into bunches to hang from the kitchen ceiling, their mingled sweetness and bitterness scenting her clothes and everything in the house.

One afternoon, while gathering the bitter leaves of basili on the ridge above the village, Vita saw a party of nobili hunting in the hills. She leaned against an apricot tree, squinting her eyes to watch them. The red horses seemed to flow across the land, their slender legs prancing, their long tails floating behind them. On their backs, the nobili were brilliant splashes of color. The women's long gowns swept the tips of bushes, and their hair surrounded their faces in masses of intricate curls and braids, woven through with colored stones. The men's cloaks and vests shimmered in the sunlight, embroidered with silken threads. The horse's bits sparkled and their harness jingled. From the nobilis' wrists their falcons, released from their jesses, flew upward into the clear sky before plummeting earthward in dazzling flight with small songbirds clutched in their talons.

One nobili man had a spyglass, long and slender, that glinted in the sunlight. He angled it skyward, watching his falcon. Then he swept it around the hills in a slow arc. Blinking in the light like an eye, the spyglass moved toward Vita, then became still for a long moment. Vita held her breath. She imagined her own face held in the spyglass's lens, floating inside its winking circle. Then the glass moved on again, and after a moment the nobili man telescoped it into a short tube that he slipped into one pocket in his velvet robe. He called something to the others, and gestured with an arm, and the whole party moved away across the hills. Vita watched until they dropped from sight into a fold of the land.

Shortly afterward, a baggage train of servants trotted past, their jennets laden with baskets and hampers. Vita tried to imagine what might be in them: the damask tablecloths, the embossed goblets and bowls, the silken tents that—according to the tale-spinners—the nobili slept in while on a hunting trip. She sighed, wondering what it would be like to ride on a red horse, to feel such prancing and such power held in one's hands, to wear her hair braided into such patterns, to feel silk against her arms.

The following morning, Aunt Carmela left the house so early that the morning star still twinkled in the eastern sky, above the dark hunched shoulders of the mountains. The widow Assondro had come knocking on the door and requesting spells for the birth of a grandchild. Aunt Carmela had gathered her bundles of herbs and disappeared up the path between the nut trees, her shoulders silhouetted briefly against the pale sky as she reached the top of the garden. The gate swung shut behind her with a whispering creak. It was much later, and brightly sunny, when Vita came down to the kitchen, rubbing her eyes sleepily, and spread honey onto bread for her breakfast.

She crossed the red tiles to the kitchen door and swung it open, letting in a flood of light and the liquid songs of the birds in the garden. The leaves of the sacred chyme tree, that grew nowhere in the village but beside the Keeper's house, hung motionless and silent in the still morning air. Vita glanced up into the tree's branches, wishing that the wombo's furry gray face and sleepy eyes would peer at her. Her glance slid down the tree's trunk of silvery, mottled bark, and across the stones of the courtyard.

She gasped suddenly in shock and stepped back.

On the stone doorsill at her feet, where the body of the wombo had lain weeks before and where Vita had scrubbed and scrubbed to remove its bloodstain, a girl huddled motionless inside a ragged shawl. At the sound of Vita's gasp, the girl opened her eyes and gazed around uncertainly.

Vita bent over and laid a hand on her shoulder. "Don't be scared. Are you hurt?"

The girl gave a slight shake of her head, and moaned softly. Her lashes flickered down over her pale skin, smooth as ivory. A dirty smear was smudged across one of her cheeks. Her hair was red, tangled and uncombed, curling over the edge of the rough green shawl.

"Please, help me," she sighed. Vita slid an arm beneath the girl's shoulders and supported her as she staggered stiffly to her feet. She was taller than Vita but light.

"Come inside," Vita said, and together they entered the kitchen where the girl slumped at the table while Vita spread honey onto bread for her and hung the pot over the fire to heat water for brewing a tea of fragranti leaves.

The girl ate her bread slowly with long, grubby fingers with ragged nails, and a hint of color seeped into her cheeks above her pouting red lips. Her shawl slipped off to reveal a roughly woven dress of pale green, torn across one shoulder.

"Where are you from?" Vita asked, pouring tea into a mug and sliding it across the table's scarred surface toward the girl. She clasped the warm mug in her hands and look fully at Vita for the first time: a blank, wide-eyed look full of empty sadness.

"I'm from a village north of the delta. Monterosso. Have you heard of it?" she asked in a tired, husky voice.

Vita shook her head.

"Four years ago, the assassini came through and raided us. I was taken to be a maid in the home of a nobili woman in Genovera and I've been there ever since. This week, the nobili were hunting in the mountains—"

"I saw them!" Vita exclaimed. "I watched them from the ridge!"

The girl nodded and sipped her tea. "My mistress was in a terrible temper. She was angry yesterday because her falcon caught nothing and then was killed itself by a great eagle. Then, when I served her supper, she said it was too cold, and that I hadn't properly mended her favorite dress that been torn on a bush. She threw her supper at me, and slapped my face."

The girl pointed to her smudged cheek as Vita listened in horrified fascination.

"Then she told me to leave her, that she didn't want me anymore. She told me to go back to my mother. I was alone all night on the mountain, but early this morning I saw the smoke from this village and I found the path that led to your garden gate."

She drained the last of her tea, tipping back her long, ivory throat.

"What will you do now?" Vita asked.

The girl shrugged. "I had news two years ago that my family

had moved away from Monterosso but I don't know where they went. So, I'm homeless. Is there anywhere in the village that I could stay?"

"You could stay here!" Vita exclaimed. "My aunt won't mind. And you can tell me all about your life in Genovera and about the nobili! What's your name?"

"Rosa."

"Come upstairs," Vita said, and she led the way up the creaking steps to where, on the second floor of the house, her bedroom looked out over the rooftops of the village to the sea shining beyond. She flung back the shutters and opened the door of her olive wood wardrobe, gesturing at the dresses that hung inside. "Choose one," she said. "Then we can wash and mend yours."

While Rosa searched for a dress, Vita ran downstairs and hauled water from the courtyard well and set it to heat over the fire. She sprinkled rosemary and lemon geranium into the water to scent it, and pulled the thickest, softest towel from the linen chest beneath the stairs. Then she went out and sat under the chyme tree while Rosa bathed in the kitchen. Excitement tickled in her. Having Rosa here will be like having a sister, she thought. The sister I should have had. We'll help each other with work, and I'll take her down to the harbor to meet Giovanni the next time he sails over. In a way, Rosa is an orphan like me because she doesn't know where her mother is.

Vita hugged herself with satisfaction. How lucky it was that Rosa had found the lavender colored garden gate and had followed the path down the valley!

When Rosa appeared in the kitchen doorway, with her red hair hanging wet and tangled down her back, Vita slid from under the tree.

"I have a comb," she offered, pulling it from her pocket. It was made of salt-pine wood, and the handle was inlaid with pink mullosk shell, and it had been given to her by Giovanni on the last Midsummer's Feast. Rosa took the comb and sat on the wall of golden stone that surrounded the well, and began to work the comb through her thick hair.

Vita sat beside her. "Tell me about living in Genovera," she asked.

Rosa glanced at her sideways, her hooded eyes brighter now and filled with secret amusement. "The houses there are wonderful," she began. "You cannot imagine how huge the palazzi are inside, with high ceilings painted with stars and wood nymphs! And on the floors are carpets of softest wool, woven from the coats of the Isfana goats that live only in the islands of Lontano. And on the walls hang mirrors with golden frames, and tapestries with ancient battles and fantastic beasts woven into them. In my mistress's room hung a tapestry with a moon goddess and a Corno d'Oro. Do you know about this mythical beast?"

A current of warning flickered across Vita's thoughts "I may have heard a tale-spinner tell of it. I don't remember really," she said casually.

Rosa didn't seem to be listening. Her eyes glowed as she thought about her old home in the city. Her words hurried on: "The nobili ride red horses, so beautiful, Vita! Their hooves spark on the cobbles. And they pull golden chariots with whirling wheels. My mistress used to go out every morning in her chariot in wonderful dresses, with jewels hanging from her ears. And every month she would order a new dress!"

Vita sighed with delight and lay along the top of the wall on her back, gazing up through the speckled sun and shadow of the chyme tree's limbs spread against the blue sky, gazing right through it all into another world. How magical and strange everything about the city seemed!

Rosa combed and combed her hair. Her husky voice seemed to weave a spell in the courtyard, while doves cooed along the rooftop of the house and the stones pressed warm against Vita's back. She felt as though she could lie there forever and listen to Rosa's wonderful stories, bound in the spell of her own longing.

Rosa began to braid her hair into a single plait. " Every equinox, there is a huge celebration in the city. Traders come with foreign goods and lay them out on stalls in the squares. My mistress bought perfume from the mistral tree, which grows only in the land of Terre where the gold mines are. And we had feasts—you can't imagine the food, Vita! We had so much fun, even the servants. And there was dancing all night, with orchestras from faraway places and music that was different each time from anything we'd heard before."

"Do you know any dances?" Vita asked. "Maybe you could teach me."

"Yes, I could!" Rosa exclaimed, and she threw her long red plait over her shoulder and slid off the wall. "This is called the giavotti," she explained. "I learned it from watching the nobili." She curtsied low, her hands sweeping out as though she held the soft folds of a shimmering gown. Lightly, humming in her husky, soft voice, she began to dance over the courtyard stones while Vita perched on the wall and watched intently until she finished with a flourish.

"It's better with music and a dancing partner."

"Let me try." Vita slid off the wall and began to dance with Rosa, mirroring her steps and the dipping and turning of her body. "I'm hopeless!" she said finally, laughing, falling breathlessly onto the grass below the chyme tree.

"You just need practice," Rosa said. "You have beautiful hair, Vita. You would have plenty of dancing partners at the feasts in Genovera. I'll show you how I did my mistress's hair for the Spring Equinox."

For half an hour, Vita sat still on the grass while Rosa, humming huskily, combed and braided her hair with long, pale fingers. When she had finished, Vita went inside to look at herself in the cracked oval of mirror that hung in her room. She turned her head from side to side and in the mirror's tarnished glow it was easy to believe that she was someone else, someone new and different. Her golden hair, shot through with silver, crowned her head in a wreath of curls and braids, making her look older, a stranger to herself. If she stared with her eyes half-shut, she could imagine that the gleams of sunlight were from precious stones woven into her hair, and that her plain dress was of Barbari silk.

"You look like nobili," Rosa whispered, her pale face a blurred oval behind Vita in the mirror's reflection. "You should meet my mistress' brother."

"Why?"

"He's called Ronaldo. He's tall. Taller than us, and the most handsome boy in the nobili families that I know. He would think you were beautiful with your hair like this. I'll braid it again for you, when he comes to fetch his horse."

"Comes—where?"

"Here, of course," Rosa said, her full lips smiling complacently, her hooded eyes intent on Vita's face. "His horse went lame while they were hunting, so he left it in my care. It's tied to your garden gate. He'll come back for it in a few weeks."

"Let's see it!" Vita said and she ran downstairs and up the valley, under the fragranti and lemon and apricot trees hung with the hard green balls of unripe fruit, to where the red horse snorted at the gate. Slowly she approached it and reached out her hand, trembling with excitement. She ran her palm down its long slender face, feeling how smooth and warm it was, how its muzzle was as velvet as rabbit ears.

"I've never touched a horse before."

"They are ordinary in Genovera," Rosa said airily, with a shrug. "Where can we keep this one?"

"Up on the hillside, in a small field my aunt owns."

Vita untied the horse's bridle reins from the gate, her fingers fumbling with excitement at the supple, oiled leather. She couldn't believe that so much luck could happen to her in one day. Leading the horse across the hillside, through the whispering grass and the cyclamen flowers, she felt more alive than she ever had; felt the unfamiliar coiled weight of her hair, the presence of

Rosa walking beside her full of stories, the warmth and power of the red horse, the promise of Ronaldo's return. She wished that Giovanni and Beatrice could see her at that moment, as she strode through the grass proudly, like a nobili woman walking onto a dance floor.

But later, in the evening when Rosa had gone to sleep in Vita's room, Aunt Carmela came in from outside and sat by the fire with a frown.

"What's the matter?" Vita asked sleepily.

Her aunt stared thoughtfully at her hard, worn hands folded in her lap.

"That horse," she said. "There's nothing wrong with its leg. It limps, but there's no swelling, no mark, no bruise. That horse is sound in all four legs. What makes it limp?"

Vita shrugged. "There must be a reason."

Aunt Carmela nodded. "I fear what it might be. To welcome strangers is hospitable, Vita, but be cautious. Be careful. We don't know who this maid is. There is something about her that troubles me..." The witch's green eyes stared into the embers of the fire, and she sighed.

"Don't fuss," Vita said lightly. "You're tired. Everything will be fine in the morning." And she kissed her aunt's forehead and took a candle up the stairs, while the embers sank low, filling the kitchen with the smell of fragranti, and Aunt Carmela rocked in her chair, muttering softly beneath her breath and staring down at her hands, that were never mistaken about the ailments of animals.

CHAPTER SEVEN

I T WAS WONDERFUL HAVING ROSA sharing her room. Waking early in the mornings, Vita would turn her head on her lavender scented pillow and stare across to where the maid lay in the new bed that the village carpenter had built. Rosa always slept on her back, with her long pale neck and face in graceful profile to Vita, and her red hair tumbling toward the floor, and her full lips pouting. I was right, Vita would think, having Rosa here is like having a sister. And we both like beautiful, rare things—dresses of Barbari silk and towels of Angoli linen—and we both like to have fun. We're both orphans, too, and neither of us can have what we want in life for Rosa is a maid and I am the Keeper. So we understand each other.

As the sun rose, and glinted through the shutters to spark bars of fire in Rosa's hair, the maid would wake. Then she and Vita would wash their faces in water with geranium leaves while Rosa explained how her mistress had bathed in huge tubs of water brought in casks from springs in the northern mountains, and how it had been filled with bubbles of foam from sea flowers, and diluted with the milk of the exotic wild asses that roamed the deserts of Terre.

"It was water that left my mistress's skin as soft as rose petals, " Rosa would say. "Soft, and with a glow to it that everyone envied."

Then the girls ate bread and honey for breakfast, and then they'd hoe the garden terraces, or gather Aunt Carmela's herbs, or wash clothes in a tub set on the tiles of the courtyard before hanging them out to dry from the balcony. Sometimes, they walked up to the meadow to check on Ronaldo's horse. Its limp had healed now, perhaps due to the amount of time that Aunt Carmela had spent wrapping the leg in poultices and muttering anxiously beneath her breath, and the horse moved easily around the small meadow, ripping up grass. Vita grew brave enough to brush its silky coat, while Rosa told her stories about Ronaldo: the tricks he played on his friends, the daring he showed shooting a boat down the rapids of a mountain river when they were out on a hunt; the fine clothes he wore.

"He'll like you, I know it," Rosa said. "Your hair is so beautiful, Vita, and you have such strange lavender eyes."

"He won't notice me. I'm just a village girl," Vita replied, trying to keep curiosity and excitement from showing in her voice.

"Of course he'll notice you," Rosa replied. "I'll plait your hair, and you'll wear your favorite dress, the one that's the same lavender color as your eyes."

Bending over to brush the horse's legs, hiding her face and her confusion against its red coat, Vita wished simultaneously that Ronaldo would hurry up and come soon, and that he'd never come at all.

Often, as they worked in the garden or the house, Rosa told Vita stories about Genovera, and sometimes they stopped what they were doing to practice dancing the giavotti, or the gazelli, or another of the many dances that Rosa knew. Vita loved to feel her feet flying through their intricate patterns. She dreamed of dancing them in a palazzo with marble walls and shining gilt mirrors and an orchestra playing, the musicians dressed in plum velvet waistcoats and white silk stockings. Rosa told her about the chandeliers, each holding a thousand wax tapers, and how their light shone on the dance floor of polished cypress wood inlaid with amber in patterns of pomegranates and grapes.

One afternoon, Vita said, "Come with me to visit Beatrice, the potter's daughter." Together, she and Rosa walked down the alleys of the village, where the shadows were cool and a breeze funneled up from the sea and the children, out of school for the summer, chased and played, their calls echoing beneath the limp, pale sheets hung out to dry.

"Beatrice?" Vita called, waiting for her eyes to adjust to the gloom inside the pottery.

"I haven't seen you for so long time," Beatrice said, dimpling and laying down her brush between the buckets of glazes. "But I've heard about Rosa."

Rosa sniffed. "News travels fast in a village," she said. "People have nothing better to do but gossip at the well."

"Look," Vita said, leading Rosa to where wooden shelves sagged beneath the weight of pots lined along them. "Look at Beatrice's beautiful work."

Rosa raised an eyebrow and shrugged. "I have been with my mistress to the mountains, north of Genovera, to visit the great potteries of Bossano. There, they use glazes made of crushed gold, and amber from Terre, and they have great kilns the size of this whole house. There are glassblowers too, and some of the pots are filled with specks of translucent glass, and others are decorated with wonderful brushwork: peacocks and tangerines and moon moths."

She turned away from Beatrice's pots and paced to the door where she leaned and stood looking out into the street.

Vita smiled at Beatrice apologetically, hoping her feelings weren't hurt. In silence they both stared at the lines of pots, and suddenly it seemed to Vita that their colors were dimmer, and Beatrice's brushwork cruder and less sophisticated than she had noticed before. It was no wonder that Rosa hadn't been impressed.

I was stupid to bring her here, Vita thought.

"Come down to the harbor with us," she said to break the silence and Beatrice nodded and untied her rough smock, covered in daubs of clay and colored glazes, and hung it on a nail above sacks of potash and silica sand.

When the three girls arrived at the little beach lying like a crescent moon at the foot of the village, a group of boys was kicking a pig's bladder around on the sand. "Let's go out on the harbor wall," suggested Vita and they walked along the hot, flat stones, past a villager trading with a pirati, stepping around the crates of sardines and black squid and purple cuttlefish, and the baskets of endives and the first ripe lemons.

"Giovanni!" Vita yelled suddenly, shading her eyes, and she ran to the end of the wall and stared across the water to where his blue boat with its yellow sail tacked shoreward, leaning over like a fine brushstroke on a blue pot. She reached out as the boat came alongside the wall, and caught the rope that Giovanni tossed up while Rosa watched curiously.

Giovanni jumped lightly up the steps and shook Rosa's hand while Vita explained how she had come to live in the village. Then he smiled at Beatrice and slung an arm casually over Vita's shoulders. "Come for a sail?" he asked, but Beatrice looked anxious because she was afraid of the water, and Rosa raised one eyebrow and said that his boat was too small for the four of them. "It would be like squeezing into a fish box," she said. So they climbed down to the base of the harbor wall instead, and leaned against it in the shade. Rosa took a cotton handkerchief from her apron pocket and brushed off the rock before sitting down, as if she was wearing a silk gown instead of her usual coarsely woven green dress. She sat decorously with her ankles crossed, and smoothed her skirt out over the rock. Vita watched in fascination. Sometimes Rosa acted more like a nobili woman than a maid; Vita supposed that she'd learned her fine manners from her mistress in

Genovera. Vita crossed her own ankles in imitation, and leaned back with her eyes closed to listen to the clear, deep water licking the rocks with gurgles and gloops. It was very warm and peaceful and for a moment Vita felt almost happy, with her three best friends sitting beside her and the sea birds crying as they soared overhead, and the breeze tickling her hair.

Then Rosa sat up suddenly with an impatient twitch of her shoulders. "This place is so very boring," she said. "There's nothing to do here. In Genovera, in summer, my mistress would pack up her household and we'd go down to Triesta, a town beside the sea. We'd go to see theatre shows on the beaches in the evenings and a band would play and people would dance on the promenade. And there was a man who had a monkey from the islands of Lontana and it could count to ten. And there was a man who sold ices, made from sugar and almonds and butter, and with ice from the high mountains. It was the best thing you ever tasted."

"Tell us some more," Vita said, for suddenly it seemed that Rosa was right, and that the sounds of sea birds and water were boring and uneventful, and that nothing ever happened here at the harbor that was worth talking about. Not the kinds of things that happened in other, more exciting, places.

Rosa thought for a moment. "I could tell you a story," she said. Beatrice and Giovanni turned to look at her with interest, and Vita gave a satisfied sigh and wriggled around until her back was more comfortable against the rocks. Rosa narrowed her eyes and stared out over the water.

"In the high and far off days," she began in her husky voice. "In the high and far-off days, a queen reigned in the Moon Mountains on the roof of the world."

A chill of amazement and shock and fear swept over Vita. The little hairs stood up on her arms, and her spine prickled, and the back of her neck turned cold. Her eyes locked with Giovanni's and she saw how his own bright blue ones were fading to dark gray.

"You can't tell this story!" she burst out. "It's a special one that only one person can tell!"

Rosa looked at her in surprise. "No, it's nothing special," she said. "I've heard it often from tale-spinners in Genovera. They tell it at fairs and festivals. Let me tell it. It's the only story that I know well."

And she gazed away across the sea and continued talking. Word for identical word, without a mistake, she repeated the Keeper's tale, telling about Luna the moon goddess, and the star lilies that sprang up behind the Corno d'Oro, and how the dark power of Lord Morte gripped the world and let greed loose into it.

Vita lay on her back, staring up at small clouds drifting overhead, and tried to breathe slowly so that the hard, sharp rattle of her heart would become calm. She had never heard this story told before in any voice but her mother's or her own. This was a sacred tale, that only the Keeper knew and that only the villagers and the pirati were told. She was sure that none of them would repeat it to strangers because they knew that it was a story that held power, and that only one person had the right to tell. So who had let the tale loose in Genovera, in the mouths of wandering tale-spinners who neither knew nor cared about the Corno d'Oro? Who had taught the tale to Rosa, a nobili maid?

"The Keeper girl had a small sharp knife hidden in her clothes," Rosa said, telling about the storm. "When the ship was wrecked, she used the knife to cut loose the ropes and cloth that bound the two Corno d'Oro, so that they might swim free and save themselves if they could. They both turned toward shore, but the sea dragon was beating the sea into a mighty froth as he whipped and stirred it with his tail, searching for every piece of gold. In the spray and waves, the two Corno d'Oro became separated. The mare swam in circles, crying for her stallion, but at last she was too weary to swim much farther and began to sink low in the wild water. At the last moment, a man called Marco— who lived on one of the islands of the archipelago—rowed out and saved her. And afterward, he sold her to the nobili for gold and they took her north to Lord Morte's city palazzo. But the waves never gave up the stallion and he was lost forever—"

"That's not right!" Vita cried out, sitting up. "You're telling it wrong. It was the stallion that was saved and the mare that sank into the waves—"

Rosa stared at her, her hawk eyes narrowed in her ivory face, her red hair shining.

Silence fell, as though for an instant in time everything ceased. In that moment, Vita realized, with a sick lurch in her stomach, what she'd done; how she had betrayed her knowledge. For that long moment, the sea lay still, the breeze held its breath, the birds hovered in midair and were silent. Giovanni had sat up and was staring at Vita with eyes as chill and dark as the sea in a storm.

"What do you mean, I'm not telling it right?" Rosa asked calmly. "Do you know this tale?"

Vita flushed. "I heard it once, told differently," she said, picking at a limpet shell with one finger and avoiding Rosa's gaze.

"How did you hear it told then?" Rosa asked. "What happened to the stallion?"

Vita shrugged uncomfortably. "I don't remember," she said. "It was long ago, when I was a little girl."

The water began again to gurgle against the rocks, and the birds to slipstream overhead and the breeze to sigh against the clouds. Vita swallowed heavily and lay down with her eyes shut, closing out Giovanni's alarm. She took a deep breath and wished that the mad galloping of her heart would slow down.

Rosa shrugged. "If the stallion didn't drown, he must be somewhere in the land of Verde. But I've never heard that this is so. No one has ever seen him."

"It's all just a story about something mythical anyway," Giovanni said.

"Only children think it's true," Beatrice agreed.

Rosa stared at them for a moment and tucked a strand of hair behind her ear. "You're right. What does it matter how it ends?

And if it were true, I would've seen the mare when I lived in Genovera, if that was really where she was taken. But I don't think she's there. And if the stallion had been saved, you would know about him living here in the mountains."

And Rosa stood up and slipped on her sandals. "I'm going home," she said. "It smells like fish down here."

Vita heard her light steps slap away across the rocks.

"I must finish painting the pots," said Beatrice. "Goodbye."

"Goodbye," Vita replied, without opening her eyes. She listened to Beatrice's steps move away, and to the sound of Giovanni breathing close beside her.

"It doesn't matter," she said at last, defiantly. "It was only Rosa. She's my friend. It doesn't matter if I let something slip out."

Giovanni remained silent, and after a moment Vita opened her eyes and sat up to meet his dark gaze.

"How does she know your tale?" he asked. "And did you hear what she said about the mare? That she was saved by Marco, and sold for gold to the nobili to take north to Lord Morte's palazzo."

"The note we found with the book in the cave—" Vita said.

"Can you remember what it said?"

"It said...something about *the great crime I have done*, and it was signed by Marco."

"So there was a Marco present at the storm," Giovanni agreed. "And if he sold the Corno d'Oro mare into the nobili hands, that might have been his great crime."

"And he stole the Keeper's book, but then hid it under a spell from the sea witch," Vita agreed. "But the mare must have perished, or else the people of the city would know about her. Rosa would have heard about her or seen her."

"Maybe Marco didn't save her...maybe letting her drown was his great crime."

Vita thought about this for a minute. "I must visit the sea witch again. Can you take me to her?"

"She's away," Giovanni said. "She was seen traveling southward on a seahorse. The sea witches meet every year in early summer, on a rocky outcropping in the Middle Sea, to talk about the oceans of the world. But I'll look for Marina and ask her what's happened with the book. And now I should go; the wind is swinging around."

Vita glanced over his shoulder and saw whitecaps riding on the crests of the waves, and the light swinging off the choppy water in hard silver bars. She scrambled up to the wall behind Giovanni, and watched him cast off.

"I'll come back soon!" he shouted. "When I've talked to Marina!"

Vita waved and shaded her eyes, watching until his bright grin and his red bandana were lost to sight and only the yellow sail remained, scudding westward toward the pirati archipelago. Then she turned and began to climb the alleys of the village toward her lavender colored gate, deep in consideration about the Keeper's Tale. Tonight, she thought, I'll make almond cakes. Then Rosa and I can sit in the courtyard to eat them, and I'll ask her questions about where she heard the Keeper's Tale, and find out whether she knows any more about the mare being taken to the city.

Vita reached the head of the alley, and glanced up at the sound of footsteps. Swiftly and lightly, Rosa was coming down the fifty worn steps that led from the gate into the alleyway, with her smiling lips caught between her teeth and Vita's lavender dress draped over one arm.

"Vita!" she called. "Ronaldo is here! You must change quickly, in the garden, and I'll plait your hair!" and she caught Vita by the arm and pulled her up the steps into the garden, and in beneath the laden lemon and olive trees, waving Vita's wooden comb in one hand.

CHAPTER EIGHT

I N THE SHELTER OF THE TREES, Rosa's fingers flew through Vita's pale hair with expert swiftness, braiding the strands into thin plaits that she wove into a crown on Vita's head. She tugged at the hem of Vita's best, lavender colored dress to straighten it. "This will have to do," she whispered. "You would look better in Barbari silk." Finally she gave Vita a strangely triumphant smile. "You look beautiful after all," she whispered. "This fabric is the exact color of your eyes. Ronaldo's in the courtyard, waiting to meet you."

"Aren't you coming, too?" Vita asked. "You could introduce us."

But Rosa shook her head. "I forgot something in the garden this morning," she said casually. "I'll be back soon."

Vita walked alone down the path as quietly as she could, the leather soles of her sandals almost silent as they pressed crumpled blossoms, recently fallen from the oleander trees, onto the flagstones. She paused at the top of the five steps that led down into the courtyard outside the kitchen door, and listened to the staccato rhythm of her own heart. It was foolish to feel so shy, so curious and expectant...this was the result, she thought, of all Rosa's stories about Ronaldo, about how he would like her. And of course, she'd never met a nobili person before. It was hard to know how she'd appear to eyes that had seen so many sophisticated and worldly things.

Vita gazed down into the courtyard. The boy was seated on the wall of golden stone that surrounded the well. His long, slender legs shone in silken tights of pale yellow, and his orange slashed jacket glowed like a nasturtium flower against the shadow of the kitchen windows. Sunlight winked on the silver spurs attached to his creamy kidskin boots, and on the ornamental hilt of the small dagger that was strapped at his belt. He yawned elegantly, waving one slim hand in front of his mouth and stretching his head back so that his long, bright yellow hair flowed across his shoulders, shining in the sun, and the light tilted across the smooth, hard planes of his face.

Vita thought he was the most beautiful boy she'd ever seen. She hesitated, in the shade of a tangerine tree, waiting for him to notice her, yet breathing as quietly as a hare hiding in the grass, so that he wouldn't ever notice her at all.

Then, he glanced up, as if her very stillness had alerted him. He rose from the wall in one swift, fluid motion and held out an arm toward her. His smile was lazy and smooth. "Vita!" he said, sounding delighted. "Rosa said you were coming. And she said how kind you've been, letting her stay here. I worried about her, after my sister sent her away."

He sprang nimbly up the five steps and reached for Vita's hand. For one moment his warm lips touched the back of it, and then he had turned and—still clasping her hand—led her into the courtyard. Vita's breath seemed stuck in her throat along with her voice, while the warmth from her hand flooded her whole body. No one had ever kissed her hand before; the act made her feel strangely regal yet flustered.

"And Rosa says she's been teaching you to dance," Ronaldo continued as they sat together beside the well. "What a shame that you've nowhere to dance here in the village."

"Well, we do—dance, I mean," Vita said, flushing as Rolando's tawny eyes lingered on her face. "We dance in the village square at the festivals."

Ronaldo waved a hand airily and the ring that he wore, set with a green stone, flashed in the light. "Peasant dances," he said. "Rosa says you're meant for better than that, Vita. And you're beautiful! When I saw you standing above the steps, I thought you must be a nobili woman who'd followed me here from Genovera."

Vita's cheeks flamed again. She slid from the wall and paced to the chyme tree, laying a hand on its smooth gray trunk and staring up into the leaves that, barely swinging in the breeze, rang in soft tones. The familiar touch of the tree steadied her and her heartbeat slowed.

"Have you come for your horse?" she asked, turning to face Ronaldo again. He had stood up, and was stretching with his arms over his head. Vita thought he had the longest spine, and arms and legs, of anyone she'd seen. Yet she could see the muscles shifting beneath the light fabrics that he wore.

"Yes, I've come for my horse. Perhaps I'll stay for a few days and have a seaside holiday. Once I go home to the city, my father will want me to return to work."

"What kind of things do you do?"

"Oh, boring stuff. Bargaining with merchants and traders. Overseeing deliveries of goods from the delta. Checking the scribes' ledgers and accounts for mistakes or theft."

"Oh, Ronaldo!" teased Rosa, skipping down the steps into the courtyard with Vita's salt-pine comb tucked into the sash at her waist. "All this talk about ledgers and deliveries! Vita will think life in Genovera is dull!"

Ronaldo smiled while Vita watched in fascination; there was something so smooth about his smile, it seemed to flow across the tawny planes of his face.

He shrugged good-humoredly. "Oh, you're right! There are other things I do at home too."

"Tell me about them," Vita asked, settling herself in a lower branch of the chyme tree. Ronaldo strolled across the grass and leaned near her. "There are parks in Genovera planted with strange trees and flowers from all over the world. I ride my horse there with my friends and we have races, or hunts where we capture animals and release them into the park for the nobili to hunt. My father has a chariot that I'm allowed to drive and sometimes, at feasts, I race it in the coliseum—"

"It's very dangerous," Rosa interrupted, looking at Vita with eyes that shone excitedly. "Sometimes Ronaldo's chariot is moving so fast that it's balanced on one wheel as it takes a corner! Ronaldo's team is of three matched tapestry stallions from the mountains north of Bossano. They are one of the fastest teams in the city!"

Vita smiled, staring through the chyme tree leaves. She imagined the countless crowds in the coliseum, their bright sea of clothing, their roaring mouths. She imagined Ronaldo standing in his chariot, lithe and strong, balanced to the vehicle's swaying and jolting while the stallions frothed at their silver bits and their arched necks fought Ronaldo's strength.

"What are tapestry stallions?" she asked.

"They're a rare breed," replied Ronaldo. "Their coats are red and white and gold hair mingled together so finely that, from several paces away, the coat looks like a tapestry stitched with tri-colored thread."

"I would love to see them," Vita said dreamily.

Ronaldo's lazy gave flickered over her face. "Why shouldn't you see them?" he asked. "You could return to Genovera with me for I came here riding another horse. I planned to ride my own horse home and lead the extra. But you could ride it if you wanted to. You could stay at my parents'. There's plenty of room in our huge palazzo."

"She could have the blue boudoir," said Rosa, sounding excited. "The one my mistress stays in when she visits you." She turned toward Vita, her hair flaming in the last rays of evening sun. "It has dolphins and Mara in the wall frescoes, and a little fountain in one corner that fills the room with the sound of water running, and a floor of marble."

Vita felt something uncoiling in her chest: her nest of hungry snakes. Restless with longing, they slithered upward, straining toward the vision of a blue room in a palazzo in Genovera. And why shouldn't she return with Rolando for a visit?

But, she cautioned herself, it was only two weeks until the summer solstice, when she would have to journey into the mountains and weave the spells of invisibility and protection around the Corno d'Oro. Could she travel to the city and return home again in less than two weeks? How would she find her way back alone from Genovera?

"I don't have anything to wear," she said.

"Maybe Ronaldo's mother will give you something. She loves to have guests," said Rosa.

"Yes," Ronaldo agreed, in his lazy voice. "It's true. But you don't have to decide right now. You can think about it while I have my seaside holiday."

In the days that followed, Vita showed Ronaldo all her favorite places: the crescent moon of the beach, the lemon groves where the fruit hung like golden balls, the stream that ran burbling into the sea through her own valley garden behind the Keeper's house, the swathes of hillside where pink cyclamen flowered. They walked along the winding path to the next village and ate freshly caught crabs in thyme sauce. Ronaldo taught Vita to ride on his red horse, and she galloped across the lower slopes of the mountains with her heart and her laughter in her mouth and the wind and the light in her eyes. She had never felt anything as fast and free as that red horse! The rhythm of its pounding hoof beats, mingled with the hoof beats of the other horse that Ronaldo had brought and that he raced beside her own, seemed to fill her head at night. She barely noticed Rosa's breathing, or the familiar susurrations of the waves on the beach, anymore. In the evenings, she and Rosa and Ronaldo sat in the courtyard and played a game called Casa that Ronaldo taught them. He had brought the flat board, made of leather and covered in finest vellum, with him in his saddlebag along with the polished pieces of agate and amber and coral that one moved on the board, using strategy to win.

On other evenings, Rosa played on the silver mouth harp that had also been packed in Ronaldo's saddle bags, and its light, bright notes filled the courtyard and drowned out the soft tinkling of the chyme tree. Then Ronaldo and Vita danced the gavotti and the gazelli and the other dances of Genovera. Ronaldo was perfect to dance with: light on his feet, elegant in his slashed vests and silk tights.

Sometimes Vita remembered that she wanted to ask Rosa more about the Keeper's Tale, and about the different ending to it that Rosa knew, but the time never seemed right. Sometimes, she wondered how long Ronaldo would spend in the village, and if she would return to Genovera with him.

"We should have a picnic tomorrow," Rosa suggested one evening, after their game of Casa. "Vita, we can invite Giovanni and Beatrice and we can go up to the tangerine grove on the top of the hill."

"Oh, yes," Vita agreed. "And Ronaldo can tell some more stories about living in Genovera."

Before darkness fell, Vita ran down the alleys to the harbor wall to see if she could find anyone to carry a message to Giovanni. A pirati whom she didn't know, with the lids of one eye stitched shut, was trading squid for lemons with Beatrice's father, who had a terrace of trees behind the pottery. The pirati agreed to carry a message to Giovanni, but secretly Vita wondered whether he was to be trusted. There was nothing else she could do, though, so she hoped for the best. On her way back through the village, she stepped into the pottery to find Beatrice, who was seated at a long workbench covered in pails of milky glazes.

Beatrice looked up dolefully as Vita entered, and no dimples appeared in her soft cheeks.

"Ronaldo has arrived!" Vita announced dramatically. "We're having a picnic tomorrow at the tangerine grove at the top of the hill. Want to come? Ronaldo has wonderful stories about life in Genovera and he drives a chariot team of three tapestry stallions and his family own a palazzo!"

In silence, Beatrice bent over the bowl that was cradled in one hand. With her free hand, she painted a row of moon snails around the rim in blue glaze. Then she dipped the brush back into the pot and waited a moment, while it soaked up more glaze and grew plump. She knew just the moment when the brush was ready to use, before it became so full of glaze that it would drip and splatter, ruining her design. Carefully, she began to paint dolphins in the bottom of the bowl. Vita watched without seeing; it was a pattern that Beatrice had been painting for years.

"Can you come?" she asked.

Beatrice sighed and set the finished bowl down onto the worktable. "I don't know," she said. "There are a lot of things to paint before my father fires the kiln tomorrow night."

She stared down at her plump fingers, rubbing smears of powdery dried glaze from them, and suddenly a fat tear rolled down her cheek and splashed onto a patch of glaze, making it shine brightly on her brown knuckle.

"Beatrice?" Vita asked uncertainly. "What's wrong?"

"I miss Sandro," Beatrice replied. "We've had no word of him since the assassini took him away. He used to make me laugh. And without his help, there's extra work here for me. My father is always waiting for me to finish one job so that I can do the next. I'm tired. And I hardly see you anymore, Vita."

Vita rubbed a toe across the dirt floor in discomfort. "I've been busy," she said defensively. "Gardening, helping Aunt Carmela with spring magic. Looking after Ronaldo's two horses. But I could see you tomorrow, if you come to the picnic."

"Maybe," Beatrice said, and picked up the next plain white bowl and dipped a fresh brush into a bucket of pink glaze. She began to paint a pattern of olive leaves and olives around the outside of the bowl in graceful, flowing lines. Her hand seemed to know exactly where the brush should go before it arrived there.

Vita lingered for a moment in guilty silence, aware of the sagging shelves lined with plates and bowls, cups, and jugs for holding goat's milk, all ghostly in the dim light.

"So...I hope you'll come," she said finally, and gave Beatrice's shoulder a squeeze before plunging outside into the alley's blue shadows. Reaching the fifty worn steps that led to her gate, she ran up them, taking them two at a time. It was a relief to leave Beatrice's gloomy company, and already her thoughts darted ahead to her own house where Ronaldo and Rosa waited in the kitchen to share supper. They were so much fun to be with; Vita loved Ronaldo's lazy lightness and the bright gleam in his tawny eyes.

The next day, it was almost noon by the creeping shadow of the sundial in the village square, when Vita and Rosa emerged from the house carrying wicker baskets full of food. Ronaldo followed with blankets tossed over an arm and his spurs jingling.

"Wait for us!"

Vita paused and glanced down the alley to see Giovanni and Beatrice toiling upward.

"You got my message?" Vita called and Giovanni nodded. Together the five of them climbed the hill, wading through the yellowing grass and the astringent aroma of the purple flowering basili, to where the tangerine grove circled the hilltop like a crown. Giovanni and Ronaldo spread out the blankets and Vita pulled food from the hampers: crumbling piquant cheese colored with nasturtium flowers, fresh figs, crusty bread, sliced ham, roasted peppers, compote of apricots, dried raisins, and a cake of mandolo nuts. There was a blue ceramic jug of nog (a delicious drink made from jennet milk and eggs and cinnamon), that Vita had been keeping cool in the well. The sides of the jug were misted with condensation.

At first, they ate in silence while the Golfo d'Levanto spread itself below them like a sparkling carpet, and the breeze whispered in the tangerine trees, and the purple flowers of the basili herb tossed in the yellow grass. Old Tomie's jennet, the one he'd wandered into the mountains to find, grazed farther down the slope, flapping its creamy ears. There was the distant crow of a cockerel from the terraces, where the mandolo nuts and the lemons were ripening. Goats bleated.

"It will soon be midsummer," said Beatrice unhappily. "And Sandro had planned to dance with his sweetheart."

"Who's Sandro?" asked Ronaldo.

"My brother, taken by the assassini."

"I don't know why you worry about him so much," Rosa said, licking nog from her full, red lips. "He's probably having a great time, learning to be a soldier. Maybe he'll be a charioteer. They have their own midsummer's feasts, in the army, anyway."

"They get roaring drunk on fig-canary, and throw each other into the river Arnona, and dance on the tables in the serving halls," said Ronaldo lazily, lying on his back and throwing up raisins into the air, that he caught in his mouth as they fell.

"I think Sandro would be happier at home," Beatrice said stubbornly. Her soft, liquid eyes seemed to have become larger lately, as though swollen with unshed tears.

"I think you'd all be happier in the city," Rosa argued, undoing the plaits in her red hair. "Even though I was just a servant in Genovera, I had a wonderful life. I danced at the feasts, and I went with my mistress to theatres and street festivals. I saw sword-swallowers from the islands of Lontana, and those weird animals, called margrazzi from the desert state of Terre."

"Didn't it bother you, that the nobili wealth comes at such cost?" Giovanni asked. Vita stared at him, and noticed how dark his eyes were in his wind-burned face.

"What are you talking about?" Rosa asked, pouting.

"All that wealth, all that leisure…while in other places people work hard for little, and give up their little in taxes, and have their sons taken for soldiers and their daughters taken for servants."

Ronaldo laughed. "You're muddled," he said smoothly. "The assassini belong to Lord Maldici. They do his bidding. But the nobili and the merchants are not evil people. My father's a merchant prince and he works long hours himself, in warehouse and riverside, supervising and planning, checking the weave of bolts of cloth, the health of imported animals, the weight in boxes of food. Some weeks he barely sleeps!"

"If the nobili didn't hire servants and support an army, the village teenagers wouldn't be taken away," Giovanni argued stubbornly, his jaw set in a hard line above his red bandana.

"If no one had hired me, what would have become of me?" Rosa asked. "I was grateful to be hired, to live in a great palazzo, to learn manners and dance steps and how to care for Barbari silk. The problem is, Giovanni, that you know nothing of the world. All you know about are a bunch of little islands, as small as pebbles in the ocean."

She ran Vita's comb through her red hair as she talked, so that the light jumped from it in sparks. Vita lay back and closed her eyes against the bright light. The arguing voices seemed to beat inside her head like the dull blows of a blunt axe falling onto soft wood.

"—maids should be in their own homes—"

"—the assassini are to blame, not the merchants—"

"—the city people are living off the hard work and sacrifice of others—"

"—but my parents don't even know Lord Morte!—"

"I'm going home."

Vita opened her eyes and watched as, outlined against a patch of blue sky, Beatrice stood up and tramped away, her eyes heavy and dark, her blanket held tightly against her plump breasts. Vita sighed and closed her eyes again. There was a rustle of silk as Ronaldo stood up, and presently his footsteps moved away to be followed by Giovanni's steps. In the sudden silence the chirring of the cicadas—a sound that usually made Vita feel sleepy and contented—seemed unbearably loud and shrill.

What will Giovanni think if I go to the city? Vita wondered. If I ride there on the extra horse, how will I get home again? I can't go anyway, until after the solstice two days from now. Will Ronaldo wait until then? I could go into the mountains first, and then go to Genovera afterward. If I want to go. But maybe Giovanni and Beatrice are right and the city is just an evil place full of people who live off the misery of others.

Oh, everything seemed so tangled and uncertain!

Vita sat up. Rosa was leaning against a tangerine tree, eating a fig. Across the slope of the hill, Giovanni and Ronaldo were having a knife-throwing contest. Giovanni was using the knife that he always carried and used to gut fish, to shave dry twigs into kindling when he wanted to start a fire on the beach, to slice through stubborn vines when he and Vita were exploring in the hills, to peel oranges. It was a plain knife, with notches in the blade and a dark handle. Ronaldo was using the little dagger from his belt. When he threw it, the slim blade gleamed in the light and the handle sparkled, for it was inlaid with precious stones and veins of gold. The point of the dagger struck the piece of wood that the boys had set up as a target, and the blade quivered. Ronaldo strolled over to pull it out, his long slim legs, in tights of aqua silk, sweeping carelessly through the grass.

"He's so elegant," Rosa said, licking fig juice from her lips. "He makes Giovanni seem so rough. Of course, he's just a pirati and Ronaldo is a prince's son, so it's silly to compare them."

Vita didn't reply. But as she watched the boys throwing their knives, and laughing, it seemed to her that Rosa was right. Compared to Ronaldo's tawny smooth skin, Giovanni's skin seemed wind-roughened. His hands were callused from handling fishing nets and oars and rope; his clothes were plain and dull, his black curling hair was tied back at the base of his neck with a piece of red twine. But Ronaldo seemed to move in a halo of sunlight that gleamed in the shot gold threads of his green vest, and shimmered in his long blonde hair. He was like an exotic animal with a beautiful pelt, as lazy-swift and loose-limbed as a leopard.

"You'd be crazy not to go with him, to Genovera," Rosa said. "Isn't this the opportunity you've been waiting for? Isn't it amazing that he's asked you to go?"

Yes, Vita supposed, it was amazing that she, a village girl, should be offered a trip to Genovera by the son of a merchant prince. She rubbed her aching forehead with her fingers and wished that someone would tell her what she should do, while Rosa sucked the juice from the fig and clapped whenever Ronaldo's knife pierced the target.

Later, when Giovanni had sailed home to the archipelago under a sky stained like a ripe apricot, Ronaldo and Vita ate supper at the café by the beach, under a striped umbrella. Ronaldo ordered a new candle lit on their table, and a fresh cloth, and a bunch of Red-Heart flowers in a blue pot. They drank wine from a tapered blue bottle that Ronaldo had produced from his saddle bag. He said that it was imported by his father from the islands of Lontano. They ate hot fresh bread and lamb's meat rolled in grape leaves. After two glasses of wine, Ronaldo reached across the table and grasped Vita's hand lightly in his long, smooth fingers. He told her stories about growing up in Genovera, about climbing walls and playing Tag and Run, and robbing orchards and commandeering boats on the river to play at being pirati, and dares he'd accepted. Once he'd accepted a dare to sneak into the courtyard of Lord Maldici and undo the cages of the wild, exotic animals there. Vita laughed until her sides ached and the lights of the village, gleaming through shutters, danced in horizontal bars across the still black waves of the harbor, danced and spun in circles. But perhaps it was the wine that made this happen.

When Vita returned home, and Ronaldo went whistling down the hill to the inn where he was staying, Aunt Carmela met her at the kitchen door. "You're late," she said shortly. She seemed to be grumpy all the time recently, and Vita was tired of it. "Did you clean Luna's shrine, and simmer the marjori leaves for me to use?"

"I forgot," Vita said lightly. She was tired of simmering leaves too, and tying them, and grinding them and mixing them. Aunt Carmela's chores seemed to have filled her days until Ronaldo arrived. She didn't see what was wrong with taking a rest from them.

"I'll do it myself then," Aunt Carmela muttered, her green eyes troubled. She stirred up the ashes of the cooling fire, and went outside to fetch kindling. Vita didn't wait for her return, for she was sure to ask about other jobs, and to mutter darkly when she found out that Vita hadn't done any of them. Vita hurried up the stairs. Rosa was already in bed, on her back with her hair hanging to the floor. Vita slipped between her own sheets, barely aware of the familiar smell of lavender and the coarse weave of the fabric, and closed her eyes to see Ronaldo's bright tawny gaze and the dancing lights in the water.

The moon rose. Downstairs, Aunt Carmela distilled the marjori over the fire, then let the flames die down, tied a linen cloth over her herbs, drew the sign against evil on the hearth with one finger, and went to bed herself. There was silence in the house. After some time, Rosa opened her eyes and listened. Then she climbed from her bed and tiptoed down to the kitchen where she wrapped a shawl around her shoulders . Like a shadow, she slipped from the house and climbed up through the garden in complete silence. The lavender colored gate swung shut behind her without a sound. Surefooted, Rosa moved across the hill in the light of the rising moon, to the meadow where Ronaldo's two horses cropped grass with a steady ripping sound.

"Ronaldo?" Rosa whispered.

"Here," came his reply from the pool of shadow beneath a crooked mandolo tree. Rosa slipped through the gate, while the horses paused in their grazing and raised their heads to watch, and crossed the grass to disappear into the shadow.

"What's happening?" she asked.

"She says she's going into the mountains."

"Will she take your horse?"

"Yes. I persuaded her that her trip would be much faster if she took it. She agreed that, with the horse, the trip might only take her a day instead of two days. But she won't say why she's going or what she's going to do there."

"It doesn't matter. We'll know soon. I have the spy stones."

Rosa reached into the pocket in her shawl and pulled out two flat, smooth stones. She carried them out into the moonlight where their slick surfaces gleamed a dark red that was almost black. For a moment Rosa stared down at them, resting in her palm, and their surfaces wavered. She glimpsed the hard planes of her father's face, his lips drawn back over his white teeth in a snarl.

"Come on," Ronaldo said nervously. "Fasten it on."

Rosa slid one stone back into her shawl and took the other over to Ronaldo's red horse. It moved nervously away from her but she gripped a fold of skin on its neck and twisted hard, and the horse immediately stood still, breathing in nervous snorts. Rosa threaded some mane hairs into a small hole that was pierced through the edge of the stone. She knotted the hairs on both sides of the stone, and then wove them into a braid over which she muttered a spell of invisibility to hide both braid and spy stone from Vita.

"There," she said. "In my stone, we'll see where Vita goes in the mountains so secretly, riding on your red horse. I'm sure that she's the Keeper. Her silver blonde hair, her lavender eyes— they're exactly as described in the Keeper's Tale that my father read in his black book. The one that Lord Morte wrote."

Ronaldo's face paled in the moonlight and he glanced apprehensively around the dark hills.

"Are you listening to me?" Rosa hissed, gripping his arm. "She knows the Keeper's Tale. She knows something that we don't, about the fate of the Corno d'Oro stallion. Tomorrow is midsummer's eve and the solstice. I'm sure that she's going into the mountains to say the spells that keep the Corno d'Oro invisible. Has she said if she'll come to Genovera with you after the solstice?"

"Yes, she'll come. And I'll keep her there for the autumn equinox, so the spells do not get said in the mountains. Then the Corno d'Oro stallion, if he exists, will be visible and unprotected, and the hunters can capture him."

Rosa's lips curled. "I didn't think this would be so easy," she said scornfully, and held out her hand. Ronaldo bent one knee and kissed her fingers, his shadow bending beside him in the dewy grass.

"We'll remember your service," Rosa whispered. "My father and I will see you rewarded."

CHAPTER NINE

MARINA SAT ON A ROCK, listening to the waves gurgling around it. She had been sitting here beneath the witch's house on the point for hours, feeling tired and despairing, while gulls cried and the sun swept across the sky and the tide fell. She'd watched the pirati gunboats slide out from the harbor early, swift and sleek as sharks, to disappear into the haze of the western horizon. They must have been expecting a merchant fleet, loaded to the waterlines with silk and spices, amber and ivory, salt and gold, to intercept. She'd watched two sailing boats filled with pirati children sail past about mid-morning, trailing fishing lines and shrieks of laughter. Although they must have seen her alone on her rock, none of the pirati had waved and one girl had made the sign with three fingers to ward off evil. Marina had stared past them haughtily, ignoring them, and pretending even to herself that she didn't care.

Now, around the point, came a battered rowing boat. It listed to port, and seemed to move heavily through the waves as though the effort of staying afloat was almost too much for it. Its wooden planking, weathered to gray, showed through in streaks along the sides where the blue paint had long since peeled off. A boy of about ten was bailing with a whelk shell. Two other boys, slightly larger than the bailer but equally skinny, were rowing while two girls sat in the bows and a fourth boy held the tiller and steered. They were sea urchins: homeless, orphaned or run-away children from coastal villages and the pirati island.

Marina smiled at them.

The girls in the bows waved and the little boat wavered closer to Marina's rock on an uncertain course until the boys rested at the oars and gave Marina crooked grins.

"What you sittin' there for?" asked one of the girls, her black hair shorn raggedly short.

"Being lonely and bored," Marina answered honestly. The sea urchins were as lost in the world, she felt, as she was herself, for neither she nor they seemed to belong anywhere. They were fellow outcasts and misfits.

"Huh," said the boy who'd been bailing. He set the whelk shell between his bare feet and stared frankly at Marina, his eyes the tawny brown of cinni spice in his narrow, golden face. His hair was remarkable, Marina noticed: dark brown shading to pure blonde streaked with bright highlights, like old honey seen in sunshine.

"What's your name?" Marina asked him.

"Ambro," he replied, straightening his narrow shoulders with a twitch of pride. "D'think as you'd be having more fun seeing as your ma's away over the water."

Marina shrugged. "She left me plenty of things to do."

"Like what?" The sea urchins drifted closer, rocking on the swell, and their six pairs of eyes stared at her curiously over their tattered clothing that had bleached, in sun and wind, to a homogeneous pale blue.

"Like reading books of spells and recording the patterns of the wind and practicing things I'm no good at," Marina replied.

"What things?"

"Well, there's this spell I'm supposed to have learned before she comes home. I have to row out into the middle of the Golfo in the night—"

"Alone?" asked one of the urchins. "Cuttlefish! You'd not catch me doin' that. That dragon lives out there. I'd take a few mates with me if I go rowing into the Golfo at night."

"The dragon only comes up once a year," Marina reminded him. Privately, she thought that a couple of mates as scrawny and bony as the sea urchins wouldn't be much help against a dragon anyway, but she didn't say this.

"Let her tell about the spell," commanded Ambro.

"Yes, the spell," said Marina. "I have to take with me seven Golden Arms—you know, those yellow starfish that live in deep tide pools and have seven legs each?"

The urchins nodded their rough heads.

"And I have to do this on a cloudy night. So I row out with my seven starfish and I make a powerful spell, and I throw the starfish up into the air. They soar up, high, high." Marina waved her arms around and the sea urchin's eyes stretched wide in their thin, tanned faces, "And then they hang in one place in the sky, forming the same pattern as the constellation called the Bright Cross. It's the one that points to the Pole Star."

"What you do that for?" asked a girl in the bow of the rocking boat.

"So that I'd never be lost at sea in the dark," explained Marina. "If I can't see the real stars, I can still use magic and Golden Arms to point to the Pole Star and then I can navigate. It's an important spell for a sea-witch to know."

"Oh, that'd be some clever to be able to do that. Are you clever?" asked Ambro with a bright, searching gaze from his amazingly clear, tawny eyes.

Marina sighed and gazed down at her toes gripping the rock's surface, engraved by barnacle shells, and at the clear water slapping against it. "No," she said in a small voice. "My mother thinks I'm stupid. I'm not good at even simple spells. I can't make the Golden Arms soar high enough , or stay hanging up there, or form the Bright Cross. I can't do anything properly."

"I hope you ain't going to cry," said one of the girls kindly, and she threw Marina a candied sea snail that was covered with fluff and dried salt from her pocket. Marina picked the fluff off it and popped it into her mouth and bit it hard until her eyes felt dry.

"Where you'd steal this from?" she teased.

The girl grinned. "That old man, the Reef-fish, he give it to me," she said. "He were out catching fresh snails and I found him one and he give me a candied snail in return."

"What old man's this?" asked Marina.

The sea urchins all swiveled in their boat, pointing toward the northern end of the archipelago.

"Lives on the last one—"

"All by hisself all the time, no mates—"

"Used to be a pirati but says he wants to be alone with his years—"

Marina nodded; it must have been this old man's house that she'd seen once when she traveled with her mother to the very tip of the archipelago to collect chitons at the full moon. The house stood near the shoreline, built of driftwood and stone, and with more beach stones holding up a terrace on the hill behind it, where several fruit and nut trees stood.

"Why do you call him the Reef-fish?" she asked.

"Why, course because the Reef-fish don't swim in schools but swims around all alone."

"But he's traveled all over the world," explained Ambro. "He has a whole room full of books, and he can tell stories about strange places—"

"And speaks hundred of languages!" added one of the girls in astonishment.

Marina smiled; it was easy to see how the sea urchins, who never attended school, would be impressed by such an man.

"We're going on now," the boy at the tiller called authoritatively, and the other boys picked up their oars and began to row, the weathered wood squeaking and groaning in the oarlocks. Like a fat, cumbersome beetle, the boat revolved slowly around until its stumpy bows pointed down the channel. The skinny boys bent their bare backs to the rowing, their vertebrae standing up in knobs. As they rounded the point, beneath the salt-pines, all the sea urchins waved to Marina, their bare arms and pointy elbows gleaming in the sun. She waved back and swallowed the last of the candied snail.

Her eyes hurt from staring into the glittering water all morning, and from unshed tears, and from staying awake to row alone into the Golfo at night, trying and trying to make the Golden Arms hang magically in the sky the way that her mother could. Why, oh why, couldn't she make this spell work? Or the other spells either, the easy, simple spells that the witch had been trying to teach her for years? Why was she so stupid, so slow, and so miserable? Marina crossed her arms over her knees and rested her face on them. She stared into the rosy darkness behind her lids.

Why did she feel the shoreline calling to her all the time, with its green terraces, its flowering trees, its smells of damp earth and lemons? Why did she long for it so, with an ache deep in her gut? She was the daughter of a sea witch and she should have loved the sea, with its clear salty depths where hundreds of fish swam, where dolphins played and sword whales cruised with their tapering horns. She should have been content with the currents and tides, satisfied with the voice of the west wind.

My mother will be angry, she thought, when she returns and finds that I still can't make the Bright Cross. But I'm too tired to try it again. And I don't even have any mates to take out into the Golfo with me. Even the sea urchins, who have no homes or families, have each other for company. I have no one. I'm like a Reef-fish, too.

She wondered how many languages the old man could really speak, and what sights he had seen traveling around the world, and if his room was really as full of books as the sea urchins had said. Books! Marina sat up and opened her eyes.

"Books," she said aloud. "Languages."

She had remembered the strange book that that girl, the Keeper, had found in the cave at the lowest tide in a hundred years, and that was still locked in the narrow cupboard in her own house. The key to the cupboard hung, in her mother's absence, around her own neck for some of the ground powders for spells were also kept in that cupboard. Maybe, if she took the book to the Reef-fish, he'd be able to help her translate the words. This would save her mother some work when she returned from her meeting in the Middle Sea, and maybe then she'd not be so angry about the unlearned spells. And then, maybe, Marina thought, I'll take the book over to the village and that haughty cuttlefish, with her blonde hair and her blue eyes and her friend Giovanni, won't be so arrogant with me. Maybe she'll be happy to have the words in her book made plain.

Marina scrambled to her feet and across the spine of rocks that stuck out into the waters around the point. She crossed the hot sand of the beach, and panted up the path to the sea witch's house where she retrieved the chest, containing the book, from the narrow cupboard before locking it carefully again. Soon she was tacking up the channel in her boat of polished salt-pine, with the indigo sail taut against the breeze and her green eyes alight with hope.

The Reef-fish was working on his garden terraces, but when Marina tacked into his bay he propped his hoe against a wall and walked down to meet her. He was a tall, bent man who looked as though he'd leaned all his life into a prevailing wind, and as though his life had already lasted longer than anyone else's. He wore gleaming spectacles perched on the end of his hooked nose, and held up his trousers of faded blue brocade with frayed sail rope, and had patches on the elbows of his black silk shirt. A golden ring shone on one little finger, and a gold hoop dangled from one ear, and a faded scar patterned his jaw. He projected the strangest mixture of elegance and poverty that Marina had ever seen.

"Please enter," he said graciously in a musical voice, and Marina went in through the weathered door. Inside, his small house was filled with objects: drums of animals, skins that Marina couldn't recognize, models of strange ships and outrigger canoes, spear heads from Terre, plants with leaves that rolled up at night like perfectly rolled scrolls.

As Marina explained the reason for her visit, the Reef-fish listened intently with his head on one side, as though he was listening for something that lay below the surface of her words. His faded blue eyes seemed to see far away things while he listened. He laid Marina's book on a table of golden fragranti wood, and bent over it until his hooked nose almost touched the pages. As he moved his head, Marina had the impression that it was his nose, held so close to the pages, that was reading the words and not his eyes at all. He scanned the words for a long time while Marina hovered anxiously at his elbow. She was afraid that her trip would have been for nothing, that her plan would fail. And what could an old pirati, know, after all, of the languages of the time of the moon goddess?

Then the Reef-fish straightened his back and said, as though he had heard Marina's unspoken doubts, "There are learned men in other places than Verde. I have studied with scholars all over the world, wise men. I may be able to read your book, given time. And the excellent resources of my collection."

He waved at the walls lined with books: small, slender volumes and thick, heavy ones randomly interspersed, their spines splitting with age, their titles burnished from many readings.

"But Sir—weren't you once a pirati?" Marina asked.

The old man stared away into one of his distances. "Young in life," he said slowly, "I learned that the mind of man is mightier than his arms, the words of man stronger than the sword, the heart of man more a force to be reckoned with than his muscle. For any man can wield a sword, but who can tell how to preserve the balance of the world, and who can number the stars? I forsook my family and went alone into far regions of the world, escaping my pirati heritage and searching for knowledge."

His hands, callused with the work of years, knotted with blue veins and yet somehow still elegant, tapped the cover of Marina's book. "The Corno d'Oro," he said softly, reverently. "Who can tell what is truth and myth? Who can tell, when the words of this book will be needed? There is a purpose here that I cannot see. Nonetheless, I gladly lend my mind to the task. Leave the book with me until the moon wanes."

Marina nodded. Sailing home, she hoped that her mother wouldn't return too soon, and that the Reef-fish would be true to his word. Impatiently she waited while the moon grew full, swollen like the pouch of a seahorse before it gives birth to live young. She tended the Golden Arms in their rock pool, and kept note of the winds and weather for her mother. She talked to the Mara women and hoed the garden of sand and salt grass and sea poppy. And all the time that she waited, the secret of the book warmed her loneliness and lightened her misery. Perhaps she wasn't completely stupid after all.

When the moon had completed its cycle and become as thin as a fish's scale, Marina sailed northward to find that the old man had translated every word. He had written the translations out between the lines of old tongue in the book, in an elegant, sloping hand using lavender colored ink made from the boiled stems of sea thistle. His eyes were grave and tired as Marina scanned his translations.

"I don't understand the verses," she said uncertainly, feeling stupid again.

"No, and neither do I," said the old man. "These words are not written for pirati and sea witches, Marina. They are written for a time of great danger and great need, and they are written for the Keeper. Let us pray that she has a discerning heart that will understand the danger and the need, as well as the riddles of these verses."

"But, which Keeper are they written for? There's a Keeper in every generation."

"Ah, that they do not tell. But I believe that you must take this book to the mainland of Verde, Marina, and deliver it to the present Keeper, who I hear is a young girl, and who lives in the village now. She must keep the book until either she or another of her line fall into need of it."

Marina smoothed her palm over the final page of the book, that remained blank but for its ghostly pattern of star lilies. "Why is there nothing written here?"

The old man shook his head, his golden hoop swinging in one ear. "Words there are, there, but written using magic. There are words in this world that have been written in certain ways, or at certain phases of the moon, or with a particular ink. Strong magic binds them. Their ink remains invisible to any but the one who can unbind the spell. Then they might be read, on the right day or in the right season. I can feel the presence of the words on that page, with my fingertips, but though I have tried many old tricks, I cannot make them appear. I have no magic, only learning. When you take this to the Keeper, tell her that the words on the last page might be for her eyes alone."

Marina nodded and, closing the book, laid it carefully into the chest and lifted it from the table. "I brought you something for your supper. It's outside the door in a pan," she said shyly, for suddenly the fish she'd caught that morning and baked into a casserole with sea lettuce dumplings seemed too small a token of thanks for the old man's many hours of hard work. But he smiled graciously and laid a hand on her shoulder.

"It was my honor to assist," he replied. "And who knows what small part my learning might have played in the events of the world? Perhaps it was to aid the Corno d'Oro and his Keeper that all my books were gathered here, to this one place, and that it was for this one task that I spent so many years acquiring languages. I would be content to have been used in so great a pattern as the Corno d'Oro weaves in the world."

Then they stepped outside, where a west wind was gusting toward the mainland of Verde and the gulls were playing in the up-draughts. "The wind will blow you straight to the Keeper's village," the old man said, and Marina nodded. She wedged the chest beneath a thwart and covered it with a piece of sailcloth while the hermit watched.

"Would you know, if there are any amongst the pirati anymore who can speak to the dolphins?" he asked.

"There is one, he's about my age and called Giovanni."

"Giovanni, Giovanni," the old man repeated. "I was such a one once." He said no more but bent to push Marina's boat into deeper water.

She rowed into the channel where, before hoisting her sail, she looked back. The hermit was standing, still bent as though into a prevailing wind, on the shoreline of his island, and Marina waved to him. Soon his house was a dot, then the island itself fell astern for the wind was brisk and Marina's light boat, with sleek hull, sped across the water.

As she steered, Marina hummed a sea chantey she'd heard the pirati sing on feast days, when she lurked around the edge of the village square trying to be inconspicuous and wishing that someone would invite her to join in. She wondered what the Keeper would say when she saw the translations in the book. Her lavender eyes would light up. She would be amazed that Marina herself had found a way in which the words could be made plain, that Marina had taken this trouble, and had even brought the book to her! Perhaps, in return, she would show Marina around the garden, for it was said that the Keeper's garden was the most beautiful place on the coastline, with birds singing in flowering trees and a burbling stream of clear water. Marina longed to wander in this garden, to stand beneath the magical tree and hear its leaves ringing. Perhaps the Keeper might even be pleasanter if Marina arrived with her book; perhaps she might want to be Marina's friend.

Buoyed up by this hope, Marina hurried through the alleyways of the village toward the fifty worn steps that a woman, hanging laundry out to dry, had told her led to the Keeper's gate. Children watched her curiously as she passed by because she was a stranger. They didn't whisper after her though, or make the three-fingered sign against evil, because they didn't know that she was the sea-witch's daughter. She wished that she had more time to enjoy the sights of the village: the flowers hanging from windows and spilling out of terracotta pots by front doors, and the cream colored jennet that an old man rode past on. She wished she could reach out and touch its soft muzzle and flickering ears, but she clutched the chest to herself instead and hurried up of those fifty steps that lay, barred with violet shadows, at the head of the steepest alley.

At the top of the steps, she found a lavender colored gate that swung open into a green paradise. She paused then, inhaling the smells of ripening fruit and oleander blossoms and green grass and fresh water. Something full and soft swelled inside her, displacing her loneliness. Dreamily she strolled down the path, and touched the fuzz on green apricots, and felt the smooth leaves of the fragranti trees, and pressed her face to the oleander blossoms.

"Who are you?" asked a husky voice in a sharp tone and Marina lifted her face from the petals to see a girl with bright red hair standing on the path and staring at her with hard, narrowed eyes. Instantly Marina felt herself stiffen inside, as if she was a crab growing a new shell. She knew that it was her pride stiffening to protect her, to give her something beneath which to hide.

"I'm Marina," she said haughtily. "Not that it's your business. I'm here to see the Keeper."

"She's busy," the other girl informed her. "She's going away to Genovera in an hour. She can't see you because she's packing."

"I have something for her."

"It can't be anything important; she didn't say you were coming."

"Why should she tell you?" Marina demanded.

"Because I'm her best friend," the redheaded girl replied with cool disdain. "You'll have to wait until she returns from Genovera. I'm sure you can wait. "

Marina felt her crab shell grow rigid and smooth as glass. She glared at the other girl and curled her lips scornfully. Without saying anything more, she turned on her heel and flounced back up the Keeper's valley with her green skirt swinging over her slender hips, and the ancient chest inside its wrapping of sailcloth clutched against her hammering heart. She could feel the other girl's eyes burning holes between her shoulder blades as she went; it was a feeling that she knew well. She had perfected the art of making a haughty exit, of knowing when she wasn't wanted, of leaving quickly.

Blindly, she stamped back down through the village, ignoring the children and the flower boxes, feeling loneliness enclose her like a dark cloud. Why had she been so stupid as to think that the Keeper would want to see her, or even be her friend? Wouldn't she ever learn to just be an outcast without hoping for something more? Stupid, that's what she was. Her mother was right. Maybe she should run away and join the sea urchins.

Her feet pounded along the harbor wall and she sailed into the Golfo with her mouth set in a straight line, and a dark cloud of loneliness dimming her eyes so that the water and the sails and the shoreline of Verde all seemed dull and dark. For hours she sailed, tacking to and fro, fighting the wind and the flood tide. She was still fuming inside her crab shell when she reached home, where to her surprise she found the pirati boy, Giovanni, sitting by her garden and splicing rope for his boat.

"What are you doing here?" she asked stiffly.

He grinned, unperturbed by her sourness. "Thought you might have a spare piece of rope I could borrow," he said. "I need a longer piece that this one."

Marina shrugged and shook her head.

"What's that in your arms?"

"Nothing much."

"Pirati treasure?" he teased.

"No."

"Dogfish got your tongue?"

"No."

He grinned and continued splicing rope. His strong, dark fingers wove the coarse fibers together until he had made one long piece. Marina set the chest down beside the sea poppies and sat hugging her knees and staring across the Golfo. The sky faded through shades of pale blue into rosy pink, gold, crimson. The waves below the point reflected each color in a liquid shimmer, and the crescent moon rose. Giovanni sighed in satisfaction at last, and stood up with his new rope in one hand.

"What are you going to do now?" Marina asked.

"I'm meeting some other boys. We're going night fishing with tapers and tridents. Thanks for the use of your garden."

He turned toward her and tripped over the chest, cursing it with a laugh. A corner of the sailcloth caught in his toes and the cloth slid off to reveal the chest. He stared at it for a moment in the dusk.

"But this is what Vita found," he said at last, sounding puzzled. "What were you doing with it today?"

Marina explained about the hermit pirati and how he'd translated the book, and how she had taken it over that day to give to Vita except that a girl with red hair had sent her away.

"That was Rosa," Giovanni said thoughtfully.

"She said that Vita was leaving, hours ago, for Genovera."

"What! How? By herself?"

"How should I know?" Marina asked coldly. Her crab shell of pride slid protectively over the memory of the deep disappointment she'd felt, standing in the Keeper's green garden, while the redheaded girl robbed her of her hopes.

"What does the book say?" Giovanni asked.

"I can't understand the riddles. They're for the Keeper. They're about wounds and tears."

"She should have it," Giovanni muttered, sounding worried.

"I certainly don't want the thing."

"Shall I take it? I can give it to Vita as soon as I see her again."

"Take it. Enjoy giving it to her," Marina said sarcastically, and lifted the chest and handed it to Giovanni who hurried down the path to his boat, frowning in preoccupation.

Marina sighed and walked inside to the round room, where the moon's glittering path reached across to touch the windowsill of bent driftwood. Soon her mother would return and ask what Marina had learned to do in her absence. I shouldn't have wasted my time, she thought, on that stupid Keeper and her stupid book.

No good had come of it and, standing in the dark room of the empty house with the sea-pine sighing against the windows and the moonlight making contorted shadows on the floor, Marina felt lonelier than ever.

CHAPTER TEN

QUICKLY AND EXPERTLY, Giovanni's strong dark fingers knotted the bow rope through a ring in the harbor wall. Then, carrying the chest in its wrapping of sail cloth beneath one arm, he strode through the village.

"Hey, Giovanni!"

"What's the rush?"

"What's in your parcel?"

He waved an arm in acknowledgement of the villagers' calls, and grinned good humoredly at the children who tumbled around him like a litter of curious puppies, but his brown, bare legs did not pause in their swinging stride. Soon, he had reached the Keeper's valley, where ripening apricots scented the air and the mandolo nuts grew fat and oily inside their wrinkled, dark purple husks. At the kitchen door, he rapped and waited. Aunt Carmela appeared after a moment, wiping her knuckles on her apron. "Giovanni! Vita isn't here; she has gone to Genovera with the maid, Rosa, and with Ronaldo."

"Will she be home soon?"

Aunt Carmela sucked in her breath and clucked her tongue, shaking her head and loosening strands of her black hair, streaked with gray. They fell across cheeks furrowed with worried lines. "I don't know when she'll return. Except that she must be home before the autumn equinox. If she doesn't come then, things will be black in this world, Giovanni. I can feel the balance trembling. They say there's a dark power stirring in the north; I don't like Vita being pulled in so close to its vortex. But she was determined to go. Do you have something for her?"

"Let me come in and show you," he replied and followed Aunt Carmela into the familiar kitchen with its red tiles polished smooth with years of usage, and its huge open hearth where summer and winter a fire burned, and iron cauldrons released the scent of bitter herbs or sweet tomatoes, the pungency of onions, the spicy tang of liniment for swollen muscles or the honey sweet fragrance of love potions into the air.

By the firelight, Giovanni and Aunt Carmela pored over the translations in the book, and the lines deepened in the aunt's face. "These words are for the Keeper. Who knows when they might be needed? I feel forces gathering against us, Giovanni. I wish that Vita was here, with the book, and not traveling unprotected in the north."

Giovanni stared into the fire for a moment. "I'll take the book to her in Genovera," he decided, and in his eyes a bright, steely blue light flared with the strength of his resolve. "I'll sail north to the delta and then follow the River Arnona inland. Maybe she'll come home with me."

"You're a true friend," Aunt Carmela said. "Wait, and I'll pack you a sack of food."

But as the aunt packed, the wind—that had been puffing uncertainly from a variety of compass points all morning—settled into the north and began to blow a steady, dry, cool torrent of air that streamed down the Golfo d'Levanto, sending white foam flying from the crests of the waves. Striding up the Keeper's valley, Giovanni felt the wind on his face and knew that he would never be able to sail north while the Bianco, the wind from the northern mountains, blew, for he would have to tack all the way to the delta and his progress would be slow. For two days, he dangled his legs over the harbor wall, fishing with a pole and waiting for the wind to change, and thinking about Ronaldo with his slashed silk doublets and his golden hawk eyes, and about Vita. He felt Aunt Carmela's worry fermenting inside him like fumes inside a cask of wine.

By the evening of the second day, he felt ready to explode with worry for he knew that at this time of the year the Bianco might blow steadily for a week or more. He slung his fishing pole over one broad shoulder and hurried up to Old Tomie's where he arranged to borrow a jennet. The next morning he set off riding northward with a sack containing salt fish and bread, and a skin holding water, hanging against his legs.

For three days he followed the tortuous mountain trails that clung to the slopes above the Golfo, winding threadlike around terraces of grape and olive, above the tiled rooftops of villages, past the warmth gathered in leaning stone walls. The Bianco stroked the Golfo into white lines far below him, and sent his dark hair streaming away from his neck, and his red bandana fluttering. The lantana bushes, flowering orange and pink on the cliffs, shook in the cool air and the jennet's creamy tail swished behind her as she jogged along, sure-footed and nimble. Giovanni talked to her from time to time, and patted her warm neck and scratched her at the base of her curly horns. When he sang sea chanteys in his clear tenor voice, the jennet's creamy ears, fringed with fine hair, flapped back and forth. Sometimes, passing a wayside shrine to Luna the moon goddess, Giovanni would halt the jennet and pause for a moment in respectful silence, and wish that Vita was with him.

On the third afternoon, Giovanni reached a junction where a trail branched off, headed westward. He knew, from directions given to him by men working in the lemon groves, that the westward leading trail climbed through a pass in the mountains and dropped down on the farther side into the inland plain. From there he could find a road leading to Genovera. He pulled the jennet to a halt and slid off her back, his legs stiff.

"Food, my girl."

At the sound of his voice, a wren chittered in the massive fragranti tree standing at the junction of the two paths, and overhead a wheeling hawk glared down with golden eyes before riding the updraft above the mountain pass. Giovanni unslung the chest containing the book from his back and tethered the jennet with a short length of rope. Then he sat down on ground sprinkled with the fragranti's tiny yellow blossoms, like fuzzy balls, and leaned his back against its huge trunk. He ripped a hunk of bread off his loaf and uncorked his water skin. As he ate, the words from the book clamored inside his head, chasing each other around and around. What did they all mean? Giovanni wiped his fingers on his short indigo breeches, patched with red cotton squares, and lifted the book from the chest. Again, he read the translations in the hermit man's elegant, sloping hand…danger and fear seemed to seep from the pages.

The wind whispered overhead, streaming through the fragranti so that its few remaining blossoms sailed southward in a glittering curtain. Down below, at the base of the tree, the sun was very warm on Giovanni's shoulders and his bare head. The jennet's teeth, ripping grass, combined with the sigh of the wind and the soft crash of waves on the rocks far below, and the words written in purple sea thistle ink wavered and swam before Giovanni's eyes. Gradually, he dropped off to sleep, the book open on his lap.

He awoke suddenly, fully alert, but held himself perfectly still because he knew that some sound—a sound that was neither from the jennet nor the wind nor the waves—had touched his sleeping mind. He awoke the way that all pirati awake: alert to danger, ready to react, with five senses searching the surroundings. It was the smells that Giovanni noticed first: male sweat and horse and old leather. After a moment, he could hear the man's breathing, just behind him and to the right of the great base of the fragranti tree. Giovanni's muscles bunched. He sprang to his feet with such force and speed that his feet hit the middle of the trail before the other person could react, and then he spun around in the gravel and dust with the book clutched to his chest and his eyes vivid with electric blue energy.

"Hey boy, what's the matter?" the man standing at the base of the tree drawled, in an accent that Giovanni didn't recognize. The man's clothes, dyed brown and green, blended into the grass so that Giovanni had to stare directly at him, in the mottled shade of the tree, to see him clearly. He looked as though he'd traveled many miles, for his trousers were white with dust and his loose tunic hung in limp creases. His legs were encased in leather riding boots, worn and darkened with age, and his long brown hair hung uncombed around his stubbled chin. He reminded Giovanni of a fox sneaking through the hills.

"Didn't mean to scare you, boy," the man tried again. "Just thought I'd stop and chat with a fellow traveler. Not often one meets a pirati boy in the hills." And his shrewd, brown eyes, squinting against the sun in a nest of fine lines, stared keenly at Giovanni.

"I'm visiting a friend," Giovanni replied.

"Uh huh. Like something more to eat?" The man moved away a few feet to where his tawny colored horse cropped grass, and reached a hand inside the panniers that hung from the saddle.

"I've eaten," Giovanni said, sounding sharper than he'd intended. He wanted to slip the book back into the chest, but the man was standing so close to the chest, at the base of the fragranti tree, that he didn't see how he could do this without drawing the man's attention to it.

"That's an ancient tome you're clutching," the man said suddenly, drawing his lips back over pointy yellow teeth. "Taking it to your friend? Must be someone interested in history. Now I myself am interested in history, or even mythology. You might say that one flows into the other. In these parts of the world, there's a myth about the fabulous Corno d'Oro—but I suppose, being a pirati, you wouldn't know anything about that?"

Giovanni shook his head and tried to look bored. He could feel alarm singing through his veins with a high pitched hum, and his muscles were tense as anchor rope.

"Hmm," said the man, chewing lazily on a grass stem he'd pulled, and running his sharp, squinting gaze over Giovanni. "Couldn't help noticing that your book said something about the Corno d'Oro, as I wandered up and found you asleep there like a baby. But maybe you can't read? Why don't you let me take a look at your book and see what it says, being as I'm interested in old stories?"

Giovanni shook his head. He suspected that at any moment the man was going to lose patience and leap at him, pin his arms behind his back, whip out a small sharp dagger from some fold of his grubby camouflaged clothes and press it to his throat.

"My friend's waiting for me," he said. "I need to keep traveling."

Swiftly, never taking his eyes off the stranger, Giovanni moved toward the jennet's tether rope. Before he'd moved three paces, the man launched himself into the air. Giovanni lunged out of the way, the man's knife cutting a bright gash through his line of vision as the sun hit the blade. Giovanni began to run, the book clutched to his chest, pebbles jetting from beneath his pounding sandals, lantana bushes whipping against his bare legs and drawing blood. It was crazy to run along these mountain tracks, where one misstep could send you plunging over the cliff to fall hundreds of feet through the Bianco's cool stream onto the rocks below. Giovanni scanned the path ahead, its pale length blurred by his speed. Over the pounding of his footsteps and his heart, he strained to hear the other man's steps giving pursuit. Instead, he heard Old Tomie's jennet give a bellow of panic, and then its hoof beats clattering along the path after him. Heard too, a curious high note blown from a hunting horn, a note that echoed and shivered through the trees, bounced off the mountains, hung in the clear air. He knew then, at that moment, that he was the animal being hunted and fear leaped through him, cold and then hot, searing his veins.

Ahead of him, a man clad in brown leaped from the bushes above the path and ran toward him with arms outspread, and a knife in one hand. Behind him, the jennet galloped and a whip cracked. Giovanni scanned the cliff side, jumped over a patch of clinging vines and landed on a tiny ledge five feet below the path. In the periphery of his vision the man in brown cleared the tangle of vines too, and a voice shouted. The horn rang out again. Giovanni ran to the end of the ledge, grasped the twisted trunk of a sea-pine with one hand and swung himself around it, feeling the bark tear his palm raw. He dropped down to a slope covered in grass, his sandals with their rough soles that were made for gripping wet decks, barely holding him on the slippery stems. He ran diagonally across the slope and saw, slightly above him, a third man moving to cut him off. The sun burned in the man's wild russet hair. Giovanni paused for a fraction of time, his eyes darting over the cliffs, aware of the great space below where only wind and water existed. But he was not afraid of heights, for he'd grown up climbing ships' masts, and hanging in rigging, and stealing eggs from the nests of cliff dwelling seabirds.

"Drop the book!" the man with russet hair shouted. "You can't escape!"

Giovanni shoved the book down inside his shirt so that he had both hands free. Then he slid to the lip of the cliff and peered over. His eyes widened at the sight below. He turned, dropped to the ground, and lowered himself down the rock face until his toes touched the crack he'd seen running through the rock like a squiggle drawn with charcoal. Wedging his toes into the crack, he slid over the cliff edge, catching crevices in the rocks with his fingers. Tenaciously, ignoring the lump of the book on his chest that caught on rocks, and ignoring too the yells from the men above, he worked his way down the cliff face. A shadow swung across his shoulders as, above him, the man in brown began to climb down after him.

Sweat ran into Giovanni's eyes. One slip, and he'd plunge into the cove below, where the pirati scouting boat—that he'd spotted from the foot of the grass slope—rocked in the swells. A sea bird beat in against him, crying harshly, and he felt the wind from its wings cross his cheek. Grit and pebbles, dislodged from the hunter above, rained down, filling his eyes so that he blinked on prisms of tears, and his throat clenched shut and he coughed. His fingers slipped from their crevice and for one moment, while his heart stopped beating, he swayed out into the Bianco's cold torrent of air. Then he grabbed another lip of rock and swung his legs down another few feet, his toes fumbling for crevices.

The roar and boom of the sea filled his ears. There was a strong swell running, pushed up by the north wind, and the water was a dark, cold blue that broke against the cliffs with a surge and fountains of white spray. Giovanni wondered how they would bring the boat in close enough to save him. Perhaps they wouldn't be able to and he'd be trapped between the boiling sea and the hunters above, trapped at the tide line with his precious book that mustn't get wet, that mustn't be given into the hands of strangers. The men, Giovanni felt sure, were spies from Lord Maldici's army.

Even if the pirati managed to bring the boat alongside the rocks, he'd only have one chance.

Down, down he climbed until the sound of the roaring water filled his mind, thundered in his heart. He jumped off the cliff face onto a flat rock, wet with breaking spray, and squinted into the boiling light. The pirati were maneuvering their long, light boat alongside with supreme skill. Giovanni glanced back up the cliff: the other man was only a few feet overhead. At any moment, he would jump to land beside Giovanni on the wet rock.

"Now!" the pirati roared in chorus, their teeth and gold rings flashing, and Giovanni saw that the boat hung just beside him on the peak of a wave. He sprang toward it, felt the air whistling past his face. He tumbled over the gunwale as the boat fell into the trough, and wooden ribs banged him across the forehead with a sharp rap. The pirati strained at the oars, swinging the boat away from the rocks before its long, thin, shining hull of varnished fragranti was splintered into firewood against them.

The man in brown jumped too late, and Giovanni saw his head tossing in the water like the head of a wet dog before it was swallowed in a smother of breaking white water.

The pirati boat turned away as the men ran the sails up the raking twin masts of polished cypress wood, and the oarsmen strained, with muscles bulging in sunburned arms, to hold the bow steady into the galloping sea and the whistling Bianco wind. Giovanni sat with his head on his arms, sucking in great gulps of salty air and waiting for his heart to fall back into his chest. The covers of the book pressed into his ribs.

A hand slapped him on the back, sending shudders through him, and he looked up to see the grinning face of Pietro, the captain of the scouting boat and a man who lived just down the alley from Giovanni's house, at home in the pirati village.

"Been doing some on-shore raiding, lad?" he asked jovially, his thick black eyebrows beetling up and down.

"Stealing tangerines and apricots!" shouted a sailor close by.

"Stealing the virtue of village girls!" roared another man and a wave of wild laughter surged through the boat.

Giovanni blushed. "Something like that," he mumbled, and Pietro slapped him between the shoulders again and knocked all the breath back out of his aching lungs.

"You're a fine young lad," he roared over the wind. "We're on our way out to the gunship and we'll take you along. Raiding party planned for some pretty ships sailing out of Lontano. You can do all the stealing you want, boy!"

And he moved away while Giovanni's heart, so recently caught in his throat, plummeted deep down into his stomach like a sounding stone on a long rope.

At home, in his village, he'd mended nets down on the harbor wall, helping out other men and joining in their songs and laughter, and he'd provided fish for the market and for his neighbor's suppers. He'd scraped and painted boats, even polished cannon on board the gunships; shown everyone what a hard worker he was. But he'd never been on a raiding trip. When the gunships nosed their slender, fierce muzzles from the inlet, he'd always made sure that he was out at sea fishing, or up on the cliffs collecting eggs, or off swimming with the dolphins.

But now, he was heading for the southern seas with a band of ruthless men who'd load the gunship to the waterline with stolen treasure. There was no way that he could see to avoid what waited in the days ahead. He stared dully at the stacked cutlasses gleaming between the thwarts of the scout ship, and then looked up as the pirati gave a throaty roar of approval.

The gunship was rushing toward them from the north, her bows smashing through green water, her cedar decks awash, her rigging thrumming. Against the sky racing with clouds, her crimson sails were brilliant as spilled blood.

CHAPTER ELEVEN

THE GUNSHIP HOVE TO, bows pointing north into the Bianco, and her sails, empty of wind, snapped with ringing cracks. Davits swung out from her deck, and the pirati in the scout ship caught the hooked ropes that were tossed down and fastened the hooks to rings in the scout ship's stern and bows. Expertly, they unstepped the two masts. Presently, the men on board the gunship hauled on winches wound around great capstans, and the scout ship was lifted from the water and hoisted upward, on the lee side, until she was level with the deck and could be swung aboard. The pirati jumped from her onto the gunship's wet decking.

Giovanni climbed out last and walked away quickly along the deck with the book still concealed inside his shirt. He would have to find somewhere more permanent to hide it, and he was worried about it getting wet now that it lacked the protection of the trunk.

"Hey! Gio !" yelled a voice, and he turned to see Pietro's son, a boy with whom he often went spear fishing off the reefs, sitting on a pile of nets against the forward bulkhead. The long needle in Antonio's hand flashed as he waved at Giovanni.

"I didn't know you were onboard!" he shouted.

Giovanni dropped down onto the rough red and blue twine of the nets. "I wasn't," he said. "The scout boat picked me up off the cliffs."

"You were getting eggs?"

"No, I was getting chased."

"For stealing?"

"For keeping something that someone else wanted to steal."

Antonio gave a shout of laughter, throwing back his strong brown neck.

The gunship swung her bows to the south again and the sails filled with wind, leaping out across the sky and casting red shadows over Giovanni's arms. He shivered in the wind, felt the boat become alive as she leapt forward like a sword whale smelling prey, heard the rigging thrum as it sliced across the clouds. Spray misted his face and the hazy shoulder of the mainland began to slip past, freckled with shadows. Somewhere over there, Vita was straying away from her home, and the ancient chest was sitting beneath a fragranti tree, and Old Tomie's jennet was either lost or stolen. Worst of all, two men were carrying word to the ears of Lord Maldici, about a boy with a book that spoke of the Corno d'Oro. All of this because he, Giovanni, had been careless enough to fall asleep in broad daylight in a strange place.

He shook his head to clear his thoughts, and noticed that Antonio was not, as he'd assumed, mending nets. "What are you making?" he asked.

"Bags for the captain's cut of salt and spices, to keep them dry after we capture the ships. You know the cured skin of the Reef-fish, that it's waterproof?"

Giovanni picked up one of the pieces of dried fish skin. It had been scraped of scales and sun-dried to create a thin, opaque sheet that was as tough as leather and pale yellow in color.

"Can I have a piece?"

"Help yourself, if you'll help me sew these bags. I'll be here for the next week."

Giovanni slipped a needle from its case in his pocket and threaded it expertly, with one swift jab, with a length of the thread that Antonio was using from a large spool. He sorted through the pile of Reef-fish skins until he found one that seemed large enough, and then he bent it in half and began to sew it into a bag with triple-folded, watertight seams.

"How far are we sailing?" he asked.

"A week south maybe, or more."

Giovanni sighed and Antonio shot him a sharp look.

"Not so good?"

"I didn't want to be away right now. There's something I wanted to do."

"Tough luck. But this will be more fun, Gio! I can't wait! My father has given me a cutlass, and I'm going on with the boarding crew!"

"To kill men doing their day's work."

"We need the gold," Antonio said defensively. "The dragon's always waiting for us. If we don't keep him happy, he may turn on us."

It was true, Giovanni reflected. The pirati, for all their courage, lived in fear of Dragomar, of his blue shining teeth and lashing tail.

"This isn't my first raiding trip!" Antonio bragged. "Last time, we captured a ship sailing out of Terre with amber. Look, I have a piece of it." And he pulled out the gold chain that hung inside his shirt and showed Giovanni the piece of amber, cut in the shape of a sword whale, that dangled from it. "And I brought my mother a necklace of seed pearls," he said. "And in the ship's hold were the weirdest animals, called magrazzi, with long thin legs and necks as long as the legs! And we saw outrigger canoes off the islands of Corallo, and we swam in the reefs and had a huge bonfire party on the beach one night. It was a great trip!"

They sewed in silence for a while, with their legs folded under them and their spines bent over their work. Their needles flashed in and out, in and out, through the tough skin of the Reef-fish. The gunship cut through the water, with the carving of a bare breasted Mara woman leaning out from her bowsprit, and the sails creaked and groaned at the masts, and the pirati men chanted at the capstans. *Heave!* they shouted. *Heave ho, my mates, for we're on our way and the sky is bright and our hearts are gay. Heave! Heave ho, my boys!* The misty spray wet Giovanni's lips with salt and the sun slipped down the western sky into clouds as soft and purple as octopus ink.

Giovanni lifted the book out of his shirt and into the large bag he'd sewn, and then he began to stitch the final watertight seam.

"Love letters?" asked Antonio mischievously.

"Maybe."

"Aha, so this is why you don't want to come with us. Can't she wait?"

"I'd rather be ashore," Giovanni replied. "Don't we put in to any port, or stop as we pass the archipelago?"

"The closest we'll come is as we pass the northernmost island. They say that a hermit lives there, who used to be a pirati."

"Yes, he does," Giovanni agreed, remembering what Marina had told him when she gave him the Keeper's book.

"Then we alter course and sail west by southwest toward the islands of Lontano. There's no land between here and—"

"Hey, Antonio! Crow's nest for you!"

Antonio nodded and bit off a piece of thread and stuck his needle back into its little leather case inside his shirt pocket. "See you later!" He sprang up, flexing his leg muscles, and swaggered away down the rolling deck before climbing into the rigging and upward through the shrouds toward the crow's nest.

Giovanni kept sewing. He wondered whether the men who'd chased him had simply come across him by accident as he sat sleeping—or if they'd been looking for him. But why should they be looking for him? He wondered if they really were spies of Lord Maldici's and, if so, why they were so interested in the book about the Corno d'Oro, and what this interest portended. Perhaps they were merely wandering tale-spinners looking for another good story? Anxiety gnawed at his stomach as the western horizon flushed with pearly pink, like a mullosk shell, and as the gunship sped onward.

Once the book was completely sealed inside the waterproof bag of Reef-fish skin, Giovanni slid it back into his shirt, and buttoned this to the throat, and tucked the hem of it more securely into his waistband. Then he leaned on the port rail and squinted toward the mainland. He reckoned that they'd be passing the northern end of the archipelago in the early hours of the following morning. He thought about the tide, and the currents, and how what he was planning was crazy and that his body might never be found.

He thought about Vita alone in the north. Her silver-blonde hair. Her lavender eyes. Her laughter.

He went down into the galley and filched a bottle of ginger beer and some crumbly sea star cakes that he ate in the shelter of the bulkhead. The sailors were still chanting at the capstans, and the gunship quivered beneath Giovanni, filled with the energy of wind and water. Giovanni noticed how the pirati men moved around the deck with spring and purpose to their steps, how they laughed and shouted. They're all looking forward to what lies ahead, he thought. The gold greed of Lord Morte is in their hearts, and they're in bondage to Dragomar's greed and their own. Yet, as he sat there eating, he thought that it might be fun to sail on a pirati raid. He too could see the strange places that Antonio spoke of, and chant at the capstan, and be part of the rowdy merrymaking. He too could bring his mother necklaces, and wear a gold chain around his throat.

My father is probably on board somewhere, he thought. If I find him and say I'm coming along, he'll beam with pride. He'll clap me on the back and shout to his mates to drink me a toast, and he'll give me a bright new cutlass to wear in my belt. For a moment Giovanni imagined the clash of arms, the ringing sound of bright steel. He imagined the holds of foreign trading ships, spilling their magnificence into his hands—the barrels and casks and trunks of treasure that he could rummage through. For a long moment, he felt the gold greed stir in his heart with a hot, sweet feel that made his mind spin, the way it had spun at the last feast when he drank fig-canary wine. For a long moment, he felt the reckless, plundering joy of all his fore-fathers coursing through his blood. It would be easy to stay on board this gunship.

I mustn't give in, he thought fiercely. I must resist.

When he'd finished every last salty crumb of cake, he craned his neck back and took a last look at the constellations overhead, marking their positions in his mind like a bright map. As the moon rose, he wriggled down into the pile of nets and fell asleep with rough twine pressed against his cheek.

He awoke fully alert and listened for a moment to the creak and roll of the ship, the wind thrumming steadily in the rigging as it had for many hours. Bianco, he thought, still coming down from the north. He smelled the salt in the wind, and the snow. He listened to the muted commands being shouted by the watch master, and to the creak of a capstan turning and the dull patter of feet on the decking. Then he stood and went out to the rail and craned his neck for another look at the sky, marking how the stars had shifted and the moon had sailed through her deep sea of darkness while he slept. Against the eastern horizon the mountains on the shore were a rumpled line, barely distinguish-able in the night. Soon, the sun's light would stain the sky above them a pale, watery yellow. But not yet; Giovanni judged that it lacked two hours until dawn.

He peered through the dark layers of air between the gun-ship and the distant shore, trying to see the northern islands of the archipelago, but if they were there they blended perfectly with the shoreline and remained invisible. Giovanni turned his head, letting the wind blow past his ear. He strained to hear the sound of distant surf breaking on the rocks of the archipelago but he heard nothing above the Bianco's steady whistle and he knew anyway, in his heart, that no pirati captain would sail so close to rocks in the darkness.

He gripped the rail and thought of Vita alone in the north.

Slipping his sandals off, he swung himself up onto the rail's cold polished brass, and tensed his muscles. For a second he paused, gathering his resolve, pushing away the last lingering sweetness of the gold greed, the temptation to stay onboard this ship. Then he sprang out away from the dark, rushing hull to plummet down and down, with air blurring his eyes, until he hit the cold, black floor of water and sank through it. Dizzily, panic-stricken, he fought upward, his arms swinging strongly and pale streamers of phosphorescent bubbles, green and blue in the moonlight, streaming from them like the ephemeral wings of moon moths. Finally, with burning lungs, he shot through the surface again and sucked in air.

The wake of the gunship lifted him up, bobbing. Its sails blotted out the moon. Its creaking voice died away as it rushed southward, and suddenly Giovanni found himself alone in the ocean and realized how small he was in its infinite vastness, and knew how very stupidly he was behaving. When you drown in the archipelago, the grandmothers of the village said, the sea doesn't give you back up for many tides and many miles. It takes you in, fathoms deep, like a jealous lover.

Giovanni turned away from the moon, floated on his back, and began to swim toward the east while the dark water rolled him up and over, up and over, on the crests of its long swells, and the Bianco lifted the crests into foam. He trailed a ribbon of phosphorescence behind himself. The moon sank lower. He flipped onto his stomach and began to swim in a long, steady crawl until his arms burned with fatigue. When he rolled onto his back again, the stars had slipped farther across the sky. Water sloshed into his mouth, a salty bitterness. He drew a ragged breath and began to swim again.

His legs were heavy, heavier than lead weights, than sacks of dragon's gold, than the chain he used to anchor his blue hulled boat. For a moment he thought of its bright yellow sail, and of how Vita loved to sit on the thwarts and watch the seabirds swing overhead. A deep sadness seemed to pull Giovanni down into the water

He was drowning, and he'd never again spend a day in his blue boat with Vita.

Water was filling his body, making it as heavy as a water-logged boat that would slip to the bottom with barely a sigh. He wouldn't make it to the islands. Anyway, he might have been miles away from them when he went overboard. He thought of Antonio sleeping on board the gunship, warm and dry, dreaming of bright cutlasses. He imagined the dragon, lying fathoms deep below him in its slimy caverns, on its hoards of tarnished gold; imagined its dreadful, gaping mouth. He thought of the Keeper's valley with its chyme tree ringing softly. Its ringing seemed to fill his head until he thought that maybe it was the stars singing to him, singing about the incredible size of the dark, mysterious heavens arched over his head. He thought of the book flattened against his chest, and he swam on with numb arms and his heavy, useless legs that were pulling him down, down, into fathoms of uncharted water.

Sea brothers! he called feebly, like a sigh or a whisper in his mind.

The stars were fading. His eyes seemed filled with salt. Waves reared up in the darkness, raced toward him. Wave after wave. Mile after mile of waves. His arms stopped moving. Water filled his mouth. He flailed helplessly, sinking down beneath the surface. The next wave submerged him, his whole head went under. He tried to kick but his legs didn't respond. Maybe they're wrapped in weed, he thought slowly, in confusion. His body rocked in the water's motion. Even fear had deserted him; he was past any feeling.

Then something boosted him skyward, and his mouth opened of its own accord and air filled it. The smooth, hard bodies beneath him held him up, his face turning toward the gray stain on the eastern horizon. Dimly he felt a rushing strength, a sleek power.

Sea brothers? he asked.

What are you doing out here all alone? one of the dolphins replied in its silvery liquid voice.

What has happened to your boat? asked another.

I am going to the hermit on the northern island. Can you help me?

We will take you there, Giovanni!

Around him, he saw their sharp dorsal fins piercing sea and sky, draining darkness from it, letting in the clear dawn light. Swiftly, playfully, they carried him through the water to the hermit's island where they nudged him to the sandy beach. He lay in the shallow water, stroking their smooth blue skin while they laughed, their small merry eyes like currants in the first rays of sunlight.

Thank you, sea brothers. Thank you.

He pressed his face to their long snouts and kissed them, making them laugh more and leap seaward. Then he crawled onto the cool rippled sand to lie face down and sleep, his hair matted with salt, his face pale with fatigue, and his wet indigo shirt plastered against the skin of his back.

He awoke to heat throbbing between his shoulder blades and a sound like a drum beating in his head and the sight of toes clad in soft leather only inches from his eyes. He staggered up, his legs buckling beneath him. The old man who'd been standing regarding him caught him just before he fell.

"Carefully, young one," the old man said, the spectacles on his hooked nose twinkling in the sun. He held Giovanni's elbow in a grip of surprising strength and peered at him with pale blue eyes.

Giovanni's head spun and his mouth was so dry that it wouldn't form words. He struggled with it and at last croaked, "Where am I?"

"You have come in with the tide, young man, to the northern-most island of the pirati archipelago. You have come to my home, for I live here alone. You may call me Giuseppe, although I believe that the sea urchins call me the Reef-fish." The old man chuckled and his eyebrows, which were curly and white and of prodigious length so that he looked like a shaggy jennet foal, bobbed up and down.

"Come," urged the old man gently. "Come inside and eat," and he steadied Giovanni with an arm around his shoulder as he walked unsteadily up the beach with stars dancing and singing in his head. Inside, in a room lined with books, Giovanni slumped at a table and silently ate the bowlful of mandolo nut porridge, and drank the tea of dried sea lettuce, that Giuseppe gave him, and as he ate and drank new strength flowed into his numb limbs. In the center of the table a candle burned before a small shrine. It was carved with the familiar tailed form of Sirena, the pirati's sea goddess with her crown of starfish and her frolicking dolphins, and Giovanni felt obscurely comforted.

"I swam in from a gunship," he said suddenly and felt the old man, seated across the table from him, stiffen. "The dolphins brought me in, not the tide."

"The dolphins," Giuseppe whispered, with a strange longing in his tone, and his gaze sharpened. He cocked his head on one side, as though listening for the meaning below the surface of the words.

"You're Giovanni," he said. "Marina told me about you. Once I was a young man such as you, the only one in my generation who could speak to the dolphins. Alas, that I lost such a gift."

Giovanni stared in surprise, for it had never occurred to him that this gift might be lost, nor had he ever met another pirati who'd had it. "But—what happened to it?"

Giuseppe rubbed his swollen knuckles together and stared into the crackling blue flames of his driftwood fire. "I wasn't true to my heart," he said. "I sailed away with the pirati, with my father and my uncles and my three brothers, and we raided a fleet out of Mombasso. I fell into the bondage of gold. Finally, I sickened of it all but I couldn't come home; I lacked the courage to face my family, my village, and tell them that I renounced my pirati heritage. So I stayed away, traveling alone through the countries of the world, seeking knowledge, collecting books, always learning and always moving on; always avoiding what I knew needed to be done. At last, I was too weary to continue and I came here, to live alone on this island."

"What? What needed to be done?" Giovanni asked.

"I should have come home and battled the old dragon that holds the pirati in thrall. I have collected a vast store of knowledge about sea dragons and their ways—" and he swept a hand toward his books "—but I lacked the courage to use my knowledge."

"Battle the dragon..." Giovanni repeated doubtfully. It had never occurred to him that such a thing was possible.

"Dragomar cannot be killed, but vanquished for a thousand years," Giuseppe explained. "But only by one with the knowledge and the true, brave heart to do it."

"What would happen to the pirati then?"

"Some would become fishermen. Others would become ship builders, making the fastest, sleekest ships the world has ever known. And they would become pilots and navigators, renowned for their skill, their knowledge of every sea. And they would be courageous explorers, drawing beautiful maps. For with the vanquishing of Dragomar, the gold greed would die in their hearts."

Giovanni emptied the last dregs of tea from his mug while the hermit stared, lost in sad dark musings, into the flames. The morning light was growing brighter outside, and it reached across the floor of flat beach stones and touched Giovanni's bare toes. It was time to continue.

"I have to reach the mainland," he said. "This package in my shirt contains the book that you translated for Marina, and I'm trying to take it to Vita, the Keeper. Would you sail me over in your boat?"

"I have no boat, Giovanni. She sank years ago and I have never replaced her. There is nowhere that I want to go."

Giovanni stared mutely out the window of thick, rippled glass at the empty beach.

"Perhaps the sea urchins will come rowing by some time, in a day or a week or a month," Giuseppe said. "Then they can take you to shore. In the meantime, I will show you my books. You can learn all that I know of dragons."

CHAPTER TWELVE

"I MUST LEAVE TOMORROW, Vita said regretfully, staring out the window into the courtyard below where a groom led a tapestry stallion in circles, its hooves striking sparks and its head tossing. Beyond the courtyard wall, the gardens of the palazzo swept uphill, divided by raked paths of golden gravel and by high dark hedges cut into ornamental shapes. Jets of water from hidden fountains sparkled in the light.

"Tomorrow?" Rosa gasped, joining Vita at the window. "But you can't leave so soon, Vita!"

"I must. I must be home for the autumn equinox in three days' time, to keep my aunt company. It's a family tradition," Vita said.

She smiled as Ronaldo strode into view from beneath a portico. Beneath a magnificent hat with a sweeping brim draped in purple feathers, his golden hair was tied back from his face. His black leather boots rapped on the cobbles and his spurs jingled. When he took the reins from the groom, the stallion pirouetted away, fidgeting restlessly. With a quick jerk on the bit, Ronaldo held it still and swung expertly into the saddle in one lithe motion, gathering the stallion's power beneath him. The horse snorted and bent its neck before prancing out through the massive gateway beneath its marble arch carved with wood nymphs and fauns.

Vita watched until Ronaldo's tall straight back, clad in a riding jacket of burgundy velvet and swaying in time to the stallion's trot, disappeared from view. She let out a sigh of admiration.

"But you can't go home now!" Rosa protested again.

"Why not?"

Rosa smiled coyly, rolling her eyes. "Well, it's a secret, Vita. But if I must tell you, I must...Ronaldo's parents are planning a party tomorrow night for your birthday! They sent out the invitations weeks ago, on cream cards bordered with gold ink. The food's already ordered too, to be served at seven, before the dancing starts. Eight courses, Vita, to be eaten at long tables. And then, at ten, a cold buffet in the courtyard, with fairy lanterns, and then fireworks to follow. It will be splendid!"

Vita listened in rapt fascination. It did sound splendid...if only she didn't need to go home to the mountains, to perform the magic at the autumn equinox and protect the grazing meadows and the resting-places of the Corno d'Oro. Would it matter, she wondered, if the magic was performed a day or two after the equinox? She'd never heard of such a thing being done...perhaps the words and spells and runes only worked when performed at the appointed time. She couldn't risk finding out what would happen if she left her task too late.

"I must go home," she repeated, turning from the window as the tile-maid, who was responsible for the palazzo floors, tapped at the door of the blue room and entered with a curtsey. She began to sweep up yesterday's rose petals and cinnamon, in preparation for strewing the floor afresh with today's lavender blossoms that she carried slung at her waist in a soft woven basket.

Rosa caught Vita by the arm, and her expression was strangely fierce. "You can't go home now," she hissed. "It would be ungrateful and rude, after all the hospitality they've shown you! And what of the expense of this party? And what would Ronaldo think if you insulted his family? If the equinox is a family time, pretend you're part of this household. I'm sure Ronaldo would like that."

Vita pulled her arm away, for Rosa's fingers were pinching. She flopped down on the pile of feather quilts that covered the four poster bed with its canopy of shimmering blue silk. Rosa perched on the edge of the bed and erased her scowl with a smile.

"Anyway," she cajoled, "if you go home, what will become of me? If I'm no longer your lady's maid, I won't have a job. I won't have a home."

Vita stared up at the draping of blue silk. It was hard here, in the city—with its ringing bells and silver clouds of pigeons wheeling around tall towers of fretted stone, with its rattling chariot wheels and brightly striped awnings over markets stalls, with its bustle and excitement—to believe that the solitude in the mountains was even real, or that the Corno d'Oro even existed. After all, she had never seen him. Perhaps, all these years, the Keepers had been telling a tale about something that had vanished long since from the world. Perhaps all that was real was this city, with its cafes and palazzi, its stately river barges and its important nobles and merchant princes with their swinging cloaks of angoli wool, their buckled shoes and ivory staffs of office.

Perhaps nothing would happen, Vita thought, if I stayed here forever; nothing would change. No one would even notice whether or not I'd returned to the mountains and mumbled my spells and waved my hands in the air and traced invisible patterns on tree trunks and rocks. What harm can it do if I stay for this party?

"I have an idea," said Rosa suddenly while the tile-maid went about her work, filling the air with the scent of lavender.

"What?"

"If you stay for the party, we can ask Ronaldo to lend you a fast horse in the morning afterward. Then you will be able to return to the mountains quickly, and be in time to join your aunt."

Vita pondered this, barely noticing as the tile-maid curtsied her way from the room and the taper-maid entered, the baskets at her hips bristling with fresh tapers in a rainbow of colors. She moved around the room unobtrusively, plucking the half-burned tapers from wall sconces and chandeliers, and replaced them with new tapers of cream wax scented with rare vanilla imported from Mombasso.

It's true, Vita thought. I could leave very early on the morning after the party. I could take one of those horses the messengers use, that can maintain their special gait for hour after hour, never faltering in their long, smooth strides. Perhaps, then, I could reach home in two days' traveling, if I ride at night, too. I'd be just in time to perform the magic. Just. If I'm lucky.

She was startled from her musings by an imperious rapping at the chamber door and, in response to her order to enter, a footman flung it open and announced: "Mistress Jacquardi."

Rosa bounced off the edge of the bed.

"The dress maker!" she cried. "Vita, you're to have a new dancing gown for the party. I forgot to tell you. But here is the fabric!"

Vita sat up to see, behind the stout, wheezing bulk of Mistress Jacquardi, three girls carrying bolts of cloth that spilled from their arms in torrents of color: lavender purple, tissue of gold, silk of sea foam shot with silver threads, coral pink taffeta woven through with satin thread of dark rose and tiny seed pearls.

"For me!" Vita cried in rapt astonishment, and slid off the bed.

"I'm here for a fitting," Mistress Jacquardi wheezed. "First we measure, then we choose the fabric, then we sew. My shop is known for the flawlessness of its workmanship, the exquisiteness of its seams, the perfection of its flounces and ruffles and necklines and trimmings. Bonnets to match. Gloves. Fans and feathers. I provide all you need."

She stopped, panting for breath, her ample bosom heaving, and gestured to Vita to step forward and raise her arms. A girl held out a measuring tape and a packet of silver pins.

"You can make it by tomorrow?" Vita asked, and Mistress Jacquardi brushed the question aside with the wave of a plump hand. "Pooh, it is nothing," she said. "I have a shop full of seamstresses."

Bending over the pink taffeta fabric, Rosa licked her pouting red lips and smiled to herself, secretly and triumphantly.

Astride the red horse, and with her pack tied to its saddle, Vita trotted from the palazzo gates into Genovera's silence. The city seemed strangely deserted at this hour, for dawn was merely a flush of ivory and rose in the eastern sky, and in the streets the shadows lay still and heavy as sleeping animals. High above the city, the castle of Lord Maldici floated atop its citadel of craggy rock, its pale towers and battlements gleaming like chalk in the first rays of light. Vita gazed up at it for a moment, in mingled fear and curiosity. In the months she'd spent here, she'd never seen Lord Maldici nor visited that lofty fortress with its curving ramp of crushed stone, its massive black gates studded with iron and decorated with the lord's insignia of condors, their huge wings spread open and their sharp hooked beaks in profile.

She tugged at the reins, swinging the horse downhill and nudging it forward with her heels. Its hoof beats echoed against the closed shutters at palazzi windows and, high overhead, disturbed pigeons cooed throatily on their towers and cornices. Vita yawned and shivered, glad that Rosa had pulled her velvet green jacket from the wardrobe and insisted that Vita wear it.

The smell of baking cakes and fresh bread wafted up cellar steps and Vita glimpsed the glowing mouths of stone ovens. Then the river Arnona appeared, a thread of light as pale yellow as the blossom of the fragranti tree, and Vita turned the horse's head toward the Verde Bridge. Beyond its graceful arches, the autumnal countryside began, stretching away into the violet and gold shadows of distance. The horse scrambled over the hump of the bridge with its nostrils stretched wide, snorting the cool air that carried the scent of wheat, ripening grapes, and the bark of magnolia trees.

From atop the bridge, Vita could see in either direction: westward the Arnona flowed steadily, its water going down to the delta and the sea. Eastward, the city of Genovera nibbled at the edges of the plains, where dust rose from the encampment of Lord Maldici's army. It was rumored that the army was swelling larger daily, its ranks supplemented with villagers brought in from the countryside by the assassini, and that they trained from dawn to dusk and even into the night. Now, in the still dawn air, Vita could faintly hear the blare of horns and the clash of steel. "Who are they preparing to fight?" she'd asked Ronaldo one day.

"Lord Maldici's brother," he'd replied. "He lives in the far south of Verde, in the stronghold of Piso. For years the brothers have ruled the land between them, but now they say that Lord Verona is planning an attack. Whoever wins the battle will be Emperor."

Now, Vita wondered about Beatrice's brother, Sandro, and whether he was there somewhere, splashing himself awake with cold water or tramping up and down the parade ground with a sword in one hand, learning how to kill. She shivered and nudged the horse forward over the bridge.

On the far bank of the Arnona, the horse quickened its pace and settled into the long, steady lope for which its breed was famous, its hooves reaching forward onto the grassy path that ran beside the dusty road. Vita held the reins loosely and rocked to the rhythm with her eyes half-closed. Her lips tilted into a dreamy smile as she remembered her birthday party, for every detail of the long night was engraved on her mind in fine detail.

First, there had been the preparations: the maids rushing around lighting thousands of tapers, until the polished floors and gilt mirrors and silken tapestries glowed. Then there had been the arrival of the guests, on clouds of imported perfumes and with swishing cloaks and gowns, while their chariot wheels rang on the cobbles and the footmen at the massive doors held flaring torches.

Then the dinner: the tables groaning with flowers and silver plates, the sauces, the carafes of fig-canary, the suckling pigs with pomegranates in their mouths, the sautéed sword whale with lemons, the grilled lamb with pine nuts, the baked song-birds, the haunches of goat with truffles, the rosemary buns, the crabs in pesto, the stuffed mushrooms, the star fish dumplings! Finally, when Vita thought she could eat no more, the desserts were carried in on silver trays by decorous serving men: fig soup decorated with marzipan hares, fried honey cookies, almond compote, vanilla meringue as light as clouds, mango ices as cold as snow, cakes as tall as the serving men and draped in ruffles of lavender colored icing, slices of golden melon imported from Lontano.

After dinner, the dancing. Remembering this, Vita's smile widened and she barely noticed the long shadows of trees stretching across the path, or the steady bobbing of the red horse's neck in front of her. Instead, she saw again the dance floor, and felt herself swirling around it in Ronaldo's arms while her dress of pink taffeta, sewn with seed pearls, floated around her legs and the heels of her silver sandals tapped in rhythm to the band. The room had swirled around her too: the other dancers in their brilliant clothes, the flashing mirrors, the fres-coes painted on the walls, the tall windows looking out into the palazzo gardens where the fairy lanterns glowed amongst the flowers as the servants set up the buffet.

"They're all admiring you, the girls. They all wish they could dance with Ronaldo," Rosa giggled behind Vita's fan between dances. "They don't know you're a village girl—they think you're nobili!"

And then, later, the fireworks—their whistling ascents, their magical blossoming into fountains and cascades of color, their thunderous reports that made the guests shriek. And Ronaldo had stood behind her, with his arms around her, and whispered

"Happy Birthday" into her ear, and slipped a necklace of silver filigree, woven with coral flowers, around her throat.

"I'll miss you," he'd said. "Come back soon. Promise?"

"Yes," she'd replied, hardly aware of what she was saying, with the fireworks shooting into her wide-open eyes and the warm pressure of Ronaldo's chest against her shoulders.

And early this morning, when she'd risen to leave, Rosa had come to her door and slipped a friendship bracelet, woven of red silk threads, into her hand before hugging her. "I hope you'll come back to Genovera!" she'd said. "It won't be any fun without you!"

"What will happen to you now?" Vita had asked.

"I'll be fine. Ronaldo's mother is going to keep me on in this house, even if I can't be your maid anymore," Rosa had reassured her. "And maybe you'll come back and we can be together again."

Now, Vita could feel Rosa's friendship bracelet, a silken touch, against her wrist as the red horse loped on and the sun climbed toward the tips of the slender cypress trees that shaded the road. Occasionally, other travelers passed Vita, heading northward to the city. The red horse flicked its ears but never ceased its steady gait, and Vita drifted again into her dream of the previous evening. It had been worth staying for; she wouldn't have missed it for anything. And now, with luck, the red horse would take her home by the morning of the day after tomorrow—and that day was the Equinox. She would be in time, as long as she rested and fed the horse at intervals, and rode for a portion of each night.

Ahead of her, as the afternoon wore on, the mountains began to take form. At first they were a misty wave that drifted across Vita's vision like a mirage. Then they became firmer, like shapes cut in wood and propped up against the clear autumnal sky. They rang a pure, hard blue behind autumn's changing yellow leaves. As she traveled closer yet, contours began to appear: slopes and passes, and valleys, all stroked into life by the sun.

Where the path running toward the mountains branched off from the main way, Vita stopped to water the horse and let it rest in the shade for half an hour as Ronaldo's groom had told her to. Then she turned its head toward the west and her thoughts traveled ahead of her over the mountains. She wondered how her aunt was, and whether she'd soon see Beatrice and Giovanni. Perhaps he would come to the equinoctial feast in the village and she could tell him all about her birthday party in the palazzo.

Suddenly, the horse slowed and its steady rhythm faltered. It broke into a jiggling trot that bounced Vita uncomfortably in the saddle and then it began to limp on its right foreleg. Vita pulled it to a halt and slid off. She ran her hand over its smooth hard leg but felt nothing, no cut or swelling. She lifted its hoof and peered at its foot, but there was nothing to be seen: no sharp piece of stone lodged there, no scrape. Mystified, Vita climbed back on but though she kicked her heels into the horse's ribs, it would only limp forward at a slow walk.

I will never get home in time, Vita thought. A chill ran through her. Genovera lay far behind her now, with its bustle and crowds, its gaiety and laughter. She was aware suddenly of how alone she was. Clearly now she could hear the voice inside her head that she'd been ignoring for days. You have neglected your trust, it said. You've betrayed the Corno d'Oro, unless you can reach home. And on this slow horse, you will never make it.

She remembered the other horse, the one that Rosa had brought months ago to the garden gate, and how Aunt Carmela had puzzled over its limping leg and said that there was nothing to account for it. Did the red horses suffer from some weakness of the legs? Was this their normal behavior?

Luna, help me! Vita entreated. What I am going to do? Fear tingled through her. Had a Keeper ever behaved so foolishly before?

Time trickled past as the horse limped forward, until finally Vita took pity on it and slid from its back and walked beside its low hanging head, for she could walk as fast as it could. Presently, up ahead, the tiled rooftops of a village came into view amongst fields of grapes, and Vita urged the horse forward for she hoped that a villager might lend her a jennet. It wouldn't be much faster than the horse, but at least it would be sound in every leg and able to carry her through the mountains by the light of the harvest moon.

Vita pulled the horse forward through the narrow streets and into the village square where a crowd was gathered around a makeshift wooden stage. Across the stage puppets gamboled, flapping their skinny wooden arms, their diaphanous garments draped over the bodies of the human puppeteers. The crowd roared in approval and Vita paused to listen. The play seemed to be about an evil lord, played by a puppet with a leering red face and black tufted hair, and his army that was pillaging the land. But now the peasant puppets were rushing onstage with hoes and sickles, bashing the wicked soldier puppets over the heads with satisfying cracks! The puppeteers' feet thundered to and fro on the echoing boards of the stage, while down below the drummer capered, playing his reed pipe and jerking his skinny knees skyward.

Vita stared at him in disbelief and a surge of homesickness ran through her. She looked around for the beetleman.

"Vita, the Keeper," said his grave, sonorous voice behind her and she swung on her heel to look into his pellucid dark eyes and his moon face with its three chins. At the end of their thread harnesses, the beetles flashed in circles, humming.

"So," the beetleman said, "it must be something of importance in Verde that takes the Keeper away from the mountains at this hour of the year, when the harvest moon ripens and the shadows lengthen toward the equinox, and the seasons tremble in their balance."

Vita felt herself flushing bright red. "I'm trying to get home," she protested, "but this horse was loaned to me and it's gone lame. I have to get over the mountains by the morning after tomorrow."

The beetleman looked westward to where the sun was falling behind the crenellated peaks. Even as he and Vita stared at it, it slipped from view and left only lingering golden stains on the clouds.

"The day is over," the beetleman informed her sternly. "The night begins, when all creatures must watch their footsteps, and pay heed to their appointed tasks. You will never reach home in time now, Keeper."

She swallowed heavily, hearing the ringing depths in the beetleman's voice. He's right, she thought in despair. I've failed.

"You had best leave this horse with me," the beetleman said. "I have something else that you may ride. Come."

Leading the horse, she followed his broad back through the crowd and around a corner of a building to where, on a patch of green grass, was tethered the strangest animal that Vita had ever seen. Its legs were skinny as sapling tree trunks and soared up to join its slender body. Its long neck, like the neck of a swan, was extended into a tree where the animal appeared to be grazing. It was covered in chocolate brown velvet and dappled with purple patches. Hearing their footsteps, the animal pulled its head from the tree and swung it down toward Vita. Its huge, gentle eyes were fringed in purple eyelashes that curled, and a fringe of purple hair hung down from between its funnel shaped ears.

"A magrazzi," the beetleman informed her. "A most curious beast, brought in a ship from far away, and arriving in the delta sick almost to death. I purchased it for my wandering entourage, and your aunt sent herbs to heal it. Its long legs will move faster than those of the red horse."

"I can ride it?" Vita asked incredulously, but as she spoke the drummer and the puppets streamed into the grassy square, for the puppet show was over. In the sudden hubbub, Vita thought she'd imagined the voice in her head.

You can ride me, it said, a shy, soft, leaf-light voice.

What? Vita asked.

She stared up at the magrazzi's wide eyes.

"In its own land, it's a night animal," the beetleman said. "It grazes in treetops by the light of the moon."

Can you take me home? Vita asked.

I can take you.

The magrazzi bent its long elegant legs, folding its knobby knees, and knelt on the grass. A puppeteer climbed from beneath his puppet and settled a purple leather saddle on the magrazzi's back, and pulled the harness tight, and Vita climbed onto it. Another puppeteer led the red horse away, and another one tied Vita's pack onto the magrazzi's saddle. The magrazzi rose slowly to its feet, swaying up and up until Vita was staring down at the top of the beetleman's shining bald head encircled with flashing wings. He tilted his head and his moon face stared back at her.

"Keeper," he warned, "do not fail, for on you we all depend. And the powers of the dark are gathering strength. Ride into the night with a true heart. Keep the magrazzi until we meet again."

Westward, night sister, Vita said, and the magrazzi strode between the houses and broke into a swinging trot, its cloven hooves jetting puffs of dust from the path that led over the mountains to the sea. Vita shivered in her velvet jacket with the collar pulled over Ronaldo's coral necklace. Anxiety cramped in her belly and she hunched miserably in the saddle. She longed for the kitchen at home with its worn tiles and its glowing fire, its familiar smells of pungent herbs and sweet tomatoes. Oh, that she would reach home by dawn, that she would see Aunt Carmela's relieved smile and feel her hard, bony hug—that she would be in time to perform her magic!

Swiftly, sister, swiftly, she pleaded and the magrazzi's long legs reached westward with eager haste.

The moon rose, a huge golden bubble that floated up from the east to shine on the carpet of fallen leaves beside the path. It shone on the slopes of the mountains, and Vita saw with a pang that they were still many miles away. Climbing higher, the moon shone into the wide, gentle eyes of the running magrazzi and onto bunched grapes hanging like jewels amongst reddening vines.

Far to the north, the moonlight slanted through the window of the highest tower of pale stone, in the palazzo of Lord Maldici where, in its light, individual strands of hair glowed like hot wire on the head of the sorcerer's daughter. The moon reached farther into the tower, sending fingers of light onto the surface of an ebony table inlaid with mullosk. There, in the moon's beams, lay a saucer of red wax that someone had softened with a candle and then shaped into a small horse. The horse's right foreleg bristled with the silver pins that had been jabbed into the soft wax.

The sorcerer's daughter lifted the china plate out of the pool of moonlight and crossed the floor, her gown sweeping over the polished marble. She tossed the red wax figure of a horse into the flames in the fireplace, beneath the mantle of marble carved with condors, and gave a husky laugh.

"She will never reach the mountains," she said. "The red horse has failed her, and now she will fail the Corno d'Oro. By tomorrow, he will be unprotected and we can take him."

Behind her, in the shadows that neither moonlight nor firelight touched, Lord Maldici pulled his fur lined cloak more closely about his shoulders. He hunched in his chair of carved mandolo wood, brooding like a great spider in the midst of a web of lies and evil intentions. Beneath his chair the black book of Lord Morte, first great sorcerer of Verde, lay in the darkness.

"What has happened to the other book, the lost Keeper's book?"

"My spies discovered it by chance with a pirati boy, but he escaped. They are searching again." The sorcerer made a growling in his throat.

The redheaded girl stared into the fire where the red horse figurine sparked and sputtered before melting into a pool of liquid wax that dribbled onto the hearthstones.

"Are the hunters ready?" she asked.

"They're ready. They have weighted nets, and your information about the places that the Keeper traveled to before, that were seen in the spy stone. The men have a box wagon with a stout door, to transport the beast here to our palazzo after its capture."

The girl sighed with satisfaction and turned away from the fire, where nothing remained of the wax horse, and stalked back to the open window. The moonlight, that shone so far away on the shoulders of Vita's jacket and on her cold cheeks, shone here on the redheaded daughter's cruel smile as she looked toward the east.

"A hunter's moon," she muttered. "Let the hunt begin."

CHAPTER THIRTEEN

Hour after hour the magrazzi's slender legs ate up the miles as the mountains loomed closer, like a breaking wave of blackness against the stars. In the darkest hour of the night, the hour before dawn, the magrazzi slowed its pace and began to climb upward while Vita hunched in the purple saddle, too cold and exhausted and sick with anxiety to move or speak. Sometimes she heard the voices of wombos muttering softly in the forest and sometimes the moon shone in their eyes as they hung on branches. A hunting gufo hooted far away and a moon moth fluttered past, its green wings translucent in the faint light.

The magrazzi moved more slowly as the path steepened until it was picking its way at a walk, its delicate cleft hooves searching for safe places on the rocky ground.

I must rest, it said shyly at last. *Sorry.*

Rest, don't worry, Vita told it and the animal moved off the trail and folded its legs, sinking into the shadow beneath a magnolia tree. Vita slid off and fell face forward, her legs too stiff to support her. She knelt and pulled a blanket from her pack, which she spread beside the magrazzi. Its wide eyes were already closed, its purple curling lashes hanging down. Vita huddled against its warm velvet side and fell into a fitful sleep.

The birds awoke Vita at dawn as the olive thrush's music and moon wren's chitter filled the forest and splashed down the mountain slopes. Vita rubbed her cold arms and aching back. The magrazzi still slept, and Vita remembered that it was a night animal in its own land. She stared at it for a moment in sympathy and admiration, wishing that she didn't have to wake it.

Sister, she whispered and the animal's lashes fluttered.

It's morning. I'm sorry to wake you. We have to go on—my journey's urgent. I must guard the Corno d'Oro.

The magrazzi's eyes widened immediately into sleepy pools. *Climb on, we will go.*

Vita hauled herself back into the saddle and the magrazzi unfolded its legs. After the magrazzi had eaten a hasty breakfast of leaves snatched from the trees as it passed them by and drunk from the rushing coolness of a mountain stream, they journeyed through the mountains. Sometimes they progressed at a trot but at other times the magrazzi could only manage a walk where the path was steep, a thread glued to the mountainside over thousands of feet of thin air and tortuous valleys that the sunlight barely entered.

Sorry, the magrazzi said. *I'm a grassland animal. I'm not good at climbing.*

Vita stroked its velvet neck. *You're doing well*, she told it but in her heart anxiety beat and fluttered. Eagerly, as afternoon wore on, she peered into the distance ahead, hoping to see the final ridge and then the bright expanse of the Golfo d'Levanto, but all that appeared was crest after crest of mountains. In the late afternoon, as blue shadows flooded the valleys and rocky peaks shone in the light, they rested once more while Vita ate leftovers from her birthday party. Here, in the deep places of the mountains where only the wind and the water spoke, Genovera seemed far away. Her party was like something that had been dreamed once, when she was younger.

The magrazzi became more energetic as the moon rose. It frisked its tail as they set off again, and trotted jauntily down the valley they were following, calling greetings to wombos and spotted deer grazing in clearings. Later, as the night grew chill, the magrazzi's breath hung in white clouds and its pace slowed. Vita swayed precariously in the saddle, drifting along the edges of sleep, waking with a start when a branch whipped across her face or the magrazzi stumbled. At dawn they rested again.

It's the equinox today, Vita mumbled in panic when she awoke after a few hours. *I must get home!*

I can smell the salt water, the magrazzi replied.

It heaved itself to its feet, stretching its sleepy eyes open and setting off stiffly, its long limbs like the wooden legs of the puppets. They ascended the final slope with the eastern sun rising warm on Vita's back, and there before them lay the shining sea sprinkled with the islands of the pirati archipelago. Far, far below them the village was a tiny jumble of red tiled roofs. Vita almost wept with gladness as the magrazzi trotted down toward the terraces and the meadows where the grapes had been harvested and the olives picked and where, tonight, the villagers would light the autumnal fires and dance in celebration of the harvest.

As they picked their way down between stony walls and banks of purple Rain Poppies—the huge, soft poppies of autumn with their downy stems and black stamens—the sun rose higher. The olive trees stood on their shadows. Vita was sweating with anxiety and she wrenched the jacket collar away from her throat, for she felt as though panic was going to choke her. I will never get through all the magic in time, she thought. The day is half over already.

Stop, sister she asked as they reached a fork in the path. One way led on downward to the village, to pass beside Old Tomie's meadow, but the other way led southward over the slopes bordering the mountains where the Corno d'Oro lived its hidden life.

Can you go farther? Vita asked the magrazzi. *Can you walk all afternoon in the mountains while I perform the magic for the Corno d'Oro? Or shall I go alone?*

The magrazzi raised its drooping head.

I can walk, it said, its voice a tired sigh.

Vita pulled dried figs from her pack and fed them to the animal; it took them one by one from her palm with its supple, velvet lips and its purple tongue. Vita rubbed her hand along its neck and scratched it beneath its purple forelock before it moved on, following the path only a little way before leaving it to climb into the mountains again. It was mid-afternoon, the heat shimmering in rocky valleys, the birds silent, and the leaves of the olive trees hanging straight down, before Vita reached the first of her fourteen magic places. She slid from the magrazzi and it fell into an exhausted sleep in the shade as she traced the runes on a face of warm rock.

They moved on, counterclockwise around the circle that marked the Corno d'Oro's range. Vita knew each one of the fourteen magic places so well that they were a part of her; she had been coming to them in rain and sun and wind, through the green spring grass and the bare branches of winter, since she was a tiny child. The tenth place was marked by an ancient acacia tree, its seedpods hanging like dark brown fingers. The eleventh place was marked by a waterfall in a mountain stream. The twelfth was marked by a grove of mandolo trees at the edge of a meadow. Vita reached it as the sun slipped down to touch the western horizon. The equinoctial day was almost over.

Hurry, Vita thought. Hurry. Hurry.

She rushed into the grove where the mandolo nuts, in their wrinkled purple husks, lay scattered. The magrazzi chewed on them as Vita stood beneath the trees, chanting the ancient words that the moon goddess had taught to the very first Keeper to guard the Corno d'Oro from the greed of men.

As the last words died on Vita's lips, the magrazzi surged to its feet in alarm, and Vita glanced across the meadow. She gasped. Noise, shape and color poured across it—a scene so terrible that for a moment Vita couldn't understand it. She knuckled her aching eyes. The magrazzi bolted toward the trees and disappeared, crashing into them.

A white animal came toward Vita, terrible and swift in its course, like a spear flung across the yellow grass. Its face was long and noble, its flaxen mane billowed around it like a breaking wave. The golden tapered horn, the golden hooves trampling the Rain Poppies, the light that shone from the animal and shimmered around it—all this Vita saw in one awestruck, horrified glance. The pounding of hoof beats hammered her thoughts into oblivion. She fell to her knees.

Behind the white beast, the red horses galloped, their mouths white with foam and their eyes rolling with terror. The red brutti bayed and howled beside them, and the assassini ran alongside. Vita saw their long dangling ears, their misshapen hands deformed to hold weapons, their thundering black boots. On their foreheads the blue brands were clear; each one with a capital M for Maldici (or was it Morte?) followed by a number. From the horses' backs, the huntsmen blew their horns. They rang harsh and strident, ripping apart the clear mountain air like thin cloth. Wind and a confused tumult of voices swept through Vita.

Then—for one long moment while the world held still on its axis—the net, flung by the lead huntsman, soared against the golden sky. Weighted at the edges with iron balls, it was a rushing dark shape woven from the fiber of the corda tree that grows only in Terre and that cannot be broken nor cut with anything but the sharpest blade. The net hung suspended. Vita stared upward, motionless with horror. Then, with a whistling rush, it fell.

"No!" Vita screamed. "No!"

The dark web fell through the nimbus of light that shone around the Corno d'Oro. It fell across the stallion's ivory shoulders, tangled in his tossing mane. A wild cry broke from his mouth, like the sound of a bell being rung too hard, a cry that resounded across the meadow, pealed amongst the trees, echoed from the mountains.

The net slipped downward, for it hadn't fallen true. It wrapped its fibers around the Corno d'Oro's golden hooves, and the stallion stumbled and fell to his knees. In the grass lay the trunk of a fallen mandolo tree, whose wood is the hardest of all wood in the forest. One broken limb stuck upward at an angle, and onto this the Corno d'Oro's shoulder fell. Instantly a red gash opened. The lips of the brutti snarled back over their gleaming teeth. The assassini whooped in triumph.

Vita's body lunged forward. She watched it from a great height, as though she too hung suspended in the air above the trampled meadow, above the shimmering white beast alone on its knees, the red swirl of horses, and the hunters' faces distorted into masks of terror and excitement.

Keeper, help me. The Corno d'Oro's voice reverberated in Vita's being.

Her hands grabbed the net and pulled it away from the Corno d'Oro's slender legs and she felt his warm, sweet breath—that smelled like star lilies—sweep across her cheek. Around her, the air turned blue and crackled with the Corno d'Oro's ancient power. His mane lashed her, tingling where it touched. She yanked at the net, sobbing. A brutti rushed at her, knocking her back into the poppies, and sprang at the Corno d'Oro's wounded shoulder. The wound was torn open in a gush of blood. Then the Corno, free from the net, soared from Vita's vision in a glistening blur, a ripple of muscle, a crackle of blue light. The last coils of net slid to the ground. Blood spattered across Vita's hands in heavy drops.

Vita leaped to her feet, facing the rearing horses, the assassini's whips, the melee of snarling creatures. She flung her arms wide. "You cannot pass!" she cried.

"Who's she?"

"The village idiot!"

"Set the brutti on her!"

"Knock her down!"

Vita opened her mouth. Magical words, the words of the twelfth magical place, poured from her. Strong and true and wild the words rang. They filled the meadow with a shining curtain of sound. Her voice was louder than it had ever been, as though it belonged to someone else. She didn't have to remember the words or think about them; they simply hurled themselves out of her open throat. The horses halted and wouldn't advance, though the huntsmen lashed them until they screamed. The cowering brutti crawled on their bellies, snarling. Behind Vita's out-flung arms the Corno d'Oro leaped toward the mandolo grove and vanished in mid-air.

As Vita's chant fell into silence, the horses stampeded forward in a blur. She held out her arms to ward them off, but a hard shoulder knocked her to the ground. A whip sliced her green jacket open and laid a burning pain across her back. Brutti snapped as they ran past. Hooves thudded on each side of her. The ground shook. A glancing blow struck her leg. She lay curled on herself, shaken, terrified, awestruck.

At the edge of the grove, the brutti milled around, whimpering, for the trail had disappeared. The huntsmen shouted and pointed in various directions. In the confusion, Vita scrambled to her feet and ran across the meadow, sobbing in panic.

Help! she shrieked as she entered the forest. *Help, help me, help!*

Night sister! The magrazzi's voice was thin and high with terror. *Here, I'm here!*

She plunged into a pool of shade and ran up against the animal's velvet sides as the magrazzi folded its knees. She grabbed its purple tufted mane and dragged herself into the saddle.

Into the valley! I must finish the magic! I must close the circle! The hunters will find the hole. They will catch him again!

The magrazzi sprang forward, shuddering.

Here!

Vita ran to the great boulder, rounded and weathered with

millennia of rain and wind, that marked the thirteenth magic place on the perimeter of the circle. She laid her hands on the rough yellow lichen and tried to speak the spell, forcing it through her parched mouth, her frozen lips, out of her heaving lungs.

The fourteenth place, the one that closed the circle, the one that would keep the hunters out, was marked by a weeping mulberry tree. Vita stumbled into the fermenting sweetness of its fallen berries, and traced the runes on its smooth gray bark and said the final words.

They're coming! The magrazzi shrieked and sprang away in panic, then rushed back again and bent its knees for Vita. Together they plunged down the mountainside, through pools of purple shadows and poppies, hearing the animals and the horns tearing the air behind them. The magrazzi found a deep thicket of trees and stood there completely still except for its quivering skin. Vita held her breath.

They aren't hunting us. They're only hunting the Corno d'Oro. She stroked the magrazzi's neck.

The hunt paused and milled around by the mulberry tree, then returned back in the way from which it had come, disappearing into the dusk. The Corno d'Oro was safe again, inside its circle—but wounded. The red gash sprang open over and over again before Vita's horrified vision. Wounded. Vita stared at her hands where the great drops of blood had dried into stiff, dark patterns. It was said that the brutti had teeth that poisoned what they tore so that the wounds festered and released a slow death into the bloodstream.

Wounded. The word tolled in her head like a heavy bell, joining the echo of the Corno d'Oro's stricken cry.

My fault, she thought. All mine. Luna, help me to heal this wound!

They waited until it was fully dark, she and the magrazzi. Then they stumbled down the mountain in exhausted silence until they came to the path that ran downhill to the village. Vita could see the fires leaping on the terraces and hear the villagers' laughter and the music of a violyno. Closer, and she could see the villagers dancing—the whirl of bright skirts, the leap of bright shirts. Their shadows capered among the olive trees while goat roasted on a spit and the new pressed wine was spilled beneath the feet of the vines in thanks for the harvest.

I can't go on, the magrazzi said, its shy voice dull with fatigue. *See, on the hill here, a grove of apricot trees? Hide here and wait. My aunt will come and care for you. Don't go away.*

Vita kissed its warm soft nose and staggered alone down the path. Her head felt as if it floated above her body, and her legs wavered over the stony path, seeming unattached to her torso. With dull eyes she stared at the lively scene on the terraces, searching for Aunt Carmela's familiar bony figure.

"It's the Keeper!" someone cried and other voices took up the joyful shout. A hand pulled her into the circle of firelight. Faces peered at her, creased with laughter and then with concern.

"She's not well!"

"Find her aunt!"

"Aunt Carmela!"

Someone pressed a cup to her lips and a sweet wine ran like fire down her throat. The dancers seem to spin. Her aunt's hard hands caught her, and Vita pressed her face into the familiar smell of wood smoke and onions, and burst into tears.

"Hush, hush," Aunt Carmela said gently, leading her away from the dancers and the violyno's singing strings.

"There's an animal—needs your help—on the hill. And the Corno d'Oro, wounded—hunters with a net— "

"Hush," Aunt Carmela said more fiercely. "Wait until we're home."

She supported Vita to the garden gate. Beside it, in the carved shrine, the pale oval of the moon goddess' stone face was remote and still, and brought Vita no comfort. With Aunt Carmela supporting her, she staggered down through the valley's fallen leaves where the poppies spread purple as bruised clouds. Faintly, from the village streets, drifted the notes of a mouth harp and the voices of women singing the equinoctial song, so sweet and sad that Vita always ached to hear it.

Rain Poppies in the woods
Are flowering, are flowering.
Rain Poppies in the woods,
It's the end of summer.

CHAPTER FOURTEEN

MARINA STOOD IN THE ROUND ROOM in her home on the island's point, and stared out its many windows over the ruffled sea. It was the first day of the autumnal equinox and the pelicans were flying southward to the islands of Lontano for the winter, their bills tucked against their snowy chins. Marina's eyes narrowed. She stared hard at a spot of white on the water, a dash of spray that was moving toward the point. Presently, she could see the sea horse's head, bright green and patterned with golden lines like lace coral. Behind this, her mother's narrow chin and silver eyes appeared. She was traveling home at last from the Middle Sea.

Marina glanced around the room. All was in order: the driftwood floor was swept, the narrow cupboards were locked, the fire crackled and shot blue sparks up the chimney of beach stone. Overhead, the sea thistles were bunched and hanging to dry. The eggs of the jellyfish were pickling in brine; and the journal of tides and winds, filled with Marina's scrawling hand, lay open and up to date on the table. Still, there was a thread of nervousness in Marina's anticipation, and she hugged herself on the window ledge as she watched the witch disappear beneath the point.

She's stabling the sea horse near the cave, Marina thought. She's tethering it with a long strand of seaweed. Now she's striding up the path with her wet skirts clinging to her legs.

The door swung open and the witch came in, her silver anklets of crabs and seaweed ringing faintly, the silver shells swinging from her ears. Marina rose from the window seat.

"Mother!" she cried.

The witch threw her green cape, lined with the breast feathers of sea doves, over the back of a twisted chair and moved to the fire to warm her pale hands.

"The Golden Arms are dead in their rock pool," she said sternly.

Marina felt her own smile dying on her lips.

"I'm sorry," she muttered. "I forgot to feed them."

"The spell for the Bright Cross? You have mastered it?" the witch asked.

"No. But everything else is in order," Marina said with a hint of defiance. "The journal is kept, the reef weed is gathered for your horse, the pelican's nest on the point has been cleaned."

The witch stared into the blue sparks of the fire, her mouth firm and the light flickering on her sharp, hooked nose.

"What have I done to deserve such a daughter?" she asked. "What is wrong with you, Marina? The Bright Cross is a spell you should have been able to work long ago. You are too slow, too lazy. You don't try."

"I do try!" Marina cried, the witch's words burning in her like jellyfish stings.

"You are to dive for fresh Golden Arms, and tonight you will sail into the Golfo, and you will stay there, night and day, until you have mastered the Bright Cross," the witch commanded.

"No, I won't," Marina shouted. "I'm tired of being alone!"

The sea witch snorted fiercely. "Witches do not feel lonely.

They are one with the wind and water, they hear the sea-pines, they watch over the birds and the creatures of the sea. What nonsense you talk, Marina."

Marina's lips thinned into a tight line. She glared at her mother, feeling a wild stubborn courage rising in herself. She had never spoken to her mother in this way before, never disobeyed her. The witch continued to stare into the fire and after a moment Marina turned away toward the open door.

"Where are you going?" the witch demanded.

"To the mainland, to the village, to find some company."

"I forbid you!" the witch shrieked, her hair crackling with silver sparks. "You are a sea witch! You are not to waste time mooning around the village. You have nothing to do with the land, nor it with you!"

"Then I'm going down to the beach," Marina replied and she darted through the door and rushed down the path with her heart in her throat. She stopped abruptly at the water's edge, listening for her mother's footsteps following her, for the witch's shriek of anger. There was silence. Marina sat on a rock and gulped air, fighting tears. She's mean, she thought. She doesn't have to be so stern. Why shouldn't I visit the village?

A wave of longing engulfed her. She imagined the Keeper's valley, that she had only been in once before, when she tried to deliver the ancient book to the Keeper. Ever since that day she had felt the memory of the valley lodged in her chest like a warm ache. She couldn't stop thinking about it. Now she imagined how the nuts would be dropping onto the carpet of fallen leaves with soft thuds. She recalled how the stream ran sparkling and laughing, and the chyme tree rang sweetly. She imagined the smells of the place so exactly that she could almost believe that they had drifted all this way across the water on the wind: the damp richness of soil, the musky warmth of jennets and goats, the peppery fragrance of autumn leaves, the sweetness of wild mushrooms.

A sob shook Marina's thin ribs.

I'm going, she thought with wild bravado. She can't stop me!

She set her jaw tight, for in her heart she suspected that the witch could easily stop her if she wanted to.

She crept across the beach pebbles, her bare feet making no sound, and glanced back up at the point. In a hammock slung between sea-pines, the sea witch was asleep, her face lined with fatigue after her travels. Marina inched her boat into the water, sliding it slowly, slowly, over the sand and pebbles, catching her breath when they grated against the keel. Finally it floated. She pulled off her scarf, patterned with shells, and tied it around one oar to silence it.

Standing in the boat's stern and keeping one eye on the witch asleep in the hammock, Marina sculled silently into the channel, never lifting the oar from the water. Half a mile from shore, where the swells rocked the boat like a cradle, she ran the sail up and set a course for the pale jumble of the village at the foot of the mountains. The thought of the Keeper's valley was like bait that she'd swallowed. She felt herself being reeled in, a hooked fish, at the end of that thought, that strong longing. She stared toward shore, watching the slopes of the mountains become clear, the trees take shape on the terraces, the chimneys become visible on rooftops. From time to time she glanced back at the archipelago as it fell astern, expecting to see her mother dashing after her on the green horse, its fins whirling the water into a fine spray. But the sea remained empty and Marina began to dare that she would get away with her disobedience.

In the village, she almost ran up the hill toward the fifty steps for the line was tight now, hauling her in faster and faster. She swung the gate open and plunged into the green funnel of the valley, then stopped still and closed her eyes. A long sigh of relief escaped from her lips. Around her the air hung soft and fresh.

I'm safe, she thought. I'm safe here.

She meandered down the valley, pausing to run her fingers over the trunks of apricot and almond trees as though they were old friends, to press her face against the pale yellow leaves that still hung in the mandolo trees, to tickle her fingertips against the fuzzy stems of the Rain Poppies. Their black pollen dusted her nose and she sneezed and laughed. Now she came down the steps into the courtyard where the leaves of the chyme tree fluttered against each other.

A woman was seated on a bench outside the kitchen door, holding a small animal in her lap. She glanced up as Marina came down the steps and her thin brown face broke into a welcoming smile. Marina felt that smile in her bones, felt the way it flowed all over the woman's face like rivulets of water. Her own mouth stretched wide in response.

She sat shyly at the end of the bench.

"This little animal is hurt," the woman said. "It was being chased last night by something, I think, and fell from the trees."

"What is it?"

"A wombo. Hold it while I fetch a poultice of herbs."

Marina held out her arms and took the furry gray body of the wombo. Its sleepy eyes peered up at her and its wet black nose whiffled, drawing in her salty scent. She laughed again in delight, cuddling its warmth. Her fingers wrapped gently around its foreleg and suddenly, a picture appeared in her mind, a pattern of pale lines. After a startled moment, she realized that the lines were bones, the bones in the wombo's foreleg. She closed her eyes, focusing on the bones, and moving her fingers slowly along the wombo's furry leg. Suddenly, she held still. Beneath her fingers nothing had changed, but in the picture in her mind she saw a thin dark line separating one piece of the bone from the other.

She blinked her eyes open to see the woman staring at her with a quizzical expression.

"I thought you'd fallen asleep," she chuckled. "The wombo has a crack in its bone. I'm going to splint it."

"Yes," Marina replied, too shy to say anything about the picture of the cracked bone that she'd seen somehow through the tips of her fingers. She watched while the woman's strong, blunt fingers laid a peeled stick against the wombo's foreleg to hold it straight. Against the other side of the leg she laid a steaming poultice of leaves wrapped in cotton, and then she bound both stick and poultice to the leg with a strip of cloth. While she worked, Marina held the wombo, its warmth comforting her the way the valley comforted her, and the way that the woman's smile made her warm inside. She forgot, in this moment, about the sea witch staring into the fire, and about the spell of the Bright Cross and all the other spells that she'd never been able to perform satisfactorily.

"Now," the woman said with a smile, "this one will heal. I'll leave it to sleep in a basket by the fire."

She disappeared into the kitchen briefly with the wombo, returning with a slab of griddle bread and a small jug of olives and a triangle of goat's cheese. "A bite?" she asked Marina.

They ate in friendly silence for a few minutes.

"Are you looking for Vita?" the woman asked.

Marina shrugged, feeling awkward. "Not exactly. I—umm—I just came to see the valley."

She hunched her shoulders defensively, waiting for the woman's derision, her sharp retort, but the woman just nodded and took another bite of bread.

"It's a good place to be," she said comfortably after she'd swallowed. "If you want to spend time here, you may. I am Vita's aunt, Aunt Carmela. And you?"

"Marina, daughter of the sea witch on the pirati island," Marina muttered reluctantly. She stared at the ground, scuffling her toes over the paving stones. Now that Aunt Carmela knew who she was, she'd send her away with a fearful glance and the sign against the evil eye.

When at last Marina looked up, she found that Aunt Carmela was gazing at her with a puzzled but kindly look. She didn't seem afraid and her fingers, that might have been warding off evil, were clasped in the lap of her rough, dark skirt.

"Well," she said in a matter of fact tone, " I must go and tend to Old Tomie's jennet, which came home from the north after being lost, with a broken hoof and a cut leg."

"Can I come too?"

"If you want to."

All afternoon, while Aunt Carmela strode around the village in her flapping shawl, Marina followed her. She stroked the creamy striped coat of the jennet, and sucked the soft flesh of the last tomatoes falling from the vines in Aunt Carmela's garden. She gathered Rain Poppies to dry by the kitchen fire, for in the long days of winter they were used for poultices to draw the chill from rheumatic bones. She gathered a basket of mandolo nuts too, cracking the purple husks in her teeth and spitting bits out, crunching the sweet yellow flesh inside. All afternoon, while the cloud shadows floated over the village rooftops and the thin sun fell warm between her shoulder blades, Marina felt perfectly peaceful.

As the sun fell into the sea far out beyond the archipelago, she followed Aunt Carmela back to the Keeper's house where they stirred up the fire and cooked a supper of goat stew with barley and onions. Sitting beneath the bunches of drying herbs, with worn red tiles under her feet and the wombo dozing in its basket, Marina wished that she could stay here forever. She wondered what would happen when Aunt Carmela grew old for she remembered, from the Keeper's Tale told at the Feast of Dragomar, that there was no young Carmela to replace her— Vita's dark sister had been swept to sea and lost when she was tiny. What would happen to the village when there was no one to tend the sick animals, to be a midwife when jennets foaled, to bind broken limbs and heal cut feet, to give love potions to girls and charms for strength to young men, to ease the passage of babies and to sooth the elderly by their winter fires?

When Marina glanced up from her pondering, she noticed that Aunt Carmela's face was anxious in the firelight. "I'm worried about Vita," she muttered, half to herself. "I thought that she'd be home from the city before now. But perhaps she's in the mountains today, for it's the autumnal equinox." She scraped the last spoonful of stew from her bowl, decorated with olive leaves in a blue glaze, and stood up stiffly.

"I must go up to the terraces," she said. "The villagers will be dancing and giving thanks for the harvest. Will you come?"

Marina swayed on the edge of such a temptation, but then she remembered the pirati festivals and how she'd always been the person at the edge of the crowd, the outcast watching from the shadows while others enjoyed themselves. She hunched her shoulders defensively again and shook her head. "They'll want to know who I am, and then they won't like me. I'll spoil their fun."

Aunt Carmela gave her shoulder a kindly shake and unhooked her black shawl from behind the door. "Stay here as long as you wish," she said, before walking away up the valley.

Marina sat in her chair by the fire and stretched her bare toes to the warmth. She knew that she should sail home to face her mother's angry silver eyes, the sparks crackling in her long, long hair, but she couldn't tear herself away from the Keeper's house. Just a little longer, she thought. Then I'll go home. She lifted the wombo into her lap where it began to wash itself sleepily with a cyclamen pink tongue. The smell of herbs and onions, honey cakes, and drying figs arranged along the mantelpiece, soothed Marina. She drifted into a fitful doze filled with jumbled images: the creamy ears of the jennet, her mother's ringing anklets, the smooth yellow leaves on the mandolo trees, the damp feel of the earth in Aunt Carmela's garden, the pale lines of the wombo's bones.

Suddenly the door swung open and Marina sat up, blinking sleepily.

A gust of cold air swirled into the room. The wombo bolted into its basket. Aunt Carmela burst in, panting, with the Keeper leaning against her. Marina stared at Vita in dismay. What had happened? Vita's face was white as a seashell. Her strange pale hair was tangled and windblown; one cheek was bruised; and her eyes, stretched wide, were filled with grief and fear. The green velvet jacket that she wore was slashed open as though a knife or a whip had cut it.

Marina started from her chair and drew back against the wall, wishing she had left the house sooner. She felt an intruder now. Vita collapsed onto a bench at the table. Aunt Carmela rushed around the kitchen like an agitated bird, her bony arms flapping in their shawl. She ladled stew from the iron pot and set it before Vita, then lifted bunches of herbs from a cupboard. "Verlaini for anxiety," she muttered, "and eyebright for grief, and sweet marjori for exhaustion." She lifted a stone pestle from the cupboard and began to grind the herbs together, releasing their bitter sweetness into the air.

"Heat water," she instructed and Marina sprang to obey, wondering what had happened.

When Vita had eaten the stew and drunk her tea, a thin flush of color returned to her cheeks.

"What do you have to tell us?" Aunt Carmela asked, stern with anxiety.

"It's terrible! I came home to do the magic," Vita said. Her voice trembled, a thin thread of sound. Marina, who'd been leaning against the wall in the shadows, moved closer to hear her. "The horse went lame—I met the beetleman and he lent me a magrazzi—a beast from some other place. I was almost in time, but the hunters—oh, the hunters were there too! They wounded the Corno d'Oro on the shoulder—I saw him! **I saw him,** Aunt Carmela! He was so beautiful, I can't explain! But everything is terrible!"

Suddenly Vita dropped her face into her hands and sobbed while Aunt Carmela let out a horrified moan.

Wounded. It didn't seem possible that such a thing could happen, Marina thought. Would the Corno d'Oro die? Then what would happen to them all, to the precarious balance in the world?

The book! Marina thought of it suddenly, and saw again the

pages on which the old hermit had written in his sloping elegant hand in purple ink. *Yellow earth,* had been amongst the words. What else? Something about wounds?

"When amongst the poppies the Golden Horn falls!" she muttered aloud, and Aunt Carmela shot her a preoccupied glance.

"What?" she asked.

"The book!" Marina cried. "Do you have it with you, Vita?"

Vita raised her face, streaked with tears, and stared at Marina blankly as though she'd only just noticed her presence in the room.

"What book?"

"The book that we found in a cave. It's been translated—"

"Oh, your mother worked on it!"

"No, but I—"

"Where is it?" Vita interrupted.

"Giovanni took it to you in Genovera," Marina said, feeling a cold puzzled fear slide down her spine.

Vita shook her head. "I haven't seen Giovanni."

"But he left weeks ago, with the book. It might help now, to heal the Corno d'Oro. There's something in it about the Corno d'Oro falling in the poppies!"

Aunt Carmela gripped Vita's arm. "Marina's right. You must find Giovanni and the book."

"Do you have a boat?" Vita asked urgently. "Will you take me to the pirati island? Perhaps Giovanni's mother will know where he is."

Marina nodded. "Yes. We can go right away..."

Vita rose abruptly, shoving the bench back too hard and over-balancing it to clatter against the tiles. They all ignored it. Vita shrugged off the slashed green jacket and Aunt Carmela handed her a shawl from behind the door. She handed a second one to Marina and then the girls went running up the path, their footsteps pounding on the gravel and sleepy birds fluttering in alarm in the fruit trees. Down through the village they ran, the sound of their footsteps bouncing off walls. Voices shouted jokingly after them. They dodged the villagers in the streets and pushed their way around the edge of the crowded square where villagers were dancing on the sundial. A fire leaped on the beach and Marina glimpsed casks of wine standing on the harbor wall and boys playing on the sand, throwing stones at cracked pots, and rolling somersaults.

Marina slipped down the harbor steps and fell in a heap into her rocking boat. Vita landed beside her as she cast off. Quickly, Marina rowed them out into the channel where a light wind played with the sail. Marina continued to row with grim determination while Vita hunched in the bows and stared miserably across the dark stretch of water that rolled between them and the archipelago. The flecks of light that marked the pirati village swung up and down ahead of them like fireflies.

"What was it like in Genovera?" Marina asked, trying to distract Vita from her anxiety.

"Fun," she said, but her voice was flat and despairing. "I was late home because of a birthday party." Her fingers went to her throat and she touched the silver filigree necklace that hung there, woven with coral flowers. "This was from Ronaldo. And there were fireworks and dancing."

The oars squeaked in their oarlocks. Water slapped the hull. The breeze rustled the sail, blew it taut, let it flap. Marina rowed on, her arms burning.

"What else did it say in the book?" Vita asked.

"Something about wounds. And something about yellow earth. I don't remember any more."

"I'm so glad your mother worked on it," Vita said fervently.

"It wasn't—"

"I must find it quickly! The Corno d'Oro is bleeding! Would the book be with your mother again?"

"It wasn't my mother—"

"What can have happened to Giovanni?" Vita interrupted once more, not listening to Marina.

Marina set her lips in a thin line. She could feel her crab shell of pride hardening back into place. Fine, she thought. Don't listen to what I have to tell you. Don't hear about the pirati hermit. Don't care that it was me, me, who got the book translated. Not my stupid mother.

She rowed on in offended silence. Gradually the wind freshened and filled the sail and she was able to rest. They sliced forward while the lights of the pirati village, at the head of its inlet, grew brighter. Across the mouth of the inlet was stretched the night chain that protected the inlet from all comers, and Marina had to light the lantern that was lodged beneath a thwart and wave it in the air. The watchman strode down from the point and stared out at them, holding his own lantern aloft.

"Who asks to pass?" he cried.

"Marina the sea witch's daughter, and Vita the Keeper!"

"What do you want here at night? Come back in the morning!"

Vita rose to her feet, the boat rocking, her pale hair streaming in the breeze. "I must speak to Giovanni. It's urgent. I'm on the Corno d'Oro's business!" she cried, her voice ringing.

The watchman ducked his head and ran to the winch, letting the chain slacken until it sank into the water and they were free to sail up the inlet. In the harbor, Vita scrambled from the boat but Marina turned her back on the village and stared out to sea.

"I'll wait here," she muttered. She had no wish to be teased and chased up dark streets by gangs of young pirati.

"Please, come!" Vita asked, and Marina saw how frightened she looked.

Together they ran through the quiet streets, for the pirati held their own festivals that celebrated fish migrations and tides, and today was not a feast day for them.

Panting, Marina stopped behind Vita at a door and waited while Vita pounded on it. After a pause, the door was opened by a tall, broad-shouldered woman with a dark, handsome face. "What do you want?" she asked, crossing her arms over her breasts. Marina thought that her lively, dark blue eyes were like Giovanni's.

"I'm looking for Giovanni!" Vita gasped.

The woman's face broke into a warm smile that revealed strong white teeth. "Now there's a coincidence," she said. "He's just home tonight, after being stranded on an island for weeks and weeks. He came home with the help of a Mara woman and a boatload of sea urchins."

"Can I see him?"

"You cannot. He's asleep in bed, and leaving for a raiding party first thing in the morning. His father's in a rare temper with him."

"But I must see him!" Vita pleaded desperately.

The woman's firm features settled into a glare. "Must?" she asked. "Only I use that word in this house."

"Then do you know if he had a book with him?"

The woman stared at Vita for a long moment, a hard look. "Ah," she said at last. "It is your book, Keeper. Giovanni said so. Wait." And she turned from the door, leaving it open a crack. Through this, Marina saw a slice of floor, beach sand swept smooth, on which the huddled shapes of several children lay sleeping in the light of a low fire. The sea urchins, their bellies full for once. Marina smiled to see them there, and recognized the marvelous honey-and-sunlight hair of Ambro, the boy with the golden face and tawny brown eyes, spilling out from the end of one blanket.

Then the door swung open again and was filled with the wide bulk of Giovanni's mother. "Here's your book, Keeper."

Vita took the package, wrapped in the yellow, leathery skin of a Reef-fish, and thanked the pirati woman. She hugged the book to her chest as she ran back to the harbor beside Marina and as they sailed back across the channel to the village under the mountains. At the steps in the harbor wall, Aunt Carmela waited for them with a lantern in her hand.

"Have you found it so soon?"

Vita climbed the steps and pulled the book from its case.

"On the first page," Marina said. In the wavering light they bent over it and Vita read the words aloud.

*"When amongst the poppies the Golden Horn
Falls, seek the high peak where the light is born
And the silver leaves of the Hare's Ears
Lay in yellow earth to heal wounds and dry tears. "*

"But what does it mean?" she asked, panic in her voice.

"Come, we'll take it home and think about it," Aunt Carmela advised. "Come, Marina," she added kindly, for Marina was hesitating by her boat. "You can sail home in the morning. You've been on the water enough tonight. It will soon be dawn."

And indeed, she was right, for after Marina and Vita had slept only a few hours in Vita's bedroom, where Marina had been given Rosa's bed, the eastern sky began to lighten. Marina awoke with a start as Vita's feet landed on the floor.

"What's happening?" she mumbled sleepily.

"The highest peak," Vita muttered. "It must be the peak they call Roccioso, two days' journey to the south. I must go there and find the Hare's Ears. Whatever they are. I don't know what I do with them then."

"Do you want help?" Marina ventured to ask, but Vita was already half out of the door, her white face smudged with blue shadows and her feet thudding on the stairs. She didn't answer. Fine, ignore me, Marina thought. I'm never wanted. I'm used to it though, she lied to herself. I don't care. She tossed her black iridescent hair and climbed from bed with a scornful expression. Crossing to the window, she looked out to where the Golfo lay in a dull sheet of pewter gray. It will rain, Marina thought. I must go home. My mother will be furious.

When she came downstairs, Vita and Aunt Carmela were already leaving for the magrazzi on the hill. "I saw it last night," Aunt Carmela was saying. "I gave it a healing draught for tiredness. It will be fine to ride south on today."

"Goodbye!" Marina called, and Aunt Carmela and Vita both sent her hurried glances, their faces tight with anxiety. Then they began to run up the garden path. Marina sighed and went downhill to her boat. Just for a little while, yesterday afternoon, she had felt a part of something as she helped Aunt Carmela around the village. This morning, though, life seemed to have settled into its accustomed rhythm and she was as alone as ever.

She sailed slowly out across the heaving water, for there was a long swell running that had traveled in from a storm far out to sea. By this afternoon, Marina thought, it will be blowing here, too. It'll be too rough to dive for Golden Arms.

Rounding the point that stuck out on one side of the pirati inlet, she squinted her eyes as a figure waved its arms and ran along the point, parallel to the water. It was Giovanni, she realized after a moment. She tacked in as close as she dared to the rocks and he scrambled down to the water's edge.

"Come closer!" he yelled. "The water's deep!"

Marina sighed theatrically and unshipped her oars, rowing in until she was a few feet from the rock on which the pirati boy stood.

"What's happening?" he asked.

"Vita's home. We came and got the book. The Corno d'Oro is wounded!"

Giovanni's eyes widened in shock.

"Will it live?"

"Who knows? Vita's traveling south to find help for it."

"How is she? Did she have a good time in Genovera?"

"Oh yes," Marina said sourly. "She's wearing a silver and coral necklace from her darling Ronaldo, and chattering about fireworks and parties."

Giovanni stared at his feet and Marina felt sorry, immediately, that she'd spoken. Even she, who knew nothing much about people, had seen that Giovanni loved Vita. It was because Vita had ignored her that she'd felt sour and spoken meanly, and yet—Vita had cause to ignore her. The Keeper was frantic with guilt and fear.

"Giovanni—" Marina called awkwardly, but she didn't know what to say to make things better. In silence she picked up her oars.

"Thanks!" he called, raising a hand, but his eyes looked away past her toward the mainland and were filled with longing. After a moment, as though remembering her presence, he looked in her direction again.

"We need to talk sometime!" he shouted. "I found out something about you and Vita in the hermit's library!"

Marina's shoulders twitched in a shrug before she could stop them. Right then, there wasn't anything more she wanted to learn about Vita. "Maybe I'll see you again soon!" she called across the widening gap of water.

Giovanni shook his head. "My father's angry at me. I'm being taken away this morning, on a raiding trip. I won't be home for weeks."

He turned and began to climb slowly back over the rocks in the direction of the village.

"Yes, and my mother's angry with me," muttered Marina. She ran the sail up the mast and turned the bows toward the island's northern point, wondering what she'd say when she reached home.

CHAPTER FIFTEEN

L ATE IN THE AFTERNOON, two days after leaving home, Vita and
the magrazzi broke through the fringe of beech and oak forest
onto the lower slopes of Mount Roccioso. The mount was volcanic in origin; above Vita, a great jumble of round rocks lay at
the base of the cone. Higher yet, smooth grassy slopes tapered
gracefully toward the summit. There the grass became sparse
and the volcanic soil appeared in dark, barren swathes.

Hare's Ears, Vita thought in worried perplexity, as she had
thought countless times in the last two days. Aunt Carmela had
never heard of such a plant—if plant it was, and not bush or
tree. But nothing of that size grew on the slopes. Perhaps she
should have been searching lower down in the forest? She slid
from the magrazzi and sank to the ground to pull the book from
the bag in which she carried it, slung across her back. Opening
it to the first page, she read aloud: *"Seek the high peak where the
light is born."*

The light is born there because the eastern sun touches the
peak before it touches anything else, she thought. Or else

because the first light was fire from the volcano. So I need to climb high up.

Then she read again, *"And the silver leaves of the Hare's Ears, Lay in yellow earth to heal wounds and dry tears."*

"Silver," she muttered, scanning the sweep of mountain above her. Nothing silver was visible. But perhaps the plant was low-lying, a creeping ground plant amongst the grass? It could be any-where on the vast sweep of slope above her. Her body sagged with tiredness at this realization; she felt as though she had spent years riding around the countryside on the magrazzi, its long spindly legs dancing with their shadows. Absently, she rubbed the inside of her own legs, chaffed and sore from the purple saddle.

You had better stay here and rest, she spoke in her thoughts to the magrazzi. *I'll go and look around higher up.*

I'll be here, it reassured her, *when you're ready to go home.* It poked its slender head into a tree and began to graze on the leathery leaves that flamed in the branches, chewing them steadily. Vita pulled a handful of dried figs from her pack, slipped the book back inside, and hoisted herself wearily to her feet. Then she began to climb, hauling herself up and over and around the piled pumice boulders. They were dull black in color and rough surfaced, riddled with irregular holes and tearing the skin on Vita's palms.

When she reached the grass at last, she walked with head bent, gazing at the ground. The grass was slippery and short with tough stems. It was turning tawny yellow and glowed in the light of the setting sun. Small black pebbles crouched between the grasses and occasionally rolled downhill from beneath Vita's boots. Few plants grew here: only a kind of low clover, and a herb with gray leaves that Vita recognized as mar-jori, and a taller plant that she didn't recognize. Its stems were already hard and brown, its seedpods rattled in the breeze and its leaves had withered into crisp brown fingers that crumbled at the touch. Had this plant been Hare's Ears? If so, was she too late or would the leaves still contain their healing properties?

She knelt beside one of the desiccated plants and closed her hand loosely around a handful of leaves, then closed her eyes in concentration. She felt nothing, just the wind at the nape of her neck and the dry prick of broken stems. Before leaving home, she'd asked Aunt Carmela how she'd recognize the Hare's Ears.

"By their touch," her aunt had advised her. "When you touch the sources of your own magic, your own power, your body recognizes them. You'll feel the tingle in your fingers."

"Yes," Vita had replied, remembering how she'd felt that power when she first touched the Keeper's book outside the cave, and how the touch of the Corno d'Oro's whipping mane had tingled on her cheek.

Now, she let the crumbled leaves fall into the grass and brushed clinging bits from her fingers. On the backs of her hands, irregular brown blotches marked where the Corno d'Oro's blood had fallen; although she'd washed and washed her hands with well water and lavender soap, the stains were immovable. She heaved herself to her feet. It was growing harder and harder to climb. Her legs burned with fatigue and her lungs sucked in mouthfuls of thin air. If I could just lie down, she thought. Only for a minute. But with every minute that passed, the Corno d'Oro might be growing weaker. Its wound might have festered, filled with the evil of the brutti's foul mouth, and be poisoning its blood. My fault, she kept thinking. My fault. No one can help it, except me.

As dusk fell over the mountains, desperation filled her. She crawled over the grass on her hands and knees, searching for anything with silver leaves. The moon sailed higher in the sky and above Vita's hunched shoulders the volcano rose black as pitch against the hazy stars. Vita began to cry, her tears dropping silently into the withering grass. Patches of bare gravel scraped her knees and a dolce-berry vine tore at her cheek.

I'll never find this plant, she thought. I'm too stupid. I've failed.

Doggedly, she searched on in the moonlight until the moon was obscured by clouds and it became too dark to see; even the waters of the Golfo so far below blended into the cloudy sky so that there was no horizon. Vita pulled a blanket from her pack and rolled herself in it, wedged into a tiny fold of mountain slope. The chill wind dried her tears. Her head swam with fatigue and she dropped into an uneasy sleep to awaken at dawn, cold to the bone, with heavy mist covering her hair and the blanket in a fine net of droplets.

I must find the leaves today, she thought, staggering to her feet. *I must.* It's three days already since the Corno d'Oro was wounded. Time is running out fast.

The morning passed as Vita clambered upward in the writhing mist. Strange shapes whirled around the mountain. Far below, she knew, the magrazzi would be sleeping in a nest of leaves and, still farther down, the villagers would be adding wood to their fires. Up here, she felt like the last person alive on the earth. It was hard to judge the passage of time for the sun was blotted out. Vita felt as though she struggled up the mountain for lifetimes with panic beating in her chest. Each passing minute seemed like a weight added to her shoulders until she felt too heavy and tired to climb anymore. Then, glancing up, she saw that the lip of the volcano was just above her, an indistinct shape in the mist. Carefully, she edged her way toward it and stopped on the edge.

At her feet, the dark cinder slope fell away, for how many hundreds of feet she couldn't tell for the interior of the volcano was a seething cauldron of mist. Vita swallowed and edged back. To slip over the edge would be like sliding into a great mouth, a place that would never spit her out. She'd shoot down forever, hurtling faster and faster toward her death...

I'm at the very top, she thought. And I've found nothing.

I've truly failed. This is what the grandmothers warned about when they spoke of betrayal. And throughout all history, I will be the one: the Keeper remembered for betraying her trust. If, that is, there is any more time to come or any one left to remember. If the Corno d'Oro dies, the green will die from the earth, the life force will falter, the balance swing down. The assassini and the darkness will rule, destroying, killing. The land will shrivel and lie waste and foul. True hearts will be killed and evil will possess the remainder that live. The flowers will die in the Keeper's valley and its sparkling stream run putrid.

It seemed such a trick of fate and time that the hunters should have wandered through that stretch of mountain, by coincidence, on the very day that she had failed to perform all the magic. They must have glimpsed the ivory flash of the stallion's coat in the trees and set their brutti to follow it. Oh, if only things had worked out differently—if the hunters had been later, or wandering elsewhere!

Despair filled Vita so that the world seemed to grow dark before her eyes. Perhaps it was the mist growing thicker, covering the sky, blocking the light from the land. She knuckled her eyes and blinked. It was at that moment that she glimpsed, as the mist thinned momentarily, a ledge of basalt rock protruding from the slope inside the cone, a little to her left and about six feet down. Lining the ledge were tiny plants with slender, tapering leaves. Even though there was no sunlight, the leaves seemed to gleam with a silver light and their hairy surfaces glittered with condensed mist.

"Hare's Ears!" Vita exclaimed.

She stared at them in wonder and then in fear.

"I can't do this," she said, but she knew that she must. She pulled off her boots and the socks that Aunt Carmela had knitted for her last winter, and in bare feet she lowered herself over the edge of the cinder cone on her stomach. Instantly, a rush of fine gravel slid down, down, rattling into the abyss. Vita froze, paralyzed with fear .

"I can't do this," she said again. She lay there for what seemed like a long time and then very carefully she moved, sliding down a little until her feet touched the ledge. The rock was wet and cold beneath her bare feet but her toes gripped onto it and she gingerly lowered herself until she was squatting by the silvery plants. She plucked the leaves carefully from their bases at the main stem, and a tingle shot through her fingers and ran through her wrist into her arm. She felt a moment of triumph.

Inch by inch, she wriggled the pack from her back and eased the book from it as a shower of gravel slid off the ledge and plunged into the volcano. She lifted her jacket and pressed the leaves against her tunic to dry them, then laid them inside the book. How many would she need? She picked more and dried them in the same way, then returned the book and the pack to her back.

Cautiously, holding her breath, she stood up and began to search for a foothold on the slope above her. There didn't seem to be one. I'm going to die in here, she thought. No one will know where to look for me. I'll never get out. She shifted her weight and more gravel slid, with a dull grating roar that set her teeth on edge, into the mist. It rattled down, for what seemed like minutes, into Roccioso's great maw.

Luna, help me! Vita thought in anguish. Her head swam. Everything seemed unreal and wavering: the dark cinder face, the mist above and below flowing in sinister shapes. It was as if she'd climbed off the world into another place where there was no sound, no light, no dimension.

Help!

She stood very still with her eyes squeezed shut, and let the Corno d'Oro run into her mind. She imagined its luminous eyes like ripest olives and the way that its mane billowed like breaking water. She watched its golden hooves, the nimbus of light that shimmered around it, and the way that it plunged through the air: straight and true, a rushing force like a flung spear.

Now, she thought. Now I'll be calm. She willed herself to breathe slowly, counting to ten, and to swallow her fear into her stomach.

I will take these leaves to the Corno d'Oro, she vowed, and opened her eyes to the swirling mist again. Then she saw it: a tiny place where she might wedge the toes of one foot. She set them in place, heaved herself upward, flung her body forward onto the grassy lip. For a moment she seemed to hang in the air, the force of her lunge fighting with the force of gravity that sought to pluck her off the lip and hurl her downward. Then she plunged face forward onto the slippery wet grass and lay still, listening to her heart crashing against the mountain.

It was raining by the time that Vita reached the forest and found the magrazzi; a thin, relentless rain that clung to the magrazzi's curling lashes and velvet coat. In old Tomie's meadow, as Vita clattered down the lane two days later, the jennet was dozing inside a shelter of olive wood and tiles left over from the roof of someone's house. Vita let the magrazzi go; it would spend the night in the apricot grove. On numb legs she limped down the valley to the Keeper's house where Aunt Carmela was waiting anxiously with clothes warmed by the fire and a chicken pie set on the table.

"*Lay in yellow earth to bind wounds and dry tears,*" Vita read from the book as she gobbled the pie, burning her tongue, barely noticing the rich taste of the gravy. "The earth on the mountain was black, Aunt Carmela. I didn't bring any home. And the soil here is reddish, in the gardens. Do you think we could use it? Do you think we grind the leaves up in a mortar and then mix them with the soil? Or do we grind it all up together into a paste? Or make a poultice from it?"

She stared anxiously at her aunt, but Aunt Carmela could only shake her head.

"You're the Keeper," she said. "This is your magic, not mine, Vita. I don't know what the words mean."

Vita pushed her empty plate away and rested her forehead on the table's scarred, polished surface. Lay in yellow earth, lay in yellow earth. The words were a refrain in her head, becoming more meaningless by the minute. She longed to sleep but felt time slipping past, running through her fingers, rushing into night. In the dark garden, the Rain Poppies were bent over, their pollen spilling like ink into the grass, their fuzzy stems beaded with moisture and their purple petals, fragile as tissue paper, beaten down with rain as time and night rushed over them. Night, and maybe death for the Corno d'Oro. Death, slow at first. Then fast.

Vita suddenly found herself thinking about Beatrice. It seemed ages since she'd seen Beatrice's dimpled smile, heard her soft voice. She imagined Beatrice's clever fingers traveling over the pots'surfaces with a brush, leaving behind them olives and fish, dolphins and apricot blossoms. Suddenly, Vita bolted upright at the table. "Yellow clay comes from the mountains north of Bossano!" she exclaimed. "Beatrice said so once!" It had been when they were younger and spending a day in the pottery, making little jennets and wombos from pieces of clay left over from the pots and jugs and bowls. Yellow clay. Was there any in the pottery right now? Vita knew that most of the clay that Beatrice's father used came from a pit only a mile or two away from the village, where he dug it himself and brought it home in panniers on a weathered jennet with one crooked ear. But occasionally, he bought clay from the north to use for special things: a jug for holding the first pressed wine at the autumnal equinox, or a bowl for a wedding gift.

Vita opened the book on the table and read the second page aloud to Aunt Carmela, hunched opposite her across the table:

"In the yellow earth the dormant power lies
To be kindled by the bright flame
Into strength, when the Keeper flies
To heal the Corno d'Oro and her shame."

The bright flame, Vita thought. The bright flame. Suddenly, she recalled a night she'd once spent with Beatrice in the pottery, feeding wood into the cone-shaped brick kiln until it glowed with a heat that radiated against her cheeks and expanded to fill the whole pottery with its suffocating force. In the bright flames, the pots had shimmered and hardened, taking on strength.

"The kiln!" Vita cried and Aunt Carmela smiled, sending rivulets of firelight across her lined cheeks.

Vita snatched the leaves and the book from the table and flew out the door with no shawl and plunged down the fifty steps, their worn surfaces slick with rain, to hammer breathlessly at the pottery door. It was Beatrice who opened it a crack, her plump face wan in the dim light.

"Vita?" she whispered, sounding surprised.

"Let me in, quick!"

Vita squeezed past Beatrice into the pottery's familiar dry, chalky smell and waited while Beatrice lit one of the lanterns that hung at intervals along the walls, the flame sending the long shadows of drying jugs across the beaten earth floor.

"Beatrice, you have to help me! The Corno d'Oro is wounded—it's all my fault! But I have an ancient book with verses that tell me what to do. Is there any yellow clay here?"

"I don't know," Beatrice replied slowly, muddled with sleep and startled by Vita's sudden appearance. "My mother's away visiting her sister. She's still grieving for Sandro. And my father is asleep; he fired the kiln last night. I daren't wake him."

"Then we must look for some yellow clay ourselves. I need it, Beatrice! Hurry! Help me!"

Together, in the lantern's glow, they began to search the pottery, squeezing between tubs of milky liquid glazes, and sacks bulging with powdered chemicals that were the glazes' raw ingredients. Vita shifted heavy slabs of clay, and pulled back the corners of the muslin cloth that wrapped them to peer at them hopefully. Red and smooth. Red and gritty. Dark brown. White, for making delicate porcelain bowls and cups with rims as thin as leaves. Jars of brushes and wooden tools for incising decorative marks into the clay. The smooth metal surface of the potter's wheel was rimmed with red streaks, dry now. The firebricks of the kiln, over in one corner of the room, were rough and still slightly warm to the touch.

"Perhaps the yellow clay is all gone," Beatrice said at last, wiping a smear of potash from one cheek.

"There has to be even a little here," Vita said in desperation, and continued shifting aside the wooden chests, lined with straw, in which Beatrice's father shipped his pottery to other villages on the backs of sturdy jennets. Stooping, she ran her hands across the rough floor in a dark corner, and her fingers touched a small lump. She hauled it into the light: a knob of clay, firm and cool, wrapped in dirty muslin. She peeled the cloth back and whooped.

"This is it!"

Beatrice joined her and together they peered at the small yellow lump, glistening with moisture. "It's all that's left," Beatrice said. "Is it enough?"

"I don't know what I'm making. Listen to the verses." Vita pulled the book from its bag and read the translated lines aloud.

"Is there enough clay here to make a small mortar?" Vita asked.

"Maybe," Beatrice agreed thoughtfully. "Then you would grind the leaves up in it and make a paste for the wound?"

"Yes. Can you help me?"

"I've never fired the kiln alone," Beatrice said doubtfully. "Once, Sandro and I did it together though."

"We have to try," Vita said. "I'll start bringing in the wood if you make the mortar."

They worked all night long, while the rain pattered on the tiled roof and hissed in the kiln chimney and fell into the dark mountains; while the poppies died in the grass and the olive trees dropped their leaves one by one. First Beatrice threw the tiny mortar on the spinning wheel, and Vita shaped a pestle by hand. The yellow clay was plastic and moist, easy to work with. Then they staggered in from the shed in the back courtyard with armloads of dried wood to fling, clattering, into the kiln's dark mouth. They lit the wood with a taper from the lantern; it flared up immediately into a crackling pyre of light and fierce heat.

For hours they fed the kiln while the heat crashed over them like waves, drying the skin on their cheeks and their lips, and shuddered against the pottery walls. The air smelled of resin and smoke. The firebricks glowed, too hot to touch, and inside the kiln the little mortar and pestle disappeared, swallowed in a heat so intense that it was like a white curtain. All night, perched on a bench with her back against the stones of the pottery wall and her shoulder wedged against Beatrice's firmness, Vita thought of the Corno d'Oro lying in the wet grass waiting for her. She bit her nails to the quick with anxiety.

As dawn crept beneath the pottery door and the lantern's light faded on the walls, the fire subsided and the roaring of its voice in the tapering chimney died to a sigh.

"It will take hours to cool," Beatrice said.

"I can't keep waiting!"

"You must; if we open the door too soon, what we've made will crack."

Hour after hour Vita paced on the beach, returning at intervals to lay her hands on the firebricks' grainy red surfaces. Aunt Carmela appeared with cold pie wrapped in a linen cloth, and Beatrice's father awoke and came downstairs to note with surprise the heat in his pottery. He opened the doors and let the misty sea air, funneling up the alley from the harbor, swirl into the room so that the smells of rotting weed and fish mingled with the fragrance of wood ash. Finally, in mid-afternoon, he said that the kiln was safe to open.

Holding her breath, Vita swung the door open. The mortar and pestle, fired to a deep golden color, stood whole and unblemished on the kiln's pale shelf. Beatrice's father handed her a pair of tongs and carefully she lifted the things from the kiln and set them down, still radiating warmth, on the shelf that ran along the nearest wall. Beatrice jostled against her, trying to see the results of their night's labor, and Vita turned to hug her, feeling her familiar solid warmth and soft cheeks. "Thank you, oh thank you so much, Beatrice."

Then she wrapped the objects in Aunt Carmela's linen cloth, and ran with them up the steps to the Keeper's house where she laid the Hare's Ears in the mortar and ground them into a thin, silvery-gray paste with water from the well. Fire, earth, air and water, she thought with sudden insight as she ground up the leaves. Already, when she emerged into the courtyard with the paste contained in a small stone jar that Aunt Carmela had given to her, the light was thin and cool, and the sun hung in the western sky in a veil of misty cloud. Vita ran up to where the magrazzi waited in the apricot grove at the top of the hill, and together they set off up the stony path at a fast trot while old Tomie's jennet nickered after them.

CHAPTER SIXTEEN

IN YEARS TO COME, the trek into the mountains to save the Corno d'Oro would seem to Vita like the memory of a dream. Light-headed with exhaustion, she rode the magrazzi to the grove of mandolo trees that marked the twelfth magical place and there, in the rain that was making the poppies bow their faces to the ground, she found the Corno d'Oro stallion lying. His damp coat was peppered with the black pollen of the Rain Poppies and fragments of dissolving petals, thin as tissue, clung in his mane. On his shoulder the wound was a festering darkness, crusty with blood and dribbling a yellow stain of poisoned fluid. The area around the wound was swollen and pulpy.

Keeper. At last. I've been waiting for you. His voice was faint in her head, a thin-tongued bell, with silvery note, tolling far away.

I would never desert you, she answered, shame flooding through her in a hot wave. She removed the lid of the stone jar and scooped out the paste, then approached the Corno d'Oro slowly as the hum of his power touched her, shivered through her. She knelt beside him. Gingerly, afraid of causing pain, she reached out a shaking finger and smeared the paste onto the wound. There was just enough to cover the torn lips of flesh, the gaping darkness between them. The paste went on as smooth as water, a silvery layer. When Vita arose from her knees, she saw that the stallion was asleep with his muzzle, softer than velvet woven for princesses in Genovera, resting on his bent forelegs. His mane fell over his face in a shining cloud. Vita sat and leaned against the damp trunk of a mandolo tree to weep with exhaustion and grief.

She awoke suddenly as the song of an olive thrush cascaded around her. In the western sky, the clouds had parted and a pale gleam of sun was reaching through like a finger. As Vita stared at it, she saw the air begin to shimmer and change. Colors began to appear: purple, orange, red, blue, as though an invisible brush was wetting the sky. The colors gathered intensity and arced in a bow across the sea toward the mountainside.

"Arcobaleno," Vita breathed, as the colors seemed to fill the air around her. She glanced at the stallion just in time to see him surge to his feet with the colors of the arcobaleno dappling him. Where the wound had been, his shoulder was an unblemished sheet of ivory coat and smooth muscle. Vita stared in amazement. The leaves had healed miraculously, their strong and ancient magic rendering the brutti's poison ineffective.

For a moment only, Vita stared at the stallion as he shook himself, flower petals cascading from his mane. His breath smoked in the chill, his flaring nostrils cyclamen pink. Around him shimmered a nimbus of light, and the dancing colors of the arcobaleno, while the air against Vita's cheek crackled with the stallion's power.

Keeper, I thank you.

Then he leaped into the shadows of the trees and was gone, straight and swift in his flight, sound on every leg. His voice reverberated in Vita's head like the voice of a great, perfectly cast bell that rings a deep, true note. She felt it vibrating in her being long after the Corno d'Oro had disappeared. Where he'd lain in the yellow grass, star lilies sprang up before Vita's eyes, their pale green stems vivid in the fading light, their white buds splitting open, their petals curling backward to fill the mandolo grove with a pure, sweet fragrance. Vita sat in a trance as rain pattered through the falling leaves to dampen her shoulders and the colors of the arcobaleno were absorbed back into the cloudy sky.

I might never see the Corno d'Oro again, she thought, and sadness filled her, blue and remote as evening.

At last, she put the lid back onto the empty stone pot and went to find the magrazzi which waited for her lower down the mountain. It was time to go home, picking their way carefully through the dripping trees, down the dark valley to the smoking chimneys of the village. Vita paused at the shrine by her gate, and laid one leaf of the Hare's Ears at Luna's feet, amongst the olives offered there, before she staggered under the silent tree and into the house.

She dragged herself upstairs to her room where she fell into the scented sheets and plummeted into hour after hour of dreamless sleep. She slept for days, like someone recovering from an illness, stirring only to wander into the kitchen and eat the hot pies and casseroles that Aunt Carmela plied her with. After this, she grew stronger and came down to sit in the kitchen and grind herbs under her aunt's fierce gaze.

"You've been foolish," Aunt Carmela said one afternoon. "I don't know what your mother would have thought of you." She sighed, separating herbs into bundles. Then she glanced at Vita's stricken face and her own expression softened. She laid a hand on Vita's shoulder and gave a sympathetic squeeze. "You're very young," she said more gently. "And all has ended well, Vita. All is safe now. You must go out again; our neighbors are asking after your health. You've been missed."

Vita wandered through the village, feeling the thin sun on her shoulders and watching as the villagers pruned the olive trees and carried the branches home in bundles for winter fires. When the chestnuts fell in the forest, Vita helped to gather them into woven baskets, their rich glossy shells promising hot porridge and sweet cakes all winter. She carried up tunny fish from the harbor wall, their swift sleek bodies gleaming silver and blue in the cool air, for it was the season when the tunny migrated and the pirati hauled them in by the hundreds in their tough dark nets. They traded the fish with the villagers for pottery, chestnuts and firewood. In the village square, Vita helped the women gut and skin the tunny, packing them into brine in oak barrels, while the autumnal sun slid rapidly around the sundial's stone face and the early evenings slid down off the mountains with a peppery smell of rotting leaves.

Vita wondered where Giovanni was and why he never came to see her, the yellow sail of his boat like a flower petal against the sky. She asked the pirati but the men to whom she spoke didn't know where he was, and hadn't seen him. She wondered if something had happened to him, or if he'd gone away, and she felt a sudden ache of loneliness. She missed his smile flashing in his dark face, the energy of his laughter, and the cheerful brightness of his bandana knotted at his strong neck. She missed his stories about wind and tides, and the confident rolling swing of his walk, and the friendly grip of his callused hands.

One afternoon, when a chill wind whistled the leaves down from the trees to whirl in the alleyways, Lord Maldici's tax collectors tramped into the village with whips coiled in their hands and with a pack of assassini and brutti to guard them and a line of jennets to carry away what they took. They scoured the village, lining up the heads of households on the sundial's flat surface, listing names in their parchment books. They raided hay lofts and nut sheds, fish smoking rooms and the press for the olives. The patient jennets were loaded with casks of oil and young red wine, with sacks of whole chestnuts and of flour ground from mandolo nuts, with jars of fragrant honey, with crates of tunny and dried apples cut into rings, with chests of pottery packed into straw.

The villagers watched, clustered in the village square, their toes lined up on the edge of the tiles where time stood still on the sundial. There was silence, until a woman let out a harsh sob, and man muttered angrily, "We will starve this winter." Then a tax collector's whip lashed out to coil around the man's legs and throw him face down on the tiles where a brutti sprang to guard him, its drool wetting his shirt.

"You surely don't begrudge food to your own sons?" a tax collector sneered. "This food is going to the army, where your sons are learning courage and forgetting they were ever scrawny village boys with no wits."

An angry growl ran through the villagers, a ripple of motion as men spat on the ground and woman raised shawls to their red eyes, but they stilled as whips cracked overhead and the brutti paced in front of their feet. Afterward, when the line of jennets had wound up through the village and followed the path away, the villagers dispersed to their homes in sullen silence. All evening Aunt Carmela rocked in a chair before the fire, sighing and frowning to herself. Vita felt the kernel of grief over her mother's death hardening and swelling in her chest again. It had been easy, in Genovera, to ignore this pain and to forget it for days at a time. It had been easy there to be light-hearted, to float like a leaf over the surface of things, to be swept away on currents of forgetfulness and pleasure.

After a month, a letter arrived at the Keeper's house, brought by a messenger in the plum and silver livery of the palazzo of Ronaldo's parents. Vita read it perched on the wall around the well while overhead in the chyme tree, the new wombo slept, its foreleg healed and strong.

Dear Vita, You've been gone so long! When are you coming back? Rosa says to tell you that she misses you—and I do, too. Things aren't as much fun without you here. Can you come back with the messenger? He's brought a spare horse in case you need one. Hoping to see you very soon. Love, Ronaldo.

Vita fingered the necklace of coral and silver filigree that she wore at her throat. Dimly, like something that had happened long ago, she remembered her birthday party—the gowns, the music, the food. Ronaldo's arms around her, his fingers fastening the necklace. Her tears blotted his elegant looping hand, on the thick creamy paper.

Dear Ronaldo, she wrote, *I'll always remember my wonderful time in Genovera. I'm sorry that I don't know where your horse is; it went lame on the journey and I had to borrow a magrazzi, a beast from another land, to reach home. I cannot come again to visit you, because my aunt needs me here at home. Love, Vita.*

The messenger bowed over her hand with a courtly flourish, slipped her reply into the leather case at his belt, and rode north with it.

The villagers pruned their grapevines and left them to rest for the winter. A storm washed a dead sword whale up on the point near the harbor, and the village boys visited it every afternoon after school until its stench became too powerful and the villagers paid a pirati to tow it into the Golfo. The pale yellow autumn crocuses flowered in the Keeper's valley and the new wombo grew fat and sleek, catching moths by the light of the moon.

Vita grew lonelier and lonelier. Still, Giovanni didn't come to see her. Beatrice was seeing a boy called Eduardo who lived in the next village down the coast; he rode to visit her on a jennet along the rocky coastal path in fog or wind or thin sunshine, and together they walked on the beach and wrote their names in the sand with sticks, or sat in the café at the waterfront and stared at each other over hot bread and mullosk chowder. Vita began to remember her birthday more and more frequently, cherishing every detail, comforting herself on the splendor of her memories. They were like small fires that she warmed herself at, growing dreamy.

Maybe I was stupid not to return to Genovera with the messenger, she thought. I could have come home again in time for the winter solstice to perform the magic. And all my new gowns, provided by Ronaldo's mother, are hanging unused in a wardrobe in the blue bedroom.

She wished she could spend a day with Rosa, shopping in the markets where the stalls were filled with things from other places: ribbons of finest organza, necklaces of pearls from Coralli, mirrors from Terre with amber handles, and inlaid lacquer boxes, cunningly painted, from Mombasso. Rosa had been a good friend and what fun they'd had, eating candied almonds and chocolates while playing Casa or walking in the palazzo gardens, or dashing through the streets in Ronaldo's chariot! Vita wished that Rosa had returned to the village with her.

Another messenger arrived on a fast horse, lathered in sweat, that stamped at the gate. The messenger handed Vita an envelope and from it she pulled an invitation card bordered with a pattern of pomegranates in red ink.

The pleasure of your company is requested at the eighteenth birthday party of Ronaldo Caselloni, she read. There followed a date, several weeks away, and the address of the palazzo in which she had stayed while in Genovera. The card promised that the party would be *A grand ball, with a Lontano theme, fancy costume, imported entertainers, dancing.*

Vita turned the card over to find Ronaldo's elegant writing on the back: *Vita—you have to come! Love, R.* She rested the card on the gate and borrowed the messenger's pen and pot of ink.

Dear Ronaldo, she wrote, *I've promised my aunt I'll stay home. Have a great birthday. Love, V.* Once again, the messenger slipped her envelope into his leather case and swung the horse's head toward the north.

Autumn faded into winter and olive wood fires crackled fragrantly on every village hearth. In the early mornings, frost sparkled on the high slopes of the mountains, or mist blotted them out in wet veils. Other days were windy, the Golfo streaked with foam and the water shuddering beneath the sky's raking touch. The pirati repaired their boats and recounted tales of raiding parties in southern seas, and cast cannon balls in their fiery forge, and honed the edges of cutlasses. Vita walked in the afternoons to the end of the harbor wall where she stood scanning the horizon, but Giovanni didn't appear. She took her Casa set, the one Ronaldo had given her, to the pottery and taught Beatrice and Eduardo to play the game, but their company was boring. They wanted to be on their own, and they wouldn't play to beat each other. Vita packed up her game in disgust.

One evening, when Eduardo couldn't come to visit, Vita and Beatrice roasted chestnuts over the kitchen fire, peeling back the brittle skins to munch on the mealy flesh inside. Vita stared dreamily into the flames, remembering the chestnut tarts served at her birthday party in Genovera, and the chestnut tree in the palazzo gardens where Ronaldo had pushed her higher and higher on a wooden swing. Her toes had seemed to sweep the crown of the tree and the sky, while Ronaldo's light, careless laughter filled the air.

"I think I'm falling in love with Ronaldo," she confided shyly to Beatrice, dropping a hot nut onto the floor by mistake.

Beatrice picked the nut up and tossed it into Vita's lap, giving her a brooding look. "Ronaldo might be nobili," she said, "but he's not worth one-half of Giovanni."

"Giovanni's still my friend," Vita retorted. "I don't see what he has to do with this, anyway." She stuffed the hot nut into her mouth, burning her tongue. What does Beatrice know about anything? she wondered crossly. All she can think about these days is Eduardo. She could at least be happy for me.

The winter solstice arrived, and the villagers decorated their homes with candleberry and boughs of leathery magnolia leaves. They lit tall tapers, smelling of honey, and carried them through the streets, singing, in the early dark as Vita came down from the mountains with the magic accomplished once more— and this time, safely. She'd wondered, deep in her heart, if she might see the Corno d'Oro again but even as she wondered she'd known that this wasn't likely. Nor did she see him, only found in the wet soil near the mandolo grove a rayed hoof print round as the sun. That evening, after she returned home, the villagers danced in the streets and the sweet wailing of the violyno drew Vita from the kitchen and down the dark alley. She danced all evening, crowned with a wreath of candleberries, and ached for Giovanni who usually danced with her.

He's forgotten me, she thought. Or else, since I went away to Genovera, he doesn't want to be my friend anymore. I'll have to manage without him.

Two weeks later a tapestry stallion arrived at the Keeper's gate and Ronaldo himself strode whistling down the path, his long legs elegant in purple silken hose, his padded winter doublet swinging open. Vita was in the courtyard sorting herbs into glass jars for her aunt; Ronaldo caught her in his arms and swung her around, humming a dance tune.

"I thought you might have forgotten the steps," he teased, while blood rushed into her cheeks and her heart leaped.

"Vita," he said tenderly, brushing her silvery hair from her eyes. "I've been waiting and waiting for you to come back."

"I didn't reach home in time—the horse you loaned me went lame, Ronaldo. It caused trouble. I can't come to the city again."

"But the same thing wouldn't happen twice!" he exclaimed with his light, careless laugh. "Bring your magrazzi to the city this time if you want. You can ride it home whenever you need to visit your aunt. Come on, Vita. It's my birthday next week, and we're having another party. I want to dance with you again. You promised. You promised you'd come back."

And he laid his pale, tapering fingers against her necklace, at the base of her throat, so that she felt the warmth in them, a warmth that her whole body seemed to gather itself around.

In the highest tower of pale stone, that rose above the sorcerer's fortress and the tumbled rooftops of Genovera, the sorcerer's daughter stretched her cold hands to the fire's blaze.

The sorcerer sat in his chair of carved mandolo wood, wrapped in a black cloak of finest angoli wool that was lined with green velvet, and embroidered with snakes and condors in lime green thread and with the silver fur of mountain hares. He hunched the cape moodily around his shoulders and watched as his daughter began to comb her long red hair; sparks crackled from it in the firelight.

"Too much time has passed," he growled irritably. "Neither the Keeper nor the beast have been brought to the city. By spring, I want to fight. The army is training daily; the spies bring news that my brother in the south is planning some foolish festivity for the spring equinox. We will launch a surprise attack when he least expects us, when his peasants are planting their fields. My men will run them down in a trice! Hah! They won't know what killed them."

His sharp teeth gleamed and his golden hawk eyes were slits of greed but his daughter paid no attention, simply ran the ivory comb hypnotically through her waving hair.

"What of your cunning plans? Heh?" the sorcerer asked sarcastically, returning to his original thought. "Why haven't the Keeper and the beast been brought to me?"

"You know what happened at the autumnal equinox, how the hunters were foiled at the last minute because the Keeper returned on a borrowed animal. The idiot who threw the net and missed has been sent to the dungeons. But the Keeper will soon come back to the city."

"We should have dragged her here months ago, in chains. What is the use of all your guile and flattery, your cajoling and sweetness?'

"You need the Keeper," the sorcerer's daughter said. "You need her on your side. There's no use dragging her here in chains—she will hate you. And she has power with the beasts. But if you flatter her and spoil her, she'll work with us. Perhaps she'll bring the beast here herself, to work your will. Perhaps she'll bring her power to our side. Even without the lost beast, we would have the Keeper and the captive beast in the courtyard."

The sorcerer stared into the fire's leaping flames beneath the mantle of smoky marble where lanterns of carved seashells stood in a row.

"Perhaps you are right," he said. "When she comes to Genovera, we will stage a banquet to which she'll be invited. We will show her our power. What does she desire? Make me a list, and she shall have it all. But I want her! There are to be no more mistakes!"

His hands, with their long yellow nails, clawed convulsively at the chair and his voice rose into a shriek. His daughter continued to comb her hair; between its hot strands, her smooth face was composed and pale.

"Don't shout at me," she said coldly. "You will have time before spring to work your black arts on the Keeper and the courtyard beast."

Rising from her seat by the fire, her hair pouring down her back and her velvet gown murmuring around her, the sorcerer's daughter paced the room.

"We will beguile her," she promised her father by the fire. "You will be Emperor before mid-summer, blacker and more powerful than Lord Morte ever was. You will crush the nations, and write your name across them in blood."

CHAPTER SEVENTEEN

HIGH ABOVE THE GUNSHIP'S polished rolling deck, Giovanni stood wedged into the crow's nest, staring over the glittering sea where occasionally a sword whale, in the school of three that had been following the boat, surfaced and blew a misty spray. They're like vultures, Giovanni thought, waiting for what we spill into the sea for them.

Just over the southern horizon, the islands of Corali floated like the backs of half-submerged turtles, their peaks of tropical forest a pale greenish-blue. All morning in the freshening wind, the gunship had cruised in circles waiting for the merchant ship the pirati spies had sent word of to come sailing north from the islands. Its cargo holds were filled with necklaces, with sharp steel daggers, with shark tooth combs and compasses inlaid with mother of pearl, with spices from the amaranth tree and with the bark of the cinni plant, that princes steeped into an exotic tea and drank with cream, with silk so fine that it was transparent, a shimmering drapery of brightest colors.

Giovanni scanned the sea, the white running crests of the waves, looking for sails. As he kept watch, he thought about what would happen next. The merchant ship would be built for seaworthiness and for carrying cargo, but not for speed. She'd come heavily across the water, beating against the northerly wind, her freeboard washed with waves. When Giovanni cried the news of her sighting, the gunship would leap forward like a brutti slipped from a leash, with the pirati lining the rails and chanting at the capstans. Sleek and fast, she'd cut through the water between the merchant ship and the islands to the south. Then she would give chase, slicing waves open to pour their green hearts into white foam that flew across her decks, while her huge sails strained at the taut rigging, making the masts groan, and the Mara woman on the figurehead stared impassively ahead beneath her delicately arched brows. The guns would be run out, their muzzles gleaming, and fired with reports that rolled deafeningly across the water.

When the merchant ship was a smashed and crippled hulk, rolling broadside with her masts and sails trailing, the pirati would board her with ropes and hooks, with their eyes alight and their hearts on fire with the gold greed of Lord Morte. Then the merchant's decks would run with blood, and the pirati would haul out the casks and chests, the trunks and coffers of loot to bring onboard the gunship. The merchant ship would be fired, a pyre full of bones, and slide into the dark depths where secrets were kept forever.

Giovanni shifted uncomfortably in the crow's nest. His father had heard that Antonio was once again going on board the merchant ship with the raiding party, and had declared that Giovanni too would be given his first cutlass and hooked rope, and sent over the gunship's sides to fight.

"You're old enough to be with the men," he'd said proudly, thumping Giovanni on the back while pirati had cheered raggedly and Giovanni's stomach had clenched. He'd wanted to say something, to refuse his father's command, but the words had stuck in his throat. This was the first time in days that his father had been pleased with him, for he'd been angry ever since he'd found out how Giovanni had gone overboard from the last raiding ship.

"A damn fool thing to do!" his father had roared. "Trying to join the bones of the dead? Trying to join the Mara? Think you're a fish? Too cowardly to fight? Ashamed of me and your uncles and all your family? Ashamed to be a pirati?" And he'd stormed out of the house, where he'd been striding to and fro before the fireplace. The walls shook as the door crashed shut.

Now, in the crow's nest, Giovanni pulled his canvas jacket more closely around his chest, for the wind had a keen edge to it. He wished that the merchant ship would never emerge from the island harbor, and that the gunship would turn and beat homeward with empty holds. Then he'd have no choice to confront. He wished that he was at home himself, fishing off the reefs, or sailing across the Golfo to climb the hillside terraces and help Vita pick chestnuts in the forest.

Vita.

She's wearing a silver and coral necklace from her darling Ronaldo, and chattering about fireworks and parties, Marina's clear, sharp voice had repeated in his head as he stood watch in starlight or on misty afternoons when the sails hung limp, as he swung all night in his hammock below decks, as he spliced ropes with his strong, clever fingers. A necklace from Ronaldo. The finest silver jewelry came from the southern islands, though gold came from Terre. If they sighted a merchant ship today, what necklaces might be coiled in strands in her chests?

If I board with the raiding party, I'll be able to find the jewel cases, Giovanni thought. I'll be able to look for them first. I'll be able to line up with the other men and take my pick of what I want, as payment for my work in the fighting and on the gunship. I'll be able to choose something fine for Vita, something of pure silver with delicate patterns of leaves and flowers, with coral inlay, with pink and golden carved flowers, with purple, deep sea pearls strung on fine silver wire. I'll choose a necklace with matching earrings to swing in her silver hair, with bracelets to chime at her wrists. What I bring her will be far finer than what Ronaldo gave her. Today is my chance. I should seize it. I should line up for a cutlass. Boarding should be easy; I'm a pirati and I'm strong and reckless. Just look at when I plunged off the lee rail of the last gunship I was on!

Heat seemed to fill his body so that he barely noticed the wind. The sky seemed suddenly bluer, blazing with a fierce cold light, and the clouds scudding southward seemed a harder, crisper white. His head spun, filled with ambitions. It was easier to think this way, to let the gold greed warm him, to forget about being disobedient and mutinous, to stop being cold and afraid. Why shouldn't he be a pirati, since he'd been born one and grown up in the pirati village, running on the wet sand at low tide beneath the towering polished hulls of the gunships, learning their shapes before he could speak words? Why shouldn't he be able to give Vita a necklace if that swaggering cuttlefish Ronaldo, with his careless laugh and his silken hose, gave her one?

A sword whale surfaced near the bows and shot mist into the air, mist to be torn away in the wind. Giovanni laughed, his strong white teeth gleaming, and shouted down to it: "Not long, my brother!" The whale's narrow, mottled back submerged as a wave washed over it and the ship heeled in a gust, and Giovanni braced himself against the nest's wooden sides and thought more about necklaces. Once, he remembered, an uncle had brought home a necklace from a raid near Coralli that was hung with silver dolphins. Giovanni wondered if he might find some-thing like this for Vita, who had been swimming with him and the dolphins although she couldn't talk to them as he could.

Once, I was a young man such as you, the only one in my genera-tion who could speak to the dolphins. Alas, that I lost such a gift. The hermit's voice, dry and creaky with disuse, filled with bitter regret, spoke in Giovanni's thoughts. He shook his head as if to dislodge the voice, and leaned against the crow's nest to stare out eagerly across the sea.

I wasn't true to my heart the voice continued relentlessly.

Giovanni pursed his lips and began to whistle. He let the melody and the wind, keening against the gunship's masts and in her red sails, fill his head. The wind felt cold again, raising a chill on the nape of his neck even though his black hair hung there in a single braid.

I should have come home and battled the dragon, who holds the pirati in thrall—but I lacked the courage.

Giovanni whistled more loudly, but it was no use. The heat and the giddy, light fig-canary feeling of the gold greed were draining out of him, and he was filling up again with cold anxiety. I am a coward, he thought, but not in the way my father accused me. I'm not afraid to fight, or to swim. I'm only afraid to be true to my heart, to step away from the pirati and make myself an outcast like Marina. I'm afraid to go down this rigging and tell my father that I won't raid the merchant ship, not even for a necklace of dolphins to take home to Vita. I'm afraid of Dragomar, of his blue teeth like polished glass and the spikes, hard as iron, lining his scaly back, and of his great gaping red mouth.

At that moment, he saw them.

He knuckled his eyes, pretending that he'd seen nothing, or only a cloud's glimmering reflection or a flock of pale seabirds skimming over the waves. Deep in his heart, he knew he'd seen the sails of a merchant ship beating northward. He licked his dry lips and opened his mouth to shout but no sound emerged. His heart hammered against his ribs.

I must choose, he thought. Now, in this moment, even though I'm not ready, even though I'm afraid and I don't know how to fight dragons. I must choose.

The sails were mosaic chips against the sky, laid in patterns that Giovanni could recognize. Three masts. Foresails. Mizzen sails. Top sails. Top gallants. He stared at them as if in a trance, feeling time slip through the air like grains of sand.

Choose, he thought. Choose.

He leaned over, staring down through the rigging to where

the pirati were small figures sprinkled over the gunship's fragranti decks.

"Ship to starboard!" a man yelled. Instantly the pale blobs of faces tilted to look over the sea and other voices took up the cry. A frenzy of organized activity broke out as feet thumped on decking and the captain shouted orders. Giovanni climbed into the shrouds, the wind tearing at his jacket like an angry dog and the ropes taut and rough in his grip. His palms were wet with sweat. Carrying his mutiny and his aloneness in his heart, he felt like a fly, suspended above the men united in their one goal. He thought that, if they glanced up at him, the pirati would be able to see right into him and know his purpose that ran against the grain of their own. He had never felt as alone as he did in that moment, knowing what he would say to his father, and how the pirati's cheerful shouts and flashing grins would fall into silence and darkness at his words. For just as long as it took him to reach the deck, he was still a part of the crew. Then, the comradeship they'd offered him would be over.

Sirena, goddess with dolphins, be with me now, he prayed silently, before dropping to the deck to land lightly amongst a crush of men heading to their stations. And there was his father, balancing over near the port rail with a brass spyglass held to one eye. Giovanni strode unsteadily toward him.

"I'm not going on board the merchant ship!" he shouted into the wind, feeling its cold torrent fill his mouth and swirl into his chest.

"What?" His father tore the spyglass from his eye, his jaw slack with disbelief.

"I'm not going on board!" Giovanni shouted again.

"But—I've ordered it! What's the matter, son? Not afraid are you? You'll be all right. It's your first time and the men will watch out for you!" His father grasped his arm in an encouraging squeeze and for a moment Giovanni's resolve wavered. How easy it would be to grin at his father and agree, to ask for a cutlass. He swallowed hard as his father turned away to the rail and raised the spyglass again.

"I am not going on board!" he repeated. "I'm not scared either! I just don't want to kill men for—for things! It's not right, Father!"

His father swung to face him, his eyes blazing a fierce and electric blue. "Then it's into the cabin with you!" he shouted. "We'll sort out this nonsense later. Get below!"

Giovanni turned away from the contempt on his father's face and rushed down the pitching steps into the dim light of the cabin. He slung himself into his hammock and lay there, clenching and unclenching his damp hands, while the sword whales leaped through his mind, with necklaces of silver wrapped around their spiral horns.

He strained listen to the clatter of running feet, the chant of men at the capstans, the groan of the ship and the fast sluice of water along her sides. He felt her come up into the wind, heard the crack of slack sailcloth. The water noise diminished to a steady slap. A shudder ran through her when the first cannon was fired. A ragged cheer, and then a great shout, rang across the water. The cannon fired again, and yet again. Giovanni heard wood cracking, a terrible groaning noise that filled his head. His mind was a black hole now, whirling with flames and images of flashing steel. He heard the gunwales banging against the hull of the merchant ship, the shriek and clash of fighting. After a long time, he heard the sound of heavy objects being dragged across the deck over his head, and then the crackle of fire. The gunship began to move again, the water rushing against her planking. Giovanni hung rocking in the dim silence and wished he was invisible as men dragged chests down the steps and past him into the hold.

"Giovanni, weaker than a woman!" a voice taunted.

"Still a baby! Only looks like a man!"

"Take away his hammock and give him a cradle!"

"Give him a wet nurse!"

Giovanni closed his eyes and thought of the dolphins, their sleek snouts touching his face with joy, their small eyes laughing and holding and the light of every new morning.

"Look at this!" said Antonio's voice, and Giovanni opened his eyes to find his friend standing beside him. The fabric of his blue canvas jacket was slashed open in two places and there was blood smeared on his collar, but his face was flushed and his eyes shone with a wild, bright gleam. He was laughing with triumph. In the dim light, the jewelry in his hands glimmered: silver strands woven together, hung with star sapphires and coral flowers.

"I know you didn't raid the ship," Antonio said. "But you can have one of these if you want. Go on, take one." And he thrust a cool silver strand into Giovanni's open palm, where it lay coiled like a snake. Giovanni felt his fingers curling shut around it; it was for Vita. Then he struggled from the wildly rocking hammock and held the necklace back out to Antonio.

"Thanks," he muttered. "I don't want it."

"Keep it, I've got lots."

"I don't want it!" he shouted. "It's got blood on it!" And he flung it toward a dark corner of the cabin where it slid across the shifting planks.

The wild laughter died in Antonio's face, and in that moment Giovanni remembered how they'd fished together so many starry nights on the reefs and how they'd dug holes on the beach looking for treasure when they were very young, and how Antonio had helped him restore the hull of his blue boat after a winter storm had stove in a plank.

Antonio's lips twisted scornfully and his blue eyes darkened into a deep chilly green. "So," he said slowly and insultingly, "the men were right about you. Giovanni—the coward."

And he swung away on a booted heel and dived after the necklace, dropping to his knees on the rolling floor. Giovanni leaped up the steps into the daylight and the wind, carrying his grief in his stomach like a cold stone. Antonio had been a good friend all these years. Giovanni would miss him now.

For a week, while the gunship rushed northward into the wind's teeth, Giovanni worked alone and in silence. At the capstans, the pirati wouldn't chant if he was with them. They excluded him from their games of cards and dice. They ignored him at mealtimes. They turned their shoulders to him as they told tales of daring and reckless skill, as they talked about what lay in the hold, as they figured out how to divide the loot and how much to sell for gold and lay aside for the Feast of Dragomar when the great sea dragon would rise from the depths and demand his tithes. Giovanni's father ignored him too, but occasionally Giovanni would feel his father's eyes and catch his father's puzzled, brooding glance lingering on his own face. At last, when the coast of southern Verde was a thin pencil line of green in the north, his father found him mending nets and squatted beside him.

"Son," he said heavily, "if you will not raid, you must sell. I'm sending you ashore in the delta, where our shore party will be waiting to unload some of the chests and sell them in Genovera for gold. You'll go with them and learn to trade, and to bring us back the gold for Dragomar."

Giovanni nodded in silence, waiting for his father's recriminations and angry muttering, but his father too remained silent and when Giovanni looked up from the needle gripped in his fingers, he saw that his father's dark face was furrowed with sad, worried lines. He cuffed Giovanni lightly across the chest. "Fair winds go with you, bright seas carry you," he said in the pirati formal tradition, before rising to his feet and swaggering aft along the deck. Giovanni's needle flashed in and out of the nets, his hands moving automatically.

The shore party left five evenings later, when the gunship had drifted into a narrow channel in the delta's sprawling miles of salty inlets where crab weed grew thick and tough, bending in the wind, and where the low tides exposed banks of yellow soil washed down in the Arnona from the mountains north of Bossano.

Here, outcasts and fishermen lived in weathered shacks perched on stilts as thin as birds' legs, and small skiffs rocked in the incoming tide. Here, the pirati shore party knew every faint trail, every sucking stretch of quicksand, and the cry of every bird. They passed through the bending, chest high grasses like ghosts, carrying their loot on their backs with tump lines of tough fabric wrapped around their foreheads and their bare feet feeling the way through sea holly and over shingle.

Giovanni hoisted a chest onto his shoulders and felt the tump tighten, squeezing the blood from his forehead. He fell into the line of silent, padding men and followed the back bent over ahead of him. Then, for two days, they waited in a cabin of driftwood while men brought jennets to load by the light of the harvest moon that silvered the delta's ruffled channels and stirred the jennet's creamy spiked manes.

The next morning they traveled miles inland, disguised as a trading party heading for Genovera, following the Arnona's winding shoreline amongst a jostle of other traders from the delta, all of whom scuttled aside for the chariots and impatient horses of merchant princes. On the river, the barges plied to and fro with their brown sails angled to catch the wind and their blunt bows pushing the muddy water into white wrinkles. Their holds were packed with porcelain and other pottery from the kilns of Bossano, with sacks of wheat from the inland plains, with casks of fine Verde wine. It was all to be exported in return for goods from other lands.

On their last night before reaching the city, they stopped to eat in a wayside inn called The Condor's Wing, with a patched roof of cracked tiles and courtyard tables littered with empty mugs and chipped plates. Giovanni slouched at a table amongst the pirati shore men. His heels were blistered and his hands smelled of jennet instead of rope. With each passing mile, he missed the sea more with its bracing wind and its vast horizon that reached far out, beckoning him, toward the sky. He knew that he was moving farther away too from the dragon, and from the task that awaited him.

As he lay awake each night on the chill ground, or sat lookout by the fire, his mind swung like a pendulum. He'd go home and fight Dragomar. He'd go home and be a pirati raider. He'd stay with the shore party and learn to use scales as the merchants did, to follow the merchants' fast tongues and their slippery minds. He'd run away and wander the world, as the hermit Giuseppe had done. But all night long, as his mind swung, he heard the dolphins calling to him in their silvery, liquid voices and he felt, in the pit of his stomach, a cold fear that never went away. He knew that he must go home to vanquish the dragon, somehow using the knowledge he'd gained in Giuseppe's library.

Now, around the table, the pirati shore men roared with laughter at some joke that Giovanni, deep in his lonely thoughts, hadn't heard.

"Go on, take him on!" someone yelled and Giovanni, glancing up, saw that another trader had challenged one of the pirati to a friendly wrestling match. In a short time, the courtyard was cleared of tables and a crowd had gathered to watch as the two men, stripped to the waist, circled each other on the tiles and measured each other with their eyes. Giovanni stood near the back of the crowd, watching with only half his attention as the cheers and shouts of the crowd filled his ears.

He thought that he'd go inside the inn and pay for the fig-canary that the pirati had drunk, and for the roasted goat meat that they'd eaten with griddlecake. He shouldered his way indoors. A couple of men were seated at one table, hunched over in whispered conversation, their drab green clothes shadowy in the dimness. Otherwise, the room was empty. Giovanni leaned on the counter and called for the innkeeper, but perhaps the man was out watching the fight for no one replied. Giovanni shouted again and waited. At the last moment, he heard the silence thicken in the room, and felt the rush of their movement. It's a trap! his senses screamed.

Too late, he whirled on the balls of his feet and threw out his arms. "Let go!" he shouted, but already the taller of the two men in green was twisting his arms behind his back until Giovanni gritted his teeth against the pain. He opened his mouth to shout for help but the other man's knife was a cold pressure against his neck. "Be silent," the man hissed and the point of the knife broke through skin with a prick like a needle. They bent his face toward the light. Giovanni saw the taller man's face hanging above him: a foxy, weather beaten face with squinting eyes. A face he'd seen before, under a fragranti tree at a branch in the mountain path.

"It is him!" the man whispered fiercely. "The pirati boy who had the book. They say he knows the Keeper. Tie him up—he's wanted."

Giovanni thrashed in desperate silence, kicking and straining for purchase on the tiled floor and trying to throw the men over with his weight, but they knocked him down instead and kneeled on his back with the knife at his throat. The gag they knotted around his mouth smelled of stale onions. When his hands and feet had been tied with rope, the men began to drag him toward a back door.

"Hey there! What's this then?" the innkeeper cried, bustling in from outside with a grubby apron over his tunic and his whiskered beard shining pale gray in the low beams of sun slanting through the open back door. Giovanni felt a flicker of hope, but the men in green stared at the innkeeper with cool composure. The taller man slipped a hand into a pocket and withdrew a silver medallion stamped with a condor, that great bird that lives in the high crags of the northern mountains, with its cruel hooked beak for tearing apart prey, its curved talons and it golden hawk eyes that see tiny creatures many miles away. The insignia of Lord Maldici. An icy chill shivered through Giovanni. The innkeeper bowed low, wiping his hands nervously.

"Out of our way," the man in green commanded, slipping the medallion back into his jacket. "We're on the lord's business. Keep your moth shut. You've seen nothing."

"Yes. No. Very good. Seen nothing, of course not," the innkeeper mumbled, and he darted nervously past Giovanni's prone body and disappeared down a hallway. The men grabbed

Giovanni's collar and dragged him over the sill of the back door and across the patch of sandy ground that lay behind the inn. A tawny pony was tethered there and they hoisted Giovanni onto its back as it sidled and snorted. They threw some dusty sacking over Giovanni and led the pony into the patch of thick magnolia trees that grew nearby. Here they waited under the dense, evergreen leaves while evening fell.

After dark, they led the pony northward until they reached a narrow plank bridge spanning the Arnona. They muffled the pony's hooves in cloth and led it across. Giovanni could hear the river's heavy flow sliding beneath the planking. The smell of the water, snowy and thin, mingled with the sweat and leather smell of the foxy man and the warm smell of the pony. On the far shore, the men left the road and plunged into the thick woods that lined the Arnona's northern shoreline and swept upward unbroken to the mountains. All night, they headed steadily northward toward Genovera, striding confidently through the dark forest although they followed no path and saw no other person. They traveled without speaking, the only sounds the scuff of boots in fallen leaves, the mumbling grunts of wombos, the hoot of a gufo.

Giovanni's tired body was jostled and shaken. The ropes chafed his wrists and ankles, and the gag bit off the circulation in his cheeks. The night seemed endless—a shadowy, impossible nightmare from which he'd surely awaken to find himself in his hammock on board the gunship—but his mind shied away from what might await him at dawn. He wondered if he was being taken to the sorcerer, Lord Maldici, and what the lord wanted. I will speak nothing about Vita, Giovanni vowed to himself. Nothing. It was said that once a prisoner was taken inside the stone walls of Lord Maldici's fortress, he was never seen again. Giovanni wondered whether even words would seep through those heavy walls to reach his parents, so that they would know what had happened to him and why he'd never come home.

CHAPTER EIGHTEEN

MARINA LIFTED THE GOLDEN ARMS from their pail that rested in the bottom of her boat. The water in the pail sloshed gently to and fro as the boat rocked in the slow swell. There were no stars and no moon tonight, for felt-like gray clouds had covered the sky all evening, and Marina stared toward the mainland, trying to see the dark shoulders of the mountains three miles away. At their foot, the lights of village harbors were pinpricks of brightness. The villages themselves lay in darkness, for it was three hours before dawn, and the villagers were all asleep.

Holding a Golden Arm in each hand, Marina straightened and balanced herself in the boat. Cool salt water ran down her arms from the starfish's horny bodies, and their arms waved lethargically. I am going to succeed in this spell, Marina thought. *I must.* She imagined the look of pleasure on her mother's face when she arrived home in the morning and proclaimed her victory. Throwing her head back, she began to chant the spell for the Bright Cross. Sometimes in the past she had forgotten the words, or faltered over their complicated pronunciations, but tonight she spoke every one flawlessly. Then she flung the two starfish upward. For a fraction of time, as they reached the tip of the boat's mast, they wavered and seemed to hang, shaking, in the air. This was the moment when, in the past, they had fallen back into her outstretched hands. Marina watched them intently, and saw how their waving arms glowed a pale golden in the light of the lantern that she'd tied to the mast. Then, suddenly, the starfish shot upward, higher and higher, dwindling to specks that began to gleam with a bright golden light of their own. Marina curled her fingers into her palms in fierce hope. Sometimes, they had failed to glow and had simply disappeared into the darkness.

Finally, when they were far overhead, the two starfish again hung suspended in the air. A breath of relief escaped from Marina. Everything had happened as it was meant to! She bent to lift two more Golden Arms from the pail but as she did so, the first two fell from the sky, descending lightly and slowly like leaves floating from a tree. Marina clenched her teeth, dropped the two starfish that she held back into the pail, and reached out with a sigh to catch the two that were falling.

For a long time, she stood holding them and trying to summon power into herself from the sea that lapped against the boat hull, from the salty water that ran down her arms. Then she began to chant the spell again, and again hurled the two Golden Arms into the sky. This time, they remained there, suspended. Marina threw another two up to join them. Twice more she repeated this until all eight Golden Arms glittered above her against the thick dark clouds. Barely daring to breath, Marina began to chant again in the ancient tongue of the sea witches, her neck craned back to watch what would happen next. The Golden Arms began to move in the sky, forming a pattern, forming the Bright Cross—that constellation of stars that points toward the North Star and that is the most important constellation for mariners to learn, so that they can navigate at sea in the night. Marina held her breath as the Bright Cross formed above her. The spell was working! She had succeeded and her mother would be proud of her!

Then Marina let out an exclamation of disbelief.

The Bright Cross was pointing in the wrong direction, toward the mainland. And the brightest, largest starfish of all, the one that represented the North Star, hung not in the north but over Vita's village. Marina groaned and spoke the words to summon the starfish from the sky into her outstretched arms. She placed them gently in the pail and leaned her head on the gunwale, resting. For a long time she listened to the sea slapping the curved wooden planks of her boat and to the wood talking back in its creaky old voice. There was no wind tonight. Marina could taste the still air, salty and with a smell like damp sand and wet rock and seaweed, on her lips. It was low tide; the shorelines of the archipelago and the mainland were exposed.

Finally, Marina rose to her feet. Again she lifted the Golden Arms from their pail and raised them overhead. She closed her eyes and imagined herself a part of the tide slipping away from the rocks, its lazy power filling her body, its depths taking her in.

"Power of the deep water, run through me!" she cried. "Power of the four winds, rush to me! Power of wave, touch me! Power of outgoing tide, pour into me!"

And finally she felt it: the tingle of magic moving through her, its heat gathering in her chest, the faint electric crackle as it ran down her arms. With one swift motion, she flung the two Golden Arms upward and, without hesitation, they flew past the lantern on the mast and soared high overhead, glittering brightly. Again and again Marina hurled the starfish into the air until all eight of them shone above her. Again, she held her breath as they moved to form the Bright Cross. Again, she stared in sinking disbelief as they pointed toward Vita's village.

Warmth and power drained from her chest, leaving her shaking with fatigue. Cold sweat beaded between her shoulder blades and her arms ached as she held them out to catch the starfish when she called them down from the sky. When they were all restored to the pail, Marina once again slumped against the boat's gunwale and sank into chill exhaustion. For a while she dozed while the boat rocked soothingly, but she awoke with a start. There was a whisper of breeze on her cheek and soon dawn would come. Still, she had failed to master the spell. What would happen, she wondered, if she performed it closer to the village? Would the pattern then point somewhere else, perhaps to the north as it should? She staggered to her feet, her legs stiff as boards, and fumbled with the heavy sailcloth as she prepared to run it up the mast. Then, as it luffed and flapped in the breeze, she bent her back over the oars and began to row toward the mainland. The oarlocks groaned in soft rhythm in the dark.

Off the end of the harbor wall, a shadowy finger in the thinning darkness, Marina threw out an anchor. The mountains loomed over her, one shade darker than the sky, and over their rolling crest a trickle of pale light eddied into the night. Dawn was an hour away. Marina steadied herself in the boat, with the breeze licking her right cheek and the smell of the shoreline, stronger now than it had been in the Golfo, filling her senses. She thought again of the falling tide, its currents eddying around rock. With all her might, she thought of water until she felt a part of it, as though her body were a current, until her arms seemed to stretch long and green and cradle rocks, until her body seemed to be slipping seaward in the darkness.

"Power of the ocean, rush to me!" she cried in the ancient tongue. "Power of salt, lift me up! Power of incoming tide, surge through me! Power of the four winds, gather in me!" She felt herself grow tall in the boat, felt darkness and salty air and water mingling with her blood, rushing into her muscles. She flung back her head and chanted the spell for the Bright Cross, the words fierce and fluid on her tongue, her mouth hot with their magic. Then she flung the eight starfish into the sky one last time.

They hung suspended against the mountains. They trembled, shifted positions. Marina waited with held breath. Now the brightest one, that represented the North Star, moved into place—and Marina, straining her eyes into the murky air, stared at it dumbfounded. It was hanging over the dark fold of the Keeper's valley.

"That isn't North!" Marina wailed despairingly. After all her efforts, she had failed. Even as she stared at them, the Golden Arms began to fade in the light of dawn that spilled, pale yellow, over the mountains.

Her teeth chattered as the magic's power drained from her. Her stiff fingers fumbled, catching the starfish as they fell. She dropped them into the pail where they lay still, their horny bodies dull. Then she crouched in the bottom of the boat and let the smells of the land wash over her: the sweet smoke of an early cooking fire, the dark waxy smell of leaves on the evergreen magnolia trees, the musky warmth of goats and jennets. A familiar ache of longing filled her chest and she imagined herself in the Keeper's valley, where the chyme tree would be ringing softly in the freshening breeze and where the wombo would be falling asleep as the dawn light touched its soft gray fur. Longing shook her thin frame.

"What's the matter, sea witch's daughter?" crooned a soft voice, and Marina glanced up in time to see the coral pink hands of a Mara woman grip the boat's gunwale. The woman's silver-blue eyes glowed like phosphorescence in the pale light, and her pale wet hair hung into the water and floated around her like a filmy curtain. Gold shone at her wrists and throat, against her soft overlapping scales that changed colors as Marina watched.

"I can't do the magic," Marina moaned. "The stars always point to the Keeper's valley instead of to the north."

With one hand, the Mara woman played with the golden beads woven into her hair.

"So, who needs to go north?" she replied flippantly. "Do you have a mirror I might borrow?"

"No, I do not," Marina retorted.

"Just as well, with a face so sour," the woman replied with a silvery laugh. "You look as though you've been eating pickles."

"Oh, go away and leave me alone," Marina complained, laying a hand across her aching forehead, although she should have been used to the teasing of the Mara by now.

They seldom took anything seriously, except their own beauty, and Marina never felt able to match their quick tongues. The Mara woman gave the boat a mischievous shove that made Marina grab a thwart for balance. She watched dismally as the woman glided away through the water, the echo of her mocking laughter washing against the boat like ripples. Her pale head submerged but then broke the surface a few feet farther away.

"Maybe you should follow the stars to the valley, and put a smile on your face," she called. "Have a lovely day, sea witch's daughter!"

Her pale arm waved languidly before she submerged again and, although Marina watched for her, nothing more appeared but a line of bubbles drifting on the surface, and a swirl where she had plunged into the depths.

At last Marina hauled up her anchor and rigged her sail, and slowly her boat tacked away from shore and headed toward the northern tip of the pirati island. Tongues of yellow light flickered across the waves while the clouds, that were parting in the breeze, glowed golden. Scraps of sky, pale blue as last season's eggs, began to show through. Marina stared at it all with bleary eyes as she slumped in exhaustion at the tiller. I tried with everything in me, she thought, with every ounce of my strength. But I couldn't command the magic. I will never be able to. And if I can't command the sea witches' magic, what will I do with my life?

Passing the deep inlet that led to the pirati harbor, Marina noticed that the slender, polished masts of both gunships were tipped with morning sun as they lifted above the harbor wall. Giovanni must have come home again, after the raiding trip he'd told her about. Maybe now she'd meet him some early morning, as he returned from night fishing on the reefs, or maybe he'd sail into her cove some winter's afternoon, asking to warm his hands at the fire that crackled salty blue in the sea witch's house on the point. He'd said that he needed to tell her something about herself and Vita.

Marina climbed from her boat when it ran ashore on the beach below the point. A glance upward showed her that the house was dark against the bright sky, beneath the whispering salt-pine, and Marina guessed that her mother was still in bed, tired from her journey, earlier in the week, to the islands of Cavalli where the sea horses breed. Aimlessly, Marina followed the path that led from the beach around to the base of the rocky point where two seahorses were tethered, just outside the mouth of the cave, with long strands of golden weed wrapped around their tails. As Marina sat down on a rock, the horses turned their long, slender faces toward her and rocked contently in the slack tide. The first sunlight arrowed down through the clear water to lick the horses with brightness. The larger one, belonging to the sea witch, was green with lacy golden patterns. The smaller, younger horse was pale blue, dappled with patterns of lavender so that it floated in the water like a cloudy flower. Marina stared at it dismally. Its tossing head and delicately scooped face filled her with a heavy sensation of despair.

Yesterday, she had turned sixteen—and this horse had been captured by her mother and brought home for her birthday present. It was a beautiful present. But I won't be able to train it, Marina thought now as she stared at the horse. I won't be able to ride it. I'll be as hopeless with the horse as with the Golden Arms, and as I am with all the other things a sea witch should be able to do. I'm sixteen, and I need to know what to do with my life. Am I always going to be an outcast, a misfit? Am I going to end up living alone like the hermit Giuseppe? A tear trickled maddeningly down her thin cheek and she swiped it away with a rough, proud gesture.

Why did the Golden Arms behave like that? she wondered. Why did the Bright Cross point to the Keeper's valley? Was it a mistake or—and here Marina felt as though her mind was fumbling forward through darkness toward someplace new—or had there been a reason for what happened? A reason. Was there some meaning in the pattern? The Bright Cross pointed mariners toward the north when they were lost at sea in the darkness. Yet her own Bright Cross had pointed her toward the Keeper's valley. It's my life I need direction in, Marina thought. It's my life I don't know how to navigate. But what if there was a message for me in the Golden Arms? What if they were sending me to the Keeper's valley?

Wasn't that what the Mara woman had said teasingly as she swam away? *"Maybe you should follow the stars to the valley!"*

Marina remembered the day that she'd laid her fingers on the wombo's foreleg and seen the image of its broken bone in her mind. There must have been magic involved, a magic that she possessed but didn't even know about. She remembered how, all that day, she'd followed Aunt Carmela around the village, and how she'd wondered what would happen when Aunt Carmela grew old and there was no young woman to replace her. Then, who would take care of the planting in the village gardens by moonlight, the protection of the seedlings, the flowering and fruiting of the trees on the terraces, the birthing of goats and jennets in their sheds filled with sweet dry grasses?

A lump filled Marina's throat. I would like to do that, all of it! she thought.

She wondered what Aunt Carmela would say if she arrived on her doorsill and asked to learn her magic. She wondered how she would tell her own mother of her decision. When she was young and lay sick in bed with a fever, the sea witch had spooned fish broth into her mouth. And even before that, when she lay at night in a cradle rocked by wind, the witch had crooned her lullabies of the sea. Marina remembered how her mother had taught her to swim in a rock pool at low tide, when the sun fell warm on their backs and the sea anemones waved their pink tentacles in encouragement, and how her mother had taught her the names of all the fish and the creatures of the sea. How can I leave her? Marina wondered. But—how can I stay, when I can't work the magic, when I'm always lonely, when I long for the Keeper's village?

The sun climbed higher in the sky as the clouds separated, like torn fabric, and their trailing scraps blew eastward on the wind. The incoming tide began to creep up the rocks, slapping and chuckling. The seahorses grazed on floating weed, their translucent fins whirring to hold them in position against the current that ran into the shadows of the cave. Hour after hour, Marina's thoughts darted anxiously through her mind until she felt as though a school of fish whirled there and she felt giddy and weak. Then, a slow certainly began to fill her. She grew warm, and relaxed against the rocks in a slump and drifted into a deep sleep.

When she awoke, the tide was flooding into the cave and the horses were asleep, bobbing like boats at the ends of their weed tethers. Marina leaned over from her rock and stared at her own reflection lifting and falling on the glassy swell. Her face was a pale oval, through which golden weed flowed. Her eyes were not the beautiful silver of her mother's eyes, but green as leaves. Green as Aunt Carmela's eyes. Marina stared at the reflection of her eyes superimposed on the silver flash of a fish, and on the dark blue water that gurgled against the rocks and whipped the golden weed. "Green like leaves," she whispered aloud to herself, and thought of the Keeper's valley as she had seen it in the summer, dancing and overflowing with green leaves, with blossom and singing birds.

"Follow the stars," she whispered.

Reaching out, she ran a hand down the little blue horse's sleek hide. "Goodbye," she told it. Then she balanced over the rocks and around to the beach where her boat lay on the sand and her mother, the sea witch, sat on a blanket woven of dried salt-grass and ate sandwiches of pickled sea cucumber. The witch's eyes flickered over Marina as she sat down on the cool sand.

"Have something to eat," the witch said.

Marina chewed nervously, her heart thumping hard and fast in her chest, then pausing, then galloping on again. She swallowed past the lump in her throat and opened her mouth to speak but it was too dry. She licked her lips.

"Have you been visiting your horse?" her mother asked.

Marina nodded, not trusting herself to speak. But she must speak, must say the words that could not afterward ever be unsaid. She swallowed again.

"Mother," she said at last, "I'm sixteen. In the villages, when the girls are fifteen, they stop going to school and are apprenticed to learn their trade. I should know how to do your magic by now—but I can't. I just can't do it! Last night, the Golden Arms pointed me three times to the Keeper's valley. They wouldn't point north. I am going to the mainland this afternoon, to see if Aunt Carmela will take me as her apprentice."

Marina ran out of breath. She picked nervously at her sandwich, the bread crumbling under her fingers. When she ventured a glance at her mother, the sea witch's face was in profile against the bright, cold blue of the sea. The familiar hook of her nose and the stern, thin line of her mouth filled Marina with sadness.

"I've tried!" Marina cried. "I've really tried to be a sea witch."

Still, her mother didn't speak, only stared to sea with those silver eyes that seemed filled with the liquid lights of sky and water. Her brown, narrow face remained still as tendrils of black hair flickered around it.

"It's my own greed that has caused this," she muttered to herself at last, and the lines on her face seemed to stretch and deepen toward her sharply pointed chin.

"I'm sorry!" Marina cried, and the witch turned to look at her.

"Yes, I am sorry too," she agreed, her voice thin and chill. "I am sorry that we have both failed. And now, Marina, the wind is freshening from the west and you had better let the Golden Arms go, and untie your horse, and fetch the things that you want from your room, and start your trip to the Keeper's valley while the sailing is fair."

"Maybe I shouldn't go. You'll be here alone," Marina faltered.

"Nonsense. I've told you before that witches don't feel lonely. Straighten your back, Marina, and stop crying."

The sea witch stood up, and her skirts swirled around her long legs and her hair tossed like a black cloud snapping with blue sparks. The silver rang at her ankles and her wrists as she strode past Marina and began to climb the path toward the house with her back stiff and straight. Marina stared after her miserably. She wished in that moment that she had never spoken, for now she had cut herself adrift from the one person who had cared for her—and who knew whether Aunt Carmela would take her in? And who could say whether, since Marina couldn't perform the sea magic, she'd be able to perform Aunt Carmela's magic either?

Marina watched until her mother disappeared toward the hammock, and then she stumbled along the path to the sea horses and untied the young one with the blue and lavender hide, but it only circled the older horse anxiously and refused to swim away into the open sea. Leaving it, Marina climbed the path to the house and in her room, where the windows faced out over the Golfo and the wind rattled the panes of glass and the salt-pine scratched against the walls, she pushed her clothes into a bag. Her room swam in her tears, and her hands were wet with wiping them away. She took her silver whelk shell earrings, that her mother had given her for her fifteenth birthday a year ago, from a chest and hooked them through her earlobes. Then she carried her bundle to the beach and dropped it into the bottom of her boat beside the pail. She lifted the Golden Arms from the pail and set them in the water, and watched as they flattened themselves against the rough surfaces of rocks, the tips of their tentacles groping for places to hold onto.

"Mother!" Marina cried. "I'm going now!"

The sea witch came down the path from the hammock slung between salt-pines with her mouth pressed in a tight line that words could not escape through. Marina waited uncertainly, anticipating her mother's flashing anger. But when the witch reached her, she clutched Marina suddenly in a fierce, hard grip. Marina smelled the witch's scent of pine and salt, of wind and sun, and she felt the witch's hard ribs pressed against her own, and the fast, light beat of the witch's heart. Grief shook her, but the witch lifted her chin and stared for a long time into her eyes with her liquid silver gaze. Then she unclasped a silver necklace hung with starfish from her bony throat and fastened it around Marina's neck.

"May they guide you toward your own North Star," she said, and then she pushed Marina toward her boat. "Go," she said gently. "May the winds speed you, and the waves carry you. May the sun shine between your shoulders, and the stars greet you."

Marina climbed into her boat and dug the oars into the pellucid water that shimmered over the sandy floor of the cove. The sail flapped up the mast and then filled with wind and winter sun, like a flower opening. When Marina glanced back at the beach, it was empty. She told herself that she didn't care, and turned with a proud toss of her dark hair to face the water, where white horses ran on the waves. She angled her bows toward the jumble of village roofs beneath the soft, wintry blue and brown of the mountains.

When she was halfway across the Golfo, her mother appeared, riding on her green horse with the young horse that Marina had set free gamboling along beside her. The witch waved to Marina and, with a sudden laugh of delight, Marina waved back. The witch kept pace with the boat until Marina dropped her sail outside the village harbor, and then she called across the water, over the horse's waving green mane.

"Marina! Don't ever take what isn't yours! Don't let greed into your heart!"

The witch waved goodbye abruptly with a thin arm and turned the horse's head toward the sea. "Goodbye!" she cried over the choppy water.

"Goodbye!" Marina called back and watched from her rocking boat until the two horses, and the witch's flying cape, disappeared into tossing light and white spray. What strange advice her mother had given her! What had brought greed to her mind? Was she warning Marina that to long for the Keeper's valley was a kind of greed? And what had she meant when she said that her own greed had caused all this to happen?

With a puzzled frown, Marina rowed into the harbor and tied up to a rusty ring in the wall. She climbed the weed-hung steps and paced along the flat, golden stones where wine casks and empty fish crates lay stacked. In the alleys between houses, the wind snatched at Marina's blue dress, swirling its patterns of fish around her knees, and she felt the seashell earrings swing in her ears. If I apprentice here, she thought, the villagers will accept me. I won't be an outcast anymore, but the girl who helps Aunt Carmela. I will belong to this place, to these alleys and these families, as she does.

This hope filled Marina with a fluttering warmth.

She went steadily up the fifty steps to the lavender colored gate, and clenched her teeth around her courage to prevent it from slipping down into the soles of her feet. This is my only hope, she thought, as she went down the valley between the lacey bare branches of the apricot and mandolo trees. The stream seemed to welcome her with its liquid chuckling, and a drift of winter crocus gleamed bright yellow on its banks. Marina laid her hands flat against the trunk of the chyme tree and closed her eyes, listening until the ringing of the hard, thin leaves seemed to fill her whole body with light.

I must be brave, she thought. I must believe that this is the right thing to do.

She wondered if Vita was at home; she hadn't seen the Keeper since the night that they had rowed together to the pirati village and fetched the Keeper's book from Giovanni's mother. Marina assumed that, from the translated verses on the book's ancient pages, Vita had found out what she must do to heal the

Corno d'Oro, for nothing had changed in the world as far as Marina could tell. The balance must have been saved, as it trembled on the autumnal equinox, for the winter seemed as winter always did, laced with sudden squalls of rain, softened with mist in which the salt-pines dripped moisture into the hushed sea.

Marina raised one hand and touched the warmth of the silver necklace that her mother had given her, and then she crossed the courtyard and knocked three times on Aunt Carmela's closed kitchen door with her back proudly straight and her chin lifted and her mouth pressed in a firm line.

CHAPTER NINETEEN

THE KITCHEN DOOR SWUNG INWARD and Aunt Carmela's kind face appeared in the widening crack. "Marina!" she cried. "Come in!" and the lines weathered in her cheeks chased each other upward in pleasure. Marina felt a sudden happiness; surely it was a good omen that Aunt Carmela seemed delighted to see her. Besides, there were few people who would swing their doors wide for the sea witch's daughter or who would draw her inside with a warm grasp on her wrist.

Marina crossed the tiles and stood by the fireplace where olive wood crackled comfortingly with yellow and blue flames, and where an iron pot of rabbit stew hung suspended and filled the kitchen with the rich smell of gravy and sweet tomatoes. Marina's mouth watered and she swallowed hard, gripping her hands together with anxiety.

I won't beg to be her apprentice, she thought. I'll ask with dignity.

She breathed deeply, drawing the smells of herbs and lavender and garlic into her lungs, as she looked around the kitchen.

Copper pots, polished to a bright glow, hung from a rack on one wall and a yellow rug brightened the tiled floor. On the table, its wood the color of old honey, a pot held a bunch of dried, yellow mandolo blossoms. Bundles of herbs, smoked cheeses in red wax, and strings of peppery sausages hung from the rafter beams, and in a blue bowl set by the edge of the fire, bread dough rose up smooth and pale as a full moon and released its yeasty odor. The watery glass in the window held the rippled silhouette of the chyme tree, and its soft ringing seeped beneath the thick door.

The stairwell leading from the kitchen was filled with shadow but Marina remembered how it led up to Vita's room, where she had spent one night listening to the sea hush into the harbor, behind the lavender colored shutters. She remembered too how the sheets had smelled of lavender, and how the mattress stuffed with goose feathers had been softer than her mattress at home that was filled with coarse salt-grass.

As Marina stared around, it seemed to her that everything was perfect. A sense of peace crept over her. She felt that, after all, she would be happy to put aside her pride and beg on her knees to become an apprentice. If I could stay here, she thought, I would never want to leave. I must ask, now. She opened her mouth to speak but Aunt Carmela moved toward her and clasped her hands in her own smooth, worn fingers.

"You've come with news of Vita?" she asked eagerly, and something sank cold and disappointed in Marina. Aunt Carmela only wants my news, she thought. Not my company. Marina's lips began to curl proudly, but then she saw the love and longing that shone on Aunt Carmela's face and in her green eyes, and she swallowed her own pride down into her stomach and uncurled her lips.

"Vita?" she asked. "Isn't she here?'

Aunt Carmela swung away and stared into the fire, her face suddenly still. "Vita left many weeks ago, with Ronaldo," she muttered. "After you were here last time, at the autumnal equinox,

Vita healed the Corno d'Oro. Then she stayed home until after the winter solstice, but Ronaldo sent messages. At last he came himself, and she left me a note on the kitchen table and went back to the city with him, riding the beetleman's maggrazi. I'm sick with worry."

"Why?" Marina asked, sinking into the bright, soft cushion on the wooden chair that stood behind her.

"I hear things from tale spinners and puppeteers," Aunt Carmela said. "I hear news of that cruel Lord Maldici, ensconced in his great fortress above Genovera. He is growing ever more evil; his assassini pillage the countryside more ferociously every day; he levies taxes that cripple us. His army swells larger by the hour, his kennels are breeding litter after litter of brutti. His smithies are ringing with hammer upon steel as they forge swords and chariot wheels. Some say..." and here the aunt's voice sank to a harsh whisper, "some say that he is practicing the dark arts, and becoming a sorcerer to equal Lord Morte, who released greed into the land of Verde and upset the balance of the world by stealing away the Corno d'Oro by treachery. Vita should not be near this man! She should be here, where we are loyal to her. And the spring equinox approaches, the winter crocus are flowering by the stream. She must return to work her magic, to keep the Corno d'Oro safe."

Marina watched helplessly as Aunt Carmela wrung her fingers, reddened with work, in her coarse apron. Marina wished that she could bring back to the aunt's face a delighted smile. If I could help her, Marina thought with sudden hopefulness, then surely she would agree to apprentice me. But how can I help?

Like a hard shove in her mind, came the thought that she could offer to journey to Genovera and find Vita, warn her of the danger, and bring her home. She sat very still and stared at the red tiles beneath her bare toes, shocked to the center of her being by such a thought. I have never been away from the pirati archipelago, she thought. And why should I care about Vita, who has never cared about me? She doesn't deserve my help! She hasn't even thanked me for getting her precious book translated by Giuseppe. She's an arrogant cuttlefish, with her silver hair and her moony eyes! I won't help her!

Marina felt her lips beginning to curl scornfully again. She glanced up from the floor as Aunt Carmela bent to the iron pot suspended over the fire and stirred the rabbit stew with a long-handled ladle. Going to a cupboard, she lifted out a blue bowl and spooned stew into it. "Come and eat, Marina," she said kindly. "You look cold."

As Marina pulled her chair toward the table, the aunt stooped again to the fire and poked the flames to fresh life, then blew on them with a leather bellows so that they shot up the chimney with a shower of sparks. Heat crept across the tiles and licked Marina's bare ankles, and the hot steam curling from the stew tickled her nose. Gratefully, she spooned it into her mouth while Aunt Carmela scooped the bread dough onto the table nearby and punched it down, then began kneading it. Marina watched how easily her hands worked, how smoothly the dough rose and fell around her shiny knuckles. She stared at Aunt Carmela's intent face, its green eyes surrounded by laughter lines and its thin mouth ready to smile, and a feeling like love swept through her.

She decided not to think about Vita, but about Aunt Carmela instead, and how to help her. She swallowed a chunk of rabbit and sweet pepper and then swallowed bravely a second time to make room in her tight throat for her heavy words.

"Aunt Carmela," she said. "I could go to the city and bring Vita home. If I found her."

The aunt's eyes widened with amazement and she paused in her kneading. "But Marina! You've never been so far!"

"I can sail north," Marina said. "I can go up the delta. No one will know me. There's no danger to me."

Aunt Carmela's forehead creased thoughtfully and she began to knead again in silence, slapping the dough with the flats of her palms while Marina scraped the last stew from the blue bowl.

"Perhaps Giovanni could take you north," she said at last. "I would be happier if you weren't alone."

"Yes," Marina agreed, wondering why she hadn't thought of this herself. "I'll sail over to the island and ask him."

"Oh, I would be so happy if the two of you went to find Vita!" Aunt Carmela cried and, looking into her shining face, Marina knew that she would not regret her offer. It was worth it, whatever it might cost her, to see the aunt's face soften with relief.

Later, when Marina walked down the alleys to the harbor, between the doorways of the village houses and their shutters rattling in the breeze and past the sundial and the village well, Aunt Carmela went with her. They carried woven baskets containing food for Marina: rabbit stew in a casserole with the lid tied down with string, dried figs, wizened apples, whole waxed cheeses and two long strings of sausage, fresh bread wrapped in cotton, small puddings of mandolo nuts and honey, almonds, grape juice in wineskins. Aunt Carmela helped to load it all into Marina's boat, and then she gripped Marina in a hug as bony and fierce as the one Marina's own mother had given her that morning when they said goodbye.

Marina jumped in and Aunt Carmela cast her off, and the boat swept quickly out past the end of the harbor wall on the falling tide. The light from the setting sun broke into splinters of orange and apricot around the bows as they sliced through the waves, and against the sun's glowing disk the tiny silhouettes of birds moved like broken stitches pulled through bright fabric. It was the pelicans, migrating north along the tail of winter. Aunt Carmela was right, Marina thought, spring will soon be here. She pulled on a rope, tightening the sail, and angled her bows close to the cold wind. Then she hunched down in the soft woven shawl that Aunt Carmela had given her, and concentrated on reaching the pirati inlet before the sun set.

The moon was rising over the mountains as she panted up the street to Giovanni's house, hoping that the shawl would disguise her from the shadowy pirati still moving around outside. She thumped hard on the door with the side of her fist and, after a pause, it was opened by a towering, broad shouldered man with a black curling beard and deep blue eyes. A gold ring flashed in his ear and his strong teeth shone in the dusk when he spoke. "What do you want, sea witch's daughter?"

Marina drew herself proudly tall and stared at Giovanni's father haughtily.

"I need to speak to Giovanni immediately," she said.

The pirati frowned before bursting into a great mocking laugh that rolled around in his chest and echoed in his throat and rang out into the cold evening wind. "Immediately!" he said. "Of course, princess!"

Marina bit her lip. She should have known better than to be haughty, but she was nervous. "Please? It's important," she pleaded.

The pirati's face became stern and his laughter died. His blue eyes deepened until they seemed black and his voice sank to a sorrowful rumble. "Giovanni has disappeared. He went ashore weeks ago with some of our men, to trade in Genovera. One night, at an inn called The Condor's Wing, he disappeared while the men were watching a fight. The men thought he had run away to come home, but he has never arrived. No one knows where he is although our men have looked for him in Genovera and at sea. I myself am leaving in the morning to search for him in the mountains, in case he was trying to reach home by land and danger overtook him. You cannot speak with Giovanni."

And the pirati began to swing the door shut. Swiftly, Marina stuck her narrow foot into the crack to prevent this from happening. "Where is this inn?" she cried.

The pirati opened the door wider and stared at her with arms folded over his barrel chest, the red bandana at his throat glowing in the light of a lamp that had been lit across the street. "It's one day's journey from Genovera. Along the River Arnona. If you travel up from the delta, you come to it."

"I'm going north to the delta," Marina said. "I'll look for him."

The pirati's black eyes sparked with surprise. "You? Alone?"

Marina straightened her back and jutted out her chin. "I am quite capable," she said, her voice haughty again and, for a moment, a smile twitched in the man's curling beard.

"You had better come in for the night, sea witch's daughter. Your boat is too small for deep water and you'll have to follow the shoreline. You can't see reefs and rocks in the dark. You'll have to sail in the morning. Come in." And he reached out to where Marina hesitated uneasily, for she had never been inside a pirati home before, and grasped her arm in a warm hand that smelled of tar and salt, and pulled her into the light of a snapping fire. Then he took a stick from the pile of kindling behind the door and moved to the ashes at the edge of the sandy hearth. "I'm going to show you something," he said. "But you must swear to me that you'll keep it secret."

Marina laid her hand over her heart. "I swear by the power of salt and wave and the four winds, and by the blood of my grandmothers," she whispered solemnly.

The man's eyes bored into her, as if they were drilling holes into her skull to look at her thoughts, and then he gave a grunt of satisfaction and stooped to the ashes with his huge, shaggy shadow leaping across the wall. "Look," he said. "This is the delta. Here is the main outflow of the River Arnona, and these are smaller channels. Here, you can find anchorage. Walk here, following the purple grasses. Watch for quicksand. Here, there is a shack on stilts. Knock twice, wait for two breaths, knock three times. The password is 'mizzen sail.' Ask for someone to shelter you, give you food, take you to The Condor's Wing. Say that I sent you."

Marina nodded as Giovanni's father swept the hearth clean again.

She slept that night in a bed of salt-grass and in the dawn, Giovanni's mother awoke her and fed her a breakfast of fried fish and flat bread. Then Marina ran down to the harbor, where the masts of the gunships stuck up into the mist, and sailed out of the inlet to cross the oily swells of the Golfo and creep north along the shoreline. The mist was like goats' wool draped across her eyes as she peered anxiously over her bows. She traveled slowly, for there was a mere breath of wind that played with her sail, and kept close to the shoreline and waited for the sun to burn the air clear. Occasionally, in the gloom overhead, she heard the whisper of beating wings and the mournful laughter of the pelicans. The mist lifted around noon, the sun already high.

All day Marina sailed north and anchored for the night in a sheltered cove where she slept huddled in her new shawl in the bottom of the boat. The next morning, she awoke stiff and sore to find a south wind blowing in a warm stream that lifted the pelicans high overhead like scattered blossoms from the apricot trees that soon, in a another month, would be flowering. Once Marina had the sail raised, the boat sprang forward and for three days, while the wind held, she rushed north to the delta, holding the tiller steady for hour after hour while her eyes, looking forward over the pointed upsweep of the bows, scanned the water for reefs and judged the tautness of her sail. Once the dolphins spent an hour with her, laughing in her bow wave, and once she waved to Mara people sunning themselves on a rock.

The closer that Marina came to the delta's windswept miles of grass and sandy channels, the stronger grew the sense of foreboding that had settled like a chill lump in her chest. Its coldness seemed to seep into her bones, and her fingers grew white at the tiller. Who knew what dark powers might be stirring in Genovera? Where was Vita and how would Marina find her—and how would she convince Vita to come home when they could barely talk to one another without Marina's crab shell of pride stiffening over her? I must keep my temper, Marina admonished herself. It would have been easier if Giovanni could have come with me. I must remember that I'm doing this for Aunt Carmela.

She worried about Giovanni too, and goose bumps crept over

her at the thought that any trouble might have befallen him, with his flashing grin and his bright eyes and his kind, steady voice. He is the only pirati who treated me with respect, she thought. I wish he could be my friend. I must look for him everywhere I go. I must find him if he's there. If I find him, I'll make sure that we become friends. But I don't know how I'm going to accomplish any of this.

On the afternoon of the third day, Marina dropped anchor in the channel that Giovanni's father had drawn for her in the ashes. She tied her bundles of food and clothes onto her back and crept through the treacherous marshes of the delta, following the purple grasses that flowed like a rivulet of water in the salt-grass and the first, early flowers of the sea holly. Breathlessly she picked her way around the edge of dark pools that the tide never cleaned, past the whitened bones of fish and dead birds, past the sucking tremble of the quicksand. At the shack, she knocked twice, waited for two breaths, knocked three times. Her heart hammered in her chest.

With her back stiff as a poker, she glared proudly at the closed door. "Who comes here?" demanded a ringing voice behind it, and "mizzen sail" she replied, her voice high and cold as the wind whipped her skirt against her trembling knees and swept her dark hair across her face. The door opened a crack, and an arm pulled her in with a hard, swift yank to a shadowy room where high tides surged beneath the cracks in the floor. Six pairs of pirati eyes stared at her, fierce over their brown hooked noses and gleaming teeth, but she returned their stares despite the cutlasses that were raised in their clenched fists. "Put your weapons away," she said. "I'm searching for Giovanni. His father sent me."

The men relaxed, lowering their cutlasses.

"It was at The Condor's Wing—"

"I think he was homesick—"

"He was very quiet. Must've run home to his mother and—"

"We'll take you and show you—"

"Stupid reef fish, everyone has to look for him now, waste of time over a boy's prank—"

Marina calmly removed her shawl, although her legs were still shaking, and sat down by the fire on a worn stool with three legs. "I'm starving," she interrupted the men's boisterous voices. "Do you have food here?"

They stopped talking abruptly and one of them laughed in an admiring kind of way that made Marina flush. Two of the pirati began to break gulls' eggs into a pan and fry them while a third gutted a fish. The other men lounged beside the fire and asked questions about Marina's boat and her journey north.

The following morning, two of the shore party headed up the river Arnona in their disguise as traders and Marina went with them, leading a creamy jennet with horns as brown as toffee. Marina loved the way that its soft nose bobbed along close to her hip, and how its rough mane hung over its shoulders. She fed it apple cores and sang along with the men as they walked inland, up the wide flat valley between the northern mountains and the inland plain.

Marina had never seen so many people in her life; she gawked at nobili chariots driven by impatient men in wool cloaks, who shouted to clear the road ahead of themselves. Barges laden with trading goods swept past on the river's current with men guarding the loads, and other traders led long lines of jennets roped together and carrying sacks of wheat from Verde and salt from Terre on their backs. Foot soldiers tramped past, their faces grim and bearded, while bruttis snarled at their feet. The closer they approached to Genovera, the more astonished Marina was with everything she saw, and the colder and darker the fear grew in her chest.

At The Condor's Wing, she questioned everyone she met but no one had seen a boy who looked like Giovanni and no one would admit to being there on the night that he disappeared. When she tried to talk to the innkeeper, he said he was too busy for chatter, and began slamming glasses down so hard on tables that Marina was afraid they would shatter. When she persisted with her questions, he roared that he didn't know what she was talking about. "Get off and leave me alone! Too much nonsense!" he roared, spittle meshed in his beard, his eyes darting nervously from side to side.

"I think he knows something," Marina told the pirati men. "But he won't tell."

The men's expressions were bleak. "There is much that happens in this part of the world that may not be spoken of," one said.

"We must travel onward to the city," the other added, and with a heavy heart Marina untied the jennet from beneath a tree and followed the men's rolling strides. At the edge of the city, on the bridge over the Arnona, they passed a strange company of puppeteers, who walked beneath their huge swaying puppets. Marina gazed in astonishment at the grins and scowls molded on their plaster faces, their waving wooden arms and trailing costumes. At the head of the puppeteers' procession came a plump, bald man with three chins hanging beneath a broad, serene face. Around his head circled green and yellow beetles, tied to a silver button on his striped vest by thread-like harnesses.

"Who is he?" Marina whispered to the pirati men.

"They call him the beetleman," one replied. "He walks all over Verde with his puppeteers, putting on shows."

The last of the puppets swayed past, its cleverly hinged arms flapping as though waving at Marina, and she followed the pirati men down the slope off the arched bridge and into Genovera.

Marina craned her neck and stared up and up to where, above the thousand tiled rooftops and the slender towers of palazzi, the fortress of Lord Maldici glowed pale and stark in the last sunlight, against the dark shoulder of the mountain. Battlement upon battlement it rose, pierced with towers and hung with balconies; half palazzo, half fortress; its thick walls studded with the slits of windows and with heavy black doors where silver condors spread their wings and glittered cold and bright in the light of the setting sun.

Marina shivered and pulled her shawl tighter around her throat, then plunged after the pirati men into a maze of narrow alleys where dogs barked and smoke from evening fires hung in a blue haze, where jennets' hooves clattered and men shouted and children ran past in ragged packs. Marina longed for the stillness of the Keeper's valley, for the chyme tree's soft ringing and the warm hand of Aunt Carmela on her shoulder. Her legs dragged tiredly and the jennet's nose hung low.

"Where are we going?" she asked.

"We'll take you to an old widow woman. You can stay with her," one of the pirati replied. "We have business elsewhere in the city." Presently Marina found herself bundled in her shawl and lying on a thin, lumpy mattress on the floor of a small room near the banks of the Arnona. She fell asleep listening to wheels rattle past from the docks, where barges unloaded, and to the crooning of pigeons.

The following morning, and for a week afterward, Marina haunted the alleys and streets, the board avenues and the crowded market squares of Genovera. At first she felt like a tiny piece of flotsam awash in a high tide of noise and motion. So many people swirled around her, and so much activity and noise filled the streets! Her eyes felt stretched wide, trying to see everything and her feet, inside the soft leather shoes that Aunt Carmela had given her, grew bruised from tramping miles of hard cobblestones. Gradually, she became used to the pealing bells that sent the flocks of pigeons wheeling upward like scraps of parchment, and used to the shouts of stall holders promoting their wares. Everywhere that she went, she asked about Vita and Giovanni, but without success. Finally, at the end of the week, she stopped to speak to a plump woman selling bunches of flowering magnolia, the blossoms creamy and thick as jennet's ears but smooth as wax. Their heavy scent wafted around Marina.

"I'm looking for a girl, about my age," Marina said. "She has silver hair and lavender eyes. She's with a nobili boy called Ronaldo."

"Do I look like a person who would know nobili by name?" the flower seller joked, her round bright cheeks creasing into wrinkles and a gap showing in the front of her mouth where a tooth had rotted and been pulled. "If you're looking for nobili," she continued after her laughter had subsided to a wheeze, "you'd best visit the dressmakers'shops, girl. The dressmakers know all the young nobili ladies. The most famous is Mistress Jacquardi who has a shop a mile from here, on Strada of Flowers. Cross this square, take that street there on your right. Follow it across the next square, then take a left and you'll come to the Strada."

Marina thanked the woman and began to walk in the direction in which she'd pointed. She was halfway across the second spacious, cobbled square lined with myrtle and bay trees when she caught a flash of bright red hair in the crowd of shoppers. She stood on her tiptoes and craned her neck. The girl with red hair was turning away from a jeweler's stall, her smooth pale face in profile to Marina. A memory flashed into Marina's mind: herself, standing in the Keeper's valley and clutching the Keeper's book that Giuseppe the hermit had translated. She was trying to take the book to Vita, but barring her way down the path was a girl with brilliant red hair, a contemptuous expression on her pale face, and a husky, condescending voice. The girl had said that she was Vita's best friend but later, Giovanni had said she was a maid. Her name? Marina struggled to remember it as she stood on tiptoe, straining to keep the red headed girl in the square in view.

"Rosa!" Marina shouted. "Rosa!" But her voice was drowned out in the rattle of a chariot's spinning wheels and the clatter of hooves as a nobili woman swept past, drawn by two red horses with foam-flecked mouths. Marina jumped back just in time, and then began to push her way through the crowds in the direction in which Rosa had been walking. Once more, Marina caught a glimpse of bright hair and then Rosa seemed to disappear. Glaring around in frustration, Marina backed against a wall, into thin shadow, and scanned the square. There—behind the myrtle trees, surely that was Rosa hurrying up an alley with a basket over her arm? She had drawn a scarf over her bright hair but Vita recognized her pale blue skirt and her graceful way of walking. She hurried after the girl, not calling now but saving her breath for running.

Entering the alleyway, she started up its slope. Rosa was already out of sight around the corner of a wall with green shutters at the windows. Marina dashed up three flights of steps and then looked around in dismay. The alley had split into two and in both directions grew even more narrow and steep, to disappear around sharp corners of ochre colored plaster. Marina hurried first up the right hand set of steps, their centers worn into smooth hollows over time, but Rosa was not in sight around the sharp corner of the wall. Muttering, Marina flew back down, scrambled up the left-hand flight of steps and sprinted up the alley. As she rounded the corner this time, she glimpsed a flash of pale blue as Rosa disappeared around another corner ahead.

Marina trotted on, panting, and burst out suddenly into a square lined with shops and cafes, whose bright awnings cast rectangles of shade and by whose doors orange and apricot trees, growing in tubs, held their spring blossoms in tiny, tight buds. Signs hung overhead: a black boot marking the shop of a cobbler, a green melon above the shop of a fruit seller, a pig creaking to and fro above the sandy floor of a butcher's where dead rabbits hung by their feet. Rosa was not in sight.

"Cuttlefish!" Marina grumbled in frustration. A structure at the far end of the square caught her eye; it appeared to be a shrine for Luna, the moon goddess. Marina wandered toward it, feeling tired and disheartened. The shrine was not a small, plain stone structure of the kind that the villagers left offerings at, but an ornate building with three tall walls covered in tiny ceramic tiles of lavender and gold. Inside the shrine, a slender statue of Luna, carved in white marble, stood surrounded by carvings of sickle moons and rayed suns. The altar, a slab of marble veined with lavender colored patterns, was bare, and as Marina entered the shrine she noticed how the ceramic tiles on the walls were chipped and dusty, how dead leaves had drifted inside to lie in piles along the edges of the floor, and how Luna herself was missing a finger from one slender, carved hand. People had scrawled words across the base of the altar in red paint: Nino was here, Marina read. Antonio loves Julia. Brutti rule! Death to Verona!

A wave of homesickness washed over Marina and she leaned against the altar and rested her face against the hard, cold marble folds of Luna's gown. She thought about the shrine at the head of the Keeper's valley, by the lavender colored gate, and of how the stone statue there was kept clean and polished, and of how the villagers laid their offerings of fruit and blossoms with humble gratitude at Luna's feet, and leaned forward to kiss her smooth brow encircled with a crown of stars.

I'm wasting time, Marina thought. A whole week in this city, where all everyone thinks about is profit and loss, selling and buying, impressing other people with their name and their chariots, their palazzi and their parties. I haven't found Vita, or Giovanni. At night, the torches flare along the battlements of Lord Maldici's fortress, and by day the condors spread wings glittering silver with malice. The city swirls with rumors of war, and the army marches endlessly to and fro on the far banks of the River Arnona with a dull throb of feet and the clash of steel. No one here cares anymore about Luna the moon goddess, or about the greed that is upsetting the balance of the world.

Her stomach rumbled with hunger. The food that Aunt Carmela had packed for her was finished, and she was hoarding the few coins that clinked in her pocket, trying to make them last for as many days as possible. Her forehead was growing numb, pressed against the marble. She moved around to the back of the shrine and sat down on the grubby tiles, leaning her back against the statue's base and screened, by the block of the altar, from the square outside. It was very quiet there, and Marina thought that if she could just rest for a few minutes, she'd feel braver again and ready to continue her search.

There was a sudden flicker of movement as a tiny lizard ran across the floor, and then a rustle of sound as someone entered the shrine. Marina held very still in her hiding place and strained her ears. Her mother the sea witch could hear things for miles across water and she had trained Marina from a young age to listen with all her being, to tease and draw out of the air—like threads pulled from a sheet of fabric—only those sounds that she wanted to focus on. For moments there was silence, and then there was a second disturbance of the air as another person entered the shrine.

"Greetings, Princess Maldici," murmured a man's voice reverently.

"What is it?" replied a female voice: a young, husky, haughty voice.

Marina stiffened in shock; she remembered that voice. Rosa? Rosa was here in the shrine, meeting a man who called her Princess Maldici? Marina pressed her back against the cold marble and stilled her breathing into silence.

"Your father asks for the list," the man said humbly.

A soft rustle of cloth and the crisper sound of parchment was followed by a breath of cruel, mocking laughter. "Here's the list—everything Vita wishes for," Rosa said. "The price we pay for her. Take it to Lord Maldici."

"Your father wishes to know about the boy, Ronaldo."

"I'll take care of him, he'll do whatever he's told," Rosa replied. "You are to tell my father that it is time to reveal the beast. Repeat it."

"It is time to reveal the beast," the man repeated.

"Leave," Rosa commanded, and Marina heard the sigh of fabric as the man moved, and the soft slap of his leather soles on the shrine's tiled floor. Then there was a moment's silence, during which the brown lizard poked its head from a drift of withered leaves and stared at Marina with its tiny, glittering black eyes. She held herself as still as the stone statue of Luna, looming at her own rigid back, until a second rustle of sound told her that Rosa too was rising to her feet. She waited until the slap of the girl's shoes had moved out of the shrine and been absorbed into the dull roar of city noise, and then she edged her way across the floor to peer around the altar's sharp corner.

There was Rosa, not hurrying but stopping to peer into the butcher's window and then to squeeze the firm flesh of a melon at the fruit seller's. She paid no attention to the tall man in a long green cape, his face hidden in shadow beneath its hood, who passed silently along the far edge of the square. He disappeared up an alley to the right with a swinging stride, his black leather boots rapping on stones, and Rosa lifted the melon into the woven grass basket that she carried slung over one arm. Money exchanged hands with a bright flash. Marina watched until Rosa too disappeared along the street at the end of the square with her shopping basket, like a maid on an errand, her hood still lifted over her bright red hair.

Danger! Marina's thoughts screamed. *Danger!* Her body hummed with the certainty of this knowledge. If Rosa was Lord Maldici's daughter, what did her involvement in Vita's life mean? What dark plot was wrapping Vita tighter in its coils, what trap was being baited?

Marina rose to her feet, her legs stiff from the hard tiles, and brushed dead leaves from her skirt with shaking fingers. The hunger in her stomach had congealed into a hard lump of dread, and she crossed the square in blind panic and hurried downhill toward the Strada of Flowers and the shop of Mistress Jacquardi, who might possibly know the whereabouts of a girl with silver-gold hair and lavender eyes.

CHAPTER TWENTY

"I CAN'T BELIEVE THIS IS HAPPENING!" Vita exclaimed, her voice soaring high and tight with excitement. Standing at her shoulder in the chariot's swaying basket, Rosa smiled briefly, a mere twitch of her pouting red lips, although for days now she'd been rushing around the palazzo with her hands full of necklaces and ribbons and samples for ball gown fabric.

"We are fortunate to be included in the invitation list for Lord Maldici's banquet. It's a great honor," agreed Ronaldo, and there was an unaccustomed tension in his lazy smile. He stood with his feet braced and his hands splayed on the long supple reins running back into the chariot from the frothing mouths of the tapestry stallions. The crimson, feathered plumes on their harness nodded and swayed in the flaring light of the torches that lined the narrow street. Their hooves clattered in the darkness and the chariot's spinning wheels, with their golden shafts, rang high and bright. Ahead of the chariot, and behind it, swayed other chariots packed with nobili arrayed in their costliest capes of pure angoli wool embroidered with pearls from the islands of

Lontano, with star sapphires from Corali, with amber from Terre, with stitches of pure silk thread. They made a splendid caval-cade as they wound uphill between the torches toward the great black mass of the mountain shoulder and the floating balconies and pale battlements of the Maldici fortress. Streaming light from every window and tower, it seemed to float in the air over-head and be a structure, not of cold stone weighing thousands of tons, but of light and soaring lines, with pillars and bridges and arches hanging magically in the sky where the late winter con-stellations arranged themselves in their cold patterns.

What a way to end my visit to the city, Vita thought. I'll remember this all my life! When I return home next week, on the magrazzi, in plenty of time for the spring equinox, I'll be able to tell Aunt Carmela all about it. Not many people in Verde have been inside the fortress of Lord Maldici!

She clasped her sweating hands together inside a fur muff and felt the bite of the two golden rings that Ronaldo's mother had generously given her. Craning her neck, she stared upward as the chariot swept through the first wall, five feet thick, and under the black lines of the raised portcullis, into the outermost courtyard of the fortress. Light gleamed on the bright steel tips of the guards' spears, on the buttons forming silver lines on their black tunics, on the steel toes of their black leather boots and the silver studs in the collars of the bruttis snarling beside them. Through another gate the chariot swept, and a third. Now lamp-light replaced the flaring tapers of torches, and liveried footmen in black, with silver condors stitched onto their chests, came for-ward to help the guests alight. Grooms sprang nimbly to the horses' heads and led them away. Breathless with excitement, Vita was swept forward through the high arched doorway into a glitter of mirrors and chandeliers, the shimmer of women's bright gowns, the brilliant painted scenes of wall frescoes. High, high overhead, the room rose into a vaulted dome lacquered with pure sheet gold, and around the walls stood lines of gleam-ing statues also covered in beaten gold.

"I'm going to join the maids," Rosa whispered. "Have fun!" and she turned away and was swallowed up in the crowd. Vita stared around uncertainly, awed by the splendor of her surroundings.

"Take my arm," Ronaldo offered, holding out a sleeve crusted with woven designs of purple pomegranates, and gratefully Vita slipped her own trembling arm through it. The line of arriving nobili pressed them forward until they reached the doorway to the banqueting hall where six bodyguards, in black and silver uniforms, barred their progress and Vita watched as the nobili men prostrated themselves in bows so low that their noses almost touched the velvet shoes of the man who stood before them in the doorway. He was clad in black velvet and draped with the silver fur of the mountain leopard, the rarest and costliest of all furs. The women curtsied to the marble floor, sinking into the pooled drapery of their gowns.

"It's Lord Maldici," whispered Ronaldo urgently, sounding nervous. "Don't stare."

Vita looked down, concentrating on the rustling folds of her taffeta dress with its decoration of looped gold beads, and at her feet advancing over the marble tiles beneath the hem of her gown, in their tiny, tight dancing slippers with damask toes and sharp, golden heels. Then the toes of the Lord's black velvet shoes were before her. Bending her head, she sank in a deep curtsy, her skirt spreading out across the tiles. She could feel the crackle of power in the air, the blue electric tingle that raised the hair on her arms and at the back of her neck. The lord's eyes seemed to burn holes in her shoulders; she held herself very still and willed herself not to flinch beneath the hot energy of their gaze. Then his hand caught her beneath the chin, sending such a shock of power through her that she began to quiver all over, and angled her face up to meet his gaze. His eyes were golden and piercing, like the eyes of a hawk or the sharpest edge of fresh-cut golden glass. His hooked nose cast shadow over his thin mouth and his beard, black and silver streaked, curled down the front of his dark robe and tangled in the silver stitching of condors and snakes that intertwined there. His grip on Vita's chin was possessive and tight: for a moment she pictured his fingers as the talons of a condor, digging into her flesh, able at any moment to rip it open into tattered shreds of bleeding tissue. Then his grip loosened and his thin lips smiled enigmatically.

"Vita, rise. I will speak with you later," he said smoothly, and his golden gaze flickered away to where Ronaldo still bowed to the floor.

Vita could barely stand; her legs trembled and her muscles were weak. She entered the banqueting hall in a daze, her heart hammering so hard that it seemed to shake her body. Lifting candied melon to her dry mouth from a golden tray, she leaned against a wall and waited for Ronaldo to join her.

Soon they were seated at a banqueting table that stretched down the length of the room with thousands of shining gold plates and crystal goblets reflecting the chandeliers' light, with the heavy scent of fresh flowers, and the white sheen of damask cloths. Course after course arrived, born in silently by nimble serving men to be placed, steaming, on the table. Vita's stomach stretched fuller and fuller inside her dress; was there no end to the food pouring up the stairs from the great ovens and preparation tables of the kitchens? She had lost count of the number of courses. Occasionally, she glanced down the long table to glimpse Lord Maldici seated at the head, his thin fingers curled around his knife, his golden eyes focused on her. Her heart fluttered and paused, and she looked hastily back at her plate. Her glass was refilled: fine fig-canary, aged for five years in casks of fragranti wood, mellowed to a sweet fire that burned her tongue and cut the breath off in her throat, and filled her head with spinning images of ripe golden figs.

After the desserts—the cakes and soufflés, the syllabubs and syrups, the pies and tartlets and candied ginger and iced cookies—had been consumed, the nobili poured in a chattering throng into the ballroom where an orchestra of fifty musicians filled the air with melodies. Vita danced with Ronaldo, but with other men too—many of them, too many for her to remember their names or even their faces, sweating and flushed, laughing and admiring.

By the early hours of the morning, Vita had lost sight of Ronaldo and wandered down a corridor and into a hothouse filled with humid, musky air. She walked down the brick aisles, her gold heels tapping, between the shadowy enormous leaves of foreign plants, the waving foliage of ferns, the sprays of pink orchids that filled the air with a spicy fragrance. At the end of one aisle, she seated herself on a chair with gilt arms and cushions of silk and listened to the distant strains of music drifting past. She wished that she could find Ronaldo and Rosa and go home. Her head ached with tiredness, and her mouth was dry from the fig-canary.

She stiffened as footsteps came down the aisle toward her, not the tapping heels of a woman's shoe but the soft pad of a man's step.

"Vita," said Lord Maldici pleasantly, and as she rose, she smelled the wild, foreign smell of his leopard furs and saw the dim light shine on his long sharp teeth and the embroidered snakes writhing around the hem of his robe. He pushed her back into her chair.

"Don't get up." He pulled a second chair from the shadows and lowered himself into it and began idly to file his long, tapering nails with a golden file he took from a pocket. Vita tried to breathe evenly and slowly, and hoped that he couldn't hear the thundering of her heart. There was a dreamy quality about the moment; it seemed impossible to believe that she was here in the hothouse with the most powerful man in Verde.

"So, Vita," Lord Maldici said. "I've been interested to meet you."

"Me, why ?" She flushed, aware of the squeak in her voice.

The lord's mouth bent into a sardonic smile. "You think that this is a great city and that I live here above it all inside my fortress walls and cannot possibly know what happens in the streets below. But you are wrong, Vita. I know everything that happens. Everything. And I heard first how you took in the maid Rosa, and how you looked after the horse for Ronaldo, whose parents are old friends of mine. From them, I've heard many more things about you: your beauty, your natural elegance, so surprising in a village girl. I have heard how the people of Genovera believe you to be nobili, never suspecting your true origin. What kind of a girl, I asked myself, could manage this deception? And so, now I have you here and may find out for myself."

He raised an eyebrow enquiringly and his sharp gaze flickered over Vita like the edge of a knife blade. She swallowed and tried to speak in a steady voice.

"I have been well treated by Ronaldo's parents," she said. "I came to the city because I had heard about how wonderful it was here. I love beautiful things, my lord. I did not come intending to deceive, but Ronaldo's parents thought it best to treat me like nobili, since I was Ronaldo's guest, and they spread the word that I was a visiting nobili from a inland town."

"How well you play the role," murmured Lord Maldici, running his sharpened nails through the streaked strands of his beard, and Vita saw the ghostly blue sparks that leapt from it to disappear into the humid, scented gloom of the hothouse. "And now, I have heard that Ronaldo is head over heels in love with you."

Vita started in surprise and felt heat rush into her cheeks. Was this true? Ronaldo had not told her that he loved her and yet—it was true, that he'd been spending more and more time with her, that he took her on picnics by the river Arnona or up in the mountain meadows, that he brought her gifts of gowns and necklaces, that he smiled lazily at her with a strange light in his eyes. It could be true, she realized, that he was in love with her.

"How do you feel about that?" Lord Maldici asked in his voice like silk being drawn over skin.

"Ronaldo is—well, I like, maybe love—him, too," Vita stuttered, blushing harder. She felt childish and stupid, under the fierce scrutiny of Lord Maldici's eyes.

"Yes," The lord agreed thoughtfully. "Such an elegant young man. There are many women who might have wanted to be loved by Ronaldo, who might have brought him large dowries of country estates and stables of horses. For I hear too that he wishes to marry you. But he fears his parents will not approve, since you are of village stock and bring no dowry. Do you have anything to bring?"

"Nothing," Vita said, staring down at the toes of her shoes. "But I am too young to marry," she said, the tips of her ears burning. Inexplicably, for one moment, the image of Giovanni's face flashed through her mind; his bright grin, and his change-able Mara eyes.

"Perhaps you are a trifle young at the present, though not too young to be betrothed. Perhaps too, I might alter your state so that Ronaldo's parents would find you more acceptable," Lord Maldici continued. "I'm a man who admires the kind of courage you've shown in coming alone to the city, who appreciates the love that you have for beautiful things. Perhaps I might intercede with Ronaldo's parents on your behalf. Do you know, at the top of the Strada of Bay Trees, that little palazzo with the roof tiled in blue?"

Vita nodded, she had once peered through the palazzo's gate into a courtyard filled with almond trees and singing thrushes, and stared wistfully at the palazzo's yellow shuttered windows and blue door and thought how perfectly lovely it was.

"That palazzo is mine," Lord Maldici said. "Perhaps, Vita, you would like to live there? It would make an ideal home for a young couple, newly married and in love. And what of servants? You have of course the maid Rosa, and I'm sure that Ronaldo's parents could supply other servants from their own household. And Ronaldo has the tapestry stallions...but what if you could bring a rare black stallion from Mombasso to the marriage? There is a foal in my stables that I could give to you, along with your palazzo."

Lord Maldici slipped his hands inside the leopard fur trimming on his sleeves, and stared at Vita consideringly. "I could make you a nobili woman in truth," he offered. "My master of lineage will confer the honor upon you."

Vita opened her mouth to speak but no sound came out. Words whirled in her brain and she felt overwhelmed with surprise and anxiety, with the humid air and the heavy food stretching her stomach, with the lingering fumes of the fig-canary. Was she dreaming? Would she awake in the morning in the blue bedroom at Ronaldo's, or even in her own bed in the Keeper's house in the village? She didn't understand why Lord Maldici was offering her all this. It was flattering to think that he admired her, but she didn't understand it and she couldn't question him. And all the time, as his voice slipped over her in the fragrant gloom, she felt the thin electric hum of his power ringing through her body like a warning.

"I don't know what to say," she croaked at last, and Maldici's lips twisted back over his teeth.

"Why, Vita, I'm surprised at you. What is there to say but 'yes' to being offered a nobili woman's status in Genovera?"

"Nothing," Vita whispered and suddenly he gripped her elbow and pulled her to her feet. "Let us take a walk," he said, his nails piercing the thin fabric of her gown. At his side, she paced long corridors and sweeping flights of marble stairs, passed miles of painted frescoes and panels of inlaid precious stones beneath a thousand gleaming chandeliers and by the obsequious bows of the guards at every doorway. At last, they came to the highest balcony of Lord Maldici's palace, where Vita saw that the dawn light was creeping over the horizon with a pale glow, like the light that lies inside a mullosk shell. Below them, the rooftops of Genovera lay in a gray tumble, and the Arnona was shrouded in mist.

Lord Maldici flung out an arm. "There it lies: Verde," he said hoarsely. "Its green hills and groves of fruit and nuts, its acres of wheat. But for my brother in the south, that half-wit usurper, I would rule it all. All! And soon, I shall do so. Soon, I shall be crowned emperor, and foreign princes shall travel far for the honor of kissing my feet. I shall make Verde proud, a name to ring through the world, the richest land on earth. I shall exalt it!"

In the rosy light, Maldici's eyes gleamed with a fiery, fanatical light, and Vita felt shivers of energy lick her bare neck and prickle over her scalp. She gripped the balcony railing for support and bit her lips to steady their tremor.

"Vita, you are not who you pretend to be," he accused suddenly and, staring into his golden gaze, she felt herself like a moth pinned to a board. "I'm not—not nobili. You know that," she stuttered.

"You are not a mere villager either. You're the Keeper, the only one who knows the power of the ancient magic, who knows the hiding places of the Corno d'Oro, who is descended from Luna, the moon goddess. Deny this if you can!" His voice rose triumphantly and Vita was aware suddenly of how alone she was, suspended here above miles of cold space, and how no one knew that she was here.

"Speak!" he commanded.

"Yes, I'm the Keeper." Her voice came out in a whisper.

"Yes! Think, Vita. Think of our power combined! Think of our power to wrest the balance of the world in our own favor. Think of the lands we might command, the western seas, the trading ships loaded with beautiful things! Then, Ronaldo would beg for your hand in marriage, to live with you in the palazzo I'm giving you, to walk in your stable of rare horses bred from the black foal that is waiting for you. Think of our triumph over my brother! Caskets of coral and star sapphires shall be yours, trains of jennets will bring the riches of the world to your door. You will be the greatest princess in the world, I can make you so!"

Vita's eyes seemed to have frozen in her head, so that she couldn't pull her gaze away from Maldici's narrow face and hooked nose, from his feverish eyes. The energy of his power crackled in her ears.

"How did you know about the Keepers, and the Corno d'Oro in the mountains?" she whispered.

"Ah, Vita, I am not some ignorant villager who thinks that myths are merely pretty tales to spin by a winter's fire, or that they are without reality and power. I have learning, am heir to a tradition of deep knowledge, to a great library filled with ancient tomes. I found you there, with your silver-gold hair and lavender eyes, in the handwriting of my ancestor. Then all that remained was to find you in Verde—but you came to my doorstep, to stay with Ronaldo. You made my task easy."

"What do you want?"

His voice dropped, became soothing and soft. "Only that you share your ancient magic with me, your words, your spells. That you bring the Corno d'Oro stallion here to my fortress where I might wrest its power to my will."

"I do not think the power of the Corno d'Oro can be used for personal gain," Vita dared to say. "Their power is for preserving balance in the world."

Lord Maldici waved his hand through the air. "Power is power," he said dismissively. "Come, I have something to show you."

He whirled to the door, his dark cape billowing at his ankles, the fur gleaming pale in the rising sun. Down long corridors he strode with Vita hurrying breathlessly after him, until they reached a door that led into a courtyard where peacocks fanned their brilliant tails across the ground, where leopards snarled in cages and a magrazzi, as shy and sleepy-eyed as the one the beetleman had lent her, peered at them through the leaves of a magnolia tree.

"I hear that you have one of these beasts," Lord Maldici said with a careless wave of his hand. "It must be the mate to this one of mine, for she sickened in the delta and the fool of a trader let her go. Perhaps we might reunite them, Vita. Perhaps you might care to keep them at your new palazzo. I am tired of this one—he sleeps all day."

Vita wished that there was time for her to speak to the magrazzi, to reassure it that it was not alone of its kind in Verde, but Lord Maldici's long stride didn't pause as he crossed the courtyard with the fine gravel crunching beneath his heels. The leopards crouched in their cages as his shadow fell across them. Vita followed him through an iron gateway and found herself at the base of a narrow, rocky fissure that climbed up through the shoulder of the mountain. Stone steps had been cut into the rock, and Vita's heels clicked on their uneven, golden surfaces as she climbed, the overhanging myrtle and lontano bushes brushing her shoulders. At the top of the steps, she waited while the lord opened another iron gateway and led her into a second court-yard, built on a terrace leveled on the side of the mountain, that was smaller than the first courtyard had been. The courtyard was encircled with walls of stone eight feet high, and thick creepers and flowering vines hung over the walls. There were no peacocks here, nor foreign and exotic animals, and only one huge golden cage stood in the center of the courtyard on the raked gravel beneath the naked branches of an apricot tree. Inside the cage lay something ivory, with a rippling mane hang-ing over its bent neck. Vita, half way to the cage, stopped as though turned to stone. Her heart hung suspended in her rib cage, her breath became still in her lungs. A force hit her: a wall of shock and pain, of recognition and disbelief.

The Lord Maldici's lips curled. "Didn't know about this, did you?" he asked softly, slyly.

Vita didn't reply. She stepped to the cage's golden bars and fell to her knees, gripping the bars in her fists, and stared in hor-rified awe at the bent neck, the golden hooves, the tapering golden horn with its spiral twist. Faded star lilies, on weak bent stems, filled the air with a thin, sickly fragrance that was nothing like their true smell.

Sentences of a story ran through Vita's mind, a story told on warm rocks beside the sea in Rosa's husky voice. She had been telling the Keeper's Tale—but telling it wrong, in a version that Vita had never heard. She'd said: "The mare swam in circles, cry-ing for her stallion, but at last she was too weary to swim much farther and began to sink low in the wild water. At the last moment, a man called Marco—who lived on one of the islands of the archipelago—rowed out and saved her. And afterward, he sold her to the nobili for gold and they took her north to Lord Morte's city palazzo."

And here she is, Vita thought. Here she's been, all these many long years in a golden cage, and I am the first Keeper to see her since that day when she and the stallion were separated in the terrible storm.

Awake, Vita called to the Corno d'Oro mare in her thoughts. *I have come, the Keeper.*

The mare's eyes, dull and dark purple as bruises, opened slowly. She stared at Vita's face pressed between the bars of the cage, and gave a melancholy sigh.

Keeper? she asked, her voice in Vita's head like the soft ringing of a muffled bell.

I didn't know you were here. I thought you'd drowned long ago, in the storm.

Not drowned, the mare said. *The stallion drowned.*

No! He's safe and alive in the mountains! Vita cried. The mare lifted her drooping head a little higher, and something shone in her eyes for a brief moment, a tongue of light like the flicker of a candle's flame.

Then the lord's thin fingers gripped Vita's arm as he pulled her away from the cage and back through the iron gate into the stairway in the mountain's crevice.

I'll come back! Vita cried to the Corno d'Oro mare, but there was no answer as the gate clanged shut.

"If you bring the other Corno d'Oro here, we can unite them," Lord Maldici said, cracking the joints of his bony fingers. "We can join their powers together, and our own powers, to create one power greater than any this world has yet known. Do you understand me, Keeper? Isn't there an ancient prophecy that says that the earth god and the moon goddess must unite their powers?"

Vita nodded numbly; the night and its dawn seemed to have lasted a lifetime and she swayed on her feet. Vaguely she recalled that the sea witch had once spoken of this same prophecy. There was something twisted, she felt now, in the lord's interpretation. For she was merely the Keeper of Luna's beasts and not the goddess herself, and Lord Maldici was not god of the earth—except perhaps in his fevered dreams.

"Come, you look tired. It's time for some breakfast."

They clattered down the steps, crossed the first courtyard with its screeching peacocks, entered the miles of fortress corridors. Vita's gritty eyes flinched away from the glitter of mirrors and the hard sheen of marble. She stumbled into the breakfast room at Lord Maldici's side and barely noticed Ronaldo's surprised stare where he stood amongst the remaining nobili eating almond waffles with honey.

Lord Maldici swung her to face himself and bent close to her ear, his hot breath stirring her hair and his fingers pinching her arm. "Come and go as you wish. The mare is lonely. She needs to be reunited with the stallion, here in the city. We'll talk again soon, Keeper. Time is running out in my hourglass, the year moves toward spring, my army flexes its muscles. Think about your future. Think of what you might do with your power."

He bent over her hand to touch it with his thin, hard lips. The kiss burned on her skin for hours afterward, while she rode home in silence in the chariot, while she lay sleeplessly in her soft bed in the blue room. She felt feverish. Conflicting desires overwhelmed her. Her muscles twitched and her eyes burned but wouldn't stay closed. She called for the tile-maid to bring lavender and strew it on the floor, filling the bedroom with its soothing fragrance, and for the taper-maid to light candles of lavender wax that burned with a pale blue flame. Still, she tossed and turned in the bed to fall, in mid-afternoon, into an uneasy sleep filled with dream images of her own face and the leering face of Lord Maldici as he chased her down long corridors of warped mirrors, the glass bending to enclose her. She awoke with a start, sweating, her heart hammering, and thought that she'd felt talons at her throat.

Sitting up in bed, she rubbed her neck and stared into the palazzo garden where late winter sunshine warmed the water in the fountains and sent birds looking for nesting materials. Tossing off the blankets, Vita forced her aching limbs from the bed and wrapped herself in a warm shawl to slip into the garden and walk its gravel paths. Gradually, her hammering heart steadied. Mild air filled her lungs and her head cleared. It was only a dream brought on by fatigue and over-eating, she thought.

She reached a viewpoint on a small knoll, and paused to lean on the railing that surrounded it and stare over the city to the Arnona's swift flow and the barges that crawled over it like beetles. To stay here always, she thought. To stay here and be a nobili princess, to live in the palazzo with yellow shutters and singing thrushes, to be a woman to whom lines of jennets were led, loaded with riches from foreign lands. To marry Ronaldo, to live with his lazy smile and light, rippling laughter. To dress every day in silk, to breed rare horses and take treats into the stables to feed to the foals...to send out dance invitations on heavy paper with delicate scalloped edges decorated with gold leaf, to keep foreign animals in her courtyards, to carry delicate hand-painted fans on summer afternoons through her gardens of roses and jasmine...

It was a heady dream, a rich mixture that wrapped itself around Vita's heart, that took her breath away and made her feel hot and giddy, as though she'd been drinking fig-canary again.

In payment: her magic, taught to her at her mother's knee, guarded and preserved through generation after generation of women. But surely, it was hers to do with as she wished. Surely, the power of the Corno d'Oro could not be used for evil purposes. If she brought the stallion to the city, if she joined forces with Lord Maldici, who knew what good they might work for the land, for the world? Who knew but that Lord Verona in the south was indeed a foolish usurper, that Verde would be better off without him? Who knew whether the gossip around the village well, about Lord Maldici's black arts, was true? It seemed unlikely that the villagers, so ignorant of state affairs, could make such judgments. As to the army, surely it was necessary, for didn't all powerful rulers need some means to protect their kingdoms? And if she herself rose to power, she would soften the taxes that the villagers paid. She would find Sandro and set him free from the army, to return home to Beatrice and their grieving mother. She would bring Aunt Carmela to Genovera and care for her in her old age, giving her servants and soft shawls and delicate food imported from other countries. She would be adored throughout Verde, as no other Keeper had been.

A dreamy smile twisted the corners of Vita's mouth. She turned away from the viewpoint and strolled toward a long hedge of candleberry that surrounded a splashing fountain, and in an alcove she sat down on a wooden bench carved with peacocks. Footsteps stirring the raked gravel paths made her glance up, thinking Rosa might be coming to join her, but it was not Rosa who approached. Vita gave a gasp of amazement for surely the figure approaching was—but how could it be? Yet it was: the sea-witch's daughter from the pirati archipelago. Whatever was she doing here, in Genovera, with her thin sharp face and her wild black hair?

"Marina?" Vita called, and the girl nodded and strode steadily toward her to perch on the far end of the bench.

"But—Marina! How did you find me?"

"I talked to the dressmaker, Mistress Jacquardi."

"But what are you doing in Genovera and what—"

"Listen to me!" Marina interrupted urgently. "I've come looking for you because Aunt Carmela is worried sick about you. You shouldn't be here, in this place. Your aunt says that the Lord Maldici is stirring up a great evil, a dark power. He will become a sorcerer like his ancestor, Lord Morte and—"

"So gossip runs, but no-one can prove it true," Vita said coolly.

"You must come home, before the spring equinox."

"Stop telling me what to do."

The sea-witch's daughter stared at her, her eyes disconcertingly green, just like Aunt Carmela's eyes, and her thin lips bent in a scornful twist.

"You need someone to tell you," she said. "You're like a baby, you're so gullible. Your fine friend Rosa, disguised as a maid, is Lord Maldici's daughter. She's been spying on you all this time."

Vita felt the words pierce her like an arrow, so great and sharp was the pain they caused in her chest.

"I don't believe you!" she cried. "Rosa's my friend and—"

"Be quiet and listen to me! When I was hiding in Luna's shrine yesterday, Rosa and a man held a secret meeting that I overheard. The man called Rosa 'Princess Maldici' and she spoke of Lord Maldici as her father. She gave the man a piece of parchment—I heard it rustle—and said 'Here's the list: everything Vita wishes for. The price we pay for her. Take it to Lord Maldici.'"

"You must have misheard!"

"I didn't."

They glared at each other, sitting so still that a thrush hopped by their feet, its beak stuffed with candleberry twigs for a nest. A snail crawled along the bench's wooden arm, and the water tinkled in the fountain and splashed the surrounding gravel a darker golden.

"What are you waiting for?" Marina asked impatiently. "We must leave, now. You must come with me."

"I have things to think about," Vita said.

"Think quickly, then! You should have started thinking months ago, instead of spending your time worrying about parties and coral necklaces. Giovanni is missing, and the army on the plain is swelling bigger by the hour."

"Giovanni? What's happened to him?"

"He disappeared from an inn, The Condor's Wing, down by the Arnona. Have you seen him?"

"No."

"Are you coming?" Marina rose from the bench and held out a thin hand toward Vita, but she shrugged. Her mind was whirling again, and the pain of Rosa's betrayal filled her chest and pressed against the back of her eyes. She wanted to be alone, to double over and sob, to sort through the muddled layers of lies and truth that filled her thoughts, to find Rosa and entreat her, or perhaps to shake her.

"Leave me alone!" she cried at Marina. "I can't think with you chattering at me! Can't you see that? I need time to think!"

Marina's eyes flashed but she bit her lip, and after a moment she spoke in a pleading tone. "Please," she entreated. "Please come away with me now. I've come all this way to find you, Vita."

The pain of Rosa's betrayal was a roaring in Vita's ears. She watched Marina's lips moving, but it was like watching someone underwater. At any moment, she was going to be swallowed by the black void of her grief like a swimmer being sucked into a whirlpool.

"I can't come now!" she cried. "Talk to me some other time!"

Without another word, the sea witch's daughter spun on her heel and strode down the path. Her hips swung with an angry flounce, and her green skirt with its pattern of fish swished from side to side. When she tossed her head, her iridescent black hair shook its long tangled tresses down her stiff back. Vita watched until Marina disappeared around the end of the hedge's interlacing branches, where a mist of green was so faint that it seemed something more imagined than seen. Then Vita drew her knees up against the pain bursting open in her chest, and bent her head onto them.

*Take this list…the price we pay for her…*a palazzo with a blue roof, a black stallion, the hand of Ronaldo in marriage, nobili status, promises of power, riches, wonders…Vita's stomach heaved. She remembered the day that Rosa had arrived in the village, how she had lain on the doorstep like a lost girl, hungry and cold, her flaming hair spilling over the collar of her rough green dress. And all the days that had followed in the village and in

Genovera: the whispers and secrets, the giggled conversations at night, the shopping and trying on dresses together. And all the time, Rosa had been spying on her. Rosa. Princess Maldici: the one who would be the most powerful princess in the land when the Lord was made emperor—not me, Vita thought. He lied when he promised that position to me. Not that I want it.

But Rosa's friendship—that she did want.

I treated her like my sister, the one I've never had, Vita thought. I told her that, I told her she was like a sister. And all the time she was spying on me, finding out about me, tricking me.

Now Vita remembered the wounding of the Corno d'Oro and for the first time she realized that it had not been coincidence that the hunters found the Corno d'Oro on the very day that she'd been late performing the magic to keep it hidden and safe. No, those hunters had been sent by Lord Maldici, and they had known where to go because Rosa had found out—and she herself had been prevented from reaching home in time because the red horse had gone lame. As had a red horse once before, bringing Ronaldo back to her village. The horses had both limped although Aunt Carmela's healing fingers could find nothing wrong with their straight, hard legs—and finally, Vita understood her aunt's concern. Not injury, but dark magic, had lamed them.

"The Corno d'Oro can never be caught by force, only by trickery," Vita remembered her mother telling her. I'm just like that first Keeper, she thought, the one that Luna chose, who was tricked into betraying the two Corno d'Oros to Lord Morte so that he could bind their slender ankles and muffle their wild cries and load them into the hold of his ship. And Marco, the captain of the pirati, who hid the Keeper's book in the cave where I found it, he too was a betrayer. It was *he* who rowed out into the storm and rescued the drowning Corno d'Oro mare, and then sold her for gold to the nobili so that they could take her north to Lord Morte's castle, to her lonely cage in a hidden courtyard where the star lilies are dying. Marco's betrayal was the 'great crime' that he wrote of, in the note lying beneath the Keeper's book in its box decorated with golden suns and moons.

And Ronaldo? Was he a betrayer too? Was it all a game—those tender glances, those fingers linked through Vita's own, those picnics in the mountains and gifts of jewels? Did he love her in truth—or had he been bought for a price, to play his part in her seduction?

The knowledge of these betrayals burned in Vita like a fire as she curled over her knees beneath the candleberry hedge. Hot tears darkened the fabric of her gown and scalded her cheeks

Rosa, she thought. Not my sister, but my enemy.

CHAPTER TWENTY-ONE

FOR TWO DAYS VITA LAY IN BED complaining of a headache and kept the blankets pulled over her face when Rosa came and went, bringing honeycakes and glasses filled with apricot juice. "Too much fig-canary," Rosa teased in her husky voice. "Too much dancing."

"Maybe," Vita croaked, the pain of Rosa's betrayal filling her throat, pressing on her chest, choking and suffocating her. She wished that she never needed to climb from the bed again, that she could just drift into its soft darkness and disappear from her own life. Her head throbbed and her limbs ached. She wished that she could sit up and smile at Rosa, that she could repeat Marina's warning and watch Rosa's face break into an incredulous smile. "Me? Princess Maldici?" she would laugh. "Are you crazy, Vita? What a dream!"

But Vita didn't ask because she knew, in her bones, that Marina's warning was true. She had only to think of Rosa's eyes to feel this truth, for they were as hawk-like and golden, as sharp and piercing, as the eyes of Lord Maldici. Why was it that she had not noticed the sharpness of Rosa's eyes until now? And then there was Rosa's telling of the Keeper's Tale, on warm rocks beside the sea. Rosa's knowledge of the tale was finally explained. It was not from a wandering tale-spinner that she'd heard it, but from her father, Lord Maldici, who'd found it in his ancient books written in Lord Morte's hand. Thus it was that Rosa knew how the Corno d'Oro mare had been saved from the sea by Marco the pirati and brought to the castle—for she had grown up from childhood in that place, where the mare languished in a cage in a secret courtyard.

Right from the start, Vita thought, I've been like clay in Rosa's hands, like the soft moist clay that Beatrice shapes into pitchers and bowls and that we formed into little wombos when we were children. But now, I must struggle from Lord Maldici's net before all is lost. I must pretend to Rosa that nothing has changed; that I know nothing of her deception. I must treat her like a friend, and in the meantime I must plan how to free the Corno d'Oro mare. Lord Maldici must never catch the stallion. And I must try to find Giovanni, who's always been my friend.

"With the pure of heart, keep your trust," rang her aunt's voice in Vita's head. Keep your trust. But I haven't, Vita thought miserably. I've forsaken Giovanni, who can talk to the dolphins, for Ronaldo's long legs in yellow silken hose, for his flattery and dance steps and lazy smile. Where could Giovanni be and what's happened to him? Has he been taken for the army? Is he on the banks of the Arnona in the valley below me, right at this moment, marching in the numberless ranks, his blue eyes dull, his shoulders bent under the blows of whips?

She longed for the grip of his callused hands, for his strong bright laughter and changeable sea eyes. She longed too for the village: for its apricot and rose colored houses, with their tall narrow facades, clustered on the slopes of the valley above the small harbor with its sickle moon of sand; for the crowing of roosters and the bang of shutters in the wind; for the sweet smoke of olive wood fires and the gleam of rain and sun mingled over the Golfo's waves.

I might never see it again, she thought, and with a moan she buried her head in the pillow and tried to shut out the chill dawn light that crept in from the palazzo garden, so that the blue room seemed like an underwater grotto where Mara might live.

Too soon, it was morning with birds trilling in the cypress trees and ruffling their feathers in the fountains. Vita's bedroom door swung open and Rosa came in, smiling, to jerk the blankets playfully off the bed. "Out, out!" she said. "There's a man in the courtyard with a black foal for you."

Vita groaned, but already Rosa was at the window swishing the damask drapes aside to let sunshine stream in, and then she opened the window and waved to someone in the courtyard below.

"Come on, Vita," she said. "You must be feeling better by now!"

"Not really," Vita mumbled, but she swung her toes out onto the wool carpet and padded across the room to join Rosa at the window. She was grateful that there was something outside to look at and she didn't have to meet Rosa's eyes. How could she ever look at Rosa again and not show her own pain? She leaned her bare arms on the sill and stared down to see a groom, dressed in the black and silver livery of the Maldici household, holding a black foal on a fine red rope. Seen from this distance the foal was like a toy with its slender prancing legs, tiny head, pricked ears and fluttering nostrils.

"Oh, how beautiful!" Rosa cried, clapping her hands, and Vita nodded but was afraid to open her mouth to speak lest the noise that came out be a sob. Dumbly she leaned on the sill, watching the groom lead the foal in circles until at last, when she waved her hand, he took it away in the direction of the stables.

"Ronaldo has been asking for you all the time!" Rosa said, tugging on Vita's arm. "Come and get dressed. He's sent you a note—I have it here."

She fumbled in her pocket and extracted a folded square of parchment that she slipped into Vita's limp hand. Vita bent over it, glad for another excuse to avoid Rosa's teasing gaze. Even the sight of Ronaldo's familiar, elegant hand made her want to give a despairing cry. *Dearest Vita,* she read, *hope you are feeling better. Can you come with me to the valley today? I'll have the chariot ready. Love, R.*

"I don't know if I can go," Vita mumbled. "I don't feel very well yet."

"Nonsense," Rosa chided. "You'll be fine once you dress. Look, Mistress Jacqaurdi has sent the new dress and a hat to match. You'll look lovely!"

Vita stared dully at the gown's soft folds woven of fine angoli wool, embroidered with peacocks, and at the hat with its drooping brim stitched with peacock feathers that gleamed in the morning light. Was it only five days ago that she'd stood in Mistress Jacqaurdi's shop, exclaiming over this fabric while Rosa held a length of it under her chin and told her that the color suited her perfectly? It seemed a lifetime ago that she'd asked the seamstress to stitch the peacock feathers onto the hat, that she'd lifted the embroidery silk from the drawer and said, "This is the perfect color!" How easily pleased she'd been, like a child with a candied seasnail, and how blind! This morning, she wished that the dress had never arrived and she didn't have to pretend to like it, but she could feel Rosa's golden eyes lingering on her face. She forced her stiff skin into a smile. "It's just right for today, for spring!" she exclaimed and even laughed lightly, but when she bent over to find her shoes underneath the bed, she felt tears spring into her eyes.

Don't cry—stop it! she scolded herself fiercely. You have to behave normally, and find Giovanni, and free the mare. You have to escape from this place when they least suspect you.

"Can't find your shoes?" Rosa asked.

"Yes, here they are! Do you think they'll suit the blue dress?"

The rattle of chariot wheels from the courtyard below almost drowned her words.

"Here's Ronaldo!" Rosa exclaimed. "I'll go down and tell him that you're just coming!"

When Vita walked outside in the blue dress, with the hat brim and its peacock feathers tilted at an angle over her fair hair, Ronaldo whistled in admiration and his horses threw up their heads nervously and stamped on the cobblestones.

"Are you coming?" Vita asked, but Rosa shook her head. Vita climbed alone into the chariot, and Ronaldo rattled the whip in its socket and loosened the reins, the horses leaping forward so that the chariot sprang after them. Vita gripped the edge with white knuckles and held onto her hat while Ronaldo gave her a sideways smile. He seemed excited, with a flush on his cheeks and a spark in his eyes. He whistled a high, bright tune as he drove, and his excitement seemed to run down the reins and infect the horses, so that they rolled their eyes and mouthed nervously at their silver bits.

"Where are we going?" Vita asked, as the chariot dashed downhill toward the river, sending shoppers scurrying from their path and pigeons wheeling upward.

"To the army camp. There's to be a review this morning! We had a personal invitation to attend, sent from Lord Maldici! You must have impressed him at the ball."

Impressed him, Vita thought sourly, the flattery bitter in her ears. I didn't impress him, you stupid cuttlefish! she wanted to yell at Ronaldo. All he wants is my cooperation with the Corno d'Oro; all he wants is power! She turned her face away from Ronaldo, so that he couldn't see the anger and misery in her eyes, and stared at the merchant stalls packed together along the road leading to the River Arnona.

As they rattled over the bridge, she thought of Giovanni and wondered if she might see him in the army camp. And if she saw him, could she attract his attention? Ronaldo appeared not to notice her silence; he had his hands full with the horses, for the chariot had to weave a path through the throng jostling toward the valley. On the far bank there was more room, and he was able to give the horses their heads and let them stretch out in a fast trot, but now his eyes were riveted on the camp a half mile ahead, with its lines of tents and its dusty parade ground where wooden reviewing stands had been built especially for the occasion. Vita was surprised when, as they entered the camp's gateway between twin watchtowers, a soldier stepped forward to greet them by name. He took the reins of the horses and Ronaldo jumped from the chariot and held out his hands to Vita.

"Come on! There's a place reserved for us!" he said, and she followed him through the crowd to climb up the wooden steps of a central reviewing stand. Inside, ranks of generals in stiff uniforms parted before her. She saw that two chairs remained empty in the front row. Beyond them, the lean, cunning face of Lord Maldici turned to greet her.

"Ahh, Vita. I trust the black colt pleased you? Be seated." His curved fingers with their long, curling nails pressed her shoulders down into the chair, and she felt the thin electric crackle of his power. Her spine stiffened. Lord Maldici remained standing at her side. He was not dressed today in his fine velvet robes, with green embroidery and leopard trim, but in the black uniform of his army. His sleeves were crusted with silver thread; ribbons held a row of medals that clattered as he moved. *Supreme Commander* was embroidered across one side of his chest and, on the other, silver condors spread their wings, their cruel beaks bent as though to rip apart prey.

Once Vita was seated, the review began almost immediately with a charge past of chariots. The charioteers balanced on their rocking platforms, giving bloodcurdling cries that resounded above the pounding of hooves and the rattle of wheels. Whips cracked over the backs of sweating horses, whose nostrils flared red and whose eyes rolled. The wooden reviewing stand vibrated beneath Vita.

"What's on the chariot wheels?" she whispered to Ronaldo.

"Knives that spin as they turn, to cut soldiers down."

Lord Maldici's hand curled on Vita's shoulder. "A pretty trick," he sneered. "My enemies will be harvested like a field of grain."

Vita closed her eyes against the sudden image that filled them: those flashing blades reaping men, slashing through legs as through stems of wheat.

After the chariots came the lines of marching soldiers, all in the black and silver of the house of Maldici. Wave after wave of men passed, the tramping rhythm of their boots filling Vita's chest, altering her heartbeat. She leaned on the stand's front rail and searched for Giovanni's familiar face. Thousands of men passed, taken from the villages and vineyards, their swinging legs and arms in perfect unison, their black boots flattening the dirt into a surface as hard as rock. Next, the assassini passed. Vita stared in revulsion at their short, brutish bodies sparsely covered in wiry red hair; at the blue brands tattooed on their foreheads, and their hands deformed to hold weapons. Their bulbous noses were always damp, and their soft long ears flapped against their swarthy necks. They existed solely for delivering terror, death, and destruction. At their sides, brutti strained at leashes, their muzzles wrinkled back over teeth gleaming with poisonous saliva.

Vita felt as though she had leaned over the reviewing stand's front rail for hours. Dust and fear thickened in her throat. Her eyes stung, squinting against the gleam of lances and shields. Nowhere could she glimpse Giovanni.

When the last assassini had passed, a series of spectacles were staged directly in front of the stand holding Lord Maldici. Prisoners, pitifully thin and begging for mercy, were dragged forward and tied to stakes before being attacked by brutti, shot at by archers, cut down by chariots.

Shudders ran through Vita; the cries of dying men filled her head. The chill, pale fingers of Lord Maldici stroked the back of her neck. "Such a wonderful thing; power," he murmured. "Never forget, Vita, what you and I could accomplish together.

The spring equinox approaches and the stallion must be captured then and brought to me. "

Vita nodded but couldn't trust her voice to speak. Her stomach heaved.

Giovanni, she thought desperately. I must keep still, and watch for him. If he is dragged out to die, I must save him. His life might depend on me. I will not be sick, or leave this stand until the end.

She clenched her fists in her lap. Each time that new prisoners were led out, her gaze flicked over them. She both longed and dreaded to recognize Giovanni's changeable sea eyes in the midst of this nightmare. Once Vita had seen that Giovanni was not amongst each batch of prisoners, she stared over the men's heads, at the horizon where drifting dust veiled the morning light like smoke, and willed her mind to go blank. One by one, each man was killed by quivering arrow, or gleaming teeth, or flashing blade. Some, Vita was aware from the roars of the crowd, fought back but were no match for the forces ranged against them; they simply died more slowly.

At long last, the spectacle ended. Soldiers tied the dead bodies to the backs of chariots and dragged them away, leaving damp trails of blood in the dust. The brutti drooled at the sight, and gave voice to ululating howls that raised the hair on the back of Vita's neck. Lord Maldici took Vita's hand and raised her to her feet.

"Time for a repast?" he asked pleasantly. "Killing makes me hungry. I trust you've had a pleasant and instructive morning. We will speak again, very soon. The equinox approaches, when the Corno d'Oro stallion will be vulnerable." Vita curtsied low in the stand's cramped confines, too petrified to meet his gaze. She felt Ronaldo at her shoulder and turned, following him from the stand to where his chariot waited. He swung the horses in a wide loop around the parade ground as men, horses and brutti scattered back amongst the tents.

"Shall we go home?" Ronaldo asked. "You look pale."

"I'm fine," she said, her jaw stiff. "But please, let's go home."

It took some time to negotiate their way over the arched stone bridge into Genovera, for many nobili had come to watch the review and the streets were crowded with chariots and footmen, as well as with the usual crowds of shoppers and traders, scribes, merchant princes, and country women selling their cheeses and sausages. The noise from the crowds was a dull roar in Vita's head, where the tramp of thousands of soldiers' feet still beat a rhythm. She glanced sideways at Ronaldo and felt an ache in her chest. She swallowed the tightness in her throat and kept her voice light. "So," she asked, "what made you suddenly think that I'd like to see the army? We've never gone to the camp before."

There was silence for a moment, and then Ronaldo gave his sleepy laugh. "I told you; we were invited by Lord Maldici. He suggested it at the party the other night. He thought that it might amuse you."

If she hadn't known him so well, Vita might not have noticed it: the faint flush that crept over the collar of Ronaldo's blue tunic and up toward his golden hair, and the tiny muscle that twitched at the corner of his mouth. But she did notice, and then she knew that Ronaldo too had been bought, and was betraying her. It was not to amuse her that he'd taken her to the army camp, but to do as Lord Maldici bid him—and Lord Maldici had a reason for wanting her there. Power, Vita thought. He wanted me to see the size of his army, to see the power that he holds in the palms of his hands. He wanted to frighten me and impress me, to persuade me that I cannot fight him but must join my own power to his. He is making sure I'll do whatever he wants me to.

"What a morning!" Ronaldo exclaimed suddenly. "What a great army! Have you ever seen anything like it? It will wipe Lord Verona and his men from the face of Verde. I wish I were a charioteer in that army, Vita. Perhaps I will ask my father about buying me a commission."

Vita ignored him. He was like a snake, she thought, so sleek and graceful and elegant, so untrustworthy. She wished that she didn't know this, that she could return to being carefree and laughing with him, to believing that he loved her. She wished that she could have confided in him. "Listen to me," she wanted to implore, snatching at the fine linen of his sleeves. "I need help!" But she turned her face away from him, and pressed her lips into a tight line.

As the chariot climbed the steep hills, the horses straining in their traces, Vita realized that she had never been able to confide in Ronaldo; that he only been a friend with whom to dance, to play games and silly jokes, to picnic and shop. He had never been a friend to confide in, as Giovanni had been. Oh, Giovanni! Was he alive, or dead long since behind a chariot's spinning knives?

"Let me out!" Vita said suddenly.

"What?'

"Let me out, here. I am going to Luna's shrine. I'll walk home."

"You can't walk around in the city alone, without Rosa your maid. It's not done by nobili women."

"Let me out," she repeated, and the cold, hard note in her voice caused Ronaldo to shoot her a look of surprise. She grabbed the reins ahead of his hands and hauled on the horses' mouths so that they slewed sideways, the chariot coming to stop at an angle beside a fruit stall.

Vita jumped lightly out. "I'll be fine!" she called. "Don't fuss, Ronaldo!"

She strode over the cobbles, her peacock hat in one hand, and ducked into an alley that led beneath sprays of flowering jasmine before entering a small square. This she crossed, almost running, and arrived panting at the shrine of Luna with its defaced altar and its drifts of leaves. The lizard that lived there scuttled up the wall and then hung in a corner, its tiny feet clinging to cracked marble tiles. Vita crouched behind the altar, out of sight of anyone in the square, and dropped her head into her hands. Dust and spilled blood, brutti and the cries of dying men swirled behind her closed lids. She sobbed dryly, her stomach heaving. Fear coursed through her.

I must escape from here, fast, soon, she thought. But the mare must come too. And Giovanni.

She felt helpless and alone; who was she, a village girl, to defy the power of Lord Maldici, his cruel hawk-eyes, his armies? How could she even hope to win?

You are the Keeper, a voice whispered in her head. *You have power. You play a role in the balance of the world.*

Vita raised her head and stared up at the cool marble statue of Luna. Her smooth brow was circled with a wreath of stars and her mouth was curved in a tender smile. Vita laid a hand on the carved drapery of her gown and felt the thin electric hum of power run up her arm. She brushed cobwebs from Luna's marble toes, and laid her face against the stone plinth to cool her flushed cheeks. Gradually, a calm resolve seeped into her.

She bent and rocked at the edges of a loose stone in the base of the altar. Dust trickled onto her fingers as the stone grated against those around it. Vita loosened it and pulled it out. She slipped her hand into the cavity she'd revealed, and touched the ancient book, the one that she had found in a sea cave at the lowest tide and then hidden here, when she came the second time to Genovera. The first time, she had not had the book with her—if only, she though regretfully, if only I'd had it translated in time, what heartbreak might have been avoided.

Vita laid her palms on the cover of the book and remembered how she and Giovanni had gone exploring the day after the Feast of Dragomar. For a moment, she felt the beauty of that morning: its luminous sky and brilliant sunlight, its rippling water that reflected the graceful, bent shapes of the salt-pines, and lapped with soft sighs at the golden sand of each floating island. How long ago that day seemed—and how much, she realized, she would lose if she failed at her task to free the mare, to find Giovanni, and to escape from the reach of Lord Maldici. If she failed, there would never be another morning like that in the world.

She opened the Keeper's book, searching for help, and tilted the pages toward the light. The first two pages held the verses that she had used when healing the wounded Corno d'Oro, those about yellow earth and Hare's Ears. On the third page lay another poem that she had paid little attention to, not understanding its meaning and not needing its wisdom. Now she ran the tip of a finger along the translations, and her lips moved as they formed the words silently.

Watch, Keeper, though your heart has slept
And through its muddled dreams slow poison's crept,
Yet watch! When the mare's horn lifts into the bow of light
Sing you the words of power, and in that hour take flight
And let the balance of the world swing into place.

Slow poison, she thought. The greed of Lord Morte, that's crept into my heart. The slow poison of Rosa's deception, of Ronaldo's flattery, of my greed for silk dancing gowns and gold from Terre to fasten at my throat.

But what was the bow of light? Vita puzzled over this line for several minutes. She thought of the light of dawn and how the first rays of the sun, emerging over the mountains, would shoot upward. She thought of sunset, and the last rays lingering in the west. Did either dawn or sunset light touch that gilded cage on the mountain terrace; did they enter that walled courtyard and gleam on the point of the mare's tapered horn?

Then Vita remembered the arcobaleno, that colored bow that had sprung from the rainy air and shimmered around the Corno d'Oro stallion as his wound healed. Perhaps, she thought, she needed to be with the mare after a storm, when the clouds parted and the sun shone and the arcobaleno shimmered across the mountain. This would be harder to accomplish than simply freeing the mare without Lord Maldici's knowledge; much harder. She did not have time to wait for this phenomena of storm and light to happen.

"Sing you the words of power and in that hour take flight," Vita whispered, the lizard in the corner turning its dark, bright eyes toward her. "When the light touches the mare's horn, I can free her—but what are the words of power?" She turned to the last page of the book and laid her hand on its blankness, feeling a thin thread of power tickle her palm. The page remained blank. Was there anything written there, that would only be revealed by a particular time? Or perhaps the words that should have been there, had never been written? Were they lost forever, in the far-off mists of time, when the world was young and its power strong, when Luna ruled in the mountains of the moon? But where else might the words be found? Were they words which Vita's mother had taught to her? Were they written somewhere else, in another book, hidden in some obscure place as this book had been?

Perhaps the words of power were simply the words of the spells that she used in the mountains to keep the Corno d'Oro safe, the words that she knew by heart already. If this was so, then she need only wait until a day of sun, when light would touch the horn of the caged mare, and then she could speak her spells and set the mare free. How they would escape from the mountain afterward, Vita didn't know.

She bent her head over the book and squeezed her eyes shut. *Luna, help me*, she prayed but there was only silence in her head.

I am the Keeper, Vita thought. I have the power to render the Corno d'Oro invisible through fourteen spells spoken in sacred places in the mountains. But what if I speak those spells here in the city—will they form a wall of invisible power around the mare? I must try this; it is my only hope.

She carefully slipped the book into the hole at the base of the altar, and worked the stone back into place to hide it. Then she dusted her hands off and stood up, her skirt swishing in leaves. In a gesture of farewell, she touched her fingers to the hem of

Luna's gown, and then crossed the shrine and stepped out onto the square. She did not walk toward the palazzo of Ronaldo's parents, where she was staying, but headed instead uphill, by cobbled streets and crooked alleyways, skirting shops and flower stalls and vendors hawking fish from the delta with high cries. She ignored the pealing bells and wheeling pigeons, the hungry rumble in her stomach as she passed cafes, the sad music of violyno and mouth harp from a ragtag bunch of musicians at a corner. She walked with her back straight and a steely determination in her eyes.

Her legs ached by the time that she toiled up the sweeping entrance to the Maldici palazzo, its pale walls soaring above her against the dark mountain, and its slotted windows staring down at her like suspicious eyes. She strode toward the ranks of guards, head high.

"I am Vita the Keeper, and I demand to enter on the lord's business," she said imperiously. The guards looked at her skeptically, but one went to confer with others, and presently the black portcullis groaned upward and the silver studded doors swung open to the first courtyard. Vita crossed it, and was admitted through the inner wall to the second courtyard.

As she reached the castle, she was met by a nobili man of high rank; at a glance she took in his costly angoli cape, his fur trimmed robe. "I have business with the Corno d'Oro mare," she said. "I do not need your assistance."

The nobleman bowed very low, scraping the dainty points of his silver shoes across the tiles inlaid with amber. "My lady, the Lord Maldici is still with his troops. He has left word that you are to be admitted to the mare whenever you wish. I shall escort you."

"I know the way," Vita lied. "If I am free to come and go, I will do so alone."

The nobili bowed low again and gestured for her to mount the staircase behind him. She swept up its steps of polished mahogany, almost tripping in her haste, fear beating in her throat. She sped down mirrored halls and under the darkened chandeliers, past frowning portraits and crossed lances with cold steel tips. She ran down echoing corridors and through humid hothouses of stiff orchids. Her heels clattered on marble and precious wood, or were muffled in thick carpets woven in the bright colors of Mombasso.

At last, with a stitch in her side, she found her way out onto the mountain and crossed the terraces of golden gravel raked into fans. The leopards in their cages watched in silence as she ran by. The magrazzi awoke from its sleep in the shade and called softly to her, but she didn't answer. She found the pathway cut into the crevice in the mountainside and rushed up its rocky stairs with the lontano bushes sweeping against her shoulders like fingers.

The gate to the walled courtyard was locked. Vita remembered how Lord Maldici had removed a golden key from his pocket to unlock it when he'd brought her here on the dawn after the ball. Vita took the lock in her hands and spoke over it the spell for freeing night creatures, when they were caught in traps and crying for her help. The lock slipped open and she swung the gate on its stiff hinges.

The courtyard was in shadow still, protected from the sunlight by a thin ridge of mountain that cut, like a serrated blade, into the sky. Even in the shadow, the mare's coat and the bars of the cage gleamed with an inner light. Vita ran past the apricot tree, its limbs starred with tiny, fragile blossoms that would yield no fruit.

I am here, the Keeper, she told the mare, who was lying down, with her pale neck bowed and her slender muzzle resting on her golden hooves.

The sickly stench of dying lilies filled the still air. The mare's eyes didn't open.

Alarmed, Vita shook the cage bars, but they were solid and strong, as though made only yesterday in the forges of Genovera, instead of generations before. It was magic that held them, she thought: the black art of Lord Morte, the spells that he had spoken over the mare when he locked her behind those golden bars.

Speak to me, awake! I am here, the keeper!

Vita pressed her face against the metal, noting with surprise how cold it felt against her skin. She watched as the mare's eyes drifted half-open, deep pools of brown with scarcely a shimmer of light or life remaining in them.

I am going to try and free you. Your stallion is alive in the mountains! The mare snorted and raised her head a few inches.

I am dying, she answered. *I have lain here for years waiting, alone. It is too late now.*

No! Vita cried in anguish. *No, no!*

The mare's head sank to her hooves again.

"There is foul magic here," Vita whispered and she stood up and began to pace around the cage. With her toe, she scuffled fourteen points in the gravel around the cage and its apricot tree, and then began to recite the spells for invisibility that she usually performed in the mountains for the stallion. She drew the runes and secret signs in the gravel, and on the apricot's scaly bark. She cried the words of power aloud, and the Corno d'Oro mare opened her eyes and lifted her head a little, watching. A shaft of light slid into the courtyard as the sun shifted in the sky, climbing higher, moving westward. It touched the topmost branches of the apricot tree, making the blossoms blaze pure white. A bee wafted in on the light and buzzed against the blooms.

Vita paused in her chanting. The light, she thought. If the mare would stand, the light would touch her horn. Maybe then, I can free her from her cage. She will be invisible and free and we can find a way out of here together.

Vita finished the spell at the twelfth place in her circle, than approached the cage again.

Rise to your feet! she cried. *Find strength in yourself. Remember when the world was young and you ran in the mountains of the moon with the stallion. Remember the scent of the lilies in those high places. Rise! Find your power again!*

The mare moaned softly, but as Vita continued to encourage her, she attempted to rise. Twice she collapsed back onto her folded legs, but the on the third attempt she staggered to her feet and stood panting and leaning against the cage for support. As she lifted her head higher, the horn caught the sunlight and flared into a shaft of dazzling gold.

Yes! Vita cried exultantly. *I will finish the circle of invisibility. Do not lie down!*

She went to the thirteenth and then, finally, to the fourteenth places she had marked on the courtyard's gravel, chanting the magic aloud. The mare's ears flickered to and fro, and she opened her eyes wider. A shiver ran through her, and she lifted her head higher.

When Vita had completed the final spell, she fell silent. The mare was protected from men's gaze, although perhaps not from the powerful gaze of Lord Maldici, and her horn was touching the light. Now, Vita thought, I should speak the words of power —but what are they? She racked her mind, trying to recall every thing her mother had ever told her, every word she had taught to her. There was nothing for a situation like this. Vita cried aloud the spell for setting trapped animals free, the one she had used already on the lock at the gate. She chanted the verses for healing, and those for finding her way in the dark. She chanted the song of the moon goddess, which was the most ancient of songs and filled with the power of stars and moonlight, the dark velvet of evening, the pure cold beauty of high places, and the tenderness of Luna. Her voice soared high and clear on the notes, ringing against the cage, echoing back from the courtyard walls. In the cages, farther down the mountain, the leopards crouched to the ground, their eyes soft and purrs vibrating their throats, and the magrazzi rested its velvet muzzle on its velvet shoulders and smiled.

As the last note died, trembling, into silence, Vita waited for something to happen. The sun fell hot across her shoulders. The bee wafted over the wall on a wisp of warm air. A petal dropped from the apricot tree. The mare shuddered.

Vita ran to the cage and flung herself against its cold bars, bruising her ribs and banging her forehead. In desperation she shook at the bars again but they stood solid and unyielding. Moisture seeped from the mare's dull eyes and trickled down her slender face and dripped onto the dying lilies. She slumped against the cage and slowly folded her legs beneath her, slipping down to lie once more in shadow.

No! Vita cried. *I will keep trying! Keep your horn in the light!*

But the mare didn't answer. Vita gave a dry sob and shook impotently at the bars again.

"You seem agitated, Keeper," said a smooth voice, drifting across the yard, curling into Vita's ear. She whirled to see Lord Maldici, a tall figure in a dark robe, standing in the deep shadows by the courtyard gate, beneath the vines that covered the walls. How long had he stood there, watching her?

In one swift lunge, he crossed the gravel to her side, his face contorted with anger. His fingers bit into her arm like talons.

"What are you doing, witch?" he hissed, staring at the Corno d'Oro mare. Vita realized that he could still see her, despite the spells. "The mare is safe here in her cage. It is the stallion you must think about now, the stallion in the mountains. The equinox approaches; we lack but three weeks until it comes. On that day, you will lead my men to the stallion and capture him alive. You will use your arts to subdue him and to bring him, alive and healthy, to Genovera. You will unite the beasts here, in the cage. They will be mine, their power at my command."

Trembling ran through Vita's body so that her legs shook. The lord's power poured into her arm; she could smell her skin burning. Her hair lifted on her head. She bit her lip against the pain.

"Do you know what happens to those who oppose me?" Maldici asked. "They die by brutti, by chariot wheel. They die with loud cries and they die in silence in deep, dark places. Some die with amazing speed, and others excruciatingly slowly. For you, Vita, I would arrange an imaginative death by torture, by spell and incantation; a slow death devised by that first great sorcerer, Lord Morte. I am not to be trifled with, Vita! I have not wasted months wooing you and bribing you, so that you could turn against me now!"

The lord's voice rose to a shriek and his fingers gripped tighter on Vita's arm. Madness filled his hawk eyes. In her cage, the dying Corno d'Oro mare moaned softly, and overhead a great condor rose up the face of the mountain on a spiral of hot air, his shadow beating across Lord Maldici's shoulders.

Vita bent her head, her face wet with Lord Maldici's spittle. "I will help you, at the equinox," she said softly. "Your power is too great to withstand, my lord. And you can give me what I desire: the small palazzo, the hand of Ronaldo. I do not wish to displease you. I was merely saying spells of healing, to bring the mare back to health before the stallion joins her. I do not think her power will be much use to you until she is healed."

Vita curtsied low, staring at the tips of her shoes, waiting for Lord Maldici to strike her, but he didn't touch her.

"Look at me," he hissed and Vita lifted her lavender moon eyes and stared a long, long moment into Maldici's suspicious anger. Her spine quivered, her arms shook, she felt the skin on her face tighten and stretch in pure fear, but she kept her gaze locked onto the lord's. *Luna help me*, she prayed, and she felt the power of the moon goddess flow into her: a cool blue balm like an evening wind that stilled the burning and the fear. For a fleeting instant, Vita thought she could smell the pure sweetness of lilies blooming on the mountains. Her quivering stilled, her chin lifted. The gaze that she directed to Lord Maldici was smooth and clear, and filled with power. Its surface veiled her true emotions as thin evening cloud veils the face of the moon, and it turned aside his anger and suspicion so that he forgot those feelings.

At long last, he nodded. "Yes," he whispered, "you are mine. We will do well, together, Vita. We will rule the earth."

He ran his fingers down the embroidery of his trailing sleeves, his rings of precious stones somber in the shadowed courtyard. Then he looked at the cage again and chewed on his lower lip.

"She does seem a sickly thing," he said. "Have you power to help her?"

"I must chant my spells over her every day," Vita said. "I will come each afternoon at this time. I must do this alone, so do not spy on me, my Lord. It will take all my power to restore her before we obtain the stallion."

Lord Maldici inclined his head. "Let us hope you can do so," he said, "for both our sakes. Do you need a key?"

Vita saw the distrust flicker in his eyes again.

She shook her head. "It is simple spell that let me in here. I cannot be kept away from the source of my power. I need no key, but you need not fear."

"Fear? You caution *me* not to fear!" He threw back his head, his dark hair hanging over his shoulders, and laughed high, cruel laughter. Then he led the way across the courtyard and through its stiff gate, and down the crooked, steep stairs cut into the mountain crevice, and through his castle's long corridors. He sent for Ronaldo to take her home in this chariot.

In the evening, when Ronaldo left home for a betting game at a friend's palazzo, and the early stars shimmered over the clipped hedges, Vita walked alone in the garden with tears streaming down her face. There was no moon tonight. "Now, Luna, even you have deserted me," Vita whispered. And why not? she thought. I am the Keeper who has betrayed her sacred trust. My power has deserted me and I am helpless. I cannot free the Corno d'Oro mare. My spells did not work. I know no other words of power. I have led Giovanni, my loyal friend, into danger. I have been betrayed by Rosa, who I loved like a sister. I have sent away Marina, who tried to help me. I am a pawn in the hands of darkness, in the talons of Lord Maldici, that dark condor feasting on power.

Beneath a hedge of rosewood, Vita crouched and rocked to and fro, weeping.

This is the end, she thought. The world is plunging toward doom.

CHAPTER TWENTY-TWO

THERE WAS NO MOON THAT NIGHT. Slumped against the stone, Giovanni remembered how at home, on nights like this, his friends would organize raiding parties onto the mainland—how they would stream home at dawn, faces blackened, bellies filled with stolen apricots and mandolo nuts, eyes alight with laughter. Once, on such a night, he had ridden a goat on a dare in the meadow of some villager, and the goat had bucked him off into a stream though he clung to its coarse beard. The laughter of his friends, which they failed to contain, had roused the villager and he'd chased them down perilous alleyways toward the sea, their snorts of laughter echoing from the walls of silent houses.

It seemed long ago, like something in a dream.

Giovanni's mind, weak with hunger and thirst, broken with the dark hours in the castle dungeons, wandered away from the memory. It dwelled for a long time on thoughts of food but no saliva wet his parched and swollen tongue or his cracked lips. Fish leaped through his mind, flickering silver and blue, salty and vibrant; fish on platters, fish his father gutted and his mother fried. He thought of seasnails candied in honey, and baby squid simmered in tomatoes, and anchovies and tunny fried in olive oil. He remembered the griddle cakes of Aunt Carmela, and a cake that Vita had baked for him once with fragranti nuts in it like nuggets of gold. He thought about gold, about gold for Vita to hang at her wrists and her neck; about caskets and merchant ships spilling with gold.

But no, it wasn't good to think of this. It was gold that had caused him to be here, starving and dying on the top of a tower above Genovera. Gold, that he had refused to plunder and kill for, and had been sent ashore to trade with instead. Gold, that had led him to The Condor's Wing, that riverside inn where the spies of Lord Maldici had captured him and brought him, bound and gagged, on a moonless night like tonight, to this place of pain.

Vita, Giovanni thought. Her face danced before his vision, but he couldn't focus on it. Perhaps by now she was betrothed to Ronaldo, with his lazy eyes and those slender legs he wrapped around fast red horses. There was too much pain here; it swelled up in Giovanni's chest like a puffer fish and his thoughts slipped away from Vita and Ronaldo to imagine food again: everything he'd ever eaten and enjoyed, cooked and raw, hot and cold.

A moan, weak as a sigh, drifted into the still night air and after long consideration, Giovanni realized that he himself had made the noise. After that, he fell into a sleep as deep as unconsciousness and did not wake until the early morning sun roused him with its brightness. He was too giddy to stand. His head pounded and his throat was too dry to allow him to swallow. Soon I shall die here, he thought, and it won't matter because Vita is with Ronaldo, and my parents are displeased with me, and the pirati scorn me.

After some time, he hauled himself into a kneeling position, using stones in the battlemented wall that he'd been leaning against. Swaying, he stared down for thousands of feet. The tower to which they had brought him, in Lord Maldici's fortress, gave him a view over the red tiled rooftops of Genovera to where the

Arnona shone in the light, barges drifting on its current like leaves, and the plain where smoke and dust from the army camp ascended into the still morning air. Giovanni stared down into the street directly below the tower, his vision blurred with hunger, and inspected the tiny ant-like forms of people hurrying to and fro. Every day, for hours, he hung here over the battlements and watched for Vita. If only, he thought, he could have one last glimpse of her, and be reassured that she was alive and well…

Presently the narrow door, at the top of the tower's spiral steps of worn stone, swung open. A surly guard in black and silver thrust a bowl of gruel and a beaker of water onto the ground, and slammed the door shut. He had once been amused to watch Giovanni crawl to the bowl, like an injured dog, but had grown tired of this jest. For a long time after the guard left, Giovanni remained slumped against the wall; the effort of crossing to the food seemed too much, and the stones beneath his knees too painful. The thirty feet that separated him from the food was a vast distance.

At last, as the sun's reflection turned orange on the Arnona and fires in the army camp began to shine like stars, Giovanni crawled toward the food. He lifted the bowl awkwardly, and scooped slowly at the gruel with his fingers, his nail beds still searing with the agony of the nails they'd pulled out. The pain gave him a kind of odd pleasure. I said nothing, he reminded himself. When they brought me before Lord Maldici, I said nothing of Vita. When they burned me with tongs, and tore out my nails and broke my ribs, I was silent.

The gruel stuck in his throat. He lifted the stale water and slurped at it noisily, with a great effort saving some for later. At last, he remembered, the lord sent word I was to be kept alive, in case he needed me—needed to use me against Vita. I will die before I will let him use me for his cruel ends.

Giovanni crawled back to the wall and leaned against the rough stones, his cracked ribs aching. Now, he reflected, the lord hopes to break my spirit up here, but I will not break. The guards told me to look out over the land and remember that soon it will all belong to Maldici, who will take the pirati alive and use them against the other nations, and who will set me free to join them if I cooperate. They said I am to be kept here, not in the dungeons, so that I can look over the land and remember, at every moment, what I am missing and how the wind calls to me, bringing me the smell of salt from the delta.

The thought of the sea brought an image of the dolphins to Giovanni and, as night fell, their silvery voices and leaping bodies flashed to and fro in his confused dreams. At midnight, he awoke to the sound of wing beats. Against the stars, he dimly saw the silhouette of a great bird circling overhead, and felt the downdraught of its wings fan his cheeks. Then he slipped into dreams again.

Next time, when he awoke, it was dawn and a pearly flush stained the sky behind the sharp rectangles of the battlements along his tower wall. Giovanni stared in awe at the huge gufo that stood beside him. He had never seen this night bird close up before, for gufos were proud, shy birds that shunned humans and their villages. For some minutes, Giovanni thought that he was still dreaming. Then the bird stepped forward delicately on its curved yellow talons softened with pale feathers, and clicked its beak at Giovanni. Its huge golden eyes, ringed with orange, stared into his own as if willing him into full awareness. He lurched into a sitting position and knuckled his eyes while the gufo waited. Then it held out one scaly leg, and Giovanni saw that something was fastened to it: a rolled scrap of parchment. His fingers shook as he struggled with the silken cord that bound the parchment in place and unrolled the scrap flat on the tattered, red cotton of his pirati breeches.

The gufo told me where you are. I will set you free. Think how. Love Vita.

Giovanni's face, burned with sun and wind, spread slowly into an incredulous grin. Vita! he thought exultantly. Vita who could talk to the creatures of the night, had sent the birds and the animals to find him. She had not forgotten him. And now this—a promise of help! Tears welled in his eyes and he licked at their bitter salt that stung his lips.

The gufo spread its massive wings in delicate fans of feathers barred gray and brown. With the lightest of thrusts, it was suddenly airborne, like an autumn leaf. It circled the tower once and then flew eastward into the rising sun. All day, huddled against the walls in an attempt to keep within their meager shadows, Giovanni thought about how Vita might help him. Over and over again, he remembered the pure joy of reading her words, and watching the beautiful soaring flight of the gufo as it returned to her. All day, battling against thirst and pain and hunger, his mind tried to devise a plan that would allow Vita to free him from the tower.

He smiled when he thought of it at last; smiled that it had taken him, a sailor, so long to think of it.

For two days, he watched the passage of pigeons wheeling below and condors rising overhead; watched the seagulls that screamed over the docks, the delicate cranes that headed for the delta to feed on shrimp, the flight of the wood grouse from the mountains behind the fortress, the flight of the gufo when it came at dawn and dusk and circled overhead, dropping him a quill and a bottle of ink that he barely caught in time before it shattered on the tower's stones. For two days, he thought of the pirati gunships, their wing-like sails bellying with air as they took flight over the long swells of the Middle Sea. For two days, his stomach cramped with fear when he considered how his own destiny might yet bring him to the dragon deep beneath the sea on its bed of looted gold.

Send light cord, a bolt of silk, tamosa wood, a knife, a needle, thread. Send them before the moon rises, he wrote to Vita with her quill and ink, that he kept hidden in his pocket—although the guard seldom looked at him any more, simply shoved the gruel and water onto the floor every morning and slammed the door shut. He rolled the parchment around the gufo's leg and tossed it into the air to flap softly away across the sea of mountain air, scented with pine and juniper, that rolled over the rooftops of Genovera.

For five days he waited, while the gufo came at night and brought him packets of fragranti nuts and honeycakes, and pieces of roast chicken wrapped in grape leaves, and once a whole baked fish with bones removed. The moon waxed to a sliver in the east. Giovanni spent his days thinking about sailing in air, like a gufo, and his nights dreaming of dolphins and Vita.

On the evening of the sixth day, as Giovanni waited for the moon to rise, and listened to the far-off sound of the city—its music and bells, its clattering hooves and shouting vendors—he heard too the familiar whooshing of the gufo's heavy wings. He turned from the parapet in time to see the bird land beside him with a great ball of strong, silken twine in its claws. Giovanni ran a length of the twine though his callused fingers; it was from the corda tree in Terre, that makes the strongest rope or twine in all the earth. Giovanni smiled. Two more gufos circled overhead, dropping a bolt of silk to land with a thump at his feet. He stooped over it, touching the fabric: smooth and strong as water. The birds flew off but barely had the sound of their wing beats died into silence than several more gufos arrived, bearing between them long pieces of tamosa wood that is the lightest wood there is, as filled with air as the bones of a bird. The last bird dropped a packet at his feet; he opened it to find an ivory-handled knife, and a sharp needle that flashed in the dim light of the rising moon, and a twist of silken thread. Giovanni wrote Vita one last note: *Meet me by the Arnona bridge, before the moon sets* and he sent it to her rolled around the leg of a gufo.

The remaining gufos perched on the edge of the parapet, between the battlements, and watched him with their round wide eyes while the city of Genovera sank into stillness, unbroken but for horses neighing in the army camp. Giovanni cut his tamosa wood to length: thin pieces that were long and light but strong. He unrolled the silk from the bolt, so that it shimmered and slid around his feet, and he laid it out flat on the stones and cut it up with the knife, its smooth handle growing warm to his touch. He forgot his pain as he worked, forgot how his chest hurt with every breath and how his fingers ached and throbbed.

He threaded the needle clumsily and began to sew, the needle flashing through the silk, in the same way that he had sewn nets for many years, seated on the harbor wall or in the bottom of his blue boat with its yellow sail. A sense of peace fell over him with the familiarity of this task, and the gufos hooted softly to one another and ruffled their feathers. When the pieces of silk were sewn together, Giovanni began painfully to sew them onto the tamosa strips, lashing them tightly around the wood with even stitches. He glanced up once, and saw that the moon was slipping far down the western sky. Grimly he sewed on, making long strips of silk into a harness that fit around his chest.

At last, he arose and went to the parapet. In the army camp, when he looked over, the fires had died to smoky glimmers, and the barges were anchored and still on the Arnona. Giovanni held up a wet finger and tested the air; the breeze was from the west, from the delta, and Giovanni thought that he could smell the salt marshes and the mouth-watering fragrance of crab roasting over a driftwood fire.

He lifted his creation to the edge of the parapet, and paused to caress each gufo in turn. Their golden eyes reflected a tiny fingernail of moon, and their feathers were warm and supple. Giovanni climbed onto the parapet beside his creation, wincing with the pain in his ribs, panting with exertion. For a moment he sat, staring giddily downward, through the thousands of feet of darkness below the soles of his very feet. It was like looking into deep water, and he remembered how he had once jumped over the rail of a gunship and swum away into dark waves. There would be no dolphins, this time, to rescue him. He swallowed hard, and looked one last time at his prison of stone, while the gufos collected all the scraps of wood and silk that were left and flew away with them. Shortly, the tower lay empty.

Then Giovanni fitted the silk harness around his body and tied it to the underside of his creation with strong seaman's knots. He stood to his feet, and lifted the light frame of tamosa wood over his head. Closing his eyes, he stepped out into cool air.

He plummeted like a thrown rock. His arms jerked and ached with strain. Terror flooded his mind. His vision whirled. Rooftops streaked up to meet him; stars wheeled in crazy patterns. Wind sucked away his breath; he was suffocating like a drowning man. No dolphins, he thought. No dolphins this time.

Then, the creaking tamosa wood began to slow his plummeting descent. The silk, filled with air, slid him sideways through the darkness, away from the Maldici walls of pale stone. A gufo was beside him now, hooting softly. Giovanni hung below his silken wings and felt his ribs bending like the tamosa wood, smelled the smoke of the city's thousand banked fires rising up to meet him. He angled his sails into the wind and soared over chimneypots and palazzi towers, over gardens of apricot and mandolo, over cobbled streets and bells hanging silent in their fretted towers.

Down he came, down, swinging softly, lightly on the wind, like a little boat running over a gentle sea. Now he was over the Arnona, its swirling, deep currents that carried the cold snowmelt from above Bossano down to the ocean, to the Golfo d'Levanto, to the water that he had been born to swim in and boat on. Giovanni tipped the tamosa wood frame and swept back to the Arnona's shore, downstream from the army camp and on the opposite bank. He landed in river grass, the jolt of landing knocking his weak legs out from under him so that he pitched forward and fell face down in the grass, feeling its new spring growth licking him like soft tongues. For a long moment, he lay there and inhaled the smell of wet earth and fresh water. Then, the gufos landed at his side and clicked their beaks.

Giovanni wobbled to his feet and dragged his wings into the shelter of a belt of trees. He peered around. The air was silent, the moon had almost set, and it lacked but an hour until dawn.

Giovanni uncurled his rigid fingers from the tamosa wood and rubbed them to restored the circulation. Then he took the knife from his pocket and cut himself out of the harness, cut through the tamosa wood and slashed the silk into scraps. He threw all the pieces into the Arnona and watched the river suck them in and sweep them away. No remains would be found, to connect him to Vita. Then he began to walk, as fast as his weak legs would take him, toward the delicate curve of the bridge. Approaching it, he fell to his stomach in the grass and surveyed the scene. There were sentries posted on the bridge. He cursed himself for being stupid; what if Vita walked into danger? For minutes he lay, undecided, then snaked forward on his belly, veteran of a hundred raids in orchard and fish drying sheds and other boyish misdemeanors, and worked his way beneath the bridge without being seen.

In the deeper darkness there, he stiffened and lay very still. The river's gurgle and suck filled his ears. Something touched his hand; he bit his lips to hold in his shout of terror. Then he recognized the touch of skin, the smooth warmth of a palm sliding up his wrist.

"Giovanni?" Her voice was a breath.

"Vita?" He felt her fall of silvery hair swing against his face, and the beating of her heart as he wrapped his arms around her. Her lips were soft, kissing his forehead, the corners of his eyes, his mouth.

He felt the moment when her fingers touched his own, the stillness in her as she realized his nails were missing. "What have they done to you?" she cried, and he pressed her face against his shoulder to keep the sentries overhead from hearing . "Hush, nothing that won't heal. We must leave before it's light," but she shook her head against his shoulder.

"You must go, but I cannot come. I have to free the mare."

"What mare?"

She pulled his ear against her mouth and quickly, the words tripping and spilling over each other, she told him about the mare in the golden cage, about Rosa's betrayal and Ronaldo's falseness, and the power and madness of Lord Maldici. "Everything that has happened is my own fault," she said brokenly. "It's my greed that has caused it all."

"Hush," he comforted her, rocking her in the grass while the river sucked and swirled around the pale arches of the bridge, and the horn of the moon slipped over the western mountains into the sea. "Hush. Where is Rosa now? How did you come here without her?"

"She is in a drugged sleep," Vita confessed. "I bought poppy from an old woman at the docks. I gave it to her in fig-canary. Forget her."

"We must think what to do next."

"Please, Giovanni, please leave."

"When they find I am gone, they will suspect you."

"No. No one knows that I have any idea you are in Genovera. There is nothing to link us together. I cannot leave without the Corno d'Oro mare."

"It is but seven days to the Equinox, Vita. What of the stallion?"

"I must free the mare within the next four days. Then, whether I have freed her or not, I must ride home with Lord Maldici's men for the equinox. But I will never betray the stallion to them."

"They will not let you perform the magic to keep him invisible," Giovanni protested.

"They will not know what I'm doing. I'll trick them. I'll pretend to be hunting the stallion with them."

"Then Lord Maldici will kill you."

"I don't know," she said, but a long shudder ran through her and Giovanni pulled her helplessly closer against himself.

"I will come into the mountains and help you," he said. "But first, I must vanquish the dragon before his feast day."

"Dragomar?"

"He can be vanquished, I think. I have read much about dragons in Giuseppe's books. Until Dragomar is vanquished, my people will never be free of the thrall of gold. And listen, Vita, there is something else I learned from Giuseppe's library. When your little sister was lost in the sea, as a babe, she did not die."

"What!" Vita's whispered exclamation was hot against Giovanni's ear and he felt the tension humming in her body.

"The sea witch made a spell, for a great wave that would sweep your sister away. She wanted her for a daughter."

"Marina—*Marina*—is my sister? I don't believe it."

"If you see her again, ask her if she has a tiny mark shaped like a leaf, under her hair at the back of her neck."

"The mark of every girl child of my family who is named Carmela," Vita breathed wonderingly.

They hugged in silence for a while, as dogs barked and horses neighed in the army camp, and the sentries banged their boots restlessly against the bridge railings overhead and complained about their hunger.

"We are running out of time," Vita said with a sigh. "You must go home and fight the dragon, Giovanni. I must stay and free the mare. You cannot do this, and I cannot battle the dragon. Don't argue with me! You know that I am right and that the balance of the world is at stake. There are things more important now than what we want for ourselves. If Luna wills it, we shall see each other again soon."

"I cannot leave you," he protested, but she laid her palm against his mouth. "Hush," she said. "You know that what I say is true. I did not free you so that you could remain here in danger. Go to your people. Marina knows some pirati shore-men here in the city. When I met her in town, she said she has arranged a boat to take you out to a gunship hidden in the delta."

"A boat?"

She took his face in her hands and turned it toward the dim archway at the bridge's eastern end, where the pearly dawn light gathered. He saw a boat, a small trading vessel, slipping easily toward them on the current. It slid into the gloom under the bridge, and Vita hauled him to his feet as it approached with water chuckling beneath the bows. "You must jump," she said. "They cannot stop long."

"And you? How will you get back to the palazzo?"

"Soon, another boat will come for me, heading upstream to the docks. Then I will run up alleys and arrive before Rosa wakes. Go, go!

"May Sirena keep you," he muttered, and kissed her one last time, feeling the rapid flutter of her heart, feeling her fear and her steely resolve. Then, for a moment, the trading vessel slowed in its course, its gunwale drifting a few feet out from the grassy bank, and in the gathering light Giovanni launched himself toward it and felt his feet land hard on the wooden deck. An arm shot out and tumbled him down a flight of steps, his broken ribs shattering him with pain. When he pressed his face to the porthole, Vita waved once, a shadowy figure backlit by morning sun, her pale hair and lavender eyes shining.

The boat shot out beneath the bridge, in the center of the current, and bore Giovanni swiftly away down the Arnona toward the delta and the sea. He lay on a bunk, gulping with pain and sadness, longing for Vita and longing, at the same time, for the moment when the first ocean swell would lift the trader's bow and rock him with that old, familiar motion he knew and loved so well.

"Soup?" a pirati asked, and thrust a bowl of steaming mullosk chowder under Giovanni's nose. "Eat up. A gunship awaits us off the delta and the wind is fair. We'll be home before the equinox."

Giovanni inhaled the soup's fragrant steam gratefully, and tried to ignore the curdle of fear in his stomach. After the equinox, one day after, came the Feast of Dragomar, a deadly foe. I am weak as a new-born seahorse, Giovanni thought grimly. How can I tackle the dragon a few days hence? And he spooned soup into his mouth as though his strength depended upon it alone.

In the highest tower of pale stone, in the fortress of Lord Maldici, the sorcerer's red-headed daughter spooned a clear liquid into a glass vial. Into this she then poured the last drops of fig-canary that lay in the bottom of a glass that she'd brought into the room wrapped inside her shawl. She swirled the two liquids together and held the vial over the fire with a set of silver tongs, chanting under her breath. A scowl pulled at her mouth as the mixture in the vial turned a smoky green.

"Poppy," she muttered angrily through clenched teeth, and hurled the vial against the back of the chimney where it shattered in a hundred sharp splinters. The girl turned as her father stormed into the room, his black robes billowing at his ankles and his eyes glittering.

"I've been drugged!" the sorcerer's daughter cried. "The Keeper—"

But Lord Maldici wasn't listening to her. He flung himself into his chair of carved mandolo wood, and ground his heels against the deep rug of golden angoli wool that lay beneath the chair. "The prisoner from the tower has vanished!" he snarled. "Vanished without a trace. There is sorcery here!"

"Perhaps he threw himself from the battlements," the girl said smoothly, unbraiding her long hair so that it crackled and sparked in the firelight.

"There is no body!" her father shrieked. "There is something afoot in my city, some power I haven't sensed!"

"What does he matter, one useless, ragged pirati boy?" the girl sniffed.

"He matters because the Keeper cares for him. He might be useful to persuade her of things."

"The Keeper drugged me last night," she repeated and this time her father's eyes narrowed on her face, and his knuckles whitened on the chair's carved arms.

"What is she up to?" he muttered. "It is but five days to the equinox. We must guard her. She has been neglecting the Corno d'Oro mare. I shall lock them up together and she shall remain there in the courtyard until we escort her south to the mountains, to catch the stallion on the equinox.

His voice rose to a shriek and spittle flew. "She shall not trick us!"

His daughter turned away from the madness in his eyes to stare into the fire. "If you provoke her, she might not cooperate with us. You said you wanted her power," she pointed out. "Why else have we flattered and seduced her all these months?"

"She's been flattered enough! She shall bow to my will!" the sorcerer raged, as he pounded on the floor with a stick to summon one of the guards stationed outside the door.

"Take four men and a chariot to the palazzo Castiglioni," he commanded, when the guard entered. "Seize the Keeper and bring her to me."

The man bowed and retreated swiftly.

"I am tired of being a maid," Lord Maldici's daughter pouted. "If the Keeper is going to be locked in the secret courtyard with the Corno d'Oro mare, I shall come home and be your daughter again."

"Soon you shall be heir to an Emperor," her father promised. "Soon the trading ships will lay open their holds for your inspection, groveling ambassadors will arrive with proposals from foreign princes, and the whole world will speak in awe of your beauty."

The girl moved to the window, holding aside the heavy draperies of ruby colored damask from the looms of Genovera, with her lips curling. She stared greedily across Verde's distances, its field turning green with spring, its trees blossoming like clouds. Her golden hawk eyes narrowed.

"Father!" she cried. "A fast horse comes over the bridge, bearing a messenger from the south. I recognize his colors. He comes with news of Lord Verona! His horse is exhausted, lathered and sweaty. It staggers on the cobbles! "

She turned from the window's leaded panes and followed her father across the tiled floor and down the winding stairs, down and down to the reception hall. Under the chandeliers the messenger collapsed at their feet, his sweat-streaked shoulders heaving, his muddy boots soiling the tiles with their inlay of marble and turquoise from Lontano.

My lord!" he panted. "The country people are rising in revolt against you. They are led by a wandering beetleman with a troop of puppeteers!"

Lord Maldici's lips snarled silently over his curved teeth.

"I tremble in my fortress," he said softly, dangerously. "Fool!" and he kicked the messenger in the ribs so that the man cried out and sprawled in the mud from his own boots. "Do not spoil my horses riding to me with such a fool's tale. Do you think the country rabble will survive a crossing of the Arnona, where my troops are stationed?"

"My lord," the man gasped, rolling away. "This is not all. The country people are joining the army of Lord Verona. Your brother is marching north to attack you!"

CHAPTER TWENTY-THREE

THE BIANCO WAS BLOWING—that strong, cold wind from the northern mountains. It filled the red sails of the pirati gunship as it ran south along the coast of Verde, so that the ship flew before it. Along the coastline, water crashed against rocks in sheets of white spray, and the wind lifted spume from the crests of the waves and turned it into mist. The sea was a dark, bright, wild thing, alive with wind. Overhead, the Bianco lifted the pelicans aloft so that their white feathers caught the spring sunshine and kindled into brilliance.

Hour after hour, as the gunship streamed south, Giovanni paced the decks, his legs wobbly beneath him after being so long a prisoner in the tower, and thought about the lore of dragons that he had memorized in the library of Giuseppe, in the books that the old wanderer had gathered from around the world. I cannot hope to fight the dragon alone, Giovanni thought. He is as tall as the masts of the gunships, as strong as a tidal wave, as wild as the sea itself. His teeth are each as big as a man. If I cannot fight him, I must use trickery against him; trickery and magic.

At evening on the third day after departing from the delta, the gunship slid silently up the inlet toward the pirati village, the watchman on the point crying a welcome as the ship's great sails were furled along the yardarms and the anchor was readied. A crowd of pirati women and children darkened the harbor wall as they waited to meet their men coming home from the sea. Giovanni went down the gangplank onto the rough stones of the wall, and looked around the harbor for his little boat. And there it was; he spotted it moored and rocking on the ripples, its paint as bright blue as he remembered, its yellow sail neatly furled. A flicker of pure joy ran through him and he began to jog, holding his ribs and gasping with pain, up the cobbled alleyways that led home.

He would never forget, in later years, the look of incredulous joy on the faces of his parents when he half-fell through the doorway. His mother turned from the fire with a cry, dropping the spoon with which she'd been stirring a simmering pot, and his father crossed the room in one stride and seized him in a hug so fierce that Giovanni thought he would suffocate in it. They fed him stew on which he burned his tongue, and bound up his ribs with strips of torn cotton, and rubbed his fingers with a salve of seabalm. While he told of his trial in the fortress, their rough, dark faces stared at him, their changeable sea eyes dark with anger and tears, their golden earrings glinting in the firelight as it flickered over their brightly patched clothes.

At last, Giovanni fell into his own bed and slept deeply for many hours. In the morning he ate griddle cakes and anchovies pickled in lemon, and went whistling down to the harbor wall to his blue boat, without telling his parents where he was going or what he was planning to do. He couldn't bear to lose their approval again so soon. When he had vanquished the dragon, changing forever the pirati way of life, would be soon enough for his father to be angry with him. Although, perhaps then he would not be alive to face his father after all. Perhaps he would be dead in Dragomar's deep sea caverns.

All day, Giovanni tacked between the islands in long reaches, for the Bianco was still blowing from the mountains of Bossano. Giovanni's blue hull shot between reefs where water boiled white over black weed and jagged rock. It swept past islands, and narrowly avoided rocky headlands where waves roared in and shot upward, hanging suspended for long moments like lace against the blue sky. Pelicans and seabirds slipstreamed overhead, and the wind thrummed in the rigging and roared in Giovanni's ears. He balanced himself against his mast and laughed aloud with the delight of being alive and free on the water again.

Around noon, he reached the island of Giuseppe the hermit and went ashore to rap loudly on the door. "It is time!" he said as the door swung open to reveal the hermit's bushy brows and crooked nose, his glinting spectacles. "It is time for you to help me; to play your part in defeating the dragon." Giuseppe's face crinkled into a thousand lines of pleasure, and his bony hand caught Giovanni and pulled him inside. He remained there for a long time, emerging at last with a parchment scroll on which were written, in the ancient dragon tongue and the hermit's purple ink, the words that Giovanni needed to know. He slid the parchment inside his shirt and buttoned it to the chin. In one hand he carried an ancient bell, its brass dome rimed with salt, its clapper silenced with a wrapping of wool. It had come from the ruins of some foreign city that Giuseppe had visited once.

On the way home, running before the wind now, his bows slicing through green waves, Giovanni stopped at the sea witch's house on the point and knocked on her door. This time, when the door opened, he went inside only briefly and emerged bearing beneath one arm a huge conch shell, striped with bands of gold and white, and carved to create a horn. Giovanni lifted the hole bored in one end to his lips, and imagined blowing through it. Then he wrapped it in seagrass and laid it carefully in the bottom of his boat. Finally, he circled the island, searching for the Mara and for the sea urchins. He found a Mara man combing his long green hair on a tiny island west of the pirati village, and spoke with him for a while. The sea urchins he found building a bonfire of driftwood on another island, amongst the rocks along the shoreline. They shared their fish with Giovanni: little sardini that they skewered on sharp sticks and roasted over the fire, and while they ate they listened to Giovanni's request. Their faces became pale and afraid, and they shook their heads and muttered and stared at the sand. One stepped forward then: the boy Ambro with his golden skin and his hair like old honey.

"I'll help," he promised bravely, and stood before Giovanni as straight as an arrow.

Finally another boy stepped forward followed by two others.

"That's enough of you, "Giovanni said. "I'll see you in the morning."

It was evening, and still stormy, when Giovanni sailed home to the village and his parents. All night, while the wind strengthened and the sea grew wilder, Giovanni lay awake in his bed stuffed with seagrass, memorizing the words in the ancient dragon tongue, and fighting the fear that caught him by the back of the neck and chilled his whole body. Restlessly he tossed and turned, imagining Dragomar's scaly back and his writhing tail that could smash a boat into splinters with one blow, and the dragon's blue shining teeth that could bite a man in half with one chomp. The night seemed endless. Giovanni rose before dawn and crossed to the window, watching the racing clouds cover the face of the moon.

Sirena, help me, he prayed to the dolphin goddess. Give me strength to battle Dragomar. Protect me and those who help me. Strengthen my tongue and make it clever with dragon words. Strengthen my heart that it doesn't weaken in its purpose. Strengthen my arm that tolls the bell. Strengthen my body, to stand before that old monster.

At dawn, the light was dirty and pale yellow, without warmth. The clouds thickened and the wind lessened. Rain began to fall. Giovanni crept from the house before his parents awoke, with a cold griddle cake in one pocket and his stomach clenched tight around a ball of fear, trying to keep it there so that it wouldn't spread through his whole body. His hands shook as he gathered rope on the harbor wall, as he untied the bow line for his boat, as he shoved off from the wall and slipped silently down the inlet toward the tossing, gray Golfo where, in its dark depths, the dragon lay with his scaly belly protecting his stolen hoard.

On the point, at the mouth of the inlet, the four sea urchin boys waited, as they had promised, and Giovanni stopped to pick them up. Their faces were thin and frightened in the cold morning light, but there was a steely resolve in Ambro's bright tawny eyes. Giovanni smiled at them all.

"Lucky for us the wind is dropping," he said. "The rain won't matter." The boys nodded but didn't reply.

It was still raining when Giovanni reached the center of the Golfo and turned the bows of his blue boat into the fitful, dying wind. The wet sails flapped and the boat rocked on the water. Giovanni waited, while gulls cried mournfully overhead. At last, the head of the Mara man broke the surface, and he swam to the boat and gripped the gunwale with strong hands covered in tiny, soft, green scales. His beard was braided and woven through with small, white cowry shells and golden beads.

"We have brought the mirror," he said. "You can look at your own faces and see how white with fear they are. Are you still going to do this, Giovanni the pirati?"

"Yes," Giovanni replied staunchly, stilling the tremor in his voice. "Dragomar has held my people in thrall too many years. And your people will no longer have to fear the dragon stealing from you, once he is vanquished."

"We look forward to such a day," the Mara man agreed gravely. "As to the affairs of pirati, we care little."

As he spoke, several more Mara heads broke the surface and swam toward the boat. Long arms, covered in pink and green and blue scales, lifted a huge mirror, framed in solid gold, above the surface. They slid it, streaming with water, into the boat, their golden bracelets chiming on their wrists.

"I will always remember your help," Giovanni said. "I will repay you whenever I can."

"We need no help from pirati," one Mara replied disdainfully, arching her pale green brows, but then she flipped her arm playfully at Giovanni and splashed him. With a silvery laugh, she dove from sight. The Mara man remained clinging to the boat's gunwale.

"We have brought the bait," he said, and he pulled up through the water a basket of fine golden wire, filled with golden coins and jeweled rings, necklaces hung with sea sapphires, and coral brooches, and earrings of gold set with fiery rubies from Mombasso, and sapphires from Lontano, and two goblets of solid gold inlaid with purple pearls. Giovanni lifted the basket into his boat and tied a great length of strong rope to it.

"Am I in the right place?" he asked, and the Mara man nodded, the beads quivering in his braided beard.

"You are drifting over the caverns of Dragomar."

"Then I shall begin," Giovanni said, and felt fear squeeze his cracked ribs so that he gasped with pain; his heart clenched like a fist before bounding up into his throat. He staggered in the rocking boat and grabbed the mast for support. The four sea urchins and the Mara man watched him gravely.

"I am ready," Giovanni insisted.

The Mara let go of the gunwale and dove deep out of sight, and Giovanni tipped back his head and called for the dolphins in his mind.

Sea brothers, help me! Come to me, sea brothers!

For several minutes, Giovanni and Ambro and the other sea urchins waited, rocking in the boat in the sullen swell while the rain trickled through their hair, plastering it to their heads, and soaking their shirts across their shoulders, and making their bare skin shine. In each of them, a ball of fear knotted and writhed, swelling bigger by the minute. Then, with a leap and a splash, the dolphins arrived beside the boat, calling, and looking at the boys with their bright dark eyes.

We have come! What do you need, Giovanni? We have come!

It is time to vanquish Dragomar, who has held my people in thrall for many generations. I need you to steady my boat!

Then the dolphins swam closer and the sea urchins peered over the gunwale in amazement to watch as their sleek green and blue bodies moved against the hull until they were touching it all around and beneath, supporting the boat and holding it still in the sea.

Giovanni sucked in a deep breath, ignoring the pain in his ribs, sucked in salt and wind and courage; thought of his people waking in their saltgrass beds unaware that today their lives would be changed forever; thought about the smooth brow of Sirena the dolphin goddess, crowned with sea stars.

"I am ready to begin," he repeated, and this time his voice rang strong.

The four sea urchins hoisted the great Mara mirror, looted centuries ago from some nobleman's castle in a foreign land and lost in a shipwreck, and balanced it on the gunwale. Their strong, callused hands gripped the gold frame with its patterns of shells and nymphs, holding the mirror steady. It reflected the cloudy sky, but the rain was stopping now, and presently Ambro pulled his shirt off and wiped the mirror dry so that it returned a clear reflection.

Meanwhile, Giovanni leaned over the boat and paid out the long length of rope that he'd fastened to the basket of gold. Down and down the basket sank, through layers of chill water, through green gloom and waving weed, trailing bubbles and phosphorescence in its wake. Giovanni gripped the rope as the basket swayed and the rope tugged at his hands, cutting into his skin. He braced himself against a thwart and slowly, slowly paid out the rope until he reached the end of it. Then he began to haul it in, faster, hand over hand, the dripping coils lying across his bare feet. When the basket reached the surface, he waited motionless, holding his breath, to see what would happen.

With a heave and a swirl like a whirlpool, the dragon's back broke the surface of the sea. His blue spines gleamed like iron spikes. Up and up he rose until he towered against the sky. His great maw opened wide as he roared in greed and frustration for the basket of gold that Giovanni had lowered to his caverns and then hauled up again, luring him after it. The sea boiled as he lashed his tail. The dolphins, with their supple strength, held Giovanni's rocking boat steady, and Giovanni stooped to the floor to pick up the horn of conch shell that he'd borrowed from the sea witch. He hid behind the mirror with the urchins, and held only the lip of the conch shell around one edge of the golden frame.

"Over here, great dragon!" he called into the conch. The shell magnified the noise so that it roared and boomed over the water. Dragomar swung his scaly head from side to side, his half-blind eyes—that were accustomed to the gloom of his deep sea caverns—shining like glass fishing floats. His terrible fetid breath, filled with the stench of rotting things, made Giovanni gag. Then the dragon saw himself in the mirror but, having never seen his own reflection before, didn't recognize himself. He lashed his tail and roared defiance at the other dragon.

"I am Scuro, the great sea serpent who was old before you were in the egg, Dragomar! I rule the Middle Sea and all its waters! I create the north wind with my breath and make the ocean swell with my swimming!"

Giovanni's boasting boomed across the water from the conch shell and Dragomar lashed the sea in a frenzy of rage.

The dolphins struggled to hold the boat steady, to lift it even higher in the water, for it floated very low with the weight of the extra people and the great mirror on board. Without the dolphins' help, it would have capsized.

"I command you to go hence, Dragomar! Tales of your fame and might have reached my ears," Giovanni continued, in the ancient tongue of dragons that sounded harsh and wild to the ears of men.

"Far beyond the Middle Sea, one of your kin has died: Nero, that black sea serpent of the west. He has died and left empty the sunken city of Atlanti where his lairs were made. For a thousand years the city has lain beneath the sea, its streets paved with gold, its temples studded with rubies, its bells tolling in the deep currents."

Giovanni bent quickly and lifted Giuseppe's old bell, tearing the woolen wrapper from the tongue so that the bell rang clear and deep across the heaving sea, a mournful note.

Dragomar became quieter. He swam closer toward the boat, until Giovanni retched for pure air to breathe, and the sea urchins' hands shook with terror on the mirror frame.

"Hold it steady," Giovanni hissed, and to the dolphins, quivering against the hull, he said, *Courage, brothers! The dragon's time here has almost passed.*

Then he lifted the conch horn to his lips again and roared around the edge of the mirror: "Approach no closer, Dragomar, to your elder, lest I smite you with my stare! I send you away now, to the golden streets of the sunken city in the west, there to take over guardianship of the hoard of your dead kinsman. There is treasure there vaster than you can imagine. Yeah, it will take all the years that remain to you to count the jewels and the chests of treasure and the crowns of long-dead kings. Be gone, Dragomar of the Golfo d'Levanto. You shall henceforth be known as Dragomar, Guardian of Atlanti! At my command, be gone!"

Giovanni bent over behind the mirror, gasping for breath, as he tolled the bell again.

There was a long pause.

Clouds thinned overhead, and a light breeze drifted across the sea urchins' aching shoulders. Waves sloshed over the dolphins' backs and slapped the hull of the boat. Dragomar lay low in the water, swiveling his head, a wisp of steam escaping from his flared nostrils, his barbed tail swinging rhythmically from side to side and sending whirlpools running through the water.

"Make haste, lest some other serpent take what is yours! Make haste to the fabled sunken city west of the Middle Sea!" cried Giovanni over the water, tasting the conch's salty roughness against his pursed lips.

And suddenly, with a roar, Dragomar turned, sending a great swell running toward the boat that almost tipped the mirror and the sea urchins into the sea, despite all the dolphins' efforts to hold the boat steady. Then Dragomar began to swim away toward the west, lashing the water with his tail, his spiked back writhing with muscle, and a white wave cresting at his breast.

Giovanni stood on a thwart and drew in a deep breath, and lifted his hands skyward.

"*I curse you from here to the horizon's horizon!*" he shouted in the ancient tongue of the sea goddess, that he had learned from the books of Giuseppe the hermit.

"I curse you by dragons' blood and the power of deep water,
by the dark of the moon and the blinding heat of the sun.
I curse you by the ancient rage of kings robbed of gold,
and by the power of your own greed.
May you be banished for a thousand years, never to return to these
waters,
lest your eyes shrivel into their sockets,
lest your skin slough from your body like seaweed
and your scales droop like jellyfish,
lest the poison in your tail turn to water
and your teeth drop from your mouth like salt crystals.
In the name of Sirena, mighty goddess of the oceans and all its
creatures,
I banish you with this curse!"

The sea urchins held very still, their eyes stretched wide. It seemed to them as though Giovanni changed as he called these words of power, as though his body stretched taller and his shoulders grew wider, as though a great wind swept from his mouth and his eyes flashed with a terrible light. Beneath the boat, the dolphins held completely still and trembled. Then the last words died on the sea air, and Giovanni was himself again: a young pirati, with a red scarf knotted at his wind-burned throat, and his sea eyes changing from deepest blue to dancing green.

"I think we succeeded," Giovanni said, and his voice—which only a moment ago had rung with power—shook and broke. He bent over in the bottom of the boat and waited for his strength to return, for the pain ringing in his ribs to subside, for his racing heart to steady. The dolphins left the boat and cavorted around it in a wide circle, leaping against the sky with joy, showering the boys with water and laughter.

"Look," said Ambro suddenly. "The pirati are coming!"

Giovanni straightened up and looked along Ambro's pointing arm, and saw the fleet of small pirati boats sailing out from the inlet toward him, floating low in the water because of the crowds that were on board.

"Now they will make me an outcast," Giovanni said solemnly, "because I have changed them from pirati into ordinary seamen." Silence fell over the boat as he and the sea urchins waited for the boats to come closer.

"It is my father in the lead boat," Giovanni said, and sadness tightened his throat. It had been a good homecoming two nights ago, good to feel his father's hug, but he had known that his father's approval would be short-lived. Closer and closer the lead boat tacked, while Giovanni stood still and straight, waiting with his chin high.

"My son! My son!" his father's voice roared across the swell, and the helmsman steered the boat so close beside Giovanni's own that his father could leap across the crack of water and land beside Giovanni. He took him in a mighty embrace and Giovanni saw that there were tears in his father's eyes.

"My son," he said again, with loving admiration. "My brave son, you have vanquished Dragomar. We are free!"

Giovanni stared at him in amazement and then he remembered something that Giuseppe had told him long before, and that he had forgotten: "When the dragon is banished, the spell of the gold greed will fall from your people. They may not remember that they were ever pirati. They may not remember their lust for gold. The generations they spent pillaging the seaways will be like a dream that is forgotten on awakening."

Now the remainder of the pirati fleet reached Giovanni and circled him like a flock of bright birds, tacking to and fro, rolling in the swell. A great cheer rang out for Giovanni, and men balanced on thwarts roaring his name and waving their neckerchiefs in their hands like bright flags. A slow grin stretched Giovanni's face, and he felt his father's arm heavy across his shoulders.

"Can we eat something now?" the youngest urchin asked timidly, and suddenly Giovanni felt laughter bubbling in his chest, the silvery laughter of the leaping dolphins.

"Look!" shouted Ambro suddenly. "What is he doing?"

Once more, Giovanni followed the line of Ambro's arm, which pointed to the scaly back of Dragomar, already miles out to sea as he swam westward. His great body was arcing skyward.

"He is preparing to dive deep, deep to the bottom, where there are no currents, and where he can swim west at greater speed," Giovanni said. The dragon plunged downward, the sea heaved and stilled. Overhead a sea bird cried. Another cheer rang from the pirati boats.

"The sun is coming out, the storm is over. I'll go fishing this afternoon," Giovanni's father said. Giovanni looked toward the east and saw that the clouds were parting. The sun pierced the soft veils of rain that still fell over the mountains. The light strengthened, reached out a long finger that slid across the sea and brightened the waves, that kindled the sails of the pirati boats into brilliant petals of color and flashed on the dolphins' bodies as they leaped from the water. Then the sun reached Giovanni's boat and touched the Mara's mirror, its sheet of smooth glass. As though the mirror were reflecting the light back to itself, the air began to thicken and shimmer.

"Arcobaleno," Giovanni breathed in wonder.

Color shone on the upturned pirati faces as the arcobaleno gathered strength, as it arced over the sea, building a bridge of light, as it reached the shore, as it bent in a great bow over the mountains and disappeared into the north, where the city of Genovera lay below the mountains of Bossano.

Giovanni tipped back his head and felt the colors fall across his face, and awe stilled his heartbeat. He thought of Vita, and wondered if she could see the other end of the arcobaleno, if it touched her in some alley or square of Genovera, or if she were in the mountains bringing the Corno d'Oro mare home to the stallion, realigning the balance of the world with their unity and freedom.

Hope leapt in his chest.

CHAPTER TWENTY-FOUR

AFTER GIOVANNI WAS SWEPT AWAY down the Arnona, Vita lay in the grass beneath the bridge and waited, while the dawn light crept toward her, kindling the grass into tongues of fire. She ached to be going home with Giovanni, with his laughter and the firm, warm grasp of his hands. She ached for the open water of the Golfo, rippling under the spring sun, and for the cries of the pelicans. Then she thought of the Corno d'Oro mare dying alone in her gilded cage, alone and forgotten on the mountain by all except Lord Maldici and his daughter, who plotted her downfall in their hearts. No, Vita could not abandon the mare, not even for Giovanni. So she lay still, and waited for the pirati boat that would bear her upstream and back to the docks of Genovera.

Once she was ashore there, she hurried up an alley to where a painted fish swung over the bright striped awning of a fish café. In the awnings shadow, Marina waited for her, as they had agreed.

"Did he escape?" she asked eagerly, starting forward.

"Shh," Vita said, grasping her thin wrist. "Walk with me. I cannot stop. If I am not home soon, Rosa will awake and miss me."

"Giovanni is on his way to the delta," Vita said as they hurried up sloping stairs and around a corner, dodging fishermen with wicker creels filled with the night's catch, and striped cats that ran crying at their heels.

"Oh, I am glad," Marina sighed.

"It was lucky for us all that you came here with the pirati and have been living near the docks," Vita said, and then she bit her lips and fell abruptly silent. The houses around the docks were not, she knew, very comfortable places to stay. At all hours of the day and night, the streets were noisy with hoof beats and rattling wheels, with hawkers crying their wares, with the thump and bang of cargoes being loaded and unloaded from barges, with the crack of whips. The houses themselves were crowded and slumped with age, their plaster peeling in the damp air, their doorways leading into dim, smoky rooms. The very paint seemed to smell of fish.

I did not consider this before, Vita thought, when I first found Marina again and told her I was sorry for being rude in the garden. I didn't even think what living near the docks was like for her. But now...now, maybe she's my sister, and everything seems changed.

Vita sneaked a sideways glance at Marina as they panted up a steep street between terracotta urns of myrtle and lantana bushes. She noticed again how very green Marina's eyes were: as green as the eyes of Aunt Carmela, and how her thin face looked sad and withdrawn. I should say something to her, Vita thought. I should tell her what I know. But a strange shyness seemed to freeze her tongue, and she couldn't find the right words.

A messenger galloped past them on a lathered horse, its nostrils rimmed with red, its eyes rolling wildly. The man on its back was soaked with sweat, his clothes muddied, his eyes as wild as those of the horse's.

"It is one of Lord Maldici's messengers," Vita told Marina.

Still hurrying, their heels a sharp statacco on the cobble-stones, they burst out into the central square before the great gates of the Caselloni palazzo.

"You're home," Marina said sharply, staring up at the gate's black bars twisted in the shapes of pomegranate flowers, and peering through them at a view of clipped candleberry hedges and leaping fountains. "I guess you won't need me now."

Already she was turning away, with her sharp shoulder toward Vita, and her lips twisted scornfully. "No one inside that place must need anything," she said sarcastically.

"Marina," Vita said softly, and she caught her by the wrist for the second time and turned her gently around.

"Marina, I do thank you for your help in freeing Giovanni. He said something about us both that he learned from the pirati hermit."

"What?" Marina said, her green eyes bright with suspicion.

"You know that my sister was lost at sea when I was a baby, Marina, and that there's no one to be the next Aunt Carmela. Giovanni says that the sea witch stole the baby away and raised her for her own daughter."

Vita was standing very close to Marina now, still grasping her wrist. She felt the leap in Marina's pulse beneath her pale skin, and heard the sharp intake of Marina's breath.

"What are you saying?"

"You're my sister. Turn around and lift up your hair."

Marina turned, lifting in both hands her thick, black, irides-cent hair that hung to her waist. Vita bent over the back of Marina's neck and saw a pale brown mark just below the hair-line, a mark shaped like a leaf. The mark of all the Carmela's, sis-ters of the Keepers in every generation.

"It's there," Vita breathed softly, and Marina let her hair go in sudden shock so that it poured over Vita's hands with soft warmth. She put her arms around Marina as she turned, and felt Marina's thin straight body stiffen.

"You're really my sister," Vita said gently, and gradually Marina relaxed. Vita saw with amazement that her sharp green eyes held tears.

"All these years," Marina said, "the sea witch has been annoyed with me because I couldn't do her spells. I thought I was stupid, Vita. I couldn't do the Bright Cross spell though I tried, over and over. The stars pointed to your valley. And when I went there, to your valley, I felt at peace. I wanted to stay forever and do village magic and heal broken bones and make green things grow and nuts ripen and help women and animals give birth. I wanted to be like Aunt Carmela. And now I shall be, Vita! Now I shall!"

Vita had never heard Marina say so much. With a sudden flash of insight, she understood how hard and lonely Marina's childhood had been, and she felt guilty for misjudging her and disliking her. I will do better in the future, she thought. I will make it up to her.

Marina had more to say. "And when I left, my moth—the sea witch—said that I must guard against greed. It was her own greed she spoke of, her greed that made her steal me as a baby and—"

Suddenly the tramp of heavy boots filled the air and Vita felt hard hands grasp her by the shoulders and wrench her away from Marina.

"How dare you? Let me go!" she shouted, struggling, but the hands held her fast with a brutal grip that bruised her collarbone and tugged at her hair. The hands turned her roughly, and she saw that she was being held by a guard in the black and silver of the House of Maldici. Behind him stood three other guards, with silver condors on their chests, and their steel lances tipped with shining points. Her mouth went dry. She drew herself up to her full height and glared at them.

"What is this?" she asked imperiously, the way a nobili woman might have.

"We are sent to bring you to Lord Maldici," the guard gripping her arm replied. "The chariot awaits you."

Vita saw the golden wheels resting on the cobbles, and remembered the knife blades for cutting down men like wheat. A shiver passed through her but she straightened her spine and nodded.

"I will come then," she said, and stepped forward.

"And I will come, too!" Marina cried.

"No. You were not sent for," the guard said disdainfully, glancing at Marina's faded dress with its muddy hem, and at her tough bare feet.

"I am the Keeper's sister and I will come with her! Out of my way!" she said with a scornful curl of her lip, and swept past the guards to join Vita at the chariot. The guards looked at one another and shrugged. "Best to bring her," one muttered. "Better to bring her than let her go free by mistake," another agreed. The girls climbed into the chariot and the driver snapped the reins across the horses' backs so that they sprang forward at a trot, the wheels rattling, and the guards running behind with their boots pounding. Early morning shoppers turned aside quickly, keeping their eyes downcast, as guards and chariot swept past and up the long incline to the fortress of Lord Maldici.

The lord awaited them in the reception hall. At the sharp pointed toes of his silver shoes lay the sweating messenger whom they'd earlier seen galloping by. Vita raised her eyes from the messenger's back and saw that Lord Maldici's daughter stood at his shoulder, still wearing her simple maid's dress of plain blue fabric but with her unbound hair falling over her shoulders in a crimson tide that snapped as she moved. Her lips twisted in a sly, triumphant smile.

Vita advanced over the marble, feeling again the stab of betrayal. "It must have amused you, how gullible I was."

"I expected nothing else from a simple village girl, not much more than a street urchin," Princess Maldici sneered.

"Rosa! I treated you like a sister! Did it mean nothing to you?"

"Why would I want to be your sister, and—"

"Silence!" roared the Lord Maldici. "You have been neglecting the Corno d'Oro mare, Keeper. It lacks but seven days to the equinox. You will travel south to the mountains in four days time, to fetch the stallion for me. Until then, I shall lock you in the courtyard with the mare, so that you can give her your undivided attention. She must be strong—I need her! My brother's army approaches from the south. We march to war! And who is this peasant smelling of fish?"

He extended a claw-like finger toward Marina.

"I am Marina, sister to the Keeper," she said with a haughty glare.

The Lord's eyes narrowed. "Sister?" he asked. "Indeed. This is most interesting. I shall consult my books. Have you power with the Corno d'Oro?"

"Perhaps," Marina answered.

"You shall join the Keeper in my courtyard, where I can keep an eye on you both. Follow me." He whirled abruptly, his green cape lined with wood doves' plumage swirling at his ankles, and the condor pin that fastened the cloak around his throat flashed a cold fire in the light of the chandeliers. Vita gave Marina a look of mingled gratitude and shame, and followed Lord Maldici up flights of marble stairs, and down echoing corridors to come at last to the steep stairs carved into the mountain crevice, that led to the secret courtyard.

When they reached the gate, Vita saw that the lock she had opened had been replaced with a new one forged of heavy black steel. Lord Maldici took it in his hand as he thrust Marina and Vita through the gate.

"Do not try to escape from here," he warned them. "Two assassini with brutti will wait at the bottom of these stairs, and this lock will not yield to your spells. I have forged it myself, in my dungeons, chanting over it the dark power of Lord Morte. It will hold more than you, Keeper."

Vita ignored Lord Maldici. She strode across the gravel to the cage, where the apricot tree had loosed all its blossoms to sprinkle the ground and the mare's back and the thin mane hanging from her bent neck. Beside Vita, Marina whispered softly, "She is dying."

"Yes," Vita agreed, staring at the bruised eyelids that remained closed, at the soft lips wrinkled on the bent foreleg. The mare's slow death filled her with infinite sorrow. She waited until Lord Maldici had retreated down the stairway, his footsteps receding into silence. Then she whispered, "I must free her. But how? Now I am a prisoner too, and there are only four days left to me. And you—you are all tangled up in my mistakes."

"I'm your sister," Marina said. "It feels strange, but true. I want to help you."

"Oh Marina, you have already done so much. I'm ashamed that you've done so much for me."

She reached out her hand and Marina gripped it and they were silent, with their joined hands pressed against the cage's golden bars, as they stared at the mare.

"If she is so weak, why does the lord want her?" Marina asked at last.

"She is weak from being alone. If the stallion is brought, the lord believes, her power will return. But I think he's wrong. I think the Corno d'Oro need freedom as well as each other to reach their full power, and to maintain the balance in the world. I can see no way to accomplish this."

She let go of Marina's hand and slumped against the cage bars, tilting her face to the thin spring sunshine and listening to the steady rhythm of her heart. The gravel was sharp beneath her and the air was sickly with the dying lilies around the mare's golden hooves. One last apricot flower drifted from the branches and fell into Vita's lap like a dying star. A bee wafted in over the wall and buzzed around the apricot tree, then flew over the wall again into the blue sky.

Vita watched it with unseeing eyes.

All day, while the mare lay still, Vita and Marina leaned against the cage, growing hungrier and thirstier and more afraid.

"We shall all be killed, or taken into the bondage of Lord Maldici's dark power," Vita whispered once, and Marina made no answer. All afternoon, while the light crept across the gravel infinitesimally slowly, the noise from the plain below drifted faintly up to them: the clash of arms and roar of chariot wheels.

"Perhaps he will go to war and forget about the stallion," Marina suggested.

"No, the stallion is part of the plan to defeat his brother, to kill him and take the whole of Verde for himself, and then to have power over all the earth. He will not forget."

"How soon will they go to battle?"

"I don't know. It is many days march from Piso to Genovera, but who knows how closely the troops follow behind the messenger who arrived this morning?"

They relapsed into silence as dusk fell softly and a moth flittered overhead. "The night creatures," Vita said suddenly. "They will help bring my book and—"

She stopped abruptly as booted steps rang outside the gate, mounting the stairs. The guard fumbled at the new lock with a key that grated as it turned, and strode in with an armful of hay and a wooden pail of water. The brutti that was with him remained by the gate, guarding it, and staring at Vita and Marina with eyes that glowed red in the dim light. Even from where she sat, Vita could smell the hot breath, and see the drool on its lips. The guard pushed the hay between the bars to fall at the mare's feet, but she didn't move. He tipped the pail against the bars, so that most of the water it contained slopped into another pail inside the cage, and the rest splattered the gravel a darker gold.

"Where's our food?" Vita demanded.

The guard shot her a surly look. "Isn't hay good enough for you?" he quipped insultingly, before reaching deep into a pocket and pulling out two small packages of chicken wrapped in grape leaves. The gate clanged shut behind the guard and the key grated in it again. Vita and Marina unfolded their grape-leaf packages. They are like the packages I sent to Giovanni, stuck on top of the tower, Vita thought dismally. Only now Giovanni is far away, and I am the one being held prisoner by Lord Maldici.

The chicken stuck in her dry throat.

When she had finished her last bite she wiped her hands on her skirt and tipped her head back to stare at the pale stars. *Night creatures!* she called in her mind. *Night creatures, help me! Come to me!*

Behind her, the mare sighed deeply and moaned in her sleep. Presently, the hanging plants that smothered the courtyard walls rustled, and a furry gray wombo jumped free and ran across the courtyard to Vita. It crept into her lap shyly, its huge eyes shining in the starlight. *Keeper, I have come,* it said, and at the same moment Vita heard the slow beat of a gufo's wings and felt the downdraught flutter her hair as the great bird landed beside her. *Keeper, I have come.*

Vita felt gratitude squeeze her heart. She touched the wombo's warm back and stroked it gently.

In the center of the city, she said, *there is a shrine to Luna the moon goddess. At the base of the altar, one stone is loose. Behind it lies an ancient book that I must have here, where Lord Maldici has imprisoned me. I need to set free the Corno d'Oro mare.*

I can fly here with the book, the gufo said.

I can pull it from its hiding place, the wombo agreed.

Go safely, Vita said, and she kissed the wombo's furry head gently and set it on the gufo's back where it clung with its tiny paws buried in feathers. With a great flap of its wings, the gufo rose over the courtyard wall and disappeared into the darkness that cloaked the mountains.

Marina looked at Vita in awe. "If I could have done my mother's spells half as well, I would still be a sea witch," she said.

"Was she kind to you, the witch?"

"Yes, in her own way. But they are not like us, the sea witches. They are not interested in green growing things, in creatures of the land, in human affairs. They do not care about hunger and cold. They do not feel lonely." Marina's voice dropped to a murmur and she stared at her hands. "I should have guessed I wasn't really her daughter. I've been lonely as long as I can remember."

"Oh Marina. You don't have to be lonely anymore. When we get out of this place, we'll go home and you can share my room with its view over the rooftops and you can run in the valley by the stream. You can care for our mandolo nuts, our fragranti and apricot trees. The village needs you, Marina. I am so ashamed that I wanted Rosa, that treacherous witch, as my sister. And all the time I ignored you, and you were my true sister."

"Don't worry about it now. Tell me more about the village and the Keeper's valley."

"It is the most beautiful place in the world, "Vita said dreamily. "I used to want to travel away from it, but now all I want is to go home to it. In spring it is filled with fragrance, and in autumn the Rain Poppies fill it with their purple petals and ..."

Vita's voice ran on softly, keeping at bay the despair that lurked in her heart, and in her golden cage the mare's ears flickered to listen to Vita's voice telling of green things and beauty.

At last, as the horned moon set, the gufo flew just over Vita's head and dropped the ancient book into her lap. Then it landed and let the wombo jump from its back and scamper away up the vines that covered the courtyard walls. Vita stroked the bird's feathers and thanked it before it flew off. As dawn spilled light into the sky, she opened the book to the last page, the parchment bare and smooth beneath her fingers but the thin crackle of power running from it. "There is something here," she said. "Oh, if only I could see it. The words of power are written here, I'm sure of it now. The words I need to free the mare."

She fell asleep at last, slumped against the wall with Marina's thin shoulder pressed to her own. When she awoke, she paced the courtyard, chanting again every spell that she knew but nothing happened. At last she leaned against the cage.

Awake, she said. *The world needs you. The stallion waits for you. Awake and talk to me about the Moon Goddess.*

The mare snorted weakly and opened her eyes.

Eat and keep up your strength, Vita told her.

The mare mouthed at the hay, chewing slowly, swallowing with difficulty. *Soon I shall join Luna in the skies,* she sighed, *and run across the stars with the wind in my mane and the moon in my eye. I am too tired to fight the darkness alone after all these years.*

No! Vita protested. *We need you here on earth.*

The mare's eyes closed and she slept again. Vita turned away and paced the gravel restlessly, listening to the trumpets and clash of arms in the camp on the plain below.

For two more days she paced and chanted, and raged in her heart at her own blind stupidity that had allowed her to be seduced by the trickery and flattery of Rosa, Princess Maldici, and Ronaldo, and brought here like a fly to the web of darkness that wrapped Genovera. On their third evening in captivity, she burst into tears.

"I shall never see home again!" she sobbed in Marina's arms. "I have failed in my sacred trust. The world is sliding into darkness and I do nothing. I am powerless, a captive here like the mare. Lord Maldici has won already. He is an emperor of the black arts. All Verde shall suffer, falling into ruin and decay, overrun with death and destruction. All the green things shall wither, all the bright things be extinguished. There will never be another morning as beautiful as the morning when we found the ancient book."

"Hush, hush," Marina soothed her.

"Tomorrow is my last day in this city," Vita said. "Then, they will come to take me for the stallion. You must promise, Marina, not to try and come with me. You must escape if you can and go home to Aunt Carmela and warn her. Flee, both of you, wherever you can go."

"We will both help you," Marina whispered bravely and she stroked Vita's hair until at last they fell asleep in the chill night air.

In the morning, they were wakened early by a ringing blast of trumpets in the camp below. Shortly, other trumpets sounded farther away. The air vibrated with the thunder of wheels and the marching of thousands of feet. Horses neighed, steel clashed, men shouted. Cannon roared. Smoke drifted upward, above the lip of the courtyard wall.

"The battle has begun," Vita said. "Lord Maldici will wipe his brother from the earth."

CHAPTER TWENTY-FIVE

I T BEGAN TO RAIN IN MIDMORNING. The water darkened the mare's coat to the pale yellow color of old ivory. Water dripped from her mane and tail and made her hooves and her golden horn shine. Droplets tricked down her pale lashes, over her closed eyes. Vita turned her face to the rain and thought of salt spray and riding in Giovanni's boat. And she thought of walking in the mountains and watching the rain fill the streams so that they frothed and leaped over their stony beds, and sang in her head with a joyful roar. She thought of rain in the chyme tree, making its hard silvery leaves ring softly together, outside the door of her home with its lavender colored shutters. At the top of the Keeper's valley, rain would be falling on Luna's shrine, glistening in the stars at the goddess' feet and on the flowers that villagers had placed there, lying like jewels on their flaming petals.

Vita ached for home.

Above the patter of the rain in the apricot leaves, she could hear the roar and clash of battle in the valley below.

Slowly the rain ceased until it was merely a mist in the air, that clung to the webs that spiders had fastened between the golden bars of the mare's cage. They gleamed like pearls on necklaces from Lontano. Vita stared dreamily at them, and thought about the pirati ship bounding free across the ocean, and of Giovanni walking the deck with his rolling gait and his eyes alight with the colors of sea and sky.

"I can't believe I ever liked Ronaldo because he could give me jewels," she said. "All the time, it was Giovanni who was true of heart. And now, I shall probably never see him again."

Marina didn't answer. She was gazing at the patch of sky visible above the wall, watching the clouds thin like wool being pulled apart, and the first shaft of sunlight slip through to gleam on the wet leaves of olive and myrtles, and on the dark somber mountain pines, drawing out their sharp fragrance.

"Look!" Marina shouted suddenly, and Vita opened her eyes and stared along the line of Marina's sharp arm.

The arcobaleno grew toward them from the west, a bridge of light. Its colors intensified, shimmering in the air, drawing into themselves all the light of the sky. Closer and closer the bridge arced until the colors flooded the courtyard, and the air danced with the arcobaleno's power. Everything glowed: the wet leaves, the sharp crystalline gravel underfoot, Marina's iridescent hair, the bars of the golden cage, and the bent neck of the mare.

"It is coming from the Golfo," Marina whispered.

Vita leaped to her feet.

"The book!" she shouted, and she raced to the wall where she had hidden the ancient book beneath the thick, broad leaves of a young magnolia to keep it dry. She opened the pages to the last one and held up its mysterious blank surface to the arcobaleno's waterfall of light.

"Luna, hear me!" she cried aloud. "Luna, have mercy on your creatures and send us freedom!"

Before her eyes, the parchment wavered and darkened. Lines appeared, lines in the ancient tongue of the moon goddess, written when the world was young and the light was clear. Vita bent her head over the book and shaped her tongue around the words and realized, suddenly, that she could understand them, even though Giuseppe the hermit had not been able to translate them for her.

She ran with the book to the cage, where the arcobaleno shimmered on the wizened trunk of the old apricot, on its tattered leaves, on the dying lilies—and on the mare's golden horn. It glowed with a light too bright to bear, and Vita looked away from it.

To your feet! she cried. *To your feet while the light touches you!*

The mare's eyes drifted open and shut again.

Up! Vita cried desperately. *Up, before the light fades and it's too late. Up!*

The mare sighed and moaned, and slowly, slowly she lifted her head and opened her eyes. Slowly she bent her legs and thrust herself into a standing position.

Then Vita cried aloud the words from the Keeper's book, the words that would save them.

"Freedom!" she cried, her voice ringing pure and cold in the shimmering air, soaring up the face of the rocky mountain, swirling through the pine and magnolia.

"Freedom I bring you!
From the snare of darkness, I release you!
From the web of evil, I send you back!
From the dark knots, I untie you!
From the deep sleep, I awake you!
From the golden bars, I take you!
From the city, I send you!
From fear and despair, I pull you!
Freedom I bring you!"

The mare snorted and sucked air into her fluttering nostrils. Her head rose higher and her eyes opened wide and filled with a lustrous sheen. As Vita chanted, the mare's mane and tail grew thick and shining, like curtains of windswept snow. Her coat gleamed, her muscles bunched. Her hooves stamped on the gravel and blue sparks crackled in the air. Her horn glowed like the sun.

The bars of the cage fell.

Vita stared at them in awe.

There they lay, those golden bars forged generations ago by Lord Morte himself, that old sorcerer of Verde; forged in fire and strengthened with evil spells. Now they clattered onto the gravel and the mare stepped over them, snorting steam from her velvety, red-rimmed nostrils. She bent her graceful neck, her mane rippling like waves, and touched her horn to the bars and instantly they blackened and flaked onto the gravel in pieces. Between the corroded metal, star lilies sprang up with juicy green stems, and opened curling petals that filled the courtyard with a sweet pure fragrance.

The air smells better here than it has for centuries, the mare said, sounding almost puzzled.

How long have you been here? Vita asked.

The mare's eyes seemed to gaze down endless corridors of time. *I do not know,* she replied. *Many moons have rolled over me, captive here. Generations of kings have ignored me, until this man Lord Maldici remembered the ancient powers and began to weave his spells around me. It has taken all my strength to fight the coils of his evil mind, the wizardry by which he sought to wrest my power to himself. Are you sure the stallion lives?*

I am sure, Vita said. *He is in the mountains to the west, where he fled after the shipwreck. He did not drown. My mother's mother's mothers have kept him safe.*

The mare flung up her head and snorted, her eyes bright. It seemed as though power flowed over her as Vita watched, as though those years of confinement and witchcraft fell away from her.

I am ready, the mare said. *Where is the stallion? I am ready to run in the mountains.*

I don't know how to get us out of here, Vita said, and she stared helplessly around at the high stone walls that enclosed them, up here on a lip of mountain, with thousands of feet of sheer rock above and below them, and two bruttis and two guards waiting at the base of the narrow steps.

"Marina!" Vita called, looking around. Her sister was kneeling on the gravel, her head bowed low to the Corno d'Oro mare.

"She is too beautiful to look at," Marina whispered.

"You'll have to stand up. We need to find a way out of here."

"Call for the wombo. He knows the wall better than anyone."

Vita called and called, trying to rouse the wombo from its sleep, and at last it swung down through the vines on the wall, rubbing its eyes with its tiny paws.

Is there any way out of here? Vita asked it.

There is another door, an ancient door that no one remembers, the wombo replied in its soft slow voice in her mind. *I will show it to you.*

"Come!" Vita shouted to Marina, and they ran across the courtyard while the wombo ran round the wall in the leaves and branches. It disappeared into thick vines and foliage on the wall's east side, and after a moment Vita heard it calling for her to put her hand into the foliage. She thrust in her arm. At first she felt nothing, only smooth wet leaves and rough bark, and then her fingertips touched solid wood. It was still dry, and deeply grooved with time.

"Help me!" she shouted to Marina, and they began to tear the bushes and foliage from the wall, ripping their skin and tearing their dresses, tripping over the strong vines.

I will open the way, the Corno d'Oro mare said and Vita pulled Marina back from the mess of shredded leaves and broken stems. The mare slashed at the foliage with her horn, severing through thick vines and branches as though using a knife. The door that lay behind was black with age, and held onto the wall with rusted hinges and corroded iron bolts. A great lock hung on the door and when Vita saw it her heart sank. The mare struck her horn against the lock and it broke and fell to the ground with a thump.

Vita pushed the door open a little, and the mare pushed her head through the crack, using her horn to slash at the vines that hung on the other side of the wall, until there was a narrow slit of light through which the mare, then Marina, could slip. Vita thanked the wombo and sent it back to its nest before she followed the others through the door.

She found herself standing on a narrow ledge of rock. Thousands of feet below, at the base of the sheer cliff, the river Arnona gleamed in the arcobaleno's fading light. Even as Vita watched, the colors disappeared, the arc dissolved. The Arnona flowed blue again, and on the last page in the ancient book the lettering faded. In a moment, the page was blank. Vita closed the book and tucked it into the sash that bound her dress at the waist.

Do you know what this book is? she asked the mare.

It was written by the moon goddess, when she was dying. She told the first Keeper that it was a work of prophecy written for dark times. I stood beside her as she wrote it, lying on her bed in a meadow on a night of full moon. That is all I know of it.

Vita nodded and stared down into the valley.

On the Arnona's far bank, spread the camp of Lord Maldici with its pale tents, its parade grounds and cooking fires and smithies. Then, on the flat plain that was the valley of the Arnona, a seething mass of men and horses, brutti and chariots fought; surging to and fro like muddy tides, filling the air with screams and death cries, with battle chants, with the ring and blare of trumpets, with the stench of blood and fear. Farther south, beyond the battle, lay the tents of Lord Verona's camp, and beyond that again lay a gentle rise of hills that marked the southern boundary of the Arnona valley and that rose to become Verde's inland plain, in the misty far distance.

The mare stared down at the scene gravely, stamping her hooves and knocking blue sparks from the stone ledge.

We must make haste, she told Vita. *Lord Maldici uses cunning and witchcraft in this war. The tide of darkness is running strong.*

Yes.

But first I will hide our passing. Wait.

The mare turned back to the door, and breathed on the vines and the slashed and trampled foliage. To Vita's amazement, it sprang up again, thick and whole, and covered the old door.

Is it growing on the inside of the wall too? she asked.

It is growing there too. No hint of our passage through the door will remain.

Then, together they followed the ledge of rock that wandered across the face of the mountain like a thin thread. At times, it narrowed almost to nothing. The mare leaped across gaps and clefts, soaring true and straight in her course as a flung arrow. It was harder for Vita and Marina. They crept along the ledge, trying to ignore the fearsome drop and the rocks that crumbled under their feet, plummeting down and down into the abyss. They trembled at the edge of clefts, gathered their courage in both hands, dashed forward and jumped with all their strength to land, breathless, on the far side.

Gradually, the ledge steepened and became a gully that ran downhill, bearing a thin thread of rushing water. They picked their way beside the torrent, grateful for the fresh, pure water which they all drank, and for the lacy green ferns and the silver splashes of flowering waterbright. The mare came behind the girls now, and she stepped where they had walked. At the touch of her golden hooves, the flattened grass and trampled ferns sprang again into straightness, so that there was no mark that anyone had passed down this narrow path. The mare herself left hoof marks shaped like sickle moons, that lasted but a minute and then faded.

At last, they had traversed the steepest slope and came to a terrace where pine trees cast pools of lacy shade and sighed in the wind eddying up from the plain. Now the girls began to run, scrambling past nut and berry trees, sliding and running, losing their balance and rolling downhill to fetch up against fallen logs. Behind them the mare flowed downhill at a trot, as smooth as running water. They stopped at the foot of the mountain, inside a sheltering fringe of dark magnolia trees, and looked out.

The army was far away across the valley, and the river Arnona lay before them, rushing down from the mountains, but narrower than it was near Genovera.

We must swim it, said the mare. *Hold on to me.*

She stepped, surefooted, down over the shingle shore and waded into the cold, fast water. Vita and Marina went bravely with her, one beside each shoulder, their fingers wrapped tightly in her ivory mane. The water swirled up over Vita's knees, over her thighs. She gasped with the cold of it, felt it clench like a fist in her stomach. Still the water rose and now, suddenly, the mare was afloat and striking out for the far bank with its fringe of water lilies. Marina and Vita clung to the mare's mane and kicked with their feet, feeling the torrent tugging and pulling at them, and the steady, powerful progress of the mare. Her tail floated out behind them on the surface. Presently they reached the shore and climbed out, dripping and chilled, and began to run along the water meadows, at the edge of the forest, gradually growing warm and dry in the afternoon sun. At last, the mare halted.

I must travel alone from here, she said, bending her velvet nose to touch Vita's shoulder. *I will run across what remains of the valley, and cross the plain to the mountains. I will call there, from the first peak, for the stallion.*

It is miles from here to the western mountains! Vita exclaimed.

It will not take me long.

You are visible to human eye. People will hunt you.

The armies have swallowed the land whole; people are concerned only for their own lives. Those who are not fighting, will not harm me. I will summon the stallion from the first peak and we will return to this battle.

It is two days journey from the first mountain to where the stallion waits, Vita said. *How can you call him from there and have him hear you?*

I can call him. From any high, free place I can call him and my cry will reach him to the ends of the earth. I am going now, but we will both return, brave Keeper. Thank you for setting me free.

What shall I do now? asked Vita.

Wait for us to return on the morning of the second day.

The mare nudged her shoulder and just for a moment, Vita felt power flow into her: power like a mighty river current, like the light of a full moon. For a moment she felt she could scale mountains, race along beaches, leap stars. Then the mare turned away, the place where her lips had rested on Vita's shoulder tingling.

Vita and Marina crouched under the magnolia and peered out, watching as the mare began to run. She slipped through the trees, gaining speed, her hoof beats silent, her legs eating up the ground, her tail flowing behind on the wind of her passage. She blazed in the sunlight outside the forest, and now she was running south, skirting the edge of the plain, flickering like sunlight and shadow at the fringes of the forest and unseen by the battalions on the plain. Faster and faster she ran, gathering light to herself, glowing with power, sure and straight in her course like a shooting comet.

For a long time after she disappeared from view, Marina and Vita crouched in awed silence, feeling as though the greatest beauty they would ever know had passed from them.

"What now?" Marina asked at last, her voice hushed.

"Perhaps now we should have a rest, and then at dark we should creep around the back of Lord Verona's army, where the washerwomen and blacksmiths work, and where the tents for the wounded are set up. We should sneak into the camp, and try to find the beetleman."

They lay back in the thin grass and the leathery magnolia leaves and fell asleep. Vita dreamed of moonlit mountains, and the smell of running water and lilies, and stars twined around the brow of a woman with ivory skin and eyes like lavender. She dreamed of waves breaking on beaches, the flight of pelicans, mandolo nuts falling in their purple husks on the mountains in the autumn, and the hoot of the gufo at dusk. She heard her chyme tree ringing, and she felt Giovanni's heartbeat. She smiled in her sleep, and awoke feeling strong and rested.

Marina awoke beside her and stretched. "I dreamed about the Keeper's valley," she said. "I dreamed my hands had the power to heal." She spread her thin, scratched brown fingers in her lap and stared at them in wonder.

"You do have that power," Vita said softly.

They peered out at the plain where the light was fading into an evening made darker by the dust and smoke of the armies. The clash of battle died. Soon, the tents of the two armies were barely visible, like drifts of pale leaves in the gloom. Campfires sprang up, bright flickering pinpoints.

"I wonder who is winning," Vita said

"They say that Lord Verona is a kinder, juster man," Marina answered. "They say that Verde should be his."

"He is the elder brother," Vita agreed. "They say he has struggled to survive in the south, with it rocky soil, but that his people would do anything for him."

"I don't see how he can win this battle."

"No, neither do I."

Vita shivered in the dusk, knowing that victory for Lord Maldici would be her doom.

"Come," said Marina, and they began to cross the water meadows, toward the camp. Vita tried to distract herself with thoughts of Giovanni. She wondered if he had battled Dragomar yet; she remembered her one view of the dragon at the Feast the previous year and shuddered as she recalled his fearsome teeth and gaping maw, his writhing, spiny back. Oh Luna and Sirena, she prayed, keep Giovanni safe. She knew, suddenly, that a world without would be a world in which the light was dim and joy never touched her again. I must heal our friendship, she thought.

They passed by the main encampment of Lord Verona's troops. In the still night air, they heard the stamp and whinny of his cavalry horses, the shouts of sentries, the subdued roar of a thousand voices. The silhouettes of men flashed to and fro before a thousand fires and Vita could smell meat roasting and the fragrance of mandolo wood burning.

Behind the main body of the army stood the tents for the wounded, and the tents where the country women washed their sons' and husbands' soiled laundry and prepared their food. Farther back yet, men toiled over the long pits where the dead were tipped, their bodies rolling from wooden carts pulled by miserable jennets. The clash of shovels on stone set Vita's teeth on edge. She stopped to tear a strip from the hem of her dress and bind all of her silvery-gold hair up into it, so that she would be less conspicuous, and then she and Marina wandered into the camp. Beneath their feet, the grass was beaten flat and its peculiar dead smell filled the air. From some tents came the moans of wounded men, or the voices of women.

"What now?" Marina asked. "How will we find the beetleman?"

"We'll have to start asking."

Vita wandered toward a fire where several men, their arms or their legs heavily bandaged with linen strips, drank thin vegetable broth from wooden bowls. "I'm searching for a person called the beetleman. He led the country people of Verde to join the Lord's troops," she said.

The men stared at her, their eyes feverishly bright in the firelight, their gaunt cheeks casting black shadows over their mouths.

"Yes, the beetleman. We know him," one of them said. "He has spent years amongst the country people, putting on his puppet shows, inciting the people against the tyranny of the nobili and their greed."

"Is he here, in the camp?"

"They say so," another man agreed with a shrug. "We haven't seen him. We are Lord Verona's men."

"What do you want with the beetleman?" another soldier asked suspiciously.

"He is an old friend," Vita replied lightly. "Come, Marina," and she took Marina's arm as they drifted off into the shadows.

Vita repeated her question at several more fires until she found a woman rubbing shirts over a washboard and turning the water in her bucket murky with blood. The woman thought she knew someone who would know where the beetleman was.

"Hey, Alfredo!" she shouted into the darkness and presently a boy, too young to fight, with muddy cheeks and dazed eyes, shambled into the light of the woman's fire.

"Alfredo, can you take a message for me to the beetleman?" Vita asked.

The boy nodded.

"Tell him that Vita the Keeper is here."

The boy nodded solemnly and jogged away, and Vita and Marina sat on the ground to wait while the woman persevered in washing the stains from the shirts, her round arms, studded with soap bubbles, pummeling and squeezing while the water slapped the inside of the pail.

Clouds drifted over the moon, blotting out the stars. Rain began to fall in heavy, warm drops that pattered on the tents with a soft rushing sound like a wind rising in salt pines. Soon the rain increased to a downpour. The campfires hissed and smoked sullenly, and men shouted curses and complaints. The long lines of cavalry horses turned their tails to the gusty wind and the rain, and hung their heads, their coats darkening with wet. The washerwoman emptied her pail of dirty water over the dead grass and jerked her thumb at a nearby tent.

"You'd best wait inside," she said. She heaved her wicker basket of wet laundry onto one hip, and lifted the tent flap to pass into the complete blackness within.

Vita heard the strike of tinder and suddenly a lantern wick burst into flame, and grotesque shadows swung and jumped over the tent's sagging canvas. As the girls ducked inside, they saw that the interior was piled with soiled laundry in Lord Verona's colors: yellow shirts slashed open by swords, green breeches stained with blood, green capes that looked as though they'd been ground into the soil by chariot wheels.

Vita wondered about the men who'd worn the garments: about whether they lay in the rain, dying slowly, or whether their bodies had already been dumped into the pits and covered with the rich alluvial soil of the Arnona's valley. She wondered about the women who had loved them, who had trimmed their hair with gentle fingers and pressed warm lips to their shaven cheeks, who had brought them roasted quail and aubergines in oil, and had washed their clothes for the very last time they were worn.

She knew, in that moment, that to be alive and to love were all that she would wish for in future. She would not long again for inlaid floors and chandeliers, fans painted with scenes of the islands of Lontano, sea sapphire necklaces and silk gowns with matching slippers of ruby damask, invitations to nobili dances. In future, she wanted only to dwell peacefully at home in her village, to see Giovanni's boat tacking into harbor as she waited for him by the lavender colored gate at the top of the Keeper's valley.

The washerwoman shoved aside a pile of damp clothes and sat down on an overturned wicker basket that creaked beneath her weight. She gestured to a pile of empty baskets and Vita and Marina took one each and sat down also, watching as the washerwoman threaded a needle with a long piece of yellow thread, and began to mend a sword slash across the chest of a shirt.

Still the rain roared in the darkness, a sound now like an equinoctial tide running up a beach. The campfires were almost all put out by the rain, and the camp sank into sodden darkness, as canvas dripped and leaked, as the ground turned to churned mud underfoot, as the sides of the pits slumped in on the dead. Vita sat hunched forward, listening to the rain and wondering if the beetleman would come, if he was even still alive. Perhaps she dozed, for the oil in the washerwoman's lamp was low, and her pile of mended shirts high, when Vita heard the tent flap move and opened her eyes again.

The beetleman ducked inside, his round face with its three chins shining with rain. He still wore his bright vest with its silver button, but no beetles were tied to it nor did any swoop around his head. At his waist was buckled a sword belt, and the hilt of a blade protruded from its scabbard. His deep grave eyes, surveying Vita and Marina, held neither alarm nor fear, but a deep inscrutable stillness. He bowed his head gravely.

"Keeper, you are free. What news have you?"

Vita told him about the freeing of the Corno d'Oro mare, about Marina being her sister, and about Giovanni going home to fight Dragomar.

"The Corno d'Oro will return," Vita said. "The mare told me to look for her return two days from now."

The beetleman considered this in silence for several minutes, sitting down upon a stool. "I hope we can hold out that long," he said at last, his deep voice thrumming beneath the roar of the rain. "The army of Lord Maldici is stronger than Lord Verona's, with well trained men and better arms. He has chariots too, which Lord Verona does not have, and his men are stronger and better fed. The southern land, as you know, is thin and poor. It is not conducive to raising fighting men, or chariot horses."

"They say that you brought the country people with you," Vita said.

"Yes, and they are brave—but not skilled in arms. They fall like wheat under the chariots."

Vita shivered. "Your puppeteers?" she asked. "Your little old man with the drum?"

"He blows a trumpet now. The puppeteers carry swords. But everywhere, at every turn, we fight the tide of Lord Maldici's evil power. It snaps our bridles and bits, and lames our horses. It weakens the sword arms of stalwart men, and freezes their hearts so that they stand in the ranks of battle like half-wits as the chariots thunder toward them. It fills our meal with maggots, our water with salt. It festers in wounds, turning them putrid and black. There are forces afoot that the troops of Lord Verona and the country people can never deal with. In another day, two at most, we shall all be slain, or ill of pestilence, or fleeing south. The end is very near."

There was a pause, and the rain seemed to come down even harder, so that the tent canvas sagged beneath its rushing force.

The beetleman cocked his head consideringly. "There is some magic afoot," he said.

"You think this rain is sorcery, called against us by Lord Maldici?" Vita asked. The washerwoman's needle stilled and she looked up, her eyes brimming with fear.

"Perhaps," the beetleman agreed. "But remember, Keeper, that the mare is freed into the mountains now. Who knows what power she and the stallion might wield together? A power never seen yet in our generation. Who knows how this tide of evil in our land might be turned at the last moment, before all is lost?"

The woman bent her head over her sewing again and the beetleman nodded thoughtfully, his chins pressing against the damp linen of his collar.

"Who knows?" he muttered one last time, his deep eyes gazing far off, through the tent wall, through the dark night and the curtains of rain.

"Who are you?" Vita asked suddenly and the beetleman's gaze returned to her slowly from some far place.

"I am a village boy from the coastal mountains," he said. "In my family, every son in every generation is raised to give his life for Verde, should need arise. We are warned to wait for the time of greatest need, when evil stalks the land. We are taught that then, we must put our hand to the plough of war and never look back."

The beetleman pulled his sword from its scabbard as he spoke and laid it across his knees.

"My father's father's fathers, for uncounted generations, have passed to their sons the knowledge that our ancestor was a young man named Eduardo. In the time after the death of the moon goddess, when the Corno d'Oro were captured and their ship wrecked, it was Eduardo who first set eyes on the Corno d'Oro stallion and the Keeper, as they struggled ashore half drowned. Eduardo helped them out of the waves, and guided them to the safety and freedom of the mountains. Then, when he was older, he married the first Keeper."

"What!" Vita exclaimed. "Then our families are intertwined, beetleman!

I thought you were just a person who liked to walk around the countryside entertaining people."

"It was a good disguise," the beetleman agreed. "A good way to travel the roads, to hear the rumors and gossip, to see the power stirring in the north, to warn the south, to rouse the people and unite them against the oppression of Lord Maldici. My feet have trodden every inch of Verde, every hill and valley, every grove of nut trees, every mile of rocky coastal path."

Beneath the sound of the beetleman's voice, his sword blade rang thinly as he sharpened it with a whetstone.

"In rain and sun and mist, my puppeteers have told the people the stories of little men who overthrow tyrants. Tonight, my heart grieves to see the people of Verde brought to their knees beneath the bitter tyranny of Lord Maldici, to witness the rabble of darkness prepare to soil Verde's green uplands and her pleasant valleys, to defile all for their greedy ends.

"But now, it grows late, Keeper. Tomorrow, perhaps, the Corno d'Oro will return. Until then, we must be strong and of good courage. We must keep hope alive a few more hours."

"Shall I see you again?" Vita asked.

"Let us hope to meet at a better hour," the beetleman said gravely, and he ducked out into the darkness and was gone.

It rained all night, a sheet of water that thrummed and rushed over the camps where men moaned in their sleep and cried out, over the streets of Genovera where the gutters swirled with waste, over the Arnona where the current swelled stronger and wilder by the hour, gnawing at the arches below the bridge. At dawn, when Vita rose stiffly from a pallet of straw in the washerwoman's tent and looked outside, the ground was saturated, and low, dark clouds pressed upon the camp.

The washerwoman shared her meager breakfast of cold, moldy griddlecake with Marina and Vita. After this, the girls set out to walk around the camp. They watched the army prepare for the day's battle, the horses hanging their heads listlessly, the men sitting on them with shoulders bowed and heads bent against the force of the rain. Beyond the camp, the Arnona's sullen voice mingled with the sound of the rain.

From a small knoll, Vita and Marina watched as the two armies advanced toward each other, the pennants and black flag of Lord Maldici and the yellow colors of Lord Verona hanging limply, the horses sinking to their fetlocks in the sodden ground, the chariots wheels cutting deep ruts that oozed water. The first charge was made slowly, with horses barely able to canter. Chariots tipped over, and foot soldiers tramped doggedly past them. There was a confused melee as the front lines met, but after some half-hearted fighting the troops were pulled back and each side retreated to its encampment, covered in mud.

"If this rain is a sorcery of Lord Maldici's, I cannot see how it's helping his troops," Vita muttered. She put a hand over her eyes, protecting them from the downpour, and stared toward the west. The coastal mountains had disappeared in the low clouds and the sheets of rain. "There is nothing to do but wait," Vita said, and she and Marina went back to the washerwoman's tent with their shoes squelching and their hair plastered against their backs. All day it rained, and all the following night while men hawked and coughed, and the wounded lay in wet beds and the Arnona flooded its banks and swirled into Lord Maldici's camp, washing away chariots and horses in its foaming, angry torrents.

On the second morning, Vita awoke chilled to the bone. The Corno d'Oro must come today, she thought. Surely, they must come today.

All morning, she and Marina waited in the tent, helping the washerwoman with her mountains of sewing, the needles shivering in their fingers so that the stitches they made were irregular and crooked.

Finally, near noon, Vita paused and laid down her needle. A thin tingle of power hummed up her arms into her chest, filling her with warmth.

"The Corno d'Oro!" she cried. "The Corno d'Oro are coming from the south!"

She plunged from the tent into the rain and shouted for Alfredo, the washerwoman's son, who was nearby in a tent with some grave-diggers.

"Fetch the beetleman! Quickly, quickly!" she cried. "Tell him the Corno d'Oro are coming from the south!" Alfredo gawked at her but ran off into the torrents. Vita caught Marina by the hand and began to run through the long avenues of tents, over the trampled grass and the puddles that stretched in every direction, past the smoldering ruins of the cooking fires. At last they arrived panting at the farthest line of tents and gazed across the water meadows to the line of hills that rimmed the southern edge of the Arnona's valley. Vita scanned the sweeping slopes of spring grass, scattered with daisies and sunlions and purple marjori that gleamed in the rain like pebbles underwater.

She stared at the crest of the closest hill and waited, her breath caught in her throat and her chest humming with the Corno d'Oro's power.

Suddenly, over the crest, the Corno d'Oro stallion and mare swept in a rushing shimmer of light. Their long legs reaching forward over the rippling grass were speckled with flower petals. Their breath steamed and their eyes shone lustrous as ripe olives. Their golden horns glowed in the dull afternoon as brightly as though the sun were on them.

Marina and Vita kneeled in the grass, and behind them the beetleman and the boy Alfredo kneeled also as the Corno d'Oro slowed to a walk and paced toward them. Vita felt the Corno d'Oro's breath on her bent neck, sending warmth through her shivering body, lifting her wet hair and filling it with wind and sunshine, flooding strength into her stiff limbs.

Arise, the stallion commanded in Vita's mind.

It is time to confront the evil, for men to choose the power of light. Arise, and send to us all who will choose to forsake darkness and greed. They have but a little time left to come here to us, in these hills. Make haste and gather them!

Power crackled along his crested neck, and up his horn.

Vita stood tall and flung out her arms. "Arise, beetleman and Marina!" she cried. "We must rouse the armies, and the people! All who forsake evil must come here to this place. All who are for the light must gather here!"

The beetleman stood and nodded. "It shall be done," he said. "We will send out men with trumpets, and heralds on our fastest horse. Hurry, Keeper. You and Marina must help."

They ran back toward the lines of tents, skirting the grave sites where mounds of dark earth slumped in the rain. As they entered the camp, the beetleman began to cry for the captains of divisions by name. Tent flaps swung open as men stumbled out into the rain and milled in confusion.

Suddenly, carrying clearly through the torrential curtains of rain, reverberated a sound such as men had never heard: the calling of the Corno d'Oro. Like a great bell tolling, so deep that it vibrated in men's chests, so high and bright that it trembled in their hearts and sang in their thoughts, the cry of the Corno d'Oro washed through Lord Verona's camp. Men flung back their heads, turning their faces to the swollen clouds, and listened in astonishment. Some shook with terror, their breath stammering on their lips, their legs bowing beneath their terrible fear, but other men smiled and felt the rain on their faces suddenly fill with warmth and the promise of green growing things and birdsong in the forests.

Farther yet, the ringing bell-like voice of the two Corno d'Oro reverberated, running through the ranks of Lord Maldici's army like a breaking wave of sound. Men howled and fell to their knees, their hands over their ears.

In Lord Verona's camp, Vita ran after the beetleman to the cavalry lines where already the captains of divisions were assembling and where the horses thrashed and lunged, trying to break free of their picket lines. "Sound the call to arms!" the beetleman cried, and the trumpets rang out clear and strong so that the foot soldiers began to form up into ranks and the cavalry men to leap onto their plunging horses.

Vita grabbed a strong-looking chestnut mare by the mane and swung herself onto the mare's soaking back. The horse danced and pirouetted beneath her but she clung on, and shouted for Marina to jump up behind her. Marina leapt and scrambled, while Vita fought for control of the mare's head, and then caught Vita around the waist with the tight grip of her thin arms. "I'm on!" she shouted breathlessly and Vita turned the mare's head and kicked her into a gallop.

"We have to find Lord Verona!" she shouted above the din of hoof beats and rain and the deep echoes of the Corno d'Oro's tolling cry.

Along the lines of tents they rushed, dodging soldiers fumbling to pull on their boots and arm themselves, past wounded men limping and men being dragged on litters, between men both running and hobbling, until they reached the great pavilion in the center of the camp where Lord Verona stood listening to the Corno d'Oro's cry with rapt astonishment.

With one hand, Vita tore the scarf that she'd made with the hem of her dress, from her head. Her silvery-golden hair streamed down her back, sparking in the dimness. She brought the mare to a skidding halt only inches from Lord Verona.

"My lord!" she cried. "I am the Keeper. The Corno d'Oro stallion and mare stand on a hillside south of your camp. Lead your men to them! Cry for every man who is brave and true, who cleaves to the light! Let them join the Corno d'Oro now, forsaking greed and darkness. Haste! Haste!"

Lord Verona stared at her. His thin face was darkened by hours spent on the battlefield, but his golden eyes were clear and lucid. Looking into them, Vita felt a rush of relief; the eyes of Lord Verona held none of the madness that lay in the eyes of his brother, Lord Maldici.

"The Keeper?" he said wonderingly. "The Corno d'Oro? Surely that mythical creature was lost generations ago, in the mists of time. Surely, it cannot appear to save us in this hour of doom."

"My lord," Vita cried, "Only lead your men south! This is not a trick nor a lie! Already the beetleman, who brought you the country people, is preparing your troops and cavalry to move south to join the Corno d'Oro. Hurry, my lord."

Lord Verona's clear bright eyes stared into Vita's as if he was searching out her heart, and then suddenly he smiled and his face changed, becoming younger and full of an eager hope. He turned, shouting for his horse and his armor. Within moments he was astride a black stallion and his standard bearer fell in beside him, the yellow pennant of the House of Verona sodden with rain.

Vita, with Marina still clinging behind her on the wet chestnut mare, plunged after Lord Verona, heading toward the beetleman mustering the troops as the trumpets rang out. Silence fell as Verona appeared, and men turned their faces toward him. He stood in his stirrups, his thin hands struggling with the stallion's hard mouth, and his voice rang true and clear through the rain.

"All men for the light, ride with me!" he cried. "Ride from the darkness!" and he turned the stallion's head and moved southward through his camp, gathering behind him a river of troops that flowed toward the hill where the Corno d'Oro mare and stallion waited, glowing in the dark afternoon as power crackled around them. Lord Verona sighed at the sight. He slid from his black stallion down into the meadow grass and knelt with his face bowed, and behind him all his troops knelt and bowed their faces.

Send the men into the hills, the Corno d'Oro mare told Vita.

She slid from her mare and kneeled by Lord Verona.

"Send the men into the hills," she repeated. The lord nodded, and the trumpets rang again, sounding the retreat. The army of Lord Verona began to tramp south, cresting the low hill in a wave of men, half-dressed, rain sodden, wounded, their stomachs pinched with hunger and foul food, their women at their sides. Vita and Marina, astride the chestnut mare, watched them pass, and saw the light of hope that shone in their eyes, despite how thin their chill and pale faces were in the teeming rain.

When the last men had passed up the hill, the Corno stallion spoke.

Now for the troops of Lord Maldici, he said. *Are there any who will join us?*

Vita stared at him.

I must find them? she asked tremulously.

Yes.

"My Lord Verona," she said. "the Corno d'Oro asks if there are any who might join us in the ranks of Lord Maldici's army. Will you lend me a trumpeter and a herald?'

"Gladly," Lord Verona replied. "There are many men in those foul ranks who wear the black and silver under protest, many a country boy or village man taken from his work, from his hearth, against his will. Gladly I will spare them if they come with us."

He called for men to ride with Vita and she was surprised to see the beetleman ride forward to join her too, astride a great war horse with feathered feet. On its high back the beetleman balanced his girth with ease, and nodded gravely at Vita.

They rode north, skirting the abandoned tents and the silent camp, and thundered across the churned plain toward the tents of Lord Maldici's camp. Vita's hair streamed behind her and she felt the grip of Marina's arms at her waist and the plunging struggle of the mare to keep her footing on the slippery ground. The rain beat in her face. At her shoulder rode the beetleman, and behind her came a trumpeter and a herald, and a standard bearer with the pennant of Lord Verona.

"The archers will shoot us," Marina gasped into Vita's blowing hair. "Do not ride too close."

Vita pulled on the reins and the chestnut mare slithered to a halt. The trumpeter blew long and clear, and the soldiers of Lord Maldici stood in the rain and stared at them.

"Step forth, all who will join the forces of light and life!" the herald cried. "The Corno d'Oro, that beast of myth and fable, has appeared in our land in this dark time. Step forth, all men who are true of heart, all who would flee the evil of Lord Maldici!"

There was a long pause. The rain drummed on the ground and the Arnona sluiced over its flooded banks and seeped higher and higher amongst the tents and chariots of Lord Maldici's army. The combined voices of the two Corno d'Oro rang out again, tolling in men's ears and minds and hearts, striking terror or awe. A surge of men burst from the ranks and moved forward over the plain to where Vita waited. The ranks became ragged. Other men came forward, orders were shouted and ignored. Unleashed brutti ran forward to attack the deserters, and assassini chased after them, cracking their whips. Still the men ran, kicking at the creatures, falling and rising to their feet again. There were nobili amongst them, Vita noticed, recognizing the bright colors of their silks and damasks beneath their swirling black and silver capes. One face blurred across her vision and passed onward: Ronaldo, his eyes stretched wide with terror, his mouth open in a soundless shout, his elegant legs plastered in mud but running, running south as fast as they could. Where was Rosa? Vita wondered. And Sandro, Beatrice's brother?

The air on the plain thickened, became smoky and dark. Into this swirling mist the deserting men disappeared. There was a long pause. "It is the Lord Maldici's sorcery," muttered the beetleman. "He is creating something into which men walk and lose their senses. They will walk in circles until he releases them."

Now the swirling cloud of darkness covered the whole plain. Vita's horse sidled and neighed as the dark cloud rolled closer.

The cry of the Corno d'Oro rang out again, clear and true, shivering between the mountains. In the sorcerer's cloud, men heard the sound and turned toward it, running south out of the swirling mist and falling, coughing and terrified, at Vita's feet.

"Keep going south! Go toward the hills!" she yelled at them, and they staggered on while a shriek of rage spiraled out of Lord Maldici's camp, keening like a rising wind, sending the condors wheeling from their mountain aeries. In a dark flock they swept over the plain, beating at the deserting soldiers with their dark wings, tearing at men's shoulders so that their shirts ran with blood.

Marina screamed and Vita flung up her arm to ward off the downward stoop of a great condor. Again and again the bird dove onto them, while the horse screamed with terror beneath Vita. The bird came so close that Vita could see its red eyes gleaming malevolently in it shriveled sockets, and the wicked sharpness of its talons and hooked beak. Suddenly a flock of gufos were overhead, diving at the condor, chasing it away with their great grey wings. They circled Vita, keeping her safe as men streamed past her, wounded or whole, on foot or on horses, until the last man who wished to had struggled from the camp of Lord Maldici.

Behind them, Vita could see the city of Genovera emptying as nobili and hawkers, street musicians and flower sellers, dress-makers and grooms struggled downhill to the docks or across the bridge. A fleet of barges and a confused melee of smaller craft rushed westward on the Arnona's raging water as people fled. Others came over the bridge and went south on foot, skirting the plain and heading for the hills. Yet others joined the army of Lord Maldici, still trusting in the sorcerer's powers to save them.

Then out from the Maldici camp shot the great golden war chariot of the Lord himself, with the condors circling above it, rending the air with their terrible screams, and with Lord Maldici holding the reins. His face was contorted with rage, his crimson robe blew about his legs with the speed of his driving, and his horses rolled white eyes and thundered over the wet ground under the snaking lash of his whip. A strange strength seemed to posses them, for they flew forward as though the chariot weighed nothing, as though they pulled it across hard packed earth rather than a sodden morass of ruts and puddles. Behind Maldici's chariot came the assassini, their blue brands glowing on their foreheads, and their deformed hands holding crossbows and catapults and spears. The brutti ran in a milling frenzy at their feet.

"Fly for the hills!" the beetleman shouted and Vita turned her mare's head.

"Hold on!" she said to Marina and they galloped southward, the horse leaping and staggering over rifts in the ground that appeared just in front of his hooves, and shying and snorting at the flickering fires of blue flame springing from the sheets of water. "It is sorcery!" Vita cried.

"Ride! Ride!" the beetleman thundered, and the herald and the standard bearer and the trumpeter clung to the necks of their frenzied horses and closed their eyes and prayed

As she neared the hills, Vita saw the shimmering shapes on the crest that were the two Corno d'Oro, but behind her thundered, ever closer, the tumultuous progress of Lord Maldici's team and the running assassini.

A great wind whistled down the mountains, swirling around the riders. Vita clung to her horse's mane and felt Marina clutch her tighter around the waist. The horses staggered and almost fell in the force of the wind, and began to stumble in circles, trying to keep their tails to the blast.

"Onward!" Vita cried, rubbing the mare's neck, pulling on the reins.

Once again the great belling of the Corno d'Oro rang over the valley, and the wind died but in its place a sheet of flame sprang up before them and hung in a trembling curtain.

"Ride!" Vita screamed, and she lashed the mare forward, straight at the flame. For a moment its electric crackling filled her ears, but the voice of the Corno d'Oro rang out again, and the curtain of flame died.

Staggering, breathless, they galloped up the sweep of the hill and halted before the Corno d'Oro. A great cheer rose from the army above them on the hill.

Vita slid from the mare, her legs shaking, and took Marina's hand. They staggered toward the Corno d'Oro, and the mare reached out her velvet nose and touched Vita's shoulder.

You are safe, Keeper.

Vita turned to stare back at the plain, where the Lord Maldici's chariot swept toward them. His chariot wheels seemed to glide just above the soaking ground. At his back the assassini surged forward, mixed with foot soldiers and charioteers: all the men who were loyal still to Lord Maldici, all the nobili in bright war colors whose hearts were hardened though years of greed and plunder.

Suddenly, above the sound of the rain, thunder boomed: a great rolling disturbance of the air that reverberated in men's chests, that shook the rain from the trees, that made the wheeling condors tremble and slip sideways in the air, their wet wings too heavy to hold them. Lightening flickered around the hilltop where the Corno d'Oro stood, so that their coats blazed with a blue-white brilliance. The army at their back fell to its knees as the Corno d'Oro's brightness dazzled their eyes. Once more the thunder rolled and boomed overhead.

Watch the mountains, the stallion said.

Vita stared to the north, across the valley, across the onward charging chariot of Lord Maldici that had almost reached them, across the heads of the assassini and nobili and charioteers charging behind him, toward the bulk of the northern mountains, black with pine trees and wet rock. They towered like a great wave behind Genovera.

The thunder rumbled a third time, shaking the ground.

Suddenly, the mountains began to move.

Vita watched, her breath in her throat, her fingers squeezing Marina's.

The mountains were slipping, sliding, falling. Trees flew through the air. Rocks shot away like cannonballs. Faces of sheer granite collapsed. With a roar, the mountains gathered momentum and surged downhill in a mighty river of debris, in thousands and thousands of tons of sodden earth. The mud slide surged over the city of Genovera, knocking flat its towers, stilling its pealing bells, burying its fountains deep in rock and broken trees and the shattered nests of screaming condors. Still the mountains disgorged rock and soil, spewing it across the Arnona, swallowing the river's swollen waters. Across the plain the mountains poured, obliterating the tents of Lord Maldici's army, covering his wounded and his dead, roaring onward.

Now the river of mountain reached the assassini and swallowed them whole, swallowed the bright chariots and the screaming horses, the foot soldiers with their pikes in their hands, the brutti howling in the rain. With one last heave the slide threw itself over the chariot of Lord Maldici and he went down into the mud and the rock, the broken trees, and shredded silk of nobili men. The mud swirled to the foot of the hills, and slowed to become a heaving cauldron of mud and foam.

It became still.

Vita let out a long breath.

The Corno d'Oro stallion and the mare reared against the sky, as the last thunder muttered behind the mountains, and as the rain stopped falling. Over the mountains, the clouds parted, opening a blue eye. The sun broke through, and the arcobaleno arced across the mud-filled valley and the grave of that great army of Lord Maldici, and of the sorcerer himself. It shimmered in the air, so that the grass sparkled and the flowers shone like jewels, so that the Corno d'Oro were radiant. A sigh of awe, like wind in the grass, swept through the people on the hill: the soldiers and washerwomen, the people who had escaped from Genovera, the men who had deserted the army of Lord Maldici, the country people, the puppeteers, the people of the south who had marched north to face a tyrant.

Lord Verona came forward and knelt before the Corno d'Oro as their prancing hooves landed back in the grass. The colors of the arcobaleno shimmered across the torn fabric of his yellow doublet.

Tell him to keep his heart pure of geed, to use his power to heal the land of Verde, to treat his people with kindness, the stallion commanded, and Vita repeated the words to Lord Verona's bent back.

"Stand, Lord of all Verde," the beetleman said, grasp his hand in his broad grip and pulling him to his feet. A cheer broke from the army and the refugees on the hill, a mighty cheer that echoed and rolled across the spring land where the nut trees opened their buds and the apricot and cherry blossoms appeared like snow along the boughs. A smell of blossoms and wet earth filled the air.

Keeper, we need you still.

Vita turned to the mare. *Isn't the land safe now?*

The land is never completely safe. Greed will seep underground, and take root in unknown places. You must still keep us hidden and safe in the mountains, preserving us from men's gaze. You must let us slip back into myth.

But the sorcerer's army is dead, Vita protested.

Some assassini escaped to the west, with brutti at their heels. The Princess Maldici went with them. They will take ship and flee this land, but who knows at what sun or moon they may return? Remember the ancient prophecy: 'Not until the powers of the earth god and the moon goddess unite will peace dwell in the world.'

I do not understand the meaning of this, Vita said.

"Time reveals all truths. Until then, you must still keep trust with us, Keeper."

I will, Vita promised. *I will come at every equinox and with every solstice, with the moon goddess's magic, and you shall roam free and safe forever, through all generations of my children, on slopes where lilies bloom.*

The mare and the stallion bowed their elegant faces into Vita's arms, one after the other, and she laid her forehead against their silken forelocks and felt the tickle of their sweeping ivory lashes.

Will I ever see you again?

You see us when the wind blows in the olive groves, Vita, when the village children's faces brighten with laughter, when the silvery tunny leap in the Golfo d'Levanto.

Tears filled Vita's eyes.

But will I really see you? she asked.

The mare blew softly on Vita's hands, warming them. *Who knows what the future of Verde might require of us?* she asked. *Be at peace, Keeper. Who can say what one will or will not see in all the years ahead?*

Be at peace, the stallion repeated and into Vita's mind crept the soft ringing of the chyme tree and the sound of the stream burbling clear and fresh in the Keeper's valley. She stepped back from the Corno d'Oro with a radiant smile.

Until the solstice, she said.

Until midsummer, the Corno d'Oro agreed, their united, bell-like voices ringing light and clear in her mind.

Then the Corno d'Oro walked down to the edge of the mountain slide and bent their necks, and sent their warm breath blowing and curling like mist over the valley. Before Vita's astonished eyes, the mud and broken debris was covered in a mist of green as grass and plants and herbs sprang from it. Within minutes, the valley began to bloom with wildflowers, and the breath of the Corno d'Oro swirled on to where the Arnona had been buried, and pure water began to bubble up through the rocks and mud, cutting a channel toward the delta. Along the new river's banks, rushes and reeds shot up and flowered. The breath of the Corno d'Oro smoked on, up over the scarred mountain, and the scars filled with juniper and pine. Over the buried city of Genovera spread a forest of mandolo and fragranti and cedars, so young and strong that the wind carried their scent all the way back to the people watching. The Corno d'Oro snorted with satisfaction and trotted together up the hill.

They paused on the crest and then, turning, leaped off it, soaring like seabirds against blue sky. Before the astonished gaze of the assembled humans, they headed toward the western mountains, lying in blue silhouette along the hazy horizon. Like shot arrows they passed over the land, like thrown spears, like white waves rushing up beaches, like moonlight slicing through darkness, like the fall of stars. They passed away into the west, and birds trilled and warbled in their wake, and where their hooves had touched the grass, star lilies thrust upward and broke into flower, filling the air with sweetness.

Vita and Marina lay in the grass beneath a mandolo tree and ate dried apricots that someone had given them. Lord Verona's trumpeters and heralds assembled the troops one last time.

"People of Verde!" he shouted. "You who have fought bravely against the darkness in the north, who have beaten your ploughshare into swords and kissed your families goodbye, I send you home! Return to your jennets and your terraces of nut trees, your grape fields and olive presses. Take into your hands the plough again, the harness of jennets, the bags of grain to plant the inland pastures, the fat grapes to press, the rough wood of your winter fires. I shall not tax you hard; I shall not send spies amongst you. I shall not breed brutti or assassini, I shall not plot war. Take into your hands the hands of your loved ones. I send you out in Verde to live in peace.

"Let there be peace in Verde!"

"Peace! Peace!" the people shouted back, a roar of sound that brought blossoms fluttering from the mandolo tree to lie in Marina's dark hair.

"Will we go home too?" she asked.

Vita nodded, thinking about Giovanni. "Do you think he has vanquished the dragon?" she asked.

"Yes," Marina said staunchly. "I believe he has."

"Then the pirati will be building shipyards, and setting out as pilots and explorers," Vita said. "But Giovanni always enjoyed fishing; maybe he will stay home and keep the village supplied with tunny and sardini, squid and crab."

"And Beatrice can keep us supplied with pots to cook all this fish in," Marina said with a laugh.

"Yes. And you and I shall live with Aunt Carmela like real sisters at last," Vita replied with a sigh of satisfaction. "Do you want to start traveling home tonight?"

"Oh yes!"

The sun was setting now, and the full moon was rising in the east. It shone on the columns of men and women winding off along the paths and roads of Verde, walking and riding home in the dark, to live in peace. It shone on Marina's hair, gleaming in its blue iridescence, and on Vita's lavender eyes, and on the three pale chins of the beetleman, when Marina and Vita met him along the road leading west.

"Keeper, and Marina," he said gravely, bowing his head. Vita saw that he had beetles attached to his silver button again. They hummed and flashed around him, their bright colors unseen in the dark but their gossamer wings trembling and bright in the full moon's light. The beetleman's bald head shone like a second moon. Behind him, Vita was amazed to see, came his puppeteers with their puppets reassembled somehow. The puppets' carved and painted faces also shone in the moonlight, grinning and leering and scowling. Their flapping garments caught the light as their wooden arms jerked.

"But your work is surely over!" Vita protested.

Something—something as close to a smile as she had ever seen him display—touched the beetleman's still, dark eyes. "We have all grown fond of the laughter of children," he said. "We are still needed in the lanes and town squares of Verde, Vita. We are needed by the children, who like things at which to laugh, and puppets with which to cavort, and beetles to fly on strings like little kites. So onto the road we march. Good-bye, Keeper and Marina."

The beetleman bowed his head once more in parting and stepped forward, his great body casting an immense shadow. Behind him the puppets jostled and danced, and the wizened old piper lifted his knees high and made the drum on his back boom, while his lips trilled a merry air on his reed pipe.

Vita and Marina watched, smiling, as the strange procession disappeared into the dark. Then they walked on.

"I can smell the sea on the west wind," Marina said after some time.

"I think you could have been a sea-witch after all," Vita teased. "All I can smell is grass and trees."

The moon was high above them now and they marched along on their own shadows. Presently, they heard the sound of hooves trotting after them. Vita pulled Marina over to the grassy verge and they peered into the darkness, waiting to see what followed them.

"There are two of them," Marina said. "Are they horses?"

The creatures' long heads were the first thing that Vita saw, silhouetted against the face of the moon. The light was so dazzling that she could see the creatures' long, curling eyelashes.

"It's the magrazzi!" she exclaimed.

"Vita!" called a voice that she loved.

She ran forward, her feet pounding, her arms outstretched. The magrazzi slowed to a halt, their tall, spindly legs with knobbed joints sending strange shadows across the road. As Vita ran, she saw the figure on the back of one animal, the figure that had called her name. It slipped to the ground down the magrazzi's velvet sides of purple and brown.

"Giovanni!" She threw himself into his arms, felt the swift, hard hammer of his heart, and his laughter, and his lips on her face.

"What are you doing here?" Marina asked in amazement from behind them and Giovanni pulled her into their hug so that the three of them stood in the moonlit road in each other's arms, while the magrazzi watched with huge liquid eyes.

"I came looking for you," Giovanni replied. "After I vanquished Dragomar, I set out for the north that same day. Old Tomie lent me his fastest jennet and it seemed to scramble over the mountains faster than any jennet has ever scrambled! Then I exchanged it for a horse that galloped north. I came tonight to the Arnona valley, and found it flooded with the mountains' fall. People told me what happened! Then I met the beetleman and he gave me this pair of magrazzi. He said one was yours, Vita, and one was in the gardens of Lord Maldici."

"But how did they escape the fall of the mountains?"

"The beetleman said he had heard, three days ago, that all the cages in Lord Maldici's fortress gardens came open, as though by magic, and all the gates swung wide and the animals walked free."

"It was the spell I said to free the Corno d'Oro mare," Vita guessed. "It set all the animals loose. And then the two magrazzi must have found each other and fled the city. I'm so glad."

She reached up her hands and the magrazzi bent their long thin necks and touched her fingers.

Greetings, she told them. *Can you help me one last time? Then you shall roam free all the rest of your days in Verde.*

We will carry you, night sister.

The animals folded their legs and lay in the road. Marina climbed onto one, and Giovanni and Vita climbed onto the other.

Take us home! Vita cried and the magrazzi trotted toward the west, their eyelashes fluttering and smiles wrinkling the soft corners of their lips.

The End

Troon Harrison is an internationally published award-winning author and editor.

She was born in Canada but grew up in Cornwall, England. After schooling, she returned to Canada and now lives near Toronto, where she writes and teaches.

She writes in a range of genres—picture books, teen novels, and junior chapter books—some 16 books in all, and is at work on the second book of her new fantasy series, TALES OF TERRE.

If you'd like to write to her, her email address is:
troon@nexicom.net.